HUNTING A KILLER

The body lay faceup at the waterline, the skin dusted with sand that glistened in the slanting early morning sun. The waves crept up, gently rocking the body and then recoiling, as if in horror at the gruesome discovery.

There was no face.

And what little skin remained was speckled with black paint.

Louis wet his lips, his stomach queasy. Tatum and Quick had been beaten, but this one . . . This time the face was gone. He steadied himself by taking a few steps away and looking out over the gulf. He concentrated on a lone sailboat, on its shape—a crisp white triangle against the brilliant blue of the sky.

Wainwright walked up to him. "We're dealing with a serial killer, Louis."

Louis nodded.

Wainwright pulled out a handkerchief and wiped his face as he looked back down at Mobley and the others.

"Dan," Louis said, "did you notice the face on this one? He's getting madder."

"But you're wrong about the pattern," Wainwright said. "He still killed on a Tuesday. That gives us six days to find the bastard."

He stuffed the handkerchief back into his pocket and trudged up the beach.

After he left, Louis stood there, not quite ready to leave, and not wanting to go back down to where the faceless body lay baking in the sand. . . .

Books by P.J. Parrish

DARK OF THE MOON

DEAD OF WINTER

PAINT IT BLACK

THICKER THAN WATER

ISLAND OF BONES

A KILLING RAIN

AN UNQUIET GRAVE

Published by Pinnacle Books

ACKNOWLEDGMENTS

You won't find Sereno Key on any map of Florida; it is a place of the imagination. But the area that inspired it—the southwest coast of Florida—is very real. In setting PAINT IT BLACK there, we have taken a few liberties with geography, but most of the places in the story are real, and we have tried to stay true to the distinct ambiance of our setting.

We were helped by some fine people along the way. A huge thank-you goes to:

Dave Jensen and Vanessa Viglione, who know where all the bodies are buried on Captiva and beyond.

George Lynch of the "Miss Barnegat Light" at Fisherman's Wharf; John Derickson of "Robin's Song" at Bahia Mar; and fishing guide Greg Rhodes, who educated us on the ways of boats, bloody fish, and the backbay.

Dr. Dave Donson of New York Methodist Hospital, in Brooklyn, NY, who inspired the original germ of the story and led us through its medical thicket.

Kara Winton, public information officer; Officer Kim Lindsay; and Major Kevin B. Anderson, all of the Fort Myers Police Department. Thanks for your insights and enthusiasm.

And last but not least, to Sam Johnson, chief investigator, Office of the Medical Examiner, in Fort Myers, for being so generous with his time and expertise.

We would also like to acknowledge some source material. The following books are excellent guides to those wishing to learn more about the early days of the Federal Bureau of Investigation and criminal profiling: *The FBI: A Comprehensive Reference Guide* by Athan G. Theoharis, Tony G. Poveda, Susan Rosenfeld, and Richard Gid Powers; *The FBI* by Ronald Kessler; and, of course, the seminal works of FBI investigator John Douglas, especially *Journey Into Darkness* (with Mark Olshaker).

March 1986

Chapter One

The car was just sitting there, its hazard lights blinking like beacons in the darkness. In a flash of lightning, he could see someone walking around the car, in and out of the shadows.

Stop here? No, no, not right. Rain. Too . . . too . . . It wasn't supposed to happen here. Stop. Stop!

He slowed the truck, pulling onto the shoulder about thirty feet behind the stalled car. A man came around the car and looked back at him, shielding his eyes in the glare of the truck's headlights.

The wipers beat with the thick pounding of his heart. He could see the man's face. And his eyes, hopeful, as they squinted back at his rescuer.

Yes . . . oh, yes.

He eased the truck forward, closing in on the car.

He left the truck idling and got out. The man seemed to relax slightly as he walked toward him. That was funny. He had to struggle to keep from laughing.

"Hey, man, thanks for stopping," the man said. "Shit, ain't nobody gonna stop to help on a night like this."

The man was talking, talking . . . about his dead battery, about the rain, about his wife being mad, his lips flapping on and on about stupid shit.

The noise hurt his head and he thought about letting the man go but he knew it would be days before he could get another. There was no reason to waste tonight.

He stared at the man's face. Something started pounding in his head, like the mad rush of waves on the beach, muffled, endless, pounding water. The face was there in front of him, the face. He put his hands over his ears and shut his eyes.

"Hey, something the matter with you?"

He opened his eyes. The man's face glistened in the headlights and his mouth was moving, but he couldn't hear anything but the rushing water in his head.

He forced himself to focus, to listen. The man was asking him something, he could hear him now, faint, like he was talking underwater. Jumper cables, the man was asking him if he had jumper cables.

The man's face was rain-slick, the color of wet leaves. It had looked different back in the parking lot. He hadn't been sure but now . . .

Yes . . . oh, yes. Perfect.

He walked back to his truck. Reaching under the seat, he pulled out a dirty rag. He could feel the outline of the knife beneath it. Carefully, he stuck it inside his jacket. Closing the truck door, he reached back into the flatbed and pulled out a long metal pole. He started back toward the car.

No! Stop! Not right . . . it's not right!

He turned back to the truck bed. He rummaged through the debris, his heart pumping faster, his hands groping for it. Where the hell was it? If it wasn't there, he would have to let him go.

Finally, his fingers closed around the wet aluminum. He pulled out the can of spray paint. He let out a breath.

Yes. Okay . . . oh, yes. It's okay now.

He walked back toward the car, the pole held at his side, the can and knife secure in his jacket. The pounding echoed inside his heading, hitting the spot behind his eyes.

The man was peering into the open hood of his car. He looked up, his eyes searching for the jumper cables. He frowned when he saw the pole.

"What you gonna do with that, hang curtains?" The man started to laugh. He laughed, falling against the car, reeling from booze and the hilarity of his own joke.

The laughter floated on the thick, wet air, like a low rumble of thunder. It rumbled inside his skull, Ping-Ponging there like a half-forgotten childhood chant.

The rain pelted on the metal hood, the blood pounded in his head, like waves hard on the beach. It hurt his ears, this noise. He didn't like it, the noise. And the man's smell, booze and sweat. He didn't like that either. He stared at the laughing face until it started to melt, the features falling away with the rain until he could see nothing left but the color of his skin.

Slowly, he raised the metal pole. He touched it to the man's leg.

A sharp bang. The man reeled back against the car and fell to the ground. The man lay there, twitching, his eyes rolled back, his mouth moving, like a fish on a dock.

He waited, standing over the man, waited for him to come to. The gaping wound in the man's leg was wet and black. The rain was coming down harder now. It was taking too long. He scanned the dark causeway road for headlights.

Do it . . . finish it.

He set the pole against the car. Lifting the man under his arms, he dragged him down the slope away from the road toward the shore. The man was limp, like a corpse, but he was still alive on the inside. He could smell the pumping blood, hear his heart still beating.

He dumped him near the rocks under a sea grape tree. A flash of lightning revealed the man's face. He was conscious, his eyes wide with terror now, his lips moving with silent questions.

What? What does he want? Why? He wants to know why? The bastard wants to know why?

He reached in his jacket and pulled out the knife. It was dark here away from the road and he couldn't see the man below him. But he could smell him. He plunged the knife blindly down but it met sand. He raised it again and this time felt the satisfying thud as it met flesh. Again, again, again, and the man was still trying to move. His moans drifted up in the darkness mixing with his own frenzied grunts. Blade against sand, blade against flesh, over and over. Finally, quiet.

He stood up, panting, his arm quivering. The lightning illuminated the man below him for a moment, just long enough for him to see that the face was still there. The man was gone but the face was still there. And the waves in his head, they were still there, too.

No! Fucker! Goddamn you to hell! You piece of shit. You should have been scraped from your mother's womb with a spoon!

With a cry, he dropped to the knees and began to pound at the face. He kept pounding, right, left, right, left in a raging rhythm, over and over, the head flopping from side to side in the wet sand.

He stopped. He tilted his head back, closing his eyes, letting the rain wash over him, letting his breathing return. The air was thick and metallic with blood and lightning. A shudder of ecstasy rolled through him. The waves had stopped.

Picking up his knife, he struggled to his feet, spent. There was just one thing left now. He reached into his jacket for the can of spray paint. It was gone. Had he forgotten it? No, he had put it in his jacket back at the truck. It must have fallen out. He scanned the darkness of the rocks. There was a lot of trash. It could be anywhere now. He felt a wave of panic closing and he knew he had to stop it because the waves would come back.

A headlight beam washed across the tree branches. He froze, waiting for the car to pass.

No . . . no. Forget the paint. Fuck it. There will be another.

Slipping the knife in his jacket, he trudged back up to the road. Picking up the metal pole, he went back to the truck.

He was putting the pole in the flatbed when another flash of approaching headlights made him look up. The car was slowing and he stood tensed, ready. But the car sped past, tires hissing on the wet road.

He smiled. *Like the dumb fucker said, ain't nobody stopping to help on a night like this.* He got in the truck and drove slowly away, leaving the empty car's red hazard lights pulsing weakly in the darkness.

Chapter Two

The jet dipped its left wing and the window filled up with turquoise.

Louis Kincaid pressed his face against the window and stared down at the water just two thousand feet below. He could see a speckling of sailboats, a race in progress maybe. They looked like white birds drifting against a cloudless blue sky, and it gave him a momentary rush of vertigo, as if he were upside down. He shook his head, a soft laugh bubbling out of him. The old woman in the seat next to him looked over, frowning slightly.

"The Gulf of Mexico," he said, pointing. "Man, that's pretty, don't you think?"

She nodded briskly and buried her face back in her Barbara Cartland paperback. Louis looked back to the window. A sweep of beach came into view and then a block of custard-colored buildings along the shoreline.

A soft voice came over the intercom, announcing they would be landing in Fort Myers in ten minutes. Louis felt a quiver in his stomach. It wasn't nerves over his first trip in a plane so much as anticipation of what lay ahead.

He leaned back in the seat, his gaze drifting back to the window, the same question in his head that had been bouncing around there for days now. What in the hell was he doing here anyway?

Dodie . . . it was all his fault. If Dodie hadn't called, gotten him out of bed. Or if it hadn't been so damn cold that morning. Or if his damn car battery hadn't been dead again. If any of that hadn't happened, he might not have accepted Dodie's offer, might not be on this plane now, going to a place he didn't know, a job he didn't really want.

Hell, not just a job. A hundred bucks a day, with a minimum of fifteen hundred, just to do some digging around and find out who killed some woman's husband. Dodie had told him his friend, the wife's lawyer, needed someone special for the job.

"I'm a cop, not a private dick," Louis had told Dodie.

"For a hundred bucks a day, you can be any kind of dick you want," Dodie said. "You want the job or not?"

He didn't want it. But there was nothing else on the horizon. He was finished as a cop in Michigan, if not technically, then practically. There was nothing to do but start over again. He shook his head slowly.

Twenty-six and starting over again. And not even with a real badge. He didn't even have a gun anymore.

He looked back out the window, at the checkerboard of white tile roofs and green palm trees.

"Shit," he muttered. "At least it'll be warm."

Southwest Florida International Airport was small, modern, aggressively upbeat, and air-conditioned to arctic levels. Louis slipped on his University of Michigan varsity jacket and waited for his bag, searching the crowd for Dodie. It struck him that the people had a different look here, lighter somehow, than they had seemed back in the cold of Michigan. Men in bermudas and baseball caps, women in sundresses and sandals. He focused on one woman standing impatiently at the Avis counter. She was thin and dry as a twig, eyes hidden behind big Jackie O shades, wearing a white pantsuit and heavy gold jewelry, with one of those yappy little cockroach dogs tucked under her arm.

"Kincaid!"

Louis spun at the sound of the familiar baritone. He was looking for a pale pitted face under a red ball cap and at first he missed him. But then, there was Sam Dodie, tan and smiling. Dodie thrust out a hand and Louis grasped it, surprised by the surge of feeling in his chest at the sight of his ex-boss.

For a second, they just looked at each other; then Dodie cleared his throat awkwardly and took a step back.

"Well, you made it. How was the flight?" Dodie said.

"Good. Long layover in Atlanta. Sat in the bar and watched the Hawks-Knicks for two hours."

"Didn't know you were a basketball fan."

"I'm not. Football." Louis smiled. "It's good to see you, Sam. You look . . . good, really good. Retirement agrees with you."

Dodie patted his belly. "Margaret's taking cooking classes, French shit."

Louis found himself staring at Dodie's outfit, a pale yellow, boxy short-sleeved shirt worn loose over his shorts. The shirt's fabric was so sheer he could see Dodie's undershirt beneath.

"Interesting shirt," Louis said.

Dodie ran his hands down his chest. "You don't like it? It's called a guayabera. It's Cuban. Lots of guys down here wear 'em. They don't pit out."

Louis laughed. "Just never saw you in anything but flannel before."

"Well, things is different here, Louis. I'm different here." He picked up Louis's bag. "Well, let's get going or we'll get caught in rush hour. Margaret's waiting supper on us."

"Hold on." Louis disappeared into the crowd. He returned, lugging an animal carrier.

"What the hell's that?" Dodie asked, staring at the black cat inside.

"A cat. Its name is Isolde."

"What?"

"Issy . . . it's called Issy."

"Shit. Where'd you get it?"

"It's a long story," Louis said with a sigh. "Come on, let's go."

They headed west, out of the airport, in Dodie's Chevy, through a scrubland dotted with scrawny cows and billboards. The pastures soon gave way to a scorched-earth suburban sprawl of Arbys, Home Depots, and tract subdivisions with names like Cape Verde Isles and Paradise Palms. As they neared downtown Fort Myers, the numbing newness fell away, replaced by a pleasing funk of mom-and-pop motels, small businesses, and palm-shaded streets.

"It's not what I expected," Louis said, eyeing a roadside stand whose sign promised JUMBO SHRIMPS AND ORANGES SHIPPED.

"What isn't?" Dodie asked.

"Florida."

"Everybody says that. What'd you expect?"

"I don't know. Coconuts. Water."

"This is the mainland. Plenty of water where we're heading."

As they approached a high-arching bridge, Louis caught sight of a gray-blue river. The Caloosahatchee, Dodie told him. They went through a pretty neighborhood, the boulevard lined with towering royal palms standing guard like a precision drill team lining a parade route. Dodie flipped down his visor and steered the car due west into the sun.

They started across a two-lane causeway. The sign said WELCOME TO SERENO KEY. HOME OF THE WORLD'S BEST FISHING.

"This is it," Dodie said proudly. "My little piece of paradise. All the water a man could want."

They were crossing a large open bay, and the confluence of water and sky was sudden and startling, like being injected into a sparkling, bright blue ball. The bay extended in all directions as far as Louis could see, broken by green islands and the razor-wakes of darting Jet-Skis.

The causeway rose over a low-slung bridge and Louis watched a pelican ride the current, keeping pace with the car. Then, suddenly, it curved out to the water and rode inches above until it suddenly nose-dived in, like a paper glider crashing into the grass. The pelican surfaced with a fish in its bill. Louis laughed.

"What's so funny?" Dodie asked.

"Nothing, nothing," Louis said softly, settling back in the seat.

Sereno Key wasn't a very big place, Dodie told him, as they touched back onto land. Only a couple thousand folks, some trailer parks, motels, landscaping nurseries, marinas, boatyards, and a small shopping area everyone called "the town center." Sereno was a dog-bone-shaped island sandwiched between the Fort Myers mainland to the east, Pine Island to the north, and the gulf barrier islands of Sanibel-Captiva to the west. The mainland, Dodie informed him, was where "regular folk" lived, and Sanibel-Captiva was where all the tourists and "money folk" lived.

"We're kinda in between here," Dodie said, slowing the Chevy to accommodate the key's two-lane main road. "Lots of retirees and folks who just want to be left alone."

Sam and Margaret Dodie's home was on the north end of the key on Tortuga Way, in a modest neighborhood cut with canals and lined with palms. It was a tidy, two-bedroom bungalow rendered charming by small touches: yellow paint with turquoise trim, a picket fence, shutters, and a porch decorated with wood cutouts of dolphins.

"Made them myself with the jigsaw," Dodie said.

He brushed his hand through a windchime as he opened the screen. "Margaret! He's here!"

Louis had never met Margaret Dodie before, had never been invited to the Dodie home in the months he had lived in Mississippi. Sam Dodie had been the sheriff, his boss, and it had been a prickly relationship, growing from distrust to respect. But it had been strictly professional right to the end. Part of it, he knew, had been the place. Born and raised in Black Pool, Margaret Dodie probably had never had a black man sit at her dinner table. And her husband had probably never thought of inviting one, even Louis.

But if Margaret Dodie now felt the slightest bit uncomfortable, she didn't show it. She greeted Louis cheerfully, like she'd known him for decades. She was a plump woman, bright blue eyes sunk in a pink pincushion face, framed by a helmet of silver-blond hair. She fussed over him, showing him to her guest room, setting up a litter tray for the cat, and finally ushering him and Dodie out onto the patio with a small cooler of beer.

The Dodies' house looked out over a canal that led out through the twisting mangrove-lined waterway to Matlacha Pass. The patio was just a concrete slab but it was furnished with comfortable lawn chairs and festooned with Japanese lanterns and orchids, another of Margaret's new obsessions, Dodie explained. Dodie's own diversion, a new Sundance Skiff, sat at a small wood dock.

"You fish?" Dodie asked.

"Nope," Louis said, smiling.

"You will, you stay here long enough." Dodie took a swig of beer.

Louis settled back into a lounge chair. He could feel his muscles unclenching, his mind slowing. Maybe it was just the combination of the breeze, the pleasant brackish smells, or just the beer. Maybe it was Dodie's cheerful yakking. Whatever it was, he found himself thinking about childhood again, his "other-child childhood," as he had only recently come to think of it. This time Higgins Lake in Michigan. A sunset over gray-blue water. The smell of marshmallows on a fire. The feel of cold sand between his toes. The first summer his foster parents had taken him up North.

A sound drew his eyes to the canal. A couple of kids were paddling out toward the open water in a canoe. Out toward the pass, Louis could see other small islands dotting the water like squat green pond turtles. It looked almost oriental somehow, like pictures he had seen of Japan.

"Another?" Dodie asked, reaching into the cooler.

"Why not?"

Dodie handed him a fresh Heineken. "I remembered."

"I see." Louis nodded to the Heineken that Dodie had just uncapped for himself. "When you start drinking this foreign shit?" he asked, smiling.

"Can't get no Jax here."

"You told me once you'd never leave Mississippi."

"Well, I thought about trying to stick around, you know, afterward." Dodie shrugged. "But Margaret, well, she always wanted to see Florida, so we came down here on that vacation I'd been promising her. After Busch Gardens, we came over to Sereno Key here and decided we kinda liked it."

"Nice place," Louis said.

"I guess I should thank you for it," Dodie said. "What you did up in Mississippi got me a nice big retirement settlement."

They fell silent, Louis lost in his memories of Black Pool.

"So you don't miss Mississippi?" Louis asked.

" 'Bout as much as a hemorrhoid," Dodie said.

Dodie let out a satisfied belch. Louis looked out at the water. A large white wading bird had appeared on the dock, its slender neck bent in a graceful S, its long legs picking carefully along. Suddenly, it took flight over the water, its huge white wings stark against the deepening sky.

"Okay, so why me for this job?" Louis asked.

"Well, I heard you were out of work,." Dodie said.

"You hear why?"

"Yeah . . . yeah, I did."

"You hear all of it?" Louis asked without looking at him. "You heard what I did?"

Dodie nodded slowly. Margaret came out to announce that dinner was in ten minutes. Dodie waited until she left.

"You don't owe me no explanation, Louis," he said. "But I'll listen if you wanna talk about it."

Louis's hands encircled the cold bottle. "Maybe later," he said. "So what exactly am I supposed to be investigating here?"

"A man named Walter Tatum was found murdered, and his wife, Roberta, is the prime suspect," Dodie said. "Her lawyer is the one who's hiring you. He wants you to find other suspects, or at least something so's a jury would find reasonable doubt."

"When do I meet this lawyer?" Louis asked.

Margaret came out onto the porch. "Sam, Mr. Bledsoe's here."

Dodie rose, looking at Louis. "How 'bout right now?"

Scott Bledsoe was a bland-looking man of about forty, tall and pale with thinning blond hair wisping over the sunburned spot on his scalp. His outfit of polo shirt, khakis, and sockless loafers spoke of family money somewhere, or at least an Ivy League diploma hanging on the wall. He moved with an odd, liquid grace that made Louis think of the white bird on the dock.

In deference to Margaret, dinner conversation was kept to small talk and compliments to Margaret on her yellowtail snapper in mango-tequila sauce. Louis learned that Bledsoe had lived in Fort Myers all his life and had never been farther north than Tallahassee, where he waited tables to put himself through law school. He and Sam Dodie had become friends after meeting at the marina; they both loved to fish.

"So, why me, Mr. Bledsoe?" Louis asked, as Margaret brought out plates of key lime pie.

"Sam said you were good," Bledsoe said.

Louis took a bite of the tart pie. "There have to be plenty of private investigators here you could have used," he said. "Why pay to bring me all the way down here?"

Bledsoe glanced at Dodie, then back at Louis. "Well . . . ah." He toyed with his fork. "Frankly, I thought a black man might be better for the job."

Louis sat back in his chair. "And you couldn't find one around here?"

Bledsoe again looked at Dodie. "Sam said you were good."

Dodie was busy with his pie. Louis looked over at Margaret, who looked embarrassed but confused as to why she should be.

"I think I'll get the coffee," she said, rising.

Bledsoe looked back at Louis, his pale cheeks coloring slightly. "Roberta Tatum is black," he said. "Her husband Walter was black. I thought having someone she could relate to might be helpful."

"You're her lawyer. You can't relate to her?" Louis asked.

Bledsoe's lips pulled into a line. "My client hired me because I'm the best criminal lawyer around here. But Roberta Tatum sometimes has trouble communicating. She's . . . well, difficult."

Louis looked over at Dodie. For a second, he was pissed, but he wasn't sure why. Then Dodie looked up at him, and over a forkful of yellow pie, his blue eyes met his.

"I just thought you could use the work, Louis, that's all," he said.

Louis's eyes slid back to Bledsoe and stayed there as he tried to reason whether he should be upset or not.

"Why don't we go outside?" Dodie said, rising.

Louis rose and followed Dodie and Bledsoe to the patio. For several minutes, the three sat quietly watching the sunset. Dodie clicked his Zippo and as he lit the citronella candles, Louis studied his face. He looked like a kid who had gotten caught doing something wrong but wouldn't apologize until he could figure out exactly what it was he did.

Bledsoe finally spoke. "Look, Mr. Kincaid . . . if I've offended—"

"Louis. If I'm going to work for you, it's Louis."

Bledsoe nodded and sank back in his chair. Even in the dim light of the candles, Louis could see the relief in the man's face. Roberta Tatum wasn't the only one who had trouble communicating.

"So, how was Walter Tatum killed?" Louis asked.

"Police believe he was first disabled with a shotgun wound to his leg," Bledsoe said. "But he died from seventeen stab wounds in his chest. He was also beaten very badly, but that was postmortem."

Louis heard a tightness enter Bledsoe's voice with the last words. He had a feeling that despite being "the best criminal lawyer around," Bledsoe had little experience with such violence.

"His body was found in some rocks along the causeway," Bledsoe said.

"The same one we drove in on," Dodie added.

"Was he killed where he was found?" Louis asked.

Bledsoe nodded. "Shot by his car, then dragged down to the rocks and stabbed and beaten."

"They think a woman did this?" Louis asked.

"Murder for hire," Bledsoe said. "She's got an ex-con brother. He's disappeared but there's a warrant out for him. They think he actually pulled it off, but that they conspired together."

"What does she have to gain?" Louis asked.

"They have some money, a very profitable store out on Captiva, and there was life insurance."

"Did you bring the file?" Louis asked.

"No, I wasn't sure Sam wanted to get into all that tonight. Stop by my office tomorrow and we'll go over things."

Louis wished Bledsoe had brought the file. Suddenly, he was anxious to get started. "Witnesses?" he asked.

Bledsoe sighed loudly. "We should be so lucky. Not a one. People fish along the causeway but no one's come forward. The ME figures it happened late, and to make matters worse, it was raining hard that night. Sereno Key is a quiet place, we close up pretty early over here. Not much reason for anyone to come over from the mainland late at night unless they live here."

Louis was silent, his mind already starting to turn over the pieces.

"So, where do you start?" Bledsoe asked.

"With your client," Louis said. "Tomorrow morning?"

Bledsoe nodded. "I'll call Chief Wainwright and arrange it."

They fell silent. The air was heavy with the scent of low tide, orchids, and citronella. The sky was ablaze, orange and pink ribbons cutting across the red backdrop.

"Nice sunset tonight," Dodie said.

Louis had never seen such a spectacular display. "Where do those colors come from?" he said, almost to himself.

"Dirt," Bledsoe said. "Just a lot of dirt in the air."

Chapter Three

He imagined that under different circumstances she was an attractive woman. She was large, maybe five-ten and a good one-seventy, but firm-skinned. Her skin was what was called blue, so dark her features seemed to blend together like ripples in an inky reflective pool. Her chopped black hair was a mess, haphazardly held back from her round face by two plastic barrettes, and she was wearing a shapeless orange jail smock. Still, Roberta Tatum held herself proudly as she paused just inside the door, staring at him.

"Where'd Bledsoe find you?" She had a sharp voice that bounced off the green concrete walls.

Louis shifted under the intensity of her eyes. They were a piercing black that reflected the florescent light like geodes.

"Michigan. A friend of a friend," he said.

She grunted out a bitter laugh. "I didn't think Bledsoe knew any black people. But then again, maybe you don't qualify as black."

She was staring at him, daring him to fight back. From his spot sitting behind the metal table, he just looked up at her calmly.

"Do you?" she demanded.

"What does it matter?" he asked, hearing a hint of weariness in his voice.

"Because!" she said sharply. She turned away. He waited while she pulled a pack of cigarettes out of her pocket and lit one. She took two long drags, blowing the smoke out in raspy streams before she turned back to face him.

"Do you think it would matter if I was some white bitch living out on Sanibel, driving a Mercedes, buying Moët and Chandon instead of selling it? Do you think I'd be in here if my skin wasn't black?"

"I don't know," he said evenly. "I imagine you would be here if you were guilty, regardless of your color."

"You *imagine?*" She shook her head, derisively.

Louis kept her gaze, trying to read her, trying to keep his own anger at bay. Shit, he was here to help the woman. He needed to hear the truth, not a recitation of all the crap she thought the world had heaped on her. He looked over her shoulder at the door. He could see Bledsoe's pale face filling the small pane of reinforced glass. His expression was hangdog, almost resigned.

"How much of my money is Bledsoe paying you?"

Louis looked back at Roberta Tatum. "A hundred a day plus expenses."

"I can get a whole box of you at the Winn-Dixie for two bucks."

He knew she meant Oreo cookies, but let the remark go. Bledsoe had told him that Roberta Tatum probably would be more cooperative without him there. So much for that theory. Well, one more try and he was out of here. He motioned to the empty chair. "Please, Mrs. Tatum, sit down."

She slid slowly into the chair across from him. His eyes dropped to her hands. Her hands were long and tapered with perfectly sculpted red nails. The pinky fingernail had a small diamond stone in it.

Louis opened his notebook. "Tell me what happened that night."

He had already read the file Bledsoe had given him earlier. He had read the police statements, but he needed to hear her version. Seconds passed. He waited, listening to the raspy intake of her cigarette smoke and the light tapping of her red nails on the metal table.

"We had a fight," she said finally.

"A bad one?"

"We didn't draw blood this time, if that's what you're asking."

"The fights got physical?"

"You know fights that don't?"

"How physical?" he asked, writing.

She eyed his notepad. "I dunno. Walter's knocked me upside the head once or twice. I guess I pulled a knife on him a couple times."

Those details hadn't been in the police reports. He stared at her.

Roberta Tatum stared back. "What, your kind don't fight like that?"

Louis set down the pencil and closed the book. All the lightness he had felt last night on Dodie's patio was gone.

"Look, Mrs. Tatum, this isn't about me or Bledsoe or the shade of anyone's skin. It's about you. You and your brother are the prime suspects in a murder and I'm trying to help you. If you don't want my help, just tell me and I'll leave."

She was staring at him. For several seconds, he sat there, debating whether to open the notebook or get up. His eyes flicked up to the door. Bledsoe was still there. He felt her touch, light on his hand.

"Look, they don't get it," she said quietly. She tilted her head toward the door behind her. "None of them get it. Bledsoe, that cop Wainwright. They don't get that what Walter and me did to each other, it doesn't mean anything. It's not like we actually hurt each other. It's just how we fight."

It was still there in her voice, that subtle exclusionary accent in "we." But her eyes had changed; the anger was backlit by fear. Roberta Tatum didn't need him to tell her she had a good chance of spending the rest of her life in prison.

An image jumped up at him out of his memory. Women. Dark-skinned women, shaking the faded paper walls of a house with their high-pitched shrieks and angry words. His mother and sister? It was loud, loud enough to make him hide under a bed. Then it was over, like a summer squall, and they were laughing. God, could they laugh.

"Did you hit each other that night?" he asked.

Roberta snubbed her cigarette out in the ashtray and sat back. "No. We watched TV, had a few beers.

He started mouthing off at me so I shoved him. We argued; then he left."

"Did he say where he was going?"

She shook her head. "He always left after we fought. Said he needed to get away from me to think."

"Were you drunk?"

"I wasn't, but yeah, I guess Walter was." She paused, looking away. "I should've hid the keys."

"After he was found, do you know if anything was missing from the car?"

She shook her head. "Nothing in there to take."

"Was he missing any jewelry?"

"Never wore none." Her voice had grown small.

"What did you do after he left the house?"

"Nothing."

"What?"

"Nothing," she whispered, not looking at him.

"You must've done something," Louis said. "Did you go to sleep? Watch TV?"

Her eyes moved slowly up to his face. Her lips parted and the words came out softly. "I took my naked ass to bed and waited for him, like I always did after we fought," she said. "I expected . . ." She ran a hand over her face. "Shit. . . ."

Louis watched her. She was staring at the far wall, shaking her head, eyes bright, jaw set hard.

"Mrs. Tatum, your lawyer told me your brother is also a suspect. There's a warrant out for his arrest."

That seemed to bring her back. "Levon doesn't got the balls to kill anyone."

"Where was he that night?"

The anger snapped back into her eyes. "I dunno.

Probably passed out somewhere. The son of a bitch is crazy." She paused. "But he didn't kill Walter."

"Three months ago, your brother attacked your husband," Louis said. According to the file, the Sereno Key police had been called to the Tatum home five times in the last year, always by neighbors. Three times, police had arrived to find that Walter Tatum had left. Roberta Tatum had never once pressed charges.

Roberta looked at him, surprised that he knew. "That was nothing," she said quickly. "Walter and me was going at it and Levon was there, so he thinks he's gonna help me by slapping Walter around." She shook her head. "I yelled at him to mind his own business, but that damn bitch next door called the cops again."

"They were both arrested," Louis said.

"I'm telling you, it was nothing."

"Your brother has a record?" Louis asked.

"You know he does," she said quickly.

"Your husband has life insurance?"

The anger flashed back into her eyes. "I expect you know that, too," she snapped. But then she closed her eyes, shaking her head. "A hundred grand," she said slowly. "Walter always had this fear, this premonition, that some kid was going to walk in the store someday and blow him away for a bottle of Jack. That man is . . . was so damn stupid sometimes."

"They're saying that's your motive," Louis said. "They say you devised a plan to kill your husband and hired your brother to carry it out. They believe your brother did something to the car's engine so it would stall out. They believe you purposely got your husband drunk, then started a fight with him, knowing he would leave. Then you sent your brother after him.''

Roberta was staring at him, her eyes wide, her mouth agape.

"That's crazy," she said.

She jumped to her feet, flinging the chair back against the wall. She turned sharply and went to the corner, her back to Louis. She stood there, her shoulders hunched, head down.

Finally, she spun back to face Louis. "Did they tell you what was done to him?" she shouted. "Did they tell you his leg had a ten-inch hole blown in it? Did they tell you he didn't have any blood left in his body by the time they found him? Did they tell you he was beaten so hard the skin came off his face?"

Her eyes welled. "I saw it!" she said. "I had to go over to that place and identify him. But I couldn't! Because Walter didn't have a face!" The tears fell down her cheeks. "Does that sound like something I *planned*? Does that even sound *normal*?"

Louis stared at her. She was waiting for an answer. He closed the notebook.

"No," he said. "It doesn't."

She stood there, her chest heaving. Finally, she walked slowly back to the table and dropped into the chair. The tears had stopped as quickly as they had come, leaving gray streaks down her face. For several minutes, she didn't move; then she slowly raked her red nails through her black hair.

"Look," she whispered, not looking up. "Levon is crazy but he didn't do this. I didn't do this. I loved Walter. And if you don't believe me, then you might as well head back to Michigan, because you're fired."

She wiped her face and folded her arms across her

chest, her eyes trained fiercely on the ashtray on the table. Her eyes were dry but he could see the veins pulsing in her temples.

Louis got up slowly.

Roberta's eyes rose to met his.

"You coming back?" she asked.

"Yes," Louis said.

Roberta ran a hand under her runny nose and turned her focus back on the ashtray. The guard opened the door, and Louis left. Bledsoe was nowhere to be seen.

Louis started down the hall, then turned and went back to the door. He looked in through the small window and saw her sitting in the chair, her arms wrapped around her chest, eyes closed. She was rocking slowly.

Chapter Four

He found Bledsoe out in the lobby, staring at the wanted posters. Bledsoe turned when he heard Louis approach.

"Well?" he asked.

"Well what?"

"Did she talk to you?"

Louis leveled his eyes at the lawyer. "I don't think I'm the 'brother' you thought I was."

"I was hoping—"

"I know what you were hoping," Louis interrupted. "It's not going to work. Your client couldn't care less what color I am."

Bledsoe let out a sigh and bent to pick up his briefcase. He straightened, gazed out the glass doors, then looked back at Louis. "I'm sorry you had to come such a long way for nothing," he said. "I'll make sure you're reimbursed for your expenses thus far." He stuck out his hand.

Louis stared at it. "I'm fired?"

Bledsoe blinked. "But you said—"

"All I said was your client doesn't like me," Louis said. "I don't like her either. But I don't think she's guilty."

Bledsoe dropped his hand. "So you're taking the case?"

Louis paused. "Yeah, yeah, I guess I am."

Bledsoe's lips tipped upward and he thrust out his hand again. Louis returned his sweaty handshake.

"I need to talk to the police chief," Louis said.

"Dan Wainwright," Bledsoe said quickly. "I already told him about you. He's retired FBI, a bit of a hard-ass, unfortunately."

Louis suppressed a sigh. "Great. How's he feel about private investigators?"

Bledsoe was steering him toward the front offices. "I don't know. All I know is he isn't crazy about me."

Dan Wainwright's door was open and Bledsoe led Louis to it. Louis watched as Bledsoe stammered out an introduction and left, actually backing out the door like some supplicant. Louis turned his attention to the man before him. Wainwright's pale blue eyes were steady on Louis's face.

"You're trapped in a room with a tiger, a rattle-snake, and a lawyer and you have a gun with two bullets," Wainwright said. "What should you do?"

Louis shrugged.

"You shoot the lawyer. Twice."

Louis didn't smile.

Wainwright stared at Louis, shook his head, then dropped down in his chair with a sigh.

"Okay, I told Bledsoe I'd give you ten minutes. Clock's running."

Louis considered the man sitting across the desk from him. Dan Wainwright was about fifty-five but had the air of an older man. It wasn't his face. It was heavily creased but ruddy with health and topped with an unruly but striking shock of thick white hair. It wasn't his body either. Wainwright was six-five, maybe two-thirty, linebacker-gone-lax, and his head almost looked too small for his robust frame. It was something intangible, like the man were some plodding, primeval creature whose species was losing the gene wars. Louis thought of Ollie Wickshaw in that moment and how his old partner used to say that some people just seemed to have old souls. Dan Wainwright looked like he had been stalking the earth for eons.

"I just saw Roberta Tatum," Louis said.

"A real sweetheart," Wainwright said.

"You think she did it," Louis said.

Wainwright nodded. "It's classic. There was a pattern."

"She has no record. Not even a speeding ticket."

"I mean the abuse," Wainwright said. "He knocked her around, she took it for years. Finally, she just snapped and bit him back."

"I don't get that feeling," Louis said.

"Well, I guess that's what she's paying you for."

Louis stared at Wainwright, trying to read what was in his eyes. He couldn't tell if the man was annoyed or amused.

"You got your license?" Wainwright asked.

"What?"

"Your PI license. You gotta have one to operate in this state."

"No," Louis said.

"What about your gun? You need paper for that, too."

"I'm not carrying right now," Louis said, avoiding Wainwright's gaze.

Wainwright pursed his lips, twirling slightly in his beat-up vinyl chair. He scribbled something on a paper and slid it across the desk. "Here's the number in Tallahassee. Call them. I won't bust your balls over the license for now."

Louis slipped the scrap in his pocket. The phone rang and Wainwright answered it. Louis used the break to look around the office. Unlike that of his last chief's, it offered no clues to the personality of its occupant. The furniture was old and spartan, a couple of scarred metal filing cabinets and a watercooler. On the walls, there was the usual glass case with police patches from across the country, a departmental photo that looked ten years old, several engraved IN APPRECIATION plaques, one from an Adrian, Michigan, civic group. There was also a glass box that held an FBI badge, a well-worn FBI sleeve patch and ID card, all mounted on a light green matte board that was scribbled with good-byes.

On the desk, there was one framed photograph of two kids, a boy of about six and a girl about eight. The only other personal item sat on a filing cabinet— an old deflated football encased in Plexiglas.

"Bledsoe said you're from Michigan," Wainwright said, hanging up the phone.

"I grew up around Detroit, worked in a small force

up North," Louis said. He wondered if Wainwright knew about his three months with the Loon Lake police. He hoped not. He needed this man's cooperation; he didn't need him to know why he had had to leave.

"I was born in Mt. Clemens," Wainwright said. "I was with the bureau in Detroit from fifty-seven till I retired in seventy-nine." He paused. "Detroit was a great town in those days. A doubleheader at Briggs, a couple of coneys at Lafayette."

He saw the blank look on Louis's face.

"How old are you?" he asked.

Louis tried not to bristle. "Twenty-six."

"And you got a feeling about Roberta."

"I'd just like to explore some things," Louis said. When Wainwright didn't say anything, he added, "And it would be easier with your help."

Wainwright let out a sigh. "Look, Mr. . . . ."

"Kincaid. Louis Kincaid."

"We all know what happened here."

"Apparently. You moved awful fast on that arrest."

"It's got nothing to do with Roberta Tatum being black. It's just the pattern."

"I don't know about patterns. I'm just after the truth here," Louis said.

Wainwright's pale blue eyes locked on Louis. "The truth. Interesting concept."

He reached behind him and tossed a file folder across the desk. "Okay, here's the truth."

Louis didn't move.

"Take it. Look at it. Whoever killed this poor bastard was really pissed. That's passion, Mr. Kincaid. Strangers . . . muggers . . . whatever, they don't have passion. Wives, now they're a whole different story."

Louis opened the folder. It was neatly organized and he flipped immediately to the crime scene photos.

Walter Tatum was on his back, spread-eagled. What looked like a green or blue shirt was soaked in blood and his face was a brown blur against the tan sand.

Louis felt his stomach quiver and he swallowed dryly. He turned the pages slowly. Knife wounds, some deep, some surface . . . gaping wounds in dead flesh. A shotgun blast to the thigh. Tatum's skin ripped apart, leaving a tattered, fleshy hole splattered with blood.

Then a close-up of his face. Roberta was wrong; Walter Tatum still had a face but it wasn't the face she had known. It was swollen with black patches visible beneath Tatum's cinnamon-colored skin.

Louis tightened his facial muscles to keep from gagging. He closed the file and put it down.

Wainwright was watching him. He nodded toward the watercooler. Louis went to it and filled a Dixie Cup. He stood with his back to Wainwright, staring at a Rotary Club plaque while he drank it.

He heard Wainwright hoist his large body out of the swivel chair and turned.

"Come on, then, if you're ready."

"Where?"

"You want to see the crime scene, don't you?"

Chapter Five

There was garbage everywhere. Beer bottles, soda cans, bits of Styrofoam coolers, McDonald's wrappers, fishing line, broken flip-flops, Cheet-Os bags, rotting bait fish, and used Pampers. It lay there in the rocks at the water's edge, a blob of color and stench, baking in the hot sun. Up on the causeway, the sun glistened on the silvery water. But there, just three feet below, the place where Walter Tatum had taken his last breath was a cesspool of human detritus.

Louis stood up on the swale looking down at it. Someone had already ripped down the yellow police tape and it lay tangled in with the junk. The rest of the shoreline didn't appear so littered. Wainwright came up to stand beside him.

"How come there's so much junk here?"

Wainwright shrugged. "The way the tide goes. It gets caught here for some reason. Usually, the crews clean it out."

"Were you able to get anything from this?" Louis asked.

"We hauled two bags out of here after we took the body. This stuff is all new." Wainwright kicked a bottle down into the rocks. "People are pigs," he said.

Louis shielded his eyes to look down the causeway road. There was light traffic, a few fishermen casting nets in the surf a couple hundred yards away. "Who found the body?" he asked.

"Some kid fishing. It hadn't been here long, the ME figures less than twelve hours maybe."

Louis stared at the nearby trees—some sea grapes and tall scraggly pines that didn't offer any real cover. "I don't think this was planned," Louis said. "If someone had planned to kill Walter Tatum, they wouldn't have picked this place."

"They would if they were following him," Wainwright said. "The wires on the distributor cap were loose. We know someone pulled up behind him, but it was too wet to get a tread."

Wainwright motioned toward the sand and gravel alongside the road. "He was shot here, then he was dragged, still alive, over there. That's where he was stabbed and beaten."

Louis kicked at the shells and gravel. Why shoot someone in the leg out in the open on the road? Why not shoot him in the chest and get it over with? Why use precious time to stab someone you could have killed instantly with a shotgun? And why the torturous postmortem beating? Maybe Wainwright was right. Maybe the murder was personal.

"What gauge shotgun?" Louis asked.

"Don't know. ME isn't done yet. I'm expecting the report later today or tomorrow."

Louis glanced at Wainwright. "You really think Roberta Tatum is this smart? Or even this lucky?" he asked.

"I think she's that mean."

Louis sighed and started back toward Wainwright's cruiser. He heard Wainwright's radio go off and someone say something about a suspect.

Wainwright shoved the radio back in his belt. "We got him."

"Who?" Louis asked. "The brother?"

"Yup. Walked right up in front of my surveillance team at Roberta's store. Let's go."

He didn't act like a wanted man. Hanging out in the shade of a gumbo limbo tree, Levon Baylis drew slowly on his cigarette and watched the blue puffs drift lazily above his head. He glanced to his right, not suspiciously, but out of boredom, tired of waiting on someone.

Reaching under a baggy orange T-shirt, he scratched at his stomach, hefted his balls, then walked a few feet across the sandy parking lot, coming out of the shadows. The sun glinted off his bald head. He was a big man, no less than six-three, with gleaming biceps and thick legs.

For a moment, Louis thought he was heading into the grocery. It was a small wooden structure, painted blue and white, with ISLAND DELI AND LIQUOR above the window. But then Levon headed toward the back.

Louis glanced at Wainwright. He calmly picked up the mike and radioed the surveillance car to stand by. He killed the ignition.

"Don't forget, you're only an observer," Wainwright said.

Louis nodded and the cruiser's doors opened. Wainwright started across the street at a stiff trot, Louis a few feet to his left. Levon heard the doors slam and looked up at them.

A thick stream of smoke rose from his lips as his mind tried to grasp what was happening. His eyes scoured the street for an escape route.

He chose backward, through the store.

Louis ran up the wooden steps, slamming into the door ahead of the others. Someone screamed and a bottle fell somewhere behind him. A flash of orange and another slammed door.

Louis jumped over a stack of Budweiser, skidded around a corner, and stopped cold in a dimly lit storage room. He pulled in a quick breath, then ran forward, hearing a clamor of footsteps behind him. Radio traffic filled the small store and suddenly there was a rush of voices and bodies.

A door banged open, flooding the room with sunlight, and Levon was gone. Louis followed him out, blinking against the sun.

He spotted Levon sprinting down the dusty street, his powerful legs pumping. Louis knew he wasn't going to catch him. Then, suddenly, there was a kid on a bike, and Levon went crashing into him.

The kid skidded into the dirt and Levon scrambled to his feet. There was just enough time. Louis launched himself, sailed over a trash can, and fell on Levon's back. It knocked the air out of him but he hung on. But Levon was not going down. Louis clung to his back, feeling the man tense to buck him off.

One of Wainwright's men caught up and grabbed Levon's arm, but Levon threw him into a fence as if he were a bag of laundry. Louis clung to Levon's back.

"Stop!" Louis grunted. "Stop!"

"Fuck you! Get off me!"

Levon veered and slammed his shoulder—and Louis—into a tree.

"Shit!" Louis yelled, gripping Levon's thick neck.

Levon lunged to his right now, crushing Louis again against another palm tree.

Pain shot through his back. He couldn't breathe. But he hung on as Levon dragged him down the street.

Suddenly they were out in bright sun. Louis could see a flash of silver blue. Water, they were near water. He was slipping and he dug his fingers into Levon's neck, trying to put pressure on his throat, but he couldn't get a grip. Levon staggered out onto a dock, jerked around, and slammed his body into a piling. Louis lost his grip and flew off the dock.

He bounced against a boat and hit the water face-first. Salt water rushed into his nose and he fought his way to the surface. He shook the water off, gasping for breath. It took a second for him to realize he could touch bottom.

Suddenly, he heard the sound of a motor. He spun around and saw Levon crouched in a small motorboat. Levon hit the throttle and the boat churned away.

Louis dragged himself up onto the dock. His face was hot with humiliation, his shoulder was on fire, and there was a strong ache creeping up his back. He heard voices and looked up to see Wainwright and the deputy who had been hurled into the fence running down the dock toward him.

They stopped short and watched as Levon's motorboat became a glint against the shimmering water.

"Notify the sheriff, Candy," Wainwright said tightly. "Tell him Levon is heading east from Sutter's Marina toward the mainland. Kill the roadblocks on the causeway. And see if you can find the owner of that boat. Go!"

Candy spun away. Wainwright went over to Louis, who was sitting on the dock, head bowed.

"You okay?"

"Yeah, I think." He couldn't move his shoulder. It was probably dislocated. "You have any idea where he's going?" Louis asked.

Wainwright squinted toward the far shore. "Depends on how much gas he's got. There's a million places he could put in."

Louis wiped his face. "I'm sorry. I couldn't hold him."

Wainwright pulled his gaze from the shoreline back to Louis. He held out a hand. "You're lucky he didn't kill you," he said flatly. "You saved me a lot of paperwork."

Chapter Six

Louis slid off the X-ray table and stepped out the door, squinting into the bright lights of the hallway. At first, all he could see was Wainwright's bulky silhouette standing near the door to exam room one. He slowly came into focus, the look of irritation on his face unmistakable.

Louis let out a breath and went toward Wainwright, holding his shoulder. He was bare-chested but still wearing his damp jeans and soggy Nikes. As he neared Wainwright, Wainwright heard the squeaking and looked up, his eyes dropped to Louis's bruised chest.

"That's going to hurt in the morning."

Louis nodded as he passed him, going into the exam room. "I know."

Wainwright followed him, leaning on the door.

Louis slipped onto the table, grimacing as he put weight on his left arm.

"Any sign of Levon?" Louis asked.

"Not yet. He's not smart enough to evade us for long. We'll find him."

Louis rubbed his shoulder, wishing the doctor would hurry up. He'd been here over an hour. "You don't have to wait," he told Wainwright. "I'll get home."

"How? Cabs will charge you an arm and a leg to take you out to the islands. I brought you here, I'll wait."

Louis glanced at the mirror above the sink, and could see Wainwright staring at him. He wished Wainwright would just go. His ribs were throbbing and he felt like a fool. Tossed into the water like a damn fish.

"Louis, we need to get a few things clear here."

Don't lecture me.

"Have you ever done PI work before?" Wainwright asked.

"No."

"The first thing you learn is that you don't have a badge on anymore."

"I know that."

"I'm not so sure you do. You had no right to chase Levon, no authority to apprehend him or anyone else. I told you that you were just an observer, there out of courtesy. You don't listen very well."

Louis stirred with anger. "I figured I could catch him."

"And what if you had hurt him in the process?

What if you had choked the fucker by accident? What if he fell into the water and drowned? What then? You'd be charged with assault or manslaughter and my department would be sued and I'd be fired. And I don't want to be fired.''

Jesus. His instincts had just taken over. When Levon ran, he went after him. He hadn't given it a second thought.

"I don't have a problem with you hanging around trying to help Roberta Tatum," Wainwright said. "But you don't have the right to detain people, assault anyone, or run after goddamn suspects. You can hang out at the office, and ask all the questions you want. But that's all. The next time you touch a suspect, you better make damn sure it's in self-defense.''

"I just reacted, that's all.''

"You're not hearing me. It's more than that. I don't want you dead, either.'' Wainwright turned toward the wall. When he didn't say anything for several seconds, Louis snuck a glance at him.

"I can take care of myself,'' he said.

Wainwright turned. "Before I joined the bureau, I spent a few years on a beat in Michigan. We had this hotshot reporter who begged us to take him on ride-alongs. Most times, he was bored stiff. Then one night, we got caught up in a domestic where shots were fired. I told him to stay in the car. He didn't.''

Louis shook his head slowly. "He wasn't a cop.''

Wainwright stared at him. He didn't have to say it. It was in his eyes. *Neither are you.*

The doctor came in, holding the X ray. "It's not dislocated, nothing's broken,'' he told Louis. "It's bruised and you've strained the tendons, but it'll be fine after the swelling goes down. I'd keep it stationary for a few days, though."

Louis slid off the table and picked up his shirt. He tried to put it on without straining the shoulder, but it dropped behind his back and he couldn't reach it. Wainwright stepped forward and held the sleeve out for him. Louis slipped into it.

The doctor looked at Wainwright. "You want the bill sent to the department, Chief?"

Wainwright nodded.

The doctor handed Louis a prescription. "Be careful, Officer."

The doctor left and Louis started to button his shirt slowly. Okay, the doc was wrong; he wasn't a cop. But Wainwright was wrong, too; he wasn't a PI, either. So what the hell was he?

He remembered a cold night not so long ago. A cop named Jesse, talking as they drove through the dark Michigan woods.

It's what we are, Louis. Taking the uniform off at night doesn't change a damn thing.

It's not what I am, Jess. I'm a man first, a cop second.

Talk to me in twenty years, Louis, and tell me then what you see when you look in the mirror.

He had been so sure. But that was before he met Gibralter, who wore the badge like a warrior shield, and before Jesse, whose life had been both saved and destroyed by the badge.

And before Fred Lovejoy, the ex-cop who lived alone with his dog on the edge of a frozen lake, spending his days fishing and polishing his service revolver, waiting to die.

He glanced up at a mirror above the sink.

Tell me what you see, Louis.

He looked at Wainwright.

"It won't happen again," he said.

Wainwright's lips drew into a thin line. "Come on, I'm driving you back to the Dodies'."

Chapter Seven

The buzzing sound filled his head, making it hurt. Where was it coming from? Damn it, it hurt, the buzzing hurt.

He looked around, left, right, but there was no one in the parking lot, just cars. He looked up. The green neon of the Holiday Inn sign towered above him. Some of the letters were missing and the neon sign was spitting, buzzing, blinking in the night.

HOLI INN HOLI INN

He covered his ears, against the buzzing, until finally it blended with the dull roar of the waves in his brain. When he took his hands down, it was gone. But the waves were still there, pounding.

He looked again at the blue car. He had followed it here, followed it for the last two hours. He had seen the man and had known instantly that he was perfect. But then, but then, he had to wait. He had to wait, wait until the man finished and got back in his car. He had to wait through the traffic. Had to wait until the fucker ate his damn burritos, bought his fucking postcards. He had to wait. And now, it was time.

What's taking him so long? Why doesn't he get out?

Finally, the taillights went dead. The driver's door opened. He heard the faint pinging of the car's ignition alarm. The man emerged.

Move! Do it now! Quick! Quick!

In three swift strides, he was at the car. The man heard him and turned. There was just enough time for something to register on the man's face—fear? confusion?—before the pole hit his leg.

A shot split the silence. The man crumbled to the asphalt, holding his thigh.

Ha! Easy now! The rest is easy! Oh, yes!

The man was moaning, writhing. Making noise. The pinging sound from the car, someone would hear it. They were far in the corner of the lot but someone could hear it.

Too much noise. Get away from here. Too much light, too much noise. Get away!

He grabbed the man's right arm and dragged him to the truck. With a grunt, he hoisted him up. Light. He was so light. He threw him in the flatbed along with the pole. The man's head made a loud clunk as it hit metal.

The man was moaning and groping at the air. He slammed his fist into the man's head and he was quiet.

He stared at the man's face. It looked green in the neon of the sign overhead.

He frowned.

Too . . . too . . . is it too? It looked different in the daylight. No . . . no, it's perfect. Finish it!

He pulled the tarp up over the man's body and got in the truck. He started the truck but then paused. He reached under the seat. It was still there. The knife was there. And the can of paint. He wasn't going to fuck it up this time. This time, he would do it right.

Chapter Eight

Louis woke to the smell of strong coffee. He grimaced as he sat up, the ache in his chest worse than it had been last night. He reached for the prescription bottle and gulped down a Percodan. Pulling on some clothes, he followed the coffee smell to the kitchen where Dodie and Margaret sat at the table, hidden behind sections of newspapers.

"Morning," Louis mumbled.

Margaret's face appeared around the edge of the newspaper. "How's your shoulder this morning?" she asked.

"Better," he lied. He had told Dodie about the episode with Levon but had told Margaret only that he had slipped on the dock. There was something about her that made him feel as if he were twelve years old and he didn't want her fussing over him.

Louis settled into the chair opposite Dodie, who acknowledged him with a grunt from behind the Sports section.

Margaret put a mug of coffee in front of him. "You want some toast and eggs?" she asked.

"That would be great," Louis said, rubbing his face. He glanced up at the clock above the sink. It was after ten. He hadn't slept so long or so soundly in years. Probably the Percodan. He felt something rub his calf and looked down to see Issy. He gently pushed the cat away with his foot. It trotted away to the bowl of kibbles Margaret had set out by the refrigerator.

"Twins lost to the Yanks in ten," Dodie muttered. He put down the paper and took a slurp of his coffee. "You wanna go see a spring training game? It's right over in Fort Myers."

"Sure. Why not?"

"I'll get us some tickets. Margaret hates baseball. It'll be nice to have someone to go with." Dodie went back to his reading.

Louis hid his smile. It was strange, this new relationship with Sam Dodie. Dodie was only forty-five, but during the last week of living in his home, Louis sometimes felt as if the man was trying to play father to a long-lost son.

The kitchen filled with the smell of bacon. The sun slanted through the sliding glass doors leading out to the patio. Louis pulled the Lifestyles section out of the *Fort Myers News-Press* and tried to lose himself in the mundane tribulations of Dear Abby's disciples.

"Jesus," Dodie said suddenly.

Louis looked up.

"They found another body," Dodie said.

"When?"

"Yesterday. Floated up out by Bakers Point." He held out the front page. Louis took it and quickly read the story. It was a tourist, another black man, but the story didn't say anything more other than that he was stabbed to death.

"Where's Bakers Point?" Louis asked.

"South end of Sereno. It's the tip of the key, part of Matlacha Wildlife Preserve. Might not be related."

"Two stabbings in two weeks. Two black men. In a town that you say has never had a murder? Too coincidental for comfort, I'd say," Louis said.

Dodie nodded grimly.

Margaret set a plate in front of Louis. "I can't believe it," she said quietly. "I mean, this place is so . . . quiet." She turned back to the stove, shaking her head.

Dodie looked at Louis, then returned to reading the story. Louis took a bite of bacon and rose quickly, going to the phone on the wall.

"Who you calling?" Dodie asked.

"Wainwright," Louis answered.

Louis waited, eating the bacon, while the operator tried to locate Wainwright. Finally, she patched Louis through to the chief's squad car.

"I thought you might be calling," Wainwright said.

"Is it the same MO?" Louis asked.

"Come see for yourself. I'm on my way to the county morgue."

Louis got directions and hung up. He picked up his coffee and took a quick drink.

"Where you going?" Dodie asked.

"Autopsy's this morning," Louis said as he put

three pieces of bacon between toast. "Wainwright said I could be there."

Dodie nodded at the food in Louis's hand. "I'd forget about that if I was you."

Louis looked at the bacon sandwich in his hand, then put it back on the plate.

It was past eleven by the time Louis got to the Lee County morgue, a squat municipal building on the edge of the Page Field airport. He found his way down the yellow-tiled hallway to the autopsy room. There was a large black man leaning against the wall outside, dressed in green medical scrubs. He took a sip from his Star Trek coffee mug and eyed Louis as he approached.

"Wainwright's in there," he said in a flat voice, jerking his head toward the door.

Louis looked through the glass to the autopsy room. He could see Wainwright's broad back in its black uniform. There was another man in green scrubs and a white apron on the opposite side of the waist-high fiberglass table, his face hidden behind what looked like a large grocery scale. On the table between them was the body, though Louis could see only the corpse's legs sticking out. He noticed a small sign above the door: MORTUI VIVOS DOCENT. Pulling in a breath, he went in.

The smell hit him square in the face, a nostril-numbing brew that immediately conjured up things and places that he couldn't quite remember. He resisted the urge to cover his nose and mouth.

Wainwright turned. "Kincaid. You're just in time for the fun part," he said.

Louis slowly approached the table. The corpse's chest had already been cut open, the Y-shaped incision running from the front of each shoulder to the bottom of the breastbone and down to the genitals. The skin, muscles, and tissue had already been peeled back, the largest flap of skin pulled upward, hiding the face.

Louis stared at the red cavity of the rib cage. A memory bubbled up from childhood, a woman's back to him as she worked at a chipped white sink and the sight of freshly skinned rabbit. And the smell . . . he could suddenly place that. Dead rats in summer, caught in the walls of their house.

He looked up and saw Wainwright staring at him with a slightly bemused look.

"First time?" Wainwright asked.

"Yes," Louis said.

"Breathe through your mouth," Wainwright said. He nodded to the man in scrubs. "This is Vince Carissimi, the ME. Doc, this is Louis Kincaid. He's working private."

Vince Carissimi was about thirty-five, tall and blue-eyed with shaggy salt-and-pepper hair. A pair of earphones hung from his neck attached to the Walkman on his belt. Louis could hear the tinny music. It was Jimi Hendrix.

"Welcome to my realm," Vince said. "Call me Vince. It's Vincenzo, actually, but only my mother is allowed to call me that. Call me Vince. Please."

Louis glanced around. The room looked unnervingly like a kitchen. He noticed a sign on the wall. HOUSE RULE NO. 1: IF IT IS WET AND STICKY AND NOT YOURS, DON'T TOUCH IT!

Louis's gaze returned to the corpse. He had seen

dead people before, but not like this. The man's limbs were bloated and mottled, like smooth pale marble. There was a gaping black hole in the left thigh just below the groin.

"How could you tell he was black?" Louis asked, without looking up.

"The anatomic position of the mandible relative to the zygomatic bones indicates a Negroid skull structure," Vince said.

Wainwright sighed. "He's bullshitting you. We found the guy's wallet." He pulled a paper from his pocket. "His name is Anthony Quick. He's from Toledo, Ohio. Forty years old. Wife and two kids." He paused. "I called Toledo PD. They're sending someone out to the house this morning."

Louis nodded. He had pulled "messenger duty" often as a rookie with the Ann Arbor force. He knew the drill: *We have some bad news, ma'am. Your husband is dead. We're sorry for your loss. . . .* Gentle but direct was the best way. But it never made it easier for them or you.

Wainwright handed Louis a file. Louis scanned the dossier and then looked at the copy of the license picture. Anthony Quick was a good-looking man, light-skinned with close-cropped black hair and dark eyes that stared out with the slightly irritated look of a man who had waited a long time in line to get his renewal. Louis had a sudden image of two kids waiting at the window for Dad's car to pull up.

"We found a Holiday Inn key in his pocket. Sheriff's guys are checking it out."

"Sheriff?" Louis asked.

"It was from the hotel over in Fort Myers Beach.

Separate city, so it's county jurisdiction," Wainwright said flatly.

Louis watched Vince use what looked like pruning shears to cut away the rib cage. "The newspaper said he was a tourist," Louis said.

Wainwright shook his head. "Not really. A computer software salesman. In town for a convention. Had a schedule in his pocket."

Vince was now carefully cutting away the last of the tissue holding the chest plate. The organs lay exposed now, an amorphic mass of pink and white. Louis stared at it, fascinated.

"Where's his heart?" he asked.

Vince pointed with his scalpel. "It's covered by the pericardial sac." He smiled. "Doesn't look like you thought it would, does it?"

"You said the MO was the same as Tatum?" Louis asked.

Wainwright nodded. "Shot in the leg, stabbed, then beaten. Show him, Doc."

Vince pulled the flap of skin off the face. Louis almost gagged. The face was bloated from being in the water but the right side was completely flattened.

"Horribile dictu," Vince said.

"We figure he was thrown in the water right after that," Wainwright said.

"So he died of the stabbing, like Tatum?" Louis asked.

"Actually, it was asphyxia," Vince said. "The guy drowned."

"Doc thinks he was still alive when he was dumped in the water," Wainwright said.

"Barely," Vince said. "If he hadn't been thrown in the water, he would have bled to death."

"Was he killed on the shore of this reserve?" Louis asked.

Wainwright shook his head. "There is no shore, no beach. Out there, just mangroves. Bakers Point is pretty isolated. There's one entrance road and no other way in except by boat. Not much of a tide there, kind of swamplike."

"Who found him?" Louis asked.

"Fishermen. He was in the water for a couple of days."

"Probably two," Vince said. "Skin and fingernails separate after about eight days." He held up one of the hands. "He had defense wounds on his hands. I suspect he was cut trying to ward off the knife. He might have even tried to grab the blade at one point."

Louis was staring at the gashes on the bloated left hand. He could see an indentation on the ring finger where Vince Carissimi had apparently cut off a wedding band.

"You match the knife yet on Tatum?" Wainwright asked, from behind Louis.

"Nope," Vince answered. "I thought at first it was one of your garden-variety kitchen Henckels. Found a butcher knife in my catalog with the same twelve-inch blade. But Tatum's wounds indicate the blade has an upward curve to it. It looks like these wounds are similar."

"So it's not your run-of-the-mill switchblade or pocketknife?" Louis asked.

Vince shook his head. "Not even close."

Wainwright sighed. "Shit. Well, keep looking."

Louis's eyes traveled the body, coming to rest on the wound on the thigh. "Do you know what gauge shotgun he used?" he asked.

"The shooter used blanks," Vince said.

Louis felt Wainwright come up behind him. "Blanks?" he said. "Damn. It looks like a real gunshot."

"The explosion of gases leaves a wound just like pellets," Vince said. "Tatum was the same, by the way. No pellets. Just the hole."

"Why the hell would he use blanks?" Wainwright murmured.

"Maybe he just wanted to disable him first," Louis offered.

Wainwright looked at him and nodded.

Vince was slicing open a thin membrane in the chest. "Oh, by the way, I found something else strange. He had minute traces of paint on him. In the pores on the neck and face."

"Paint?" Wainwright said, blinking. "What kind of paint?"

"I don't know. It was black."

"New? Old?"

Vince shrugged. "Hard to say. There wasn't much, but it could have washed off. You want me to send it out?"

Wainwright nodded, lost in thought. Louis was looking again at the corpse. If there was black paint on the mutilated, mottled body he sure couldn't see it.

"Did Tatum have paint on him?" Louis asked.

Vince's blue eyes met his. "Not a trace."

"You're sure?" Wainwright asked.

"Of course I'm sure. After I found the paint on this one, I went back and checked. No paint on Tatum."

Wainwright shook his head. "Damn."

Vince snapped off his gloves. "Well, I'm done here. You guys wanna go for coffee and bagels?"

"That's it?" Louis asked.

"Oh, no," Vince said, taking off his scrub shirt. He was wearing a gaudy Hawaiian shirt beneath. "Octavius runs the gut."

They followed Vince Carissimi out into the hall. The large black man was still there, reading a paperback copy of Edith Hamilton's *The Greek Way.*

"He's all yours, Octo," Vince said. "Don't forget to tie off the subclavian. I don't want to get a call from some pissed-off mortuary jockey in Ohio."

The man grunted and went into the autopsy room. Vince saw Louis watching him.

"Octavius is the diener," Vince explained.

"What's a diener?" Louis asked.

"It's a German word that means servant, but he's really an assistant. Octo's been here forever. Sometimes I think he knows more about carving than I do. *Experto crede* . . . trust one who has experience." Vince turned to Wainwright. "So, breakfast or lunch?"

"Already ate, thanks," Wainwright said. "You go if you want, Kincaid."

Louis shook his head.

Vince looked disappointed. "Well, next time you make it over to the mainland, my treat." He held out a hand to Louis. "Good to meet you." The ME disappeared, trailing Hendrix after him.

"Strange guy," Louis said.

"Vince knows his stuff," Wainwright said. "Likes to try to impress you though, with the Latin shit."

Louis looked up at the sign above the door. "*Mortui vivos docent,*" he read.

" 'The dead teach the living,' " Wainwright said. "Come on, let's get out of here."

They walked out into the bright sunshine toward

the parking lot. It was about seventy-five and the breeze had a briny tang even though they were miles from any water. Louis pulled the air deep into his lungs, trying to clear his head of the smells from inside. He watched a small airplane lift off from nearby Page Field and hover like a balsa glider until it disappeared into the clouds.

"You need a ride?" Wainwright asked.

"No, thanks. I borrowed Sam Dodie's car," Louis said.

"Nice folks, the Dodies," Wainwright said. "I met 'em at a Rotary party."

"Yeah," Louis said with a slight smile. "I've been staying with them."

"How's your ribs, by the way?"

"I'm okay."

"I should have warned you about Levon," Wainwright said. "He's got a history of drug abuse. From the looks of it, I'd guess he was on something yesterday. Maybe PCP. Like I said, you're lucky he didn't kill you."

Louis slipped on his sunglasses. "You're still convinced he killed Tatum?"

Wainwright nodded. "Like I said, he's got a history."

"Have you known Levon to ever carry a knife?"

"He had a switchblade on him last time we arrested him."

"But these wounds aren't from a switchblade."

"He could've used a different one."

"But why Anthony Quick? Levon has no motive for that."

Wainwright hesitated. "Like I said, Levon has a

history. He's got some mental problems. And the MO was the same."

"Except for the paint."

Wainwright looked at Louis. "Maybe the paint means nothing. Maybe Quick painted his house or something before he got here."

"His dossier said he sold software for Novel," Louis said. "You ever know a computer geek who got his hands dirty?"

"Look, right now I don't even know if these two murders are related. Right now, I gotta find Levon."

"Any sign of him yet?"

"No," Wainwright said. "We got an APB out, and I have someone watching Roberta's house and the store. Levon stayed in a room in the back sometimes. But he's not coming back."

"So what's your next move?" Louis asked.

Wainwright was looking out at the airstrip again. "I don't know," he said tightly.

For several seconds, they just stood in the warm sun, soaking it in. Wainwright seemed absorbed in watching the planes.

"I came here to retire," Wainwright said softly.

Louis waited, sensing Wainwright wanted to say something more. But Wainwright just let out a deep breath.

"Well, I gotta get back," he said, turning.

Louis watched Wainwright walk toward his cruiser. He noticed he had a subtle limp.

Wainwright stopped and turned suddenly. "Hey, Kincaid," he called. "I just thought of something. I think I know where Anthony Quick was killed. Wanna come along?"

Chapter Nine

He expected pine trees, mossy paths, and maybe a deer or two. That's what preserves looked like in Michigan. But he was in Florida now, where the earth smelled of rotting things and the spindly trees were packed dense, their branches twisting up to the sun like tortured fingers, their roots curving down into the water like inverted rib cages. Mangrove trees, Wainwright called them, as they drove past a sign that said MATLACHA NATURE PRESERVE. They didn't look like trees to Louis. They looked like skeletons frozen in the black water.

The reserve was on the southern tip of Sereno Key, where the neat little neighborhoods ended and the land trickled off to melt into the brackish water. The water here was different than over on the bay. There, out in the open, it caught the sun and was moved by the tides and the wake of human activity. Here, it was dark, still, and primordial, frosted with a thin layer of algae.

Louis looked out over the mangroves. "There's no way someone could get through those trees and wade out to the water," he said. "Where do you think he threw him in?"

Wainwright lowered the visor as he took a curve in the narrow, hard-packed dirt road. "There's an old boat ramp up here somewhere."

They passed a small wooden sign that said NATURE WALK. Louis craned back to look for a path but saw nothing but dense brush. "What the hell is there to see out here?"

"Birds mostly," Wainwright said. "Tree huggers like this place. It's kept natural on purpose. I guess they feel it makes them one with God and all that shit. Me, all I see is a swamp."

Wainwright took another curve and stopped suddenly. They had come to a clearing where the trees opened abruptly onto blue sky. In front of the squad car was a wooden boat ramp that dipped down into the tannin-brown water.

"This is it," Wainwright said. "The only place he could have dumped him."

Louis thought suddenly of the garbage on the causeway. "How do you know Quick wasn't dumped somewhere else and the tide carried the body to where it was found?" he asked as he got out.

"I checked with a fishing guide I know," Wainwright said. "Bakers Point is a small basin, with little water movement. Plus I just got a feeling."

Wainwright was walking the ramp, his eyes scouring

the planks. Louis joined him. The warped wood was old and sun-bleached to gray. But there was no sign of blood or paint. The air was hot and still, with no sounds—from animals or water.

"Jesus, this place stinks," Louis said.

"Tide's out. That's nature for you," Wainwright said. "Lots of things in nature stink."

Louis chuckled. "See anything?"

"Nothing," Wainwright said, crouching to peer at the planks. "Shit, there has to be some blood. He was stabbed eighteen times."

Louis wandered over to the edge of the road, scanning the dirt around the ramp. It was flat and smooth, as if it hadn't been walked on in years.

"When did it rain last?" he called back.

"The night Tatum was killed," Wainwright said. "But even so, a man bleeds this much, it doesn't matter. There would still be something to see on this old dried-up stuff."

Louis turned. "Like spray paint?"

"Spray paint? Why do you think it was spray paint?"

"I doubt he'd take the time to use a brush."

Wainwright started to stand up with a groan and Louis extended a hand. Wainwright accepted it, rising to his feet.

"I still don't think the paint means anything," he said.

"Maybe it does to the killer," Louis said.

"Then why didn't he paint Tatum?"

"I don't know," Louis said.

Wainwright glanced around. "Shit, I was so sure this was the place."

Louis wiped his sweating brow. The boat ramp emptied into a narrow channel of mangroves. Louis spotted a beer can in the mangrove roots. From far off came the faint whine of a boat's motor. Louis thought of the fishermen who had found Quick's bloated body. They probably thought they were looking at a clot of trash, like the garbage caught in the rocks up on the causeway.

He turned to Wainwright suddenly. "Dan, could you call your office and have them pull the evidence sheet from the Tatum scene?"

Wainwright stared at him. "Why?"

"I got a hunch about something."

Wainwright radioed in and Louis waited until Wainwright's man had the evidence sheet. Louis started to speak, but Wainwright held up a hand. "Never mind, I think I just figured out what you're looking for. Jones, check the sheet of all that garbage we picked up around Tatum on the causeway and tell me if you got a can of spray paint on it."

They waited. Something splashed. Louis eyed the trees, expecting to see a gator come crashing out.

Finally Jones's voice came back. "Yes, sir. One half-full can of Krylon spray paint. Black satin. No prints."

Wainwright looked at Louis. "The motherfucker dropped it in the rain," he said softly. He told Jones to run the can over to the lab, then signed off. He slid the radio back and looked at Louis.

"Any other ideas?" Wainwright asked.

"Yeah. The Nature Trail," Louis said.

They backtracked to the trail sign and parked. The trail itself was a primitive, twisting boardwalk of old planks over the swampy ground, seemingly heading nowhere.

Louis opened his shirt, growing hot from the afternoon sun, and wiped his brow with his sleeve. Wainwright forged ahead on the boardwalk, unfettered by the heat, making his way through the tunnel of mangroves like a bear in the woods.

As they walked, Louis eyed the planks for signs of a struggle, drops of blood, ripped clothing, but there was nothing.

"Watch out for snakes, Kincaid," Wainwright called back. "Don't worry about the gators. They're usually asleep in the heat of the day."

Louis stopped, his eyes darting to the brush. He heard Wainwright chuckle but then go silent as he came to a stop.

"Well, I'll be damned," Wainwright said softly.

Louis hurried up behind Wainwright. Wainwright stood next to a sign that said SCENIC OVERLOOK. In front of him was a wooden platform.

"I didn't even know this was here," Wainwright said.

"Well, you're not into this nature shit," Louis said, walking ahead.

They went to the base of the platform and stopped cold. There were dark brown stains on the gray wooden steps.

"Bingo," Wainwright said.

Some of the bloodstains were splatters, others streaks. "It looks like he dragged him up," Wainwright said. "Careful going up."

Slowly, avoiding the bloodstains, they ascended the ten steps. The platform was about six-foot square and it left them just above the tree line. To the east, across the narrow inlet, there was another body of land. But Louis didn't focus on it. His eyes were drawn immediately to the large brown bloodstain in the middle of the platform. It radiated out nearly three feet. On one edge of the stain, black overlapped the brown.

"Paint," Louis said, pointing.

Wainwright nodded.

For several long seconds, neither man said a word. Louis was rooted, unable to take his eyes off the huge brown stain. It was hard to believe Anthony Quick had any life in him when he was thrown into the water.

"Kincaid, over here."

He looked up to see Wainwright standing by the railing. The rail was peppered with blood splatters and there was one large brown smudge.

"This has to be where he threw him in," Wainwright said.

Louis stretched to look down into the water, dark as coffee grounds. "Where exactly did they find the body?" he asked.

Wainwright looked around, then pointed to a spot about ten yards away where the mangroves formed a point.

"So the tides didn't move him," Louis said. "Your hunch was right."

"Yeah," Wainwright said quietly. There was something in his eyes, but he blinked it away. "Well, I guess I'd better get a tech unit out here and call Bledsoe. He and the DA will need to know about this."

They headed down to the squad car and Wainwright radioed in to his office. Louis leaned against the car, staring back at the wooden platform, trying both to see and not see what Quick must have gone through up there. Had he been able to comprehend what was happening to him as he was dragged up those steps? Had he known his killer? That was unlikely, given the fact that the same man probably also killed Tatum. Unless there was some link between the two dead men. But what could a liquor-store owner from Sereno Key and a computer sales-man from Toledo have in common?

"Well, the county guys are on their way over," Wainwright said. "By the way, Sheriff found Quick's rental in the Holiday Inn lot, keys on the ground. And they found a clerk who said Quick asked about going fishing. He was supposed to get back by six for some awards dinner but never showed."

"Can we talk to the clerk?"

Wainwright pursed his lips. "Sheriff says they're handling it." He looked out over the water. "Damn," he said softly. "I hate to have them in on this."

"This is your jurisdiction, isn't it?" Louis asked.

"Technically. But I don't have the men to do this kind of work and that asshole Mobley knows it. I have three uniforms on my little force, Kincaid. None of them has ever done anything harder than trying to take down Levon the other day."

Louis guessed Mobley was the Lee County Sheriff and that there was some bad blood between the two men. Or maybe Wainwright was just embarrassed about having to admit his department's inadequacies. The same thing had happened back in Michigan. What was it with cops and turf wars?

"Kincaid," Wainwright said.

Louis glanced back at him.

"You've got good instincts."

"Thanks."

"Why'd you give up the badge?"

Louis felt himself tighten. The words *I didn't have a choice* came to his mind, but he didn't say them.

"I needed a break," Louis replied.

Wainwright was looking at him. Louis waited, hoping he'd let it drop. Finally, Wainwright just nodded.

"Yeah, this shit can get to anybody," he said.

It had been Margaret Dodie's idea to bring Roberta Tatum some fresh clothes. Margaret said she didn't think Roberta had any kin who cared about her—outside of her dead husband and her brother. And it didn't seem right, she said, that an innocent woman should have to go home wearing dirty clothes. So she had Wainwright take her to the Tatum home and she selected an outfit. She asked Louis to deliver it.

Roberta had eyed him suspiciously when he handed her a blue linen pantsuit, shoes, and underwear. She offered no thanks.

Louis waited for her in Wainwright's office. He paced, left alone with images of Quick's splattered blood and Walter Tatum's battered face. It was unfamiliar and unsettling, and he allowed himself to wonder if, given another twenty years, he would have the same sense of coolness that Wainwright had.

His eyes fell to the photo on the desk. Two kids but no wife. Where was she and how old were the kids now? Teenagers or young adults, far removed from their old man's life?

"You still here?"

Louis turned to face Roberta Tatum. The linen pantsuit and matching shoes were probably meant for a dressy occasion and Roberta had not been able to do anything with her hair. Still, she looked different.

"You look . . . nice," Louis offered.

She grimaced and tried to smooth back her hair. He sensed he amused her. "I suppose you think I should thank you," she said.

"I didn't do anything. Chief Wainwright is the one who got the state's attorney to move on dismissal."

"They think I'm capable of killing one man but not two?" she said.

"Something like that," he said. He didn't see the need to explain the legal thinking behind it, that this case was no longer a domestic gone bad. It was obviously beyond that now, turning into something very different.

"You find my brother yet?" she asked.

Louis shook his head. "You want to tell us where he might be hiding?"

"You still think he did this?"

Louis stared at her evenly. "We've got two violent homicides that are, at this point, without motive. They seem to be the work of someone who is . . . unbalanced."

Roberta Tatum held his eyes for a second, then looked away.

"Mrs. Tatum, is there anything you're not telling us about your brother?"

"Levon ain't been right in the head for a while now," she said slowly.

"What do you mean?"

"It started when he was about sixteen, when we were living over in Fort Myers," she said. "He got in with a bad bunch. Then the drugs started and Mama and me couldn't do anything with him after that."

Louis waited, not sure she was going to offer anything more.

Finally, she sighed. "Levon wasn't a bad boy. He still isn't when he's clean."

"That's not often, is it?" Louis said.

She shook her head slowly. "I've tried to look out after him. Me and Walter moved over here to make a fresh start. We put every dime we had into the store on Captiva, and finally started making a little money." She paused. "Levon kind of came and went. We gave him a room in the back of the store and Walter paid him to do some work. He was okay for a while, but then he got messed up again and stole some stuff and Walter threw him out."

Louis wondered how much of this Wainwright knew.

"Mrs. Tatum," he said, "I have to ask you again. Do you believe your brother could kill someone?"

She didn't answer. She didn't even look at him. "You got a cigarette?" she asked softly.

"I don't smoke. Sorry."

Roberta pulled in a deep breath and turned to face him. Her black eyes glistened but she had retreated back into her hard shell. "You got any other suspects besides my brother?" she demanded.

He could tell she was waiting for something from him, anything that might help her believe her brother was innocent.

"No," he said finally. "Not yet."

Her eyes bore into him. "I read there's another dead black man now. They think Levon killed that other man, too, don't they?"

"Mrs. Tatum, Chief Wainwright—"

"Wainwright," she snapped. "He thinks Levon did

it because it's easier. It's easier to think that 'cause Levon is sick he did it. It's easier 'cause black men kill black men every day and it's easier than finding who really did it.''

Louis turned away. His head was pounding and his ribs ached like a son of a bitch. "Your lawyer is waiting outside to take you home, Mrs. Tatum," he said.

"I know, I know," she said.

When he turned to look at her, she was facing the wall again, seemingly examining the plaques on Wainwright's walls. He sensed she wanted to say something more. He waited until she finally turned to face him.

"I suppose you're still expecting your money," she said.

"Your lawyer already took care of that," Louis said. Bledsoe had paid him the fifteen-hundred flat fee. Not bad for a week's work and he still had the return portion of his plane ticket.

"Who do you think killed Walter?"

The question caught him off guard. "I have no idea," he said.

"Well, could you?"

"Could I what?"

"Have an idea? I mean, if you stayed around to look."

She was staring at him, waiting for an answer.

"I think the police will work hard to find your husband's killer, Mrs. Tatum," he said.

Roberta stared at him a moment, then shook her head. "You really believe white men care about black men laying dead in the swamps?"

When he didn't answer, she started for the door. She stopped and turned.

"I'm putting up a reward," she said. "Twenty grand for anyone who finds out who killed my Walter. I want to know. Even if it is Levon." She narrowed her eyes at him. "Maybe that'll get you motivated."

She turned on her heel and was gone. Louis watched her stalk out the front glass doors and get into Bledsoe's Honda waiting at the curb. He let out a sigh.

He went outside, lingering for a moment on the sidewalk, feeling the balmy night breeze on his face. Well, that was over. So where would he go from here? He sure as hell didn't want to go home to Michigan. But he had no job here and couldn't get one. Not without telling a potential employer everything. He had seen a few ads for security officers in the paper, but the thought turned his stomach. And no matter how desperate he got, he didn't want to work on his own, hanging up some shingle and busting cheating husbands for fifty bucks a day.

Hell, maybe he could go back to school. Get his law degree, make his foster mother proud. Prosecute these motherfuckers after people like Wainwright caught them.

He stared at the darkening sky.

God, he missed it. He missed the job.

The day out in the sun with Wainwright had brought it all back, and he had almost come right out and asked Wainwright if he wanted help on the case. But Wainwright was ex-FBI and he knew how that could be. Retired or not, he was obviously a one-man show. So Louis hadn't brought it up. But now here was Roberta Tatum, dangling her own twenty-thousand-dollar carrot.

He sat down on the station house steps.

He missed everything. The surge of energy that came from using his brain, the rush of adrenaline in the veins. The sifting through evidence to find that one shred someone else missed. The feel of a gun on his hip and the weight of the badge on his shirt. He missed, too, the feeling that at the end of the day, he had done something right. He missed all of it, despite everything that had happened in Michigan.

"Thought you were long gone."

Louis hadn't heard Wainwright come out the door. "Evening, Dan."

"You look like you were a hundred miles away."

"Yeah." Louis rose and took a deep breath. "I think you did the right thing droppping the charges against Roberta Tatum."

"You're probably right," Wainwright. "But I still got some concerns about the brother. I think it's possible Levon got pissed enough at Walter to kill him, and maybe that pushed him off the deep end and he took it out on Anthony Quick, too."

"Maybe," Louis said. "Roberta told me something interesting. Walter Tatum threw Levon out once for stealing from the store."

"Levon did some jail time here and there for assault and he got into some court-ordered drug rehab program. I didn't know about the stealing though. It adds to motive."

"It still doesn't explain why Levon would kill Quick. He was a stranger," Louis said.

"Drugs can mess up your head," Wainwright said.

Wainwright was staring off down the street, his brows furrowed. "Roberta put up a reward," he said finally.

"She told me," Louis said.

"Do you know what that'll do? The screwballs are going to come out of the woodwork now. People would turn in their mother if they thought they'd get some bucks out of it. Not to mention the reporters and PI's. Goddamn amateurs."

Wainwright looked quickly at Louis. "Didn't mean you, Kincaid. You're not a real PI anyway."

Louis forced a smile. He guessed that was a compliment.

Wainwright cleared his throat. "So, when you heading back to Michigan?"

"Soon," Louis said.

"I guess that means you didn't send away for that PI license application then."

Louis shook his head. He knew it was time to say his good-byes and walk away, but he didn't.

Wainwright leaned against the railing, looking out at the parking lot. Across the street, some people were coming out of the Lazy Flamingo, laughing as they piled into a car.

"Whoever it is, I don't think he's finished," Wainwright said.

Louis nodded. "I had the same feeling."

Wainwright looked at him. "You ever work a case like this before?"

Louis shook his head. The car peeled out of the Flamingo's lot, trailing laughter in the warm night air.

"You don't realize at first what it can do," Wainwright said. "You're working, trying to catch the fucker, doing your job, and you don't even notice what it's doing to you. It gets inside you until one day you realize looking at stiffs isn't any harder than cleaning up cat shit."

Louis stared at him. *Ask me to stay.*

The moment lengthened. "I better get going," Louis said finally.

"You wanna go across the street and get a beer?" Wainwright asked.

"Margaret locks up at ten. I'd better go."

Wainwright nodded and started up the steps. Louis turned to the parking lot.

"Hey, Kincaid. Have a nice flight," Wainwright said.

Chapter Ten

Wainwright sifted slowly through the autopsy photos. Tatum's battered face. Quick's bloated body. Two men. Two strong, healthy men without enemies. Men from different states and different professions. And nothing to link them but the color of their skin.

Across from him, Officer Greg Candy craned his neck to look at them. Wainwright noticed Candy made no move to turn them around for a better viewing.

"The doc call yet with his final report?"

"No, sir," Candy said. "You want me to try him again?"

Before Wainwright could answer, there was a knock. Wainwright hollered, "Come in" and a man entered. He wore a suit, and Wainwright knew instantly he was a cop.

Officer Candy started to rise, but Wainwright waved his man back into his seat.

"Can I help you?" Wainwright asked.

"Sergeant Driggs," the man said. He flipped open his badge and slapped it shut in one flick of his wrist. But not before Wainwright saw the Lee County Sheriff's emblem.

Wainwright looked at Candy over the desk and smiled. "I've always wanted to learn how to do that." He looked back at Driggs. "Can you do that again?"

Driggs sneered at him. He was short and balding and looked stretched too tight, as if he felt the need to constantly overcompensate for both his lack of height and hair.

"I'm here on behalf of Sheriff Mobley," Driggs said.

"And what business does Mobley have with me?" Wainwright said.

"Homicide," Driggs said.

Wainwright looked at Driggs and calmly gathered the photos and slipped them back into the manila file. "Really. Who died?"

"You know what I'm talking about. Two dead men in less than three weeks."

"True enough, true enough. But I don't see why you're interested, Driggs. Both bodies were dumped here on Sereno Key. There's a whole lot of water and a big-ass causeway between Sereno Key and your turf, isn't there?"

"Anthony Quick's car was found at the Holiday Inn on Fort Myers Beach," Driggs said. "That's unincorporated, so he was abducted from our *turf.*"

"Who's to say Mr. Quick didn't go voluntarily?" Wainwright said.

"You and I both know the odds are against that."

"Right now, we have no reason to believe he didn't. Therefore, I don't think you have any jurisdiction here, Sergeant Driggs."

The top of Driggs's head was red. "Look, Chief Wainwright. You don't have the resources to work this alone."

Wainwright looked down at the manila folder. Part of him wanted to hand off the file and forget about it. Let the jokers have it. He knew Mobley. He was an ambitious son of a bitch who was probably looking to use the murders as a springboard for reelection or even DA. The county did have the technology, the money, and the manpower. What did it matter who caught the bastard?

"Don't make me embarrass you here, Chief," Driggs said softly.

Wainwright's eyes shot up. "Excuse me?"

Driggs glanced at Candy, who was sitting off to one side, failing miserably at looking disinterested. "Chief," Driggs said calmly, "you have three men on your force here, one who's near retirement and two who never wore a badge before you took them on." He paused just a beat. "And you are retired from the FBI, the OPR, to be exact. Why don't you just give us what you've got and let us do our job?"

Wainwright took a breath. "You mean let you do *my* job. They're my bodies on my island. Now why don't you see if you can get yourself safely back across the bridge without driving into the goddamn bay?"

Driggs pulled a folded newspaper from under his arm and slapped it down on the desk. "Okay, Chief. Have it your way. But when this case blows up in your face, you'll reconsider."

Wainwright looked down at it. It was that morning's *News-Press* with a headline big enough to be read from a car speeding by a newsstand box: NAACP: MURDERS ARE HATE CRIMES

Wainwright had already read the story. An anonymous source in the sheriff's office was quoted as saying they were looking at a racially motivated crime. The Southwest Florida NAACP was demanding swift investigation.

Driggs held out a card. "When you change your mind, give me a call."

When Wainwright didn't take it, Driggs slipped the card back in his pocket. He left, leaving the door open. The office was quiet. Wainwright could hear his own breathing. Officer Candy picked up the newspaper, scanned the story, then put it down.

"Chief," Candy said, "what are you going to do?"

"I don't know." Wainwright turned to look out the window.

Candy stood up. "Anything else you want me to do before I sign out?"

Wainwright turned and picked up the case folder. "Yeah, get Louis Kincaid on the phone."

"Move, damn it."

Louis pushed Issy off the bed, but the cat jumped back up, strolling across his open suitcase.

"Are you taking her back with you?"

Louis looked back over his shoulder at Margaret Dodie standing at the door.

"Unfortunately."

"You could leave her, you know."

Louis stood up, stretching his back. The cat was

sprawled across his shirts, looking up at him with calm green eyes.

"No, I can't do that."

Margaret came into the bedroom and walked over to Issy, petting her gently. "How'd you end up with her? It's obvious you don't like her very much."

Louis frowned. He had *tried* to be nice to it. "She was abandoned. A friend of mine left suddenly. I took her until . . ." Louis paused.

Until what? Until he saw Zoe again? Until she came back? Until he went back?

Margaret smiled and sat on the corner of the bed. Louis kept his eyes down, folding his things, hoping Margaret would leave, wishing she didn't seem to *know* everything.

"We'll miss you, Louis," she said. "Sam especially."

Louis busied himself rolling socks. "He's a good man. I'm glad he's happy down here." Louis shoved his socks down the side of the suitcase.

"He likes you, Louis. He likes you a lot."

"Well, I like him, too, Margaret."

A screen door banged shut and Margaret rose as Dodie came to the bedroom door.

"All packed, eh?"

Louis scanned the room. There was nothing else to pack, but it was easier than beginning the good-byes. "I guess so." He closed the suitcase and finally looked over at Dodie, who was scratching the cat's head. Margaret was looking at her husband.

"So. What time is your plane?" Dodie asked finally.

Louis glanced at his watch. "Two hours. Guess we'd better get going."

"I'll make you a sandwich," Margaret said, setting the cat aside. "They only give you crackers now, you know. Me, I've never been on a plane, but that's what I heard.''

"Peanuts," Dodie said.

Margaret looked confused.

"Peanuts. On the plane," Dodie said. "They give you peanuts, Margie, not crackers."

"Peanuts, crackers. Still not enough for a man to eat. You still need a sandwich."

"It's okay—" Louis said, but Margaret was gone. Issy jumped down after her. Dodie came into the room and handed Louis the newspaper.

"Still no suspects," he said. "Or any sign of Levon. And the black folk are asking for answers."

Louis looked at the headline and then tossed the paper aside. "They'll catch him."

"Not interested?"

"It would only drive me nuts."

Dodie sat down on the bed. "You could get work down here, Louis. You don't have to go back up North."

"Sam, we both know I can't work down here, not at what I want to do."

"Can't work up there at what you want to do, neither, Louis."

"Sam . . . please."

Dodie nodded and started for the door. "I reckon I overstepped. Sorry."

"You didn't overstep—"

But Dodie was gone. Damn it.

Louis grabbed the suitcase and the cat carrier and walked to the living room. Dodie was nowhere to be seen, but Louis could pick up the smell of his cigar coming from the patio. He called for Issy and heard her meow from the kitchen. He went to the kitchen.

The cat looked at him from between Margaret's thick ankles.

"Come here, cat."

Issy trotted away into the laundry room.

"Damn it," Louis said.

Louis started after the cat. The phone rang. Margaret was busy making the sandwich and motioned for Louis to pick it up. It was Wainwright.

"Kincaid," he said, "I just had a visit from one of the sheriff's boys and I kind of put my foot in it. They want to help and I threw him out of my office. He pissed me off, Kincaid. I probably shouldn't have done it, but it gave me a chance to do something I've been wanting to do since I met you."

"Who is it?" Margaret asked.

"Go on, Chief," Louis said.

Margaret scurried out of the room. Louis could hear her calling to Dodie.

"Do you want to stay and help me with this case?" Wainwright asked.

"Are you offering me a job?" Louis asked.

"Well, yeah, there's one thing, though."

Jesus. Background check. Reference check. Why did you leave your last job? He had to tell him.

"I can't pay you much," Wainwright said. "I got a little money in petty cash that I can funnel your way, and I'll have to label you as a consultant or something until I can get the town to approve you being hired as anything else."

Louis fell back against the wall. He glanced over to see Dodie and Margaret standing at the door.

"Kincaid? Can you live with that?"

"Yeah, yeah," Louis said, smiling. "I can live with that."

Chapter Eleven

Louis ducked under the Japanese lanterns and joined Wainwright and Dodie out on the lawn by the barbecue. Dodie was turning pieces of chicken. The sauce sizzled onto the coals, sending magnificent smells into the evening air.

Wainwright nudged Louis. "Can he cook?"

"I don't know. Only food he ever offered me in Mississippi was a bowl of crawfish."

Dodie glanced at him. "I never told you this, Louis, but you're not suppose to eat the heads."

Louis smiled. "I know that. Now."

Wainwright looked confused and Dodie told the tale of how Louis bit off the head of a crawfish.

"Trying to impress me, he was," Dodie said. "Well, better let this bird bake a few. Let's go pop open some brews."

They retreated to the patio and sat watching the sky darken, listening to the evening's overture of frogs and crickets. Margaret came out, glanced at the three men, then went over to check the chicken.

"I just turned it, Margie."

Margaret turned it again, then disappeared back into the house. Louis watched Dodie's eyes as they followed her round body with open affection.

Wainwright sat forward in his chair. "Louis, you see this morning's *News-Press*?"

Louis nodded.

"They're calling it a racially motivated crime. A fucking anonymous source in the sheriff's department," Wainwright said. "Someone leaked it on purpose. They knew the reporter would jump on it."

"But why would someone inside leak it?" Dodie asked.

"To put the screws on me, Sam," Wainwright said. "Mobley wants the case and he knows if there's enough pressure, I'll have to give it to them."

"That kind of talk is only gonna make everyone nervous," Dodie said quietly.

"Just black men," Louis said, taking a sip of beer.

"Well, do y'all believe that's what it is?" Dodie asked.

Louis glanced at Wainwright, but he didn't seem inclined to answer. "Racially motivated crimes are usually messages," Louis said. "The offender is sending a message to a certain group that they are . . . unwelcome. The crimes are usually generalized and not normally filled with such rage."

Wainwright was nodding. "Which is why I don't think these murders fit. They seem *personal* somehow. My money's still on Levon."

"But you haven't found any connection between the two men, have you?" Dodie asked.

"Just their race," Wainwright said.

Louis hesitated. "It's got to be more," he said. "I think Tatum and Quick *are* connected, but only in the killer's mind. They are symbols."

"Of what?" Dodie asked.

"I don't know. Maybe they are symbolic threats. Maybe the killer believes black men are taking something away from him, usurping his place."

Margaret came back out and the three men remained silent while she gathered up empty beer bottles. When she was gone, Dodie spoke.

"How does this Levon fit in then?"

"I'm not so sure he does," Louis said.

Wainwright took a drink of beer. "Well, I'm not ready to give up on Levon yet. He's fucked up in the head. He's capable of murder."

"Levon doesn't have motive. The *why* just isn't there," Louis countered.

Margaret came out onto the patio. "Sam, I'm almost ready in here. You keeping an eye on those birds?"

Dodie got up reluctantly and trudged out to the barbecue. Margaret went back inside.

"He wants to be included," Wainwright said quietly, nodding after Dodie.

"I know," Louis said. "I don't know how much to tell him."

"Have you told him about the details, like the black paint?"

Louis nodded. "But I explained that we're keeping that from the press as a control."

Wainwright nodded. They were silent for a moment.

"You know," Louis said, "we have to consider the possibility that we have two perps."

"We don't have any evidence to indicate that."

"We don't have evidence to the contrary either," Louis said. "The rain messed up the Tatum scene. And there was nothing at the overlook to say one way or the other."

"The stab wounds are consistent with one killer. Same angle, same knife."

Louis shook his head slowly. "That doesn't mean someone else didn't help. Most hate crimes aren't committed by individuals. It's usually a couple guys together."

Wainwright gave a grunt and drained his beer. Dodie came back onto the patio.

"Couple of guys what?" Dodie asked, sitting down.

"Hate crimes," Louis said. "It's usually a group effort."

"He's right, Dan," Dodie said. "These types are cowards and need to gather up their courage in packs. I mean, if I was you, I'd be looking for somebody with a hard-on toward black folk with a couple of buddies to help him out."

"You got anybody like that around here?" Louis asked Wainwright.

Wainwright leaned back in the lawn chair. "A couple months ago, I arrested a guy named Van Slate."

"What for?"

"He and two friends almost beat a black guy to death. It started at the Lob Lolly over on Pine Island. The black guy was with a white girl and Van Slate was shit-faced and made some remarks. They followed the couple out of the bar, tailed them back here, forced them off the road, and whaled on him.''

"Does Van Slate have a record other than this?" Louis asked.

"No, but he's a hothead."

"He lives here on Sereno?"

Wainwright nodded. "His father owns a big boatyard here on the key, and he's had enough pull in the past to keep his kid out of jail."

"I still can't believe whoever killed these two men is living right here among us," Dodie said quietly.

"Sam, you had killers living right next to you in Black Pool," Louis said.

Dodie looked at his beer. "True enough."

The crickets had stopped. It was quiet until a fish jumped out in the canal.

"Have you noticed the dates?" Wainwright said finally.

"What dates?" Dodie asked.

"Tatum was killed on Tuesday, March first. Quick was found on Thursday, nine days later, and the doc says he was in the water about two days."

"Could be just a coincidence," Louis said.

"Could be Tuesday's the killer's day off from his regular job," Dodie interjected. "If he has one."

Louis looked at him. "Well, Tuesday is three days away," he said.

Wainwright drained his beer and sat forward. "Okay, this is what we're going to do," he said. "Louis, you check out Van Slate. We'll put twenty-four-hour surveillance on the causeway to check every suspicious vehicle. If anyone sees anything, he'll radio me to do a stop."

"We don't have the manpower," Louis said.

"Chief Horton over in Fort Myers is a friend of mine and might lend some uniforms," Wainwright said. "And I know my guys will do what it takes on our end."

"I'll pull a shift, Dan," Dodie said quickly.

Wainwright paused and glanced at Louis. "Sure, I'll fit you in, Sam."

Wainwright pulled out his notebook and began to draw a diagram of the causeway and key. "Okay, we've got the Sereno Key causeway with two lanes going into the town center and—"

Margaret came back out carrying a platter. Wainwright fell silent. The three men looked up at her.

She gave them a stern look, then went out to get the chicken off the grill. She came back onto the patio, holding the platter, and paused, looking at them.

"You'd think y'all were CIA or something," she said. "It's not like I don't know anything. I read the paper. I watch *Hill Street Blues.*"

Louis glanced at Wainwright, who lowered his head. Dodie sat very still. The silence lengthened.

Louis looked up at Margaret. "So, you think Furillo and Joyce will ever get married?" he asked.

Margaret smiled. "Yes, I do, and if y'all would get your butts inside to supper, I'll tell you why."

She went in. Louis glanced at Dodie, who looked mildly embarrassed. He looked at Wainwright. He was gripping his beer bottle, staring out at the black canal beyond, his face tight in the spare light of the Japanese lanterns.

Chapter Twelve

Louis stood outside the chain-link fence of the boatyard, watching Matthew Van Slate. If Van Slate had noticed him, he didn't show it. He was up on a ladder, sanding the wooden hull of a sailboat that was propped on scaffolding. The yard was crowded with dry-docked boats—everything from beat-up bassers to a forty-foot white Hatteras that hung in a massive metal lift like some exotic captured bird. At the entrance was a large sign: VAN SLATE BOAT WORKS.

Louis opened Van Slate's criminal folder. Van Slate and two other boatyard employees had been arrested last May by Wainwright's officers for assault and battery on Joshua Zengo. Van Slate had served ten months of an eighteen-month sentence, and his two friends had served seven. According to Zengo's girlfriend, the drunken Van Slate had picked a fight with Zengo in the bar, making racial slurs about him being with a white woman. The couple left, but about ten minutes later they noticed a car following them. Van Slate ran Zengo's car off the road in Sereno and pulled him out of his car. The girlfriend said the three men beat Zengo unconscious before fleeing.

According to a witness statement from a patron in the bar, Van Slate was angry because his wife had recently left him and Van Slate suspected she was seeing a black man.

Louis closed the file and stared back at Van Slate. He looked to be about thirty, at least six feet, with a body honed by day labor and nights spent in a gym. He was wearing paint-stained jeans and an old denim shirt with the sleeves cut off. His knotty shoulders glistened in the sun and his oily blond hair hung over his forehead.

Louis could see two other men painting a hull. From what he could tell from the mug shots in the case folder, they looked to be Van Slate's two friends. Louis tossed the file in the car and went through the gate.

"Matthew Van Slate?" he called as he approached him.

Van Slate looked down, the sander in his hand. His knuckles were dirty and raw, several scraped nearly to the bone.

"Who are you?" Van Slate asked, turning off the sander.

"Louis Kincaid. I'm working with the Sereno Key Police Department. I need to ask you a few questions."

Van Slate's eyes narrowed. "Get lost," he said. He went back to his sanding.

Louis waited, knowing Van Slate would eventually turn around again. After almost a full minute, Van Slate looked back down at Louis.

"I thought I told you to get lost."

"All you have to do is answer a few questions." Louis could tell Van Slate was trying his damnedest to figure out who he was—and what authority he actually had here.

Finally, Van Slate set the sander on the ladder and climbed down. His eyes locked on Louis, and he reached into his back jeans pocket for a cigarette. Louis waited while he lit it. The pungent smell of paint thinner drifted on the breeze.

"Be careful, you might go up in flames," Louis said.

Van Slate slipped the lighter back in his pocket and blew out smoke. "Okay, what?"

"Two black men were found murdered here in the last month. Both were beaten. You heard about it?"

"Why would I care?" Van Slate's lips, gripping the cigarette, barely moved when he spoke.

"Past history."

Van Slate pointed the cigarette at Louis. "Look, that shit with my old lady is over with. I don't care anymore how many—who she fucks." Van Slate looked at the gravel, then out over the yard. "I got a new life now."

"Must be hard, though."

"What?"

"Your buddies still talk about it?"

Van Slate's eyes drilled into Louis. "Get the fuck out of here."

Louis glared back, feeling a surge of anger. Van Slate stepped forward. For a second Louis thought he was going to hit him and he braced himself.

"You'd like to kick my ass, wouldn't you?" Van Slate said.

"Yeah," Louis said.

"But you can't. Cops got rules. Too bad."

Van Slate took a drag from his cigarette. Louis focused on Van Slate's bruised knuckles. Images of Anthony Quick's battered face came to his mind. He inhaled and forced his words out evenly, meeting Van Slate's eyes.

"Where were you a week ago Tuesday, about six-thirty P.M.?"

Van Slate shook his head. "I don't have to talk to you."

"You'll talk, Mr. Van Slate. If not to us, then to the sheriff's department."

"You fucking people . . ." Van Slate muttered, turning away.

Louis reached out and hit his shoulder, spinning him around. "What?"

Van Slate stared at him, shocked, then smiled. "Cops. You fucking cops."

Over Van Slate's shoulder, Louis noticed the two friends staring at them. Van Slate followed his gaze, then said, "Touch me again and they'll be all over your ass, you son of a bitch. This is my boatyard. There's not one fucker in here who will come to help you. You understand that?"

Van Slate's friends were edging forward. Louis resisted the urge to look around.

"Don't threaten me, Van Slate," Louis said. *Cops have rules.* Little did this asshole know.

Van Slate flicked the ashes of his cigarette at Louis and they landed on his chest.

"I don't feel sorry for either of those two . . ." Van Slate deliberately let his voice trail off, eyeing Louis.

Louis reached out and threw an arm around Van Slate's neck, spinning him into a quick choke hold and backing up against the boat so he could see the other two across the yard.

"This is police brutality. I'll report your ass," Van Slate hissed.

Louis pulled tighter, keeping his eyes on Van Slate's friends. "I'm going to ask you again. Where were you last Tuesday night?"

Van Slate gagged. "I was at home, watching a basketball game."

"Who was playing?"

"Shit, I don't remember. I was drinking. Let me go, you're fucking choking me."

"Anyone with you?"

Again, silence.

"Anyone with you?" Louis shouted, jerking on Van Slate's neck.

"Yeah! Both of them guys. Now let me go!" Van Slate yelled, bucking against him. Louis released him and Van Slate stumbled away. He spun back to face him.

"I'll have your fucking badge!" he screamed.

Louis watched the friends, who suddenly didn't look too eager to deal with a cop.

"Good luck," Louis said.

"I'll see you again!" Van Slate shouted. "You can bet on that!"

"I'll be holding my breath."

Louis walked toward the gate, hearing the crunch

of his shoes on the gravel, listening for a rush of bodies behind him. But there was nothing except the beating of his heart and the clang of the boatyard gate as he slammed it behind him.

Chapter Thirteen

Louis drove aimlessly, turning the encounter with Van Slate over in his head. Van Slate didn't seem too bright. Most likely, Van Slate senior ran the office, leaving junior to bust his nuts sanding hulls. It occurred to Louis suddenly that the hull of the huge white Hatteras was painted a nice shining black. Vince Carissimi still hadn't reported back on whether the Krylon can found near Tatum matched the paint on Anthony Quick's body. Maybe it wasn't spray paint after all. He made a mental note to bring it up to Wainwright.

Louis glanced at his watch. Just after nine-thirty. He decided to go check in with whoever was pulling surveillance on the causeway.

Louis spotted Officer Candy's face behind the

wheel of a Toyota in the small parking lot nearby where fishermen routinely left their boat trailers. Candy was sifting through that morning's *News-Press*, looking tired after what was probably a long and boring shift. He smiled as he saw Louis approach.

"You didn't bring any coffee, did you?" Candy asked.

"Sorry, man," Louis said, leaning into the window. "Anything going on?"

Candy yawned. He was in civvies and looked like a tourist, not a cop. "Not a thing. We had four cars come over all night and I knew every one of them."

A Cadillac came by and Candy eyed the occupants: an elderly couple with a Chihuahua hanging out the window. He dutifully recorded their Palm Beach County tag number as they passed through.

"You here to relieve me?" Candy asked hopefully.

"Sorry," Louis said. "I'm thinking of heading over to Fort Myers Beach to talk to the hotel clerk."

Candy nodded and looked out over the sun-silvered bay. "You really think we're gonna catch this guy?" he asked.

"We're going to try," Louis said. He slipped his sunglasses on. "Later, man."

Traffic was light on the mainland but twice Louis had to resort to the map spread on the passenger seat. The map had been his bible in the last two weeks as he labored to familiarize himself with the area. Fort Myers wasn't a big town by any standard, but he had managed to get lost in its tangle of two-named streets, subdivisions, and waterways.

Water . . . it seemed to touch everything here. Dodie had told him that life here revolved around the water, that you were never very far from it, what with the gulf, the Caloosahatchee River, and all the bays and inlets. What God or glaciers hadn't carved out, man had added, with canals and waterways that interlaced every neighborhood.

Back in Michigan, water had been a simple thing he had never given much thought to—rivers, lakes, and creeks. But here—here, water was like a pantheon of exotic-named deities.

He had noticed it back at the 7-Eleven when he stopped to get coffee and study the map in an effort to figure out the easiest way over to Fort Myers Beach. He had never seen so many different names for bodies of water. It was like he had heard about Eskimos having a hundred different names for snow.

Hell Peckish Bay. Matlacha Pass. Hardworking Bayou. Pine Island Sound. Buck Key Channel. Big Dead Creek. Old Blind Pass. Kinzie Cove. Gator Slough. The Rock Hole. The Mud Hole. Long Cutoff. Short Cutoff. Glover Bight.

What the hell was a "bight" anyway?

It took one more look at the map before he found San Carlos Boulevard, the main drag leading to Fort Myers Beach. He drove through a commercial clot of marinas and stores, then over a high graceful bridge that deposited him onto the long narrow spit of land that formed the town of Fort Myers Beach.

Louis had to slow the car to a crawl as he started down congested Estero Boulevard.

Fort Myers Beach had little in common with its namesake city on the mainland and even less with Sereno. Out on the key, a glimpse of blue water and sky was never out of eyesight and the loudest noise was the squawk of a gull. Fort Myers Beach was a carnival crush of hotels, T-shirt shops, and fast-food joints. The sidewalks were choked with seared-skinned tourists who waddled along with the stomach-full, head-empty gaits of winter parolees. The air smelled of sea spray, caramel apples, pizza, and Coppertone.

Louis spotted the Holiday Inn and pulled in.

He parked under a palm and got out, his eyes scanning the crowded lot. It was black asphalt, freshly repaved, the oily smell baking in the sun. Most of the cars were basic sedans with out-of-state or lease plates.

The sheriff's deputies had already questioned the hotel clerk and told Wainwright that nothing had come of the interview. Louis wasn't sure what he expected to get out of the clerk, maybe some vibration someone else had missed.

A young man with neatly cropped hair looked up at him as he approached the front desk. His brightness quickly faded.

"Oh, man, another cop?"

"How'd you know?"

"Maybe it's the walk."

Louis smiled. "Sereno Key." He glanced at the kid's name tag. "You're Kevin Grunow?"

"One and the same." He sighed. "Look, I told everything I know to the other guys."

"I'm just here to clarify some things," Louis said.

Kevin stood up straight. "Okay. I was on duty that afternoon. I had just gotten off, around eight, and I heard a bang."

"Go on."

"I figured it was a car backfiring and I just forgot about it until the police showed up a week later. My boss called me in and they asked me what I saw. But I saw nothing, nada, zilch.''

"Do you know if there were any other witnesses?"

Kevin shrugged. "This is a hotel, man, people come and go. We were busy that weekend because of that computer convention. The boss gave them a list of everyone who was registered. I guess you're trying to track them all down for questioning, huh?"

Louis nodded. Luckily, the kid wasn't bright enough to figure out the sheriff's department and Sereno Police Department weren't the same thing. Most civilians weren't.

"I made copies," the kid said suddenly. "You need one? I got the guy's phone list, too."

"That would be helpful to us, Kevin." Blind dumb luck.

Kevin disappeared and came back a few seconds later with a copy of a computer printout. Louis glanced at the phone list. Quick had made four calls, all back to his home in Toledo. Nothing.

"Anything unusual about Mr. Quick, Kevin? Did he have any visitors? Put anything in your safe?"

Kevin shook his head. "Not that I know of."

Louis folded the papers and glanced around the lobby. "I understand Mr. Quick asked about going fishing the morning he was killed. Do you know where?"

"Well, there's lots of fishing around here."

"Such as?"

"You could do back bay, where you hire a guide. Or you can go on one of the charters that go out to the gulf. Or you could just go down to the pier and rent a pole."

"What do most tourists do?"

"Charters. I think I remember him looking at those brochures." He pointed to a rack behind Louis.

Louis plucked out the four brochures on fishing charters. There were trips on everything from small skiff rentals to large overnight charters that went to the Keys. Most of the charter boats were located at Fisherman's Wharf, near the bridge he had passed over that led to the beach.

He thanked Kevin and left. As he backtracked to the bridge, he had a sinking feeling that this, like the trip to see Van Slate, was going to be another waste of time. If Quick had shown up at Fisherman's Wharf, the sheriff's deputies probably had it covered. Besides, there was no proof Quick had gone fishing the day he died. The check Wainwright had run on Quick's credit cards had revealed no charges to fishing boats. And as the hotel clerk pointed out, Quick could have gone to any number of places to fish. To top it all off, Quick's car was found back at the hotel.

The docks fronted a narrow baylike body of water that faced Fort Myers Beach. The slips were crowded with boats: fancy sailboats, fishing skiffs like Dodie's, and at the far end a couple of shrimp boats, great hulking contraptions festooned with nets and huge poles extending outward like antennae.

Louis scanned the charter boat office and bar that fronted the docks. The office was closed but there was music and laughter coming from the bar.

He started by showing Anthony Quick's picture at the bar, but no one could remember seeing him. Back outside, there was only one charter boat in dock, a beat-up-looking tub with a sign announcing CAP'T ED'S FISHING CHARTERS.

It appeared deserted but as he drew closer, Louis heard a banging sound inside the cabin.

"Hey! Anyone around?" he called out.

It took some more yelling before a man emerged brandishing a hammer. He was squat and bandy-legged, wearing grimy cutoffs and worn Docksiders. His bare chest was suntanned to a dark mahogany, his sparse hair bleached out to white.

"Ain't hiring out today," the man said.

Louis came forward. "I'm not here for fishing. I'm looking for some information."

The man squinted up at him. "Oh, yeah? 'Bout what?"

Louis held out Quick's photo. "You ever seen this man?"

The man didn't move. "You a cop?"

"Yes."

"What'd he do?"

"Nothing." Louis extended the photo. "You seen him around here in the last two weeks?"

Slowly, the man came forward and took the picture, glanced at it, and held it out. "Nah. Never seen him."

Louis took it back. "He was a tourist. You're sure?"

The man shrugged. "Hell no, I ain't sure. We get lots of tourists down here. I can't say for certain he wasn't one of them."

Louis slipped the photo back in the file. "How many other boats are usually here?"

"Five of us. We come back 'bout four-thirty. I'd be out myself if it weren't for the damn generator."

Louis's eyes wandered over the empty slips. Shit, he would have to come back. He started to his car, then doubled back to the bar and ordered a hamburger and beer. He stood at the open bar, sipping a beer and watching a large brown pelican waddle down the dock. There was a stink of rotting fish in the air. Louis thought of Dodie, who had been bugging him to go out fishing. As long as he lived, he would never understand the allure of sitting for hours waiting for a damn fish to bite.

He finished eating and returned to the parking lot. He was about to get in the car when he noticed a ramshackle wooden structure on the far edge of the lot. It had a loading dock open to the parking lot and a rusted corrugated-roof carport filled with junk. Fishing nets were strung below a sign that said DIXIE FISH CO. WHOLESALE AND RETAIL. WE SHIP UP NORTH. There was a toilet on the dilapidated porch. It was planted with bright pink geraniums.

Louis trudged up the steps and pushed open the screen door.

It was dark as a cave inside, except for a lighted refrigerator case. Behind the frosted glass, Louis could see slabs of fish and piles of pink shrimp. The weathered plank walls were covered with bumper stickers, pictures, and junk.

"Howdy."

The voice was husky female. Squinting, Louis made out a figure silhouetted against the far open window. He went forward and she came into view.

Medium height, shapely, blond hair piled on her head, hand propped on cocked hip. And very large tanned breasts barely covered by a bright pink bikini top.

He had to struggle to keep his eyes on her face. She noticed and gave him a smirky smile.

"You want something?" she asked.

He pulled out Quick's photo. "Have you seen this man around here?"

She didn't even look at the picture. Her smile faded. "I got fish. You want fish?"

"Not really. I—"

She turned away, grabbing a remote and aiming it at the wall. The place filled up with the sound of Charlie Parker's buttery sax.

"Okay, okay!" Louis yelled.

She punched the remote, lowering the volume, and looked back at him.

He glanced at the glass fish case. "Give me some shrimp."

"How much?"

When he hesitated, she sighed. "How many you feeding?"

"Three," he said.

"What size? We got small, medium, and jumbo."

"You decide."

She smiled and moved languidly to the case. He could see her breasts clearly in the light of the case as she shoveled the shrimp, but not her face. She plopped a plastic bag down on the counter. "That's forty-five bucks."

"What?"

"They're jumbos, hon."

Louis dug into his pocket and pulled out two twenties and a ten. "Keep the change," he said.

She gave him a smile as she deposited the money in a drawer. His eyes were getting used to the dim light. She wore her ponytail high on her head like that little girl in the *Flintstones* cartoon. She could have been eighteen or forty; he couldn't tell.

"I hate cops," she said.

"Most people do," Louis said. He held out the photo. "This man might have been here about two weeks ago. Did you see him?"

She glanced at it, shrugged, and turned away, bending down to pick up some paper, making sure Louis got a prime view of her ass in the tight cutoffs.

"How's business?" he asked.

It took a moment, but she smiled. "Beats flipping burgers in a hair net at Wendy's. I get a lot of men customers off the boats."

"I don't doubt it." Louis held out Quick's photo again.

"I saw him," she said.

"Are you sure?"

"Positive. I'm here every day and I notice things."

"How do you know it was him?"

She shrugged. "We don't get many black guys coming in here. But this guy I remember. He had just come in off a charter and he came in here to buy some fish to ship home."

"Why would he buy fish?"

She smiled. " 'Cause he didn't catch anything and he wanted to send a big fish home to impress his kids."

"Do you know what boat he chartered?" Louis asked.

She shook her head. "They all get back in around four-thirty or so."

"Thanks. I'll be back." Louis picked up the bag of shrimp. At least he'd have something to take back to Margaret for dinner. He started to the door.

"You're the first, you know," she said.

"The first what?"

"The first cop I told this to."

Louis stepped back toward the woman. "Did the sheriff's deputies come talk to you?"

"They talked to me. But I didn't talk to them."

"Why not?"

She smiled. "They didn't buy my jumbos."

Chapter Fourteen

Louis walked in the door to the Sereno Key station and paused, looking around for somewhere to put the shrimp. Greg Candy looked up from his desk, spotting the bag in Louis's hand.

"Those look good. Where'd you get them?" he asked.

"From the shrimp woman at the wharf. Cost me forty-five bucks to find out Quick stopped there after his fishing trip. You guys got a fridge?" Louis asked.

"Yeah." Candy came forward and took them from Louis.

Louis headed toward the bathroom to wash his hands. He walked into Wainwright's office, still drying them. He stopped short at the door. Wainwright was seated at his desk and two black men stood in front of him, both in dark suits and ties. The taller of the two was slender and bald, with an earring in his right ear. The other one was built like a wrestler.

Wainwright caught Louis's eye and waved him in.

"Kincaid, this is Oscar Mills," Wainwright said, motioning toward the taller one. "And Wallace Seaver. Southwest Florida NAACP. Gentlemen, Louis Kincaid."

Mills looked back at Wainwright. "And his position is?"

"Consultant."

Seaver and Mills gave Louis the once-over as he came farther into the room.

Wainwright handed Louis a newspaper, folded to an inside page. Louis scanned it quickly. It was an editorial that took all the local law enforcement agencies to task for their failure to officially acknowledge the two murders as hate crimes.

Louis looked back at Seaver and Mills. "I see their point," he said. "But right now, we're not sure what we're looking at."

"The chief already made that point," Mills said. "We disagree."

Louis glanced at Wainwright.

"We're doing all we can," Wainwright said. "We've committed as much manpower as we can to the case, and we've got a couple of solid leads we're pursuing."

It wasn't true. They didn't have anything really, and Louis resisted the urge to look at Wainwright again.

"We're not here to bust your chops, Chief," Mills said. "We're here to offer our help."

"How?" Wainwright asked.

Mills set his briefcase on the desk and withdrew a

file. He held it out to Louis, who stepped forward to take it. It was filled with computer sheets, mailing lists, bad copies of white supremacist literature, and photos of white men.

"We've compiled this over the last few years," Mills said. "We like to know who's hiding under the proverbial rocks, if you get my meaning. There are a hundred and five names there, all confirmed to be members of various white power organizations or convicted of race-related crimes."

Louis looked up from the file, glancing at Wainwright. He looked mildly annoyed.

"Have you shown this file to anyone else?" Louis asked Mills.

"No. We hoped you would act on it first. We don't want to have to release these men's names to the media. But we will if we have to."

Louis stared at Mills. "They're not suspects yet, Mr. Mills," he said. "At least not in these murders."

"We just want you to do your job."

Louis glanced at Wainwright. It was obvious Wainwright was going to let him take the lead on this.

"We'll check into all of them. You have our word," Louis said.

Mills nodded and snapped his briefcase shut. He extended his hand. Wainwright rose and shook both men's hands. They left.

Louis waited for Wainwright to say something. Wainwright moved to the watercooler.

"Do our jobs," he muttered.

"They're just doing theirs," Louis said.

"I know, but I just hate outside interference, especially from people who don't know a damn thing about police work. Everything's so damn political with them."

"Them?"

Wainwright turned. "Outsiders. District attorneys. Civil liberty groups. Activists. Bleeding hearts. Reporters. Mayors. All of them."

"You getting more pressure?"

Wainwright came back to the desk and slid into his chair. "Mayor Westoff called this morning. Said he'd been hounded by reporters and he's tired of listening to Hugh Van Slate. Wanted to know if we had any suspects."

Louis held out the folder. "Tell him we got a hundred and five of them."

Wainwright smiled weakly. "Right. I guess I should go over there and talk to him, try to calm him down."

Candy poked his head in the door. "Chief, someone wants to see you."

"Now who?"

"Matt Van Slate," Candy said.

Wainwright glanced up at Louis. "Did you see Van Slate today?"

"This morning. Didn't get anything."

"Let him in," Wainwright said to Candy. Wainwright stood up as Van Slate appeared at the door.

Van Slate's eyes shot to Louis.

"I want to file a complaint against him," he said, pointing.

"Really?" Wainwright said. "What'd he do?"

"He hassled me. Put me in a choke hold."

"And I'll bet you didn't do anything to provoke it, right, Van Slate?"

Van Slate came toward them. "That's right. Nothing."

"Why do I find that hard to believe, Van Slate?"

"I got witnesses that'll say I never touched him," Van Slate said. "And I know my rights and I know what you guys can do and can't do. I want his file to have a complaint in it. I want him suspended or something."

Wainwright put his hands on his hips. "Well, Matt, my friend, we got a problem then. I can't discipline him for anything. Kincaid is not a cop. He's a private citizen. If you got a beef with him, you'll have to sue him."

Van Slate glared at Louis. Then he thrust a finger at Louis.

"We'll meet again."

"You're starting to repeat yourself, Van Slate," Louis said.

Van Slate turned and stalked out.

"He's a jerk," Louis said.

"Did he take a swing at you? Draw a weapon?" Wainwright asked.

"No."

"Did you?"

Louis hesitated. "I used a show of force."

Wainwright moved to the door, closing it softly. He faced Louis.

"Look, Louis, I know this might be hard, but you have to play it smart right now."

"What do you mean?"

"It's like I told you at the hospital after you chased down Levon. You don't have the protection of a badge anymore. That means little credibility for you when it comes to who's telling the truth. If he had been smart enough to want to press criminal charges, I would've had to take his statement."

Louis sighed. Neither he, Wainwright, nor the investigation needed shit like this right now.

Louis nodded slowly. "Sorry."

"No more assaults on suspects," Wainwright said. "Not in front of witnesses, anyway."

There was a knock on the door.

"Now what?" Wainwright said in exasperation. "Come in!"

Candy poked his head in. "Chief, there's someone else here to see you."

"Jesus, can't it wait, Candy? I've got to—"

"I don't think so, Chief. It's Mrs. Quick."

"Mrs. Quick? Anthony Quick's wife? Shit," he said softly. "Show her in, Candy." Wainwright looked at Louis. "Stick around, okay?"

Louis nodded.

She came slowly into the office, a small woman in a blue dress, carrying a black wool coat over her arm. Her soft brown eyes went from Wainwright to Louis questioningly.

"I . . . I spoke to someone on the phone a couple days ago," she began. "I'm Anita Quick, Anthony's wife."

Wainwright came forward, holding out a chair. "That was me you spoke with, Mrs. Quick, I'm Chief Dan Wainwright. Sit down, please."

Louis watched her closely. He had seen the look on her face before, back on the force in Ann Arbor. It was a stunned look of calm that took over people when they were trying to hold on to reality while their brains were screaming in disbelief. He had come to think of it as the grief mask.

Anita Quick looked like her mask was about to break. Louis glanced at Wainwright. He looked suddenly wound too tight, and his blue eyes, even as they were focused on the woman before him, signaled that he was somewhere else.

Anita Quick was waiting—for one of them to speak, tell her that there had been a mistake, that the man they had pulled out of the water was not her husband after all. Suddenly, she began to cry, putting one hand over her eyes.

Ah, shit. Louis felt something give in his chest.

"Mrs. Quick . . ." he said.

The crying grew into sobs.

"I'll get her some water," Wainwright said. He hurried out, leaving the office door open.

Louis went to the bathroom, grabbed some Kleenex, and came back to sit down in the chair next to Mrs. Quick. He gently pushed the Kleenex into her palm, lying open in her lap. She didn't seem to notice it. The lap of her blue dress was spotted with tears.

Louis looked up at the door. *Damn it, where is Wainwright?* His eyes focused on the watercooler by the wall. *Why did he leave to get water?*

He went to the cooler and drew a cup, taking it to Anita Quick. Her sobs had slackened to weeping punctuated with sharp intakes of breath.

"Mrs. Quick, take this, please."

She finally accepted the cup. She took a sip and handed it back. "I would have been here sooner," she whispered, "but I couldn't find anyone to stay with the boys."

"You didn't have to come," Louis said gently.

"Yes, I did. I have to take Anthony home." She hesitated. "I can do that now, can't I?"

"Yes. I'll make the call." Louis hesitated. "Will you be all right here for a moment?"

She nodded, wiping her eyes with the Kleenex.

Louis rose and started for the door.

"Officer?"

He turned.

"Did Anthony . . ." Her eyes welled. "Did Anthony suffer?"

"No," Louis said.

She nodded slightly. "Thank you," she whispered.

Louis left, pausing outside the door to let out a deep breath. He knew that the Toledo police had been instructed to tell her as little as possible. He knew, too, that few people really wanted to hear the truth, even when they asked. He was thankful that whoever had gone to her home that day to break the news had been kind.

He glanced around the outer office but there was no one there except the dispatcher. Wainwright was gone.

"Myrna, did you see where Dan went?" he asked.

"He left a few minutes ago, but didn't say where," she replied. "Maybe to see the mayor?"

More likely he just didn't want to face Anita Quick, Louis thought grimly. He had known other cops like that, cops who were as cold as ice when confronted with decomposed bodies but who fell apart when they had to talk to a mother whose teenage kid had just been pulled out of a smashed car. Wainwright's steely exterior was apparently just that—a shell.

Well, so what? Wainwright had enough on his plate with the mayor, Van Slate, and the NAACP. He'd give him a pass on this, and handle Anita Quick himself.

He picked up the phone to call Vince Carissimi. He just hoped they'd get a break soon. He didn't want to lie to any more widows.

Chapter Fifteen

Shit. Look at him.

Just sitting there. Just waiting for me . . . Ready to die.

A surge of power raced up through his chest. He slid the truck to a quiet stop, his eyes jumping around quickly. A 7-Eleven sign loomed to the left, but back here, behind the store, no one would see. No one ever saw.

He slipped out of the truck, grabbed the stick from the back, and walked up to the man slumped against the bricks. He had seen him on the beach and known he was perfect. He had followed him, down the crowded sidewalks, staying back, waiting, until now.

The bum lifted a soggy head and squinted at him. "Hey, you got some change, man?" he asked.

He looked down at him. This was too fucking easy.

The shit wanted money. He'd offer him something better.

"Got beer," he said.

The bum smiled as he tried to lift himself up.

He extended a hand and the bum took it, rising. He pulled the bum toward his truck, opened the door, and pushed him inside.

Down the busy street, past the moms and dads and kiddies, moving silently under the flashing neon lights, past the cars. Past the fucking cops. Stupid fucking cops.

The bum started talking.

Shut up . . . Shut the fuck up!

This was all wrong. What the hell were all these people doing out so late? It was busy here. Too busy to stop and kill the bum. He would have to drive farther.

Water . . . he wanted the water. It always helped, having the water there. It quieted the pounding in his head, made things clear enough so he could do it. The water. He needed the water.

Slowing down at the booth . . . the woman inside not even looking at him as he handed over the money. Not like the other causeway, where they were waiting for him now.

Moving on now, slowly. Moving through the dark tunnel of trees, way out to the end.

He opened the window and the ripe night air rushed in. The sting of the salt was in his nostrils, seeping up into his brain.

He killed the ignition. The water . . . faint . . . he could hear it.

It wasn't hard dragging the bum out. He thought he was going to drink.

Stupid nigger. You're going to die.

He shoved him and the bum hit the sand with a thud. The bum's eyes were glazed, not with the booze, but with a confused fear.

He stepped forward, his knife glinting in the moonlight. He dropped to his knees, straddled him, and pushed the knife quickly into the bum's chest. Then again. And again.

Yeah . . . Yeah.

Fuck! No! No! Shit! Motherfucking piece of shit!

He stopped. *Damn it, damn it. Where is it? Where did it go?*

Stupid . . . stupid!

The stench of blood drifted to his nostrils.

Find it! Find it!

There was too much blood, too much blood, he couldn't find it. The murmur of the waves at his feet was drowned out by the pounding in his head.

He looked up at the moon just as it slipped behind the clouds. He pulled the can of paint from his jacket.

Finish it!

Chapter Sixteen

The body lay faceup at the waterline, the skin dusted with sand that glistened in the slanting early morning sun. The waves crept up, gently rocking the body and then recoiling, as if in horror at the gruesome discovery.

There was no face.

The cheekbones and eye sockets had disappeared into the mushy tissue, and what was left was blackened and puddled with foaming water. Only the teeth were left, smashed and distorted against swollen lips. What little skin remained was speckled with black paint.

Louis wet his lips, his stomach queasy. Tatum and Quick had been beaten, but this one . . . this time the face was gone. He steadied himself by taking a few steps away and looking out over the gulf. He concentrated on a lone sailboat, on its shape, a crisp white triangle against the brilliant blue of the sky.

"Damn it, these waves are killing us."

Louis looked back. Wainwright and another man were standing over the body. Wainwright was the one who had spoken. Louis didn't know the other man but he recognized the uniform: Lee County Sheriff. He walked back to them. The deputy's nameplate said G. VARGAS.

"Any evidence left will be crab food," Wainwright said. "Christ, it's almost seven. The rubberneckers are going to be out in force soon. Where are your techs, Deputy?"

"They're on their way, Chief Wainwright." The deputy hesitated. "I better get things taped off."

"Good idea," Wainwright muttered.

Louis heard a car and looked up the beach to the road, but it was just another sheriff's department unit. He looked back and saw Wainwright watching as the two men, one a suit, the other a uniform, started down to the shoreline. The shorter one in the suit looked like a detective. The other was broader and taller in his dark green uniform, with a windswept tuft of blond hair, sunglasses, and a large square jaw. He was walking with a quick, determined stride and Louis suspected it was Sheriff Mobley.

Louis wondered what Wainwright would do. They had no jurisdiction here and had beaten the sheriff's department to the scene only because they heard Deputy Vargas's call come in and had a shorter distance to drive.

This wasn't Sereno Key, but Captiva, the barrier island on the gulf, one bay west of Sereno. Captiva didn't have a police department of its own and relied on the sheriff's office for law enforcement.

Louis saw Mobley's face sour as he noticed Wainwright. Wainwright looked like he was ready for a fight. Louis decided to make himself scarce until the air cleared.

He turned and walked a few paces down the beach, careful to avoid the footprints in the area around the body. His eyes swept over the broad white beach. They were out on the northern end of the island, with only a few cottages set back at least twenty yards from the beach. The cottages were up on low dunes, hidden by waist-high tufts of sea oats and palms. The beach itself sloped gently toward the gulf and the body was further obscured from view by some rocks. The shoreline was not visible from the road. If there had been any witnesses, they would have had to have been right on the beach to see anything.

He walked farther down the beach, finally spotting a clearing in the trees. He went up the dune and through the sea oats. There was a restaurant, its rough-hewn exterior fronted by a patio that was obviously there to offer patrons a view of the sunsets on the gulf. The sign said THE MUCKY DUCK and listed the hours as 5:30 P.M. to 9:30 P.M. He peered in the windows, but saw no one inside. It was unlikely any customers might have been around late last night, but employees might have lingered. He made a mental note to come back and question possible witnesses.

He retraced his steps back to the beach. When he passed one of the cottages, he noticed a man standing on the bluff. He hadn't been there before, and he was shielding his eyes against the sun, trying to see what was going on.

The man suddenly started down toward the water. Louis braced himself to rebuff him.

"What is going on?" the man demanded. He had an accent.

"Nothing, sir. Please go back up where you were."

The man was fiftyish, fat and bald, wearing too-tight red swimming trunks and a pink guayabera shirt open over his tanned belly.

"Did someone drown?"

"No, sir—"

"But there is something bad?"

"No—"

"No? No? *Les flics* . . . the cops. They are there, no?"

The man started forward. Louis pushed gently against his shoulders.

"Yes, there's been an accident. A man is dead."

The man drew back slightly. "Dead? Here? Before my house? *Grand Dieu!*"

"You live here?"

"Yes, I am *le proprio,* the . . ." He frowned. "The landlord for the cottages there." He pointed to the nearest one, a wood-frame place painted soft gray with a screened-in porch.

"Did you see anyone on the beach here late last night or very early this morning?" Louis asked.

"*Moi? non* . . . nothing. *Rien.*"

"You're sure?"

He started to nod but then stopped. "A man, I saw a man on the beach last night."

"What time?"

"Nine, ten? I don't remember. He was walking near the cottages there. People do that. But this is *propriété privée.* I must run them away."

"What did he look like?"

"I don't know. It was dark. He . . . *il a une sale tete.*"

"What?"

He flapped a hand impatiently. "You know, ugly look."

Louis stifled a sigh and pulled out a notebook. "Can I have your name and phone number, please?"

The man looked alarmed. "Why?"

"We might need to talk to you again."

"Pierre Toussaint," he said. "You can phone me at the office," nodding to a rental sign with a number on it.

The place was called Branson's on the Beach. It offered rentals by the week, month, or season. Louis jotted down the number and turned to leave.

"How did he die?" the Frenchman called out.

Louis turned back. "He was stabbed."

"Sad, so sad," the man said. "*Mourir comme un chien.*"

Louis nodded and started back toward the scene below. To die like a dog. His French was good enough to at least pick up that much.

Wainwright and the others looked up as he approached. "Where'd you go?" Wainwright asked.

"Thought I had a witness," Louis said. "He saw someone but can't give a description."

Louis glanced at the sheriff and his detective, both hiding behind their sunglasses. Mobley had the sculptured arms of a bodybuilder and his skin was a golden bronze. He looked like a forty-year-old surfer in a uniform. Louis's eyes were drawn to the shirt's epaulettes. There were five stars, like a general would wear. Most sheriffs or chiefs settled for two.

Mobley nodded toward the body. "You've seen the other ones. This look the same?"

Louis glanced at Wainwright, surprised Mobley would ask. Wainwright didn't say anything, so Louis spoke up.

"Black male, same approximate age, same manner of death." He knelt to look closer. "There's a tattoo on his right forearm."

"Who's this guy?" the suit demanded, jerking a thumb at Louis.

"He's working for me," Wainwright said. "You got a problem with that, Driggs?"

"I got a problem with you being here, Wainwright," Driggs said, mopping his bald head. "Your prints are screwing up the scene."

"So cast my shoes, asshole." Wainwright squatted next to Louis. "Can you make out the tattoo?"

Louis nodded. It was old and faded but still visible on the corpse's light brown skin. "It's a dog, I think," Louis said. "And the name 'Bosco.' "

Louis avoided looking at the crushed face. "His shirt has old stains, pants are ripped, probably not from this struggle. No belt, badly worn sneakers. Not a tourist, I'd guess."

"That's a brilliant observation," Driggs said.

Louis carefully checked the pockets. "No wallet."

"Homeless, most likely," Wainwright said.

"Right," Driggs said. "How'd a homeless guy get out here on Fantasy Island?"

Wainwright rose slowly, dusting the sand from his hands. "He was probably abducted, Driggs. Quick was."

Mobley pressed forward, edging Driggs out of the way. He gave them a tight smile of capped teeth.

"I've heard enough. Driggs, go help Vargas with the crowd," Mobley said.

Driggs trudged up the beach toward his squad car.

"Thanks, gentlemen," Mobley said. "Nice of you to stop by."

Louis rose. Wainwright didn't even look at Mobley. "Fuck you, we're staying around for a while."

"I could have you removed from the scene," Mobley said.

"Can the crap, Lance, there's no cameras here."

Mobley ignored him and bent to poke at the body. Louis pulled Wainwright off to the side. "What makes you think this one was abducted from somewhere else?"

"This isn't like Sereno, Kincaid. Sanibel-Captiva is tourist territory, lots of money. You pay a three-buck toll just to get out here. No way this man is from here."

"But why did he dump him here instead of Sereno?"

"Maybe he knows we're watching the Sereno causeway."

"Shit," Louis muttered.

"What did you have going today?" Wainwright asked.

"I was going to go back to the marina and show Quick's photo around again. But the boats will be out by the time I get there now. There's a restaurant down the beach and I thought—"

"Let that go for now. I want you to check Matt Van Slate's alibi for last night."

"Dan, I've been tailing him. He's been laying low. All he does is drink beer and shoot pool."

"Check him anyway."

Louis suppressed a sigh. "Anything new on Levon?"

Wainwright shook his head. "We thought we had a sighting in Cape Coral. Didn't pan out."

Wainwright looked back at the body. "We have to get an ID on this poor bastard. There's a shelter over in Fort Myers. After you check out Van Slate, head on over there."

Louis heard a car door slam and looked up to see a white van with D.M.E. on the side. Vince Carissimi was coming down the sandy slope through the sea oats.

"Hey, Doc," Wainwright said. "What are you doing here?"

Vince was holding a Styrofoam cup from 7-Eleven. "When the call came in, I decided to come out with Ted," he said, nodding toward the ME office's investigator making his way down from the road carrying a black case. "I wanted to see it firsthand," Vince added.

Vince went over to the body. "Morning, Sheriff."

"Took your time, Vincenzo," Mobley said.

Vince ignored him and took off his sunglasses, letting them dangle on his chest by their neon-green cord. "Would you mind?" he said to Louis, holding out the cup. Louis took the coffee and stepped back. Vince knelt beside the body.

"Who found him?" he asked.

"A jogger," Deputy Vargas said. "Honeymooner staying over at 'Tween Waters. She went out for her morning run and stumbled on it. Literally."

Vince looked up. "This one wasn't shot."

"You sure?" Louis asked quickly.

"Won't know for sure till we get the clothes off, but look at the legs. No wounds."

For several seconds, they were quiet. Louis heard only the lapping of the waves. His gaze traveled over the sand, up to the road, and beyond. He was thinking about the woman jogger and the horror she must have felt when she finally realized what she was looking at. Some honeymoon.

"How long you think he's been dead?" Mobley asked, drawing Louis's attention back.

Vince shrugged. "He's cool to the touch. Quick guess . . . less than four hours."

That would set the time of death at about 3 A.M., hours after the Frenchman saw the trespasser and long after anyone would have been on the beach.

"Can I have my coffee back now?" Vince asked.

Louis handed him the cup. The investigator was starting his work now, taking Polaroids. Louis heard a car door slam and looked up to see the CSU guys coming down the slope.

"He's changing his pattern," Louis said quietly to Wainwright.

Wainwright nodded, staring at the body.

"He shot the others but not this one. And he killed Tatum where he came upon him," Louis went on. "But he picked up Quick in Fort Myers Beach and killed him on Sereno. Now he dumped this one here. Why?"

"Why not?" Wainwright said.

"Seems like more of a gamble he'd get caught here," Louis said. He thought of the map back in his car. "There's a million little bays and swamps he could have dumped him instead. Why here?"

Wainwright was looking out at the gulf.

"Why is he changing his pattern?" Louis asked.

"Christ, I don't know, Louis," Wainwright said. "Maybe he didn't need to shoot this guy. Maybe he forgot his gun this time. Maybe he dumped him here because he works here. Maybe he just likes the water. We don't need to read the fucker's mind to catch him. We need physical evidence."

Louis remained silent. He knew Wainwright's sharpness came from frustration. Shit, he felt the same. Three dead men and they had nothing concrete to go on. He had followed Van Slate. Nothing. They had taken photos at Tatum's funeral and staked out the cemetery for eighteen hours hoping the killer would show. Nothing. They had manned the Sereno causeway around the clock and the bastard had just moved to another one.

Now the killer was switching his MO and they didn't know a damn thing about whom they were looking for. And no matter what Wainwright believed, he knew they would never find him until they did.

Mobley looked at Wainwright. "I think you two have seen enough. Watch where you walk on the way out."

"I've got a right to be here," Wainwright said.

"Let's get real, Wainwright. You're out of your league here."

Louis looked up. *Christ.*

"The first two washed up in my territory, you asshole," Wainwright said.

Mobley tilted his head up to the sun, his glasses catching the light. "Well, now we've got one, too."

Wainwright reached up and pulled the sunglasses off Mobley's face. "You're an idiot if you think you can handle this alone, Mobley," Wainwright said. "You're going to get eaten alive come election time."

He shoved the glasses into Mobley's hands and turned, walking quickly up the hill. Louis hurried after him.

"Dan—"

"Later, Kincaid," Wainwright said.

"No, now."

Wainwright stopped.

"What difference does it make if we help him or he helps us?" Louis demanded.

"I know the man. You can't put him in charge," Wainwright said. "He's got an eye on the DA's office and he'll drag this thing out forever just to keep his name in the papers. He doesn't care about those dead men because he doesn't care about people. It's all about him and how much face-time he gets on TV."

Wainwright started walking again. "Besides, I have another idea."

"What?"

"I'll tell you later."

"Tell me now."

Wainwright stopped. "We're dealing with a serial killer, Louis. That means we can get help. I'm calling the bureau. I still got a few friends over there. I'm going to ask for Malcolm Elliott. Great guy. Worked a half dozen of these things."

Louis nodded. Good. That was good.

The sun was rising in the sky. Wainwright pulled out a handkerchief and wiped his face as he looked back down at Mobley and the others.

"Dan," Louis said, "did you notice the face on this one? He's getting madder."

Wainwright nodded. "But you're wrong about the pattern changing," he said. "He still killed on a Tuesday. That gives us six days to find the bastard."

He stuffed the handkerchief back in his pocket and trudged up to the street.

Louis stood there, not quite ready to leave, and not wanting to go back down to where the faceless body lay baking in the sand. The sun was hot on his neck, and the murmur of the crowd gathering behind the yellow tape mingled with the whisper of the waves on the beach. He heard something rise above it. It was Vince Carissimi. He was whistling "Sitting on the Dock of the Bay." Louis looked out at the water. The sailboat was gone.

Chapter Seventeen

After leaving the beach on Captiva, Louis headed over to the homeless shelter in Fort Myers. No one there knew of a man who had a dog tattoo, but the director promised to post a notice about it. He also told Louis about a man nicknamed The Saint who ran a soup kitchen on Fort Myers Beach. Louis detoured over to the beach but The Saint had already packed up his makeshift operation by the time Louis arrived.

On the way back to the station, Louis made a quick stop at the boatyard, intending to question Van Slate about his whereabouts last night. But a secretary told him Van Slate was off on Tuesdays and Wednesdays. She cheerfully gave him Van Slate's home address.

Back at the station, he went directly to Wainwright's

office. Wainwright was on the phone and motioned for Louis to wait. Louis walked to the watercooler and poured himself a cup. Wainwright had a photograph on the desk in front of him. It was of the homeless man's body lying on the beach. Louis was glad it wasn't a close-up of the face.

"Back from the shelter already?" Wainwright asked, hanging up the phone.

Louis nodded. "Nobody there recognized the tattoo, but the director promised to post a notice. Maybe someone will recognize it. Also found out about a soup kitchen over on Fort Myers Beach, but the guy was gone when I got there. I'll check into it tomorrow morning."

"Good."

"Van Slate's off work today. I'm heading over to his apartment," Louis said. "You want to come?"

Wainwright stood up, groaning. "Can't. Mayor Westoff's coming by in twenty minutes."

"No problem. I'll handle it," Louis said, tossing the cup in the trash.

"Take Candy with you."

Louis eyed him. "I can handle it."

"Van Slate doesn't like you and he knows you're not a cop and he can do anything to you he wants," Wainwright said. "Candy can step in if he gets out of line. Take backup, Louis."

Louis bit back his response. Backup. That was a nice way to say "baby-sitter." He knew Wainwright was right but he still didn't like it.

Outside, he spotted Candy waiting near the door. Candy tossed down his cigarette and fell into step with Louis as he walked to the cruiser. Candy walked to the driver's side and Louis paused, then climbed into the passenger side.

"Know where we're going?" Louis asked.

Candy nodded. "I arrested him the first time."

Louis put on his sunglasses, hiding his souring mood. *Van Slate knows you're not a cop.*

God, he was really beginning to hate this, trying to work in limbo, not knowing where his limits ended and the suspect's rights began. There had always been a definite line before. Now the line was drawn in sand, constantly shifting. It was all so much clearer with the badge.

He leaned back in the seat. No. That wasn't really true. He had learned that much in Michigan. They had all been cops but they had not known their limits. And he had almost allowed himself to be pulled right in with them.

They pulled out and turned onto a narrow asphalt road, shaded by a tunnel of trees. Louis glanced out the window, catching occasional glimpses of the water between the houses. Candy started whistling a tune. Louis glanced over at him, trying to place it.

"What is that?"

"What?" Candy asked.

"That song."

" 'I Walk the Line.' Johnny Cash."

"Right."

"I keep a close watch on this heart of mine . . ."

Louis looked away.

Candy kept singing, sounding less like Johnny Cash and more like a bullfrog. He nudged Louis. "C'mon . . . because you're mine . . ."

"I walk the line," Louis sang softly.

Candy laughed. "Man, you got a terrible voice."

Louis smiled.

Candy was quiet for moment as he slowed for a stop sign. "Chief going to take you on eventually?"

Louis was surprised he asked. "Nah, I think I'm going home after this."

"Where's home?" Candy asked.

Louis was about to answer, but hesitated. Who knew anymore?

"Up North," Louis said finally.

"I'm from a place called Everglades City," Candy went on. "Ever hear of it?"

"I'd guess it's in the Everglades."

"Yeah. Armpit city. I came up to Fort Myers to go to college, got my bachelor's, met the girl I'm going to marry, and landed this job. I figure in three years I'll have one of those cool old condos on the Atlantic and be wearing a Miami-Dade patch on my arm."

"Why Miami?" Louis asked.

"That's where all the shit happens, Louis. Sereno's great and so is the chief, but I'd be bored to death if I had to spend the rest of my career here."

"You call this case boring?"

"Well, no, but I'm twenty-three, man. I want to be where life really happens. That's why I have it all planned out, right down to the month."

Louis smiled to himself.

Planned out. Right.

Just like all those great plans he had made for himself. Prelaw at Michigan but always with an eye to the police academy. Then the first job with the Ann Arbor force and the plan was officially launched. Two quick seasons in the minors and he'd move up to the Detroit PD, the real work. A couple more years in uniform, making his mark, and then a nice gold detective badge hanging on his dress shirt. All without ever having to leave the great state of Michigan. Nice and neat.

Life is what happens when you're busy making plans, Louis.

Who was it who had told him that? Phillip Lawrence . . . his foster father. He remembered now. A rainy afternoon in May 1980. College graduation ceremony. It was what Phillip had said after Louis had finally worked up the guts to tell him he wasn't going on to law school after all.

I've got it all planned out, Phillip. It's what I want. I want to be a cop and stay here in Michigan, near you and Frances.

Phillip Lawrence had been disppointed. Frances had cried. But they supported his plan. It was three years later when Phillip finally told Louis what he really thought, that Louis's life plan was "safe."

Safe? What's safe about being a cop?

You're looking for what you didn't have as a kid, Louis, assurances that life is neat and tidy and safe. But life, real life, is messy. It's what happens when you're busy making plans.

He sat up in the seat. A thought that had been just a swirl in his brain was starting to coalesce. He wasn't going back to Michigan. He could see that now. He didn't know where he would go when this was done. But he knew now that he wasn't going back.

"We're here."

Candy pulled to a stop in front of a pale pink apartment building. There were four units. Louis got out and followed Candy to the door of one on the ground floor. They knocked and waited. Candy was tapping his nightstick lightly against his thigh, whistling softly.

Van Slate opened the door, squinting into the sun.

"Oh, Jesus Christ . . ."

"May we come in, Mr. Van Slate?" Candy asked.

"What do you think?"

Candy glanced at Louis. "Where were you last night after eleven?"

Van Slate started to close the door. Candy shoved his foot in to brace it. Van Slate looked down at Candy's shiny black shoe, then up, his eyes sliding to Louis.

"Get off my property. You're trespassing."

"He's with me," Candy said.

"Ain't that too bad." Van Slate shoved on the door and Candy was forced to withdraw his foot. The door shut in their faces.

"So much for cooperating," Louis said, turning. He spotted Van Slate's truck in the drive and walked to it. It was a new Chevy pickup, painted a bright custom blue. Louis went to it, his eyes scanning the flatbed. It was immaculate. Not a speck of dirt, let alone an empty spray paint can.

He moved to the doors and peered in the dark-tinted windows, tempted to try the door handle. He knew he couldn't open the doors as a cop, but he wasn't sure where he stood as a private citizen. He also knew it would bring Van Slate storming from his apartment. He decided to take the chance.

He opened the truck door. The interior was clean, except for sand on the driver's-side floorboards.

"You can't touch that without a warrant!" Van Slate shouted, bursting from his apartment.

Louis turned, facing him. Candy was standing to Van Slate's left, watching.

"Get away from my truck."

"Where were you last night?" Louis asked.

Van Slate was panting. Louis glanced back at the truck. There was definitely something in there that Van Slate didn't want them to see. What was it? Gloves? A knife hidden under the seat?

"Where were you last night?"

Van Slate took a step toward Louis and Candy gently slapped the nightstick sideways against his belly. Van Slate looked down at it.

"I can puncture your spleen and never leave a bruise with this, Van Slate," Candy said calmly. "Want to see?"

Van Slate took a step back.

"Answer the man," Candy said.

"I went out drinking with my friends. I was at the Lob Lolly till after two. Then we went to the beach."

"What beach?"

Van Slate glared at him. "Fort Myers."

"You weren't on Captiva?"

"Captiva? Hell no."

Louis was looking behind the seat now. On the floor, he saw what looked like the handle of a knife, but he wasn't sure.

Damn.

He wondered what the chances were of getting a quick warrant for the truck. He looked over at Candy.

"Watch him."

He walked back to the cruiser and radioed Wainwright, and told him about what he thought he saw. He asked about a search warrant.

"All we got is his past crimes," Wainwright said.

"Unless you can break his alibi, it's weak. Damn weak."

"I know."

"Can you call it plain view exception?" Wainwright asked.

Louis glanced back. "Yeah. Let's try it."

He clicked off and returned to the truck, reaching under the seat.

"What are you doing?" Van Slate yelled.

Louis used a pen to carefully extract the knife handle so he could see the blade. But it wasn't a blade. It was a putty knife, dull and gobbed with a hard mud-brown paste.

Louis let the seat fall back into place. *Damn it.*

"What? What?" Van Slate asked.

"Let's go," Louis said to Candy.

They got back in the cruiser and pulled away. Louis was watching as Van Slate moved quickly to his truck and started rummaging inside.

"What a nightmare," Louis muttered.

"What?" Candy asked.

"He might be destroying evidence and there's not a damn thing we can do about it."

It was late when he got home that night. Inside, the house was quiet and dark except for the patio lanterns out back.

Louis grabbed a beer from the refrigerator, picked up his files and notes, and slipped out the sliding glass door to the patio. He dropped into a chair and took a drink. It was pitch-black, no moon, no stars.

A cool breeze drifted in from the mangroves bringing with it the dank smell of low tide. The quiet was broken only by the groan of Dodie's boat against the pilings.

Serial killer.

When Wainwright had come out and said those two words, something had ignited inside him—horror, fear. He wasn't afraid to admit it. More dead men, more dead black men, more crushed faces and broken families.

But with the horror had come something else—a ripple of adrenaline coursing through his veins.

He had spent most of the day after the visit to Van Slate wading through the NAACP files. One hundred and five angry white men, all with axes to grind, rage to vent. All looking for someone to blame for their own misery.

He thought back to the encounter with Van Slate. The guy hated blacks, that much was obvious. But did he hate them enough to kill? He didn't know that much about serial killers, but he did know enough about people in general, that sometimes what you saw on the surface wasn't what simmered beneath. Did enough rage boil below Matt Van Slate's bigotry to turn him into a murderer? Was there a seed of evil there?

"You're in late."

Louis turned to see Dodie standing near the patio door. He was wearing boxers, a T-shirt, and white socks. His little spikes of gray hair shimmered in the lantern light.

"Need a fresh one?" he asked, nodding at Louis's beer.

Louis shook his head. "No, thanks. Did I wake you?"

"Nah, I was watching the news in bed. The guy said cops think it's a serial killer now. That true?"

Louis nodded and took a drink.

Dodie sat down across from Louis. "You know much about serial killers?"

"Just a little, from reading," Louis said. "They weren't such a hot topic when I was in school. Kind of a new breed."

"They caught Bundy down here, you know."

"I know. Stopped by a traffic cop. We could stop our killer tomorrow and not know it was him. We have no idea who he is."

"You'll catch him. You and Wainwright make a good team. He's got a damn good reputation down here."

Louis laid his head back. "He's calling in his buddy from the bureau."

"Well, that's gotta help."

Louis got up abruptly. He tossed his beer into the trash can and stood there, staring out at the canal. It was so dark out here. So quiet.

"What's the matter, Louis?"

"Nothing."

Dodie was quiet for a minute; then Louis heard the chair squeak as Dodie got up. Louis turned and watched him walk toward the sliding glass door.

"I need to tell Wainwright about Michigan."

Dodie came back and sat down across from Louis.

"I don't want him to hear it from someone else. I want him to know why I had to quit the force." Louis looked away. This was hard. "I don't want to lose his respect."

"Then tell him."

"It's hard to explain."

"Tell me first then," Dodie said. "It'll be easier the second time around."

The darkness seemed overwhelming. Louis could feel the sweat on his forehead.

"It all came down to one night," Louis began slowly.

Twenty minutes later, Dodie sat back in the lounge chair, his eyes leaving Louis's face for the first time. For a long time, Dodie just sat there, staring at his hands. Then he looked up at Louis.

"Sounds to me like you had no choice, Louis," he said.

"Should I tell Dan?"

"If you feel like you need to, yeah. If it's bothering you that much, tell him."

Louis shook his head. "But he's got so much on his mind right now. He doesn't need this."

Dodie nodded. "You'll know when. It's your choice." He rose, stretching. "Well, I'm going in to bed. Night, Louis."

"Night, Sam."

Dodie left. A few minutes later, the light in the bedroom went out.

Choice . . . had he had a choice that night in Michigan? Yes, he had plenty of choices he could have made. Not to go into the woods, not to pull the trigger. Men were dead because of his choices. And he was just now learning to live with that.

The question was, could others see it the way he had that night in the woods? Could a cop like Wainwright see it and not condemn him?

Louis gathered up the files. He would tell Wainwright. But not now, not until this case was over. They needed to catch a murderer and to do that, they had to believe in each other. The rest could wait. It would have to.

Chapter Eighteen

The large bulletin board took up the entire wall near the watercooler. Wainwright told Louis he had put it up that morning, and this was the first time Louis had seen it.

It was divided into three columns, one for each victim, and covered with photos and colored note cards. Wainwright had told him it was a method he learned back at the bureau.

Louis stared at the cards. If there was a system to the color code, he couldn't figure it out. He was reading a yellow card that detailed Anthony Quick's job when Wainwright came in from the bathroom.

"What are the yellow ones for?" Louis asked, pointing.

"Background. Maybe we'll find a thread," Wainwright answered. "You want some coffee?"

Louis shook his head as he went back to reading the cards. Wainwright yelled out the door for Myrna the dispatcher to bring him a coffee.

"I got a call from the bureau yesterday," Wainwright said. "We're not getting Elliott."

"Why not?" Louis asked, turning.

"They didn't say. They're sending someone else, though. Named Farentino. Out of the Miami office."

Wainwright fell silent. His old chair squeaked as he rocked it back and forth. Louis took a chair opposite the desk and stared at the colored cards on the bulletin board.

"How you doing with those NAACP files?" Wainwright asked.

"I've gone through all hundred and five and pulled out about thirty that could be legitimate suspects," Louis said.

"Christ, thirty?"

Louis nodded. "But of those, there are only five that I think we should really concentrate on." He pulled his notebook out of his jeans pocket and flipped it open, slipping on his glasses.

"I've got a Fort Myers man who used to run a white supremacist group in Texas, but he's fifty-seven with emphysema. Two other men who were arrested for starting a brawl at a Jessie Jackson speech. And there's a twenty-two-year-old guy named Travis Durring suspected of a 1984 church burning in Immokolee. Where's that?"

"Town southeast of here in Collier County. You check into him?"

"Yeah. The file says he is also suspected of spray-painting racial slurs on a synagogue in Naples."

"Travis gets around. Coincidence?"

"The paint? I think so."

"You sound like you don't think this one is worth pursuing."

"Churches, synagogues . . . they're vulnerable targets of white rage," Louis said. "But the rage behind these murders is more focused. Like you said, they're personal."

"Is Van Slate in the files?" Wainwright asked.

Louis nodded, taking off his glasses. "He's one of the five I pulled out. They've been keeping an eye on him since he was in high school. He's got a mouth and he uses it."

Wainwright sighed. "I got a call from Hugh Van Slate today," Wainwright said.

"Matt's father?" Louis asked.

Wainwright nodded. "Warned me to lay off his damn kid. Shit . . . kid. The *kid* is thirty years old and still has to have his daddy clean up his messes."

"Can he apply pressure?"

"He's got the mayor's ear, if that's what you mean. And you can find three generations of Van Slate tombstones in the key's cemetery. Hugh's the biggest fish in our little pond here."

Wainwright's face creased in a deep frown. "Sereno used to be like Captiva, getting its police protection from the county. Five years ago, the council voted to start its own force. Hugh was the only dissenting vote. He's never quite warmed up to me. It got worse after we arrested Matt for that beating."

"How does everyone else here feel?" Louis asked.

"Crime is low, property values are high. Folk here like living in the Emerald City and are happy to let me stand behind the curtain and pull the switches. At least, they were."

"I don't think we should give up on Van Slate," Louis said.

"Me either." Wainwright let out a deep sigh. "God-damn it, where's my coffee? Myrna!"

It was Officer Candy who appeared at the door a moment later. "Chief, someone here to see you," he said.

"Who?"

"Agent Farentino." Candy blinked rapidly several times. "FBI, Chief."

"Well, get him in here," Wainwright said, rising quickly and straightening his tie.

Candy disappeared and was back a second later. "Agent Farentino, sir," he said.

Louis turned. It took every ounce of his self-control not to show his shock.

Agent Farentino was small, maybe five-three, with milky white skin, short curly hair the color of a bright copper penny, and large black-rimmed glasses perched on a small freckled nose. The black suit and white shirt showed the wear and tear of the drive from Miami, but there was no mistaking what it didn't hide. Agent Farentino was a woman.

Louis rose slowly and glanced at Wainwright. Wainwright's face was gray, his mouth slightly agape. Agent Farentino didn't wait for things to get worse.

"Emily Farentino," she said, coming forward and thrusting out a hand.

Her voice was deep and melodious, like a late-night disk jockey. Louis had half expected a high-pitched peep. He watched as Emily Farentino's tiny hand disappeared into Wainwright's mitt.

Wainwright pulled himself together enough to mutter out a greeting and ask her to sit down. He glanced at Louis, and coughed up a quick introduction, adding that Louis was a "consultant" on the case. Louis came forward, offering his hand to Agent Farentino. Her handshake was overly firm.

Louis glanced at Wainwright, whose eyes seemed to be pleading for something. He gave Wainwright an imperceivable shake of the head and slid into a chair.

Agent Farentino set her briefcase down next to the chair. She sat back, elbows resting lightly on the arms, fingers interlaced. She was making things easy for Wainwright, tossing out bits of small talk about how nice Sereno Key was, how different it was from Miami. She looked at ease. Or at least she was putting on a damn good show of it, Louis thought. Unlike Wainwright, who still looked like he was having a bad hemorrhoid attack.

The small talk suddenly trailed off.

"So, where do we start?" Farentino said briskly.

Wainwright sat forward in his chair, picking up a file folder. "Well, I guess I should fill you in—"

"I've already read the case file," she said quickly.

Wainwright dropped the file and settled back in his chair. He was staring at Farentino, like she was some alien life-form. Louis also saw something else there in Wainwright's eyes. Disappointment? Anger? He couldn't tell. He glanced at Farentino, suddenly feeling sorry for her.

He saw Emily Farentino's eyes drift up to the colored note cards and back to Wainwright.

"There are some things we should probably go over," she said, hoisting the huge, battered briefcase onto her lap and snapping it open.

Wainwright held up a hand. "We have plenty of

time, Agent Farentino," he said. Louis watched in amazement as Wainwright squeezed out a smile.

"Actually, Chief Wainwright, from what I have read in your files, the last thing we have is time," she said firmly.

Wainwright's smile faded. "What I meant was, I suspect you'd like to get settled first. You have a hotel yet?"

Emily Farentino blinked twice behind the large glasses. "Well, no, I didn't—"

Wainwright rose quickly. "You might try the Sereno Key Inn down the road," he said briskly. "I can have one of the men—"

Farentino paused, glanced at Louis, then back at Wainwright. She closed the briefcase latch. "I have a car, thank you," she said.

She rose and started for the door. She turned back. "What is the activity for the day?" she said.

"Activity?" Wainwright asked.

"What were you and Mr. Kincaid going to do? Before I arrived."

Wainwright hesitated. "We're due at the medical examiner's at eleven."

"Good," Farentino said. "I'll meet you there."

And she was gone. Wainwright sank down into his chair.

"Jesus H Christ," he said softly.

Chapter Nineteen

Louis hated reading in the car, but he forced himself to concentrate. He had nearly filled one spiral book with notes about the three dead men and now, as Wainwright's cruiser zigzagged through the choked traffic on Cleveland Avenue, he tried to make some sense out of what he had written.

Friday. Today was Friday. Four days before he would strike again, if the pattern held true.

The last thing we have is time.

She was right.

He felt nauseated and closed the notebook. He looked over at Wainwright.

His jaw was set, almost clenched, and he hadn't said much since Emily Farentino had walked out of his office. He didn't need to say what Louis suspected, that he was embarrassed about the choice his friends at the bureau had made. Farentino was a rook. And she was female. Was Wainwright's reputation worth no more than that?

"Dan," Louis said softly.

Wainwright grunted.

"About Farentino . . ."

"What about her?"

"She must have something going for her for them to send her."

Wainwright grunted again, this time more softly.

"At least they sent someone," Louis said.

Wainwright glanced at him, then looked back at the road. "It's a token offer of assistance, Louis. In the old days, a request from someone like me would've carried some weight."

They stopped at a light. Louis watched a small plane take off from Page Field and lift quickly into the cloudless blue sky. It gave him a moment to work up the guts to ask the question that had been on his mind all morning.

"Dan, what division did you work?" Louis asked.

Wainwright didn't look at him and didn't answer until the light turned green and they started moving. "OPR," he said. "Office of Professional Responsibility. Retired early on a medical."

Louis stared out the window, lightly tapping his notebook on his knee. Office of Professional Responsibility? Man, he had thought Wainwright's past was a colorful blaze of manhunts, priority investigations, and high-tech forensics. What was this OPR thing?

"We're here. And so is she."

Louis saw Emily Farentino waiting for them outside

the medical examiner's building. She was talking to a man in a suit whom Louis recognized as Driggs.

They climbed out and Farentino turned to watch them approach, pushing her glasses up her nose with her middle finger.

"Chief, this is—" Emily began, motioning to the suit.

"We know each other," Wainwright mumbled, without looking at Driggs.

Driggs was staring at Louis. A wind gust off the nearby airstrip made his comb-over take sudden flight. When he saw Louis looking at it, he smoothed it down over his sunburned head.

"Let's get this over with," Wainwright said.

They followed him inside, down a tiled hall to the autopsy room. Louis trailed, watching Emily Farentino walk—strong, determined steps, a sense of purpose to her stride. She was still dragging that big briefcase but her small shoulders handled it well.

She had changed into jeans and a long-sleeved white shirt that Louis suspected might be a man's. Her tiny ankles were pale and bare, her feet covered in black slip-on flats.

Odd uniform. Odd cop.

Octavius was at his station at the door and nodded silently as they approached. When he held the door for Emily, she thanked him.

"He's the diener," Louis said. "It's German—"

"For servant. I know," she said.

There was no sign of Vince Carissimi except the tape player on the counter. Louis could make out Lynyrd Skynyrd singing "That Smell." He realized suddenly that the sickly sweet death smell that had surrounded Anthony Quick's water-bloated corpse was absent this time. The room now smelled just vaguely musty, like a refrigerator that wasn't quite clean. He looked at Emily Farentino. She didn't seem fazed by it or anything in the room, including the body on the table.

Vince came in. "Welcome back, guys," he said. His eyes immediately picked up Emily. "And you are . . . ?"

There was no sarcasm to his voice, Louis thought, just a hint of . . . what? Interest?

Emily motioned toward the badge hung on a chain around her neck. "Agent Farentino. FBI."

"FBI? Well. Good to meet you. What office?"

"Miami."

"Let's get to it, Doc," Wainwright said.

Vince drew his eyes off Farentino and went to the fiberglass table where the corpse lay, head slanting toward the stainless-steel sink. "No name yet for victim number three?" Vince asked.

Wainwright shook his head. "Got his description, prints, and that dog tattoo posted all across the Southeast. Nothing."

Vince lifted the sheet covering the body from the feet, leaving the face covered.

"The man sorely neglected himself," Vince said. "Don't imagine he'd been to a doctor in years, didn't bathe regularly. He had a scrape that had been infected for weeks."

"Unless the infection killed him, I don't think we care about that," Driggs said.

Vince looked over at Driggs, then went on. "He's about forty, maybe less, no drugs, but a BAC of point-two."

"I don't suppose that killed him either," Driggs said. "Get to the point."

Vince didn't even give Driggs the courtesy of a look this time. He lifted the corpse's hand. "He had motor oil on his palms and on his clothing. Might give you a starting point for a pickup. Unlike the last one, he had no defense wounds. And I was right. No sign of a shotgun wound this time."

Driggs sighed loudly.

"Eighteen stab wounds in the chest cavity and shoulders, but here's the kicker, my friends . . ."

Vince paused. "The wounds are different sizes," he said. "At first I thought I was seeing two different knives, but upon closer inspection, I discovered the killer had broken his knife about halfway through his rage. Look."

Vince pointed to a gaping split in the neck. "This was done with what was left of the knife. The wound depth is only three inches as opposed to up to twelve for the others. Those bruises were made from the butt hitting the skin."

"He broke the knife and he just kept stabbing?" Louis asked.

"Apparently."

Emily squeezed forward between Louis and Driggs. "Tell me we have the blade," she said.

Vince turned and picked up an object wrapped in plastic. He opened it to reveal a thin, bloody blade, with an upward bow to its nine-inch length. "It was stuck in his spine. I believe the killer tried to retrieve it with his hand. I found massive injury to internal tissue that was inconsistent with knife wounds."

Louis felt sick.

"You make the knife yet?" Wainwright asked.

Vince shook his head. "Not yet. But at least I've got the blade to send to the lab now. *Ignotum per ignotius.*"

"So he was stabbed to death," Driggs said.

"Technically," Vince said.

Vince lifted the sheet off the face. Louis tensed, feeling his stomach begin to swirl. Without the blood and seawater, the sunken face looked like a pile of week-old hamburger meat and mushy shredded wheat.

"The beating was postmortem, just like the others," Vince went on. "And he was painted, as you can tell from the flecks still visible. Most of the paint washed away with the tide."

"Same kind of paint?" Wainwright asked.

"Consistent with glossy black Krylon. He used satin on Mr. Quick."

"At least that part of the pattern still holds," Wainwright said.

"It didn't match the boatyard paint?" Louis asked Vince.

"Nope. Definitely plain old Home Depot spray paint."

"That still doesn't eliminate Van Slate," Wainwright said.

"Who's Van Slate?" Driggs demanded.

Wainwright ignored him.

Driggs stepped forward. "Look, Wainwright, I don't care if you bring in half of Quantico's graduating class. If you're holding out—"

"Could this wait, gentlemen?" Vince interrupted. "I moved this case to the top drawer for you boys and now I've got bodies stacked up like 747s at Newark. Let's move on here."

Driggs stepped back. Louis glanced at Farentino. She was staring at Driggs.

Vince cleared his throat. "Now, here's something really interesting. I found nonhuman tissue in the chest wounds."

"Nonhuman?" Wainwright asked. "Like what? Animal?"

"Don't know yet. Give me a couple of days."

Driggs scratched at his bald head. "So, what are you telling us? We got some kind of supernatural monster here?"

Vince smiled and Louis thought he detected a wink in Farentino's direction. "I don't speculate, Sergeant. That's your job."

Driggs slapped his notebook shut. "Send me your full report." He headed for the door.

"Sergeant Driggs," Farentino called out.

He turned impatiently. "What?"

"What kind of bullets you got in that gun?" she asked.

"Copper-jacketed hollow-points. Why?"

Farentino gave him a smile. "Maybe you should pick up some silver ones. And some garlic."

Louis laughed. Driggs stared at Emily, then at Louis. He turned quickly and left.

Louis glanced at Wainwright. He wasn't smiling. Wainwright's radio went off and he turned away, moving out of earshot. Louis turned his attention back to Vince.

"You think the lab can match that knife to something in their catalogs?" he asked.

Vince shrugged. "It's a really odd blade. I'm guessing foreign made. I'll get you some photos of it so you can show it around on your end."

"Kincaid."

Louis turned to Wainwright.

"Some guy at the homeless shelter recognized the tattoo," Wainwright said. "He says he doesn't know who the man is, but he remembers seeing him hanging out at that soup kitchen on Fort Myers Beach."

"The place run by The Saint?"

"Yeah. The guy says The Saint is there right now. But he says to hurry because he folds up his tent right after he's done dishing out lunch."

"I'm on my way," Louis said, starting for the door.

"I'm going with you," Emily said quickly.

Louis glanced at Wainwright. He couldn't hide it. He looked glad to be rid of her.

Chapter Twenty

"I don't think Driggs appreciated your comment," Louis said.

"Do you think he even got it?" Emily said.

They were in a Sereno Key squad car, heading toward Fort Myers Beach. They passed the turnoff for the marina where Louis had questioned the jumbo shrimp woman, and then went up over the bridge and onto Fort Myers Beach. Louis had to slow the car to a crawl on congested Estero Boulevard.

"Sodom and Gomorrah," Emily said, eyeing the crowds.

"Good place for The Saint," Louis said.

The Blue Heron was a mom-and-pop hotel with fading pink stucco that spoke of a heyday sometime in the late fifties. It was sandwiched between a 7-Eleven and a new Taco Bell. Louis parked in the convenience store lot and he and Emily set out for the beach.

As they waited to cross the street, Louis looked south down Estero Boulevard. Barely visible in the glare of the sun was the familiar green sign of the Holiday Inn, the site of Anthony Quick's abduction.

On the beach, they spotted The Saint's operation immediately, a couple of old card tables set up under a palm. About twenty shabby men milled around, trying to find some shade as they quietly ate sandwiches and drank coffee from Styrofoam cups. There were two men manning the line and Louis zeroed in on the older one, a gaunt, deeply tanned man of about sixty, with a white beard, wearing shorts and a Tampa Bay Bucs T-shirt.

"Excuse me, are you The Saint?" Louis asked.

The man peered at him with milky blue eyes. "Nope."

"You know where I can find him?"

"Nope."

Louis stifled a sigh. Emily stepped forward. "We're trying to find someone, and we were told he might have come here." Emily paused. "You are The Saint, aren't you?"

The man slapped a bologna sandwich on the plastic tray. "Look, we're not hurting anybody here. Why can't you cops just leave us alone?"

"We're not—"

The old man turned away to hand a cup of coffee to a man who had trudged up beside Louis. "Hey, Willie, where you been? Ain't seen you around."

"Was up in Jersey for the summer. Took me a while

to get back this time. Good to see ya, Saint," the man said. He took his food and moved away.

The bearded man looked at Louis and extended his wrists. "Okay, take me in again. I don't care. I'll just find another place. This is public property. You can't stop me from giving away food."

"We're not here to harass you," Louis said. "We just need some help."

The man stared at Louis and slowly let his arms fall. "Help," he said with a snort. "Who doesn't need help?"

"We're trying to identify a man, a dead man, who might have been homeless," Louis said. "Have you ever seen a man here with a tattoo on his left arm of a dog and the name Bosco?"

The Saint was staring at Emily now. "You really a cop, a little bitty thing like you?" he asked. He didn't wait for her answer. He looked back at Louis.

"Bosco . . ." he said. "Yeah, I know that tattoo." He paused and looked at some kids playing in the surf. "Shit. You say he's dead?"

Louis nodded. He was glad when The Saint didn't ask for details. "Was Bosco his last name?" Louis asked.

The Saint shrugged. "Who knows? Lots of folks here don't use their real names. It's like a family, I guess. We just call each other by whatever name fits, you know?"

"You called him Bosco?" Emily asked.

The Saint eyed her, still unsure he should reveal much more. "Nope. We called him Harry."

"Do you know where he was from, where he lived?" Emily asked.

"Lived?" The Saint gave a small smile. "Well, you

could try behind that 7-Eleven over there. Other than that, I don't know much about him. He always showed up for his food here. I haven't seen him in weeks now. I thought he just moved on. Or disappeared. Most do." He glanced back out at the ocean.

Emily reached in her pocket and pulled out a card and pen. She scribbled a number on it. "If you think of anything else, call, okay?"

The Saint took the card and slipped it into his shorts pocket. "Sure, miss."

"Thanks for your help," Louis said. He paused, then reached into his pocket and pulled out some bills. When The Saint saw the two twenties, he shook his head.

"I don't need it," he said. He smiled. "I've got plenty of my own money. I spent my share of time on the street but my brother left me a bundle when he croaked. Asshole never called me when he was alive but then . . ." He gestured toward the sandwiches. "Sixty grand buys a lot of bologna."

Louis and Emily left The Saint and trudged up the beach to the street. Louis waited while she emptied the sand from her shoes and they continued on to the 7-Eleven. The clerk had never heard the name Bosco or Harry and they had no photo to show her. But she said the management was constantly chasing away the homeless who slept behind the store near the Dumpster.

Behind the store, Louis and Emily discovered a heap of discarded boxes and dirty blankets, the remnants of a dismantled homeless camp.

"Lots of motor oil back here," Emily said, nodding at the stained asphalt.

"Yeah. But whoever was here moved on," Louis

said. He kicked at an empty bottle of Mad Dog. "Let's get out of here."

They wound their way back through the tourists, toward the squad car. Louis climbed in and as soon as they were away from the crowd, he radioed in to Wainwright, telling him what little they had found. Wainwright's response was clipped. Louis knew he was aware that Emily was listening.

"He doesn't like me much, does he?" Emily said as they inched along in the traffic. She said it more as a statement than a question, but Louis sensed she wanted an answer.

"He was expecting the bureau to send an old friend," Louis said.

"Malcolm Elliott retired a year ago," Emily said. "They sent me instead."

A tightness had crept into her voice. He wasn't sure if it was defensiveness. Whatever it was, it made him uncomfortable.

"Look, Farentino," he said, "Wainwright is kind of old school."

"The good old boy network," she said softly. "I know all about it."

"Give him time."

"I told you. We haven't got time."

She pulled her briefcase onto her lap and started rooting through it.

Louis stared at the cars inching along in the baking sun. He felt the need to say something conciliatory.

"So, how'd you come to work for the bureau?" he asked.

"I joined after getting my master's degree at Stanford."

"And before that?"

She leveled her eyes at him. "If you're trying to find out if I was ever on the street, the answer is, no, I wasn't." She turned her attention back to the briefcase. "Except for the week they made us ride with the NYPD."

Louis glanced at her. "I wasn't—"

"Yes, you were," she said quickly.

They crept along in silence. Emily rummaged furiously through the briefcase. She finally pulled out a file and tossed the briefcase to the floor with an impatient grunt. She started reading the file.

Louis kept silent. Great. Emily Farentino didn't have any real experience. Wainwright was going to go nuts when he found out. He wasn't exactly happy about it himself. Shit, he wasn't happy about Wainwright retiring from some obscure division of the FBI, for God's sake. He found himself wondering how long it would be before they were forced by public pressure to lateral the case over to the sheriff's department. Wainwright would be back to busting shoplifters at the Sereno Key drugstore. And he himself would be on a plane back to Michigan.

He let out a sigh.

"What?" Emily asked.

"Nothing," he said. They finally made it to the bridge. This was nuts. If he was going to have to work with this woman, he had to find a way to get through her armor.

"So, what division you work?" he asked.

"BSU."

Louis glanced at her again.

"Behavioral Science Unit."

"I don't know—"

"Nobody does," she said abruptly. She let out a sigh. "It's new, the unit, and what we do. It's . . . new."

Louis tried to recall what little he had read about serial killers. He had read something about how police departments were starting to use psychologists as consultants. They were calling them "profilers," the idea being they could figure out the twisted minds of criminals by poking around in the messes they left.

"So you're what's called a profiler?" Louis asked.

She looked surprised he knew the term. "I prefer 'forensic psychologist.' "

"Ah. A shrink," Louis said.

She shook her head. "I'm not a doctor."

You're not a cop, either, Louis thought.

They were up on the bridge now, heading back toward Fort Myers.

"Wainwright doesn't know any of this," Emily said finally. "Unless he's checked."

"He hasn't checked," Louis said. "You going to tell him?"

She took off her glasses and began to clean them on the tail of her shirt. "I heard things about Dan Wainwright before I came. I think he is—" She stopped herself. "There are some people who aren't open to new ideas."

Louis let a few moments pass in silence. For a moment, he considered asking her what the hell OPR was. But he didn't want Wainwright to think he was checking up on him. He also didn't want to do anything to make this case harder than it already was. Men were dying and he didn't want to waste time playing referee between Farentino and Wainwright. They needed to get going in the same direction.

"Listen, Farentino," he said finally, "if I've learned one thing it's that you don't get much by muscling your way into things. We're outsiders here, both of us. Wainwright is in charge, at least for now. You ought to respect that."

She lasered her eyes back to Louis. "And how many more bodies do we bury while showing this respect?"

Louis tensed, a quick knot forming in his belly. *How many more men are you going to bury, Chief Gibralter?*

Did she know? Had she checked *him* out? Did she know what had happened back in Michigan? She knew about Wainwright. She had all the resources in the world at her fingertips. She could easily have checked out his background. He would have done the same thing.

He inhaled thinly, determined not to let her rattle him. He stared hard at the road, slowly allowing himself to digest her remark differently. He had to appreciate her sense of urgency; he felt the same thing. He was seeing faceless black men in his dreams. He didn't want to see any more real ones.

"Okay," he said slowly. "So let me hear your theory."

"About what?" she asked.

"About how this guy picks his victims."

"I need to study the pattern first."

"There is no pattern," Louis said. "We thought there was, but he keeps changing. Except for the day he kills."

"Tuesday," Emily said.

She was quiet for a moment. "He has two needs," she said finally. "He needs a place to live where he won't stand out. But he needs a place to do his work that's secluded."

Louis thought her choice of the word "work" was odd.

"I'd say he lives near Fort Myers Beach," Emily went on. "It's crowded there, with lots of tourists and transients, and he would blend in. He wouldn't live on Captiva or Sereno. The locals would know him. Also, serial killers tend to dispose of bodies away from where they themselves live."

"So you think he stalked them?"

"It fits the usual pattern. He seems very impatient. I don't think he stalks them for days on end. I think he zeroes in on them and then follows them until he feels the moment is good."

"Well, what about Tatum then?"

"What about him?"

"We think his murder was pure impulse."

Emily closed the file on her lap. "Why would you think that?"

"Tatum was different than the other two. Tatum's car broke down. When Wainwright's men found it, the hood was still up, so we're guessing Tatum was stranded there for a while before the killer came along."

"Came along," she said. "Just came along, conveniently armed with his shotgun and can of spray paint."

Louis glanced at her, glad the sunglasses hid his eyes. "So you think Tatum was followed, like the others?"

"Yes."

"From where?"

"That's what we need to find out."

Louis turned on his blinker as he slowed at a corner. She was making sense. Shit. Wainwright was going to love this.

Chapter Twenty-one

It was Emily's idea to go see Roberta Tatum. When Louis told her that Roberta had already been questioned, Emily said simply, "Wives know things their husbands don't know that they know."

The Tatum home was a yellow stucco cottage, buried behind a riot of banana trees and purple bougainvillea vines. A storm was gathering over the bay by the time they arrived, and deep shadows moved in the junglelike yard where the windswept palm fronds played treble to the bass of approaching thunder.

They had called ahead and Roberta was waiting for them. She stood behind the wooden screen door, a stocky silhouette in a caftan of orange and green that billowed around her in the breeze. Her hair was concealed beneath a matching turban, giving her round, fresh-scrubbed face a stretched and youthful look.

Emily spoke first. "Mrs. Tatum, we're sorry to bother you—"

"Have you found him?" Roberta said, her eyes going to Louis.

"Levon, or your husband's killer?" Louis asked.

"Either."

"No."

Roberta sneered. "That's what I thought."

"May we come in, Mrs. Tatum?" Emily asked.

Roberta's eyes slipped to Emily, then back to Louis. "Who's she?"

"This is Agent Farentino. FBI."

Roberta made no move to open the screen door. She was staring hard at Emily.

"Mrs. Tatum, please," Louis said.

Roberta shoved open the door. "This is what they give Walter," she said as she moved away. "A cookie and a meatball."

Louis entered first and Emily followed slowly. He found himself in a small living room, with a kitchen off to his left. The rough-textured walls were painted a soft gold and the furniture was a pleasant mishmash of overstuffed sofas and rattan. A rainbow-hued Kilim rug covered the tile floor, and there were several beautiful wood sculptures around the room that looked to be good copies of African primitives. The jalousie windows were open to the breeze, and with each waft of air came the smell of stewing tomatoes and distant rain.

"You have a lovely home, Mrs. Tatum," Emily said, edging forward through the archway. Louis followed, his gaze going past the tiny dining room to the open

French doors that offered a glimpse of pool and greenery. He could hear wind chimes dancing.

Roberta grabbed a pack of cigarettes off an end table. "All right, what do you want?"

"The night your husband was killed—" Emily started.

Roberta's sharp glance silenced her. Roberta waited until she was sure Emily didn't plan to speak again, then looked at Louis.

"Where did Walter go when he left here?" Louis asked.

Roberta shrugged. "How would I know?"

"Give us a break here, Mrs. Tatum," Louis said. "We're here to help you. You told me you want this bastard found and we're trying to do that."

"You and I both know why they aren't looking too damn hard." Roberta turned away, picking a bit of tobacco carefully from her lip.

Louis could almost hear Emily bristle and he lifted a hand to keep her from intervening. She was no match for Roberta.

"We're doing everything we can," Louis said.

"It's been almost a month," Roberta said. "And what do you have? You can't even find Levon."

Louis rubbed his forehead. "We will."

Roberta laughed softly. "I heard about your piggyback ride. I wish I could've seen it."

"Mrs. Tatum," Louis said slowly, "are you going to help us, or not?"

Roberta suddenly seemed deflated and she sat down, resting her forearms on her knees. The cigarette dangled from her long fingers.

Emily seized the moment. "Mrs. Tatum, we think if we can recreate your husband's whereabouts the night he was killed, we might have a better idea what happened."

Roberta looked up at Emily, then at Louis. He could read in her eyes that she wasn't going to tell Emily Farentino a thing. He was about to ask Emily to go outside when Emily spoke again.

"You were his wife, Mrs. Tatum. You know things that could help us. Please."

Roberta took a deep drag on the cigarette. She fell back in the chair, staring at the wall.

"I wasn't his wife," she said. "Not legally, anyway. But we were together for twenty-two years and that counts for something."

Emily hesitated, then sat down on the sofa opposite Roberta. "My parents were together for thirty-five years, and they weren't married, either," she said.

Roberta looked up at Emily.

"It counts," Emily said.

Roberta's eyes welled. She looked away.

"Mrs. Tatum," Emily said, "is there anything you can tell us about the night Walter died?"

Roberta wiped a hand across her eyes. "He used to like to go over to Hibiscus Heights in Fort Myers," she said softly. "They got a couple of joints over there that run all night. He'd drink and then I'd feel him crawling into bed when the sun was coming up."

Louis waited, glancing at Emily.

"I used to worry he'd drive off that bridge one morning and kill himself," Roberta went on. "Never thought . . . never dreamed somebody would do it for him."

"What are the names of these places?" Louis asked.

"You can't miss them," Roberta said. "There's a string of them on a little street called Queenie Avenue. But they don't get going till after eleven. Anyone who works late there will know him."

Her voice had gone flat, her gaze vacant. The long ash from her cigarette fell to the rug. She didn't seem to notice it.

Louis spotted a framed photo on the television and went to it. It was a photograph of Roberta and Walter. It had been taken on a cruise ship and they were in formal wear. They were smiling like prom-goers.

"Can I take this, to show around?" he asked.

Roberta looked up at him. It took a moment for her to focus on the frame. Then she rose suddenly and disappeared into another room. She came back and thrust something at Louis.

"You take this instead," she said.

It was a snapshot of Walter, taken at a Christmas party. Walter was smiling and wearing a Santa hat. His face was blurry.

"Mrs. Tatum—" Louis began.

She snatched the frame from Louis and set it back on the television. "You use that one," she said, nodding at the snapshot.

Louis motioned to Emily and she headed toward the door. Roberta followed them. As they reached the door, Roberta grabbed Louis's arm. He turned, but Roberta waited until Emily had walked toward the car before she spoke.

"Don't let them fuck around on this," she said. "Make them understand Walter is important. Walter is important, you hear me?"

"I hear you, Mrs. Tatum," he said.

Roberta let go and Louis stepped out, letting the screen slap shut behind him.

Emily was standing at the squad car, waiting. The

temperature had dropped at least ten degrees with the coming rain and she was hugging herself, as if cold.

Louis glanced at his watch. "It's only five o'clock. No point in going to Queenie Boulevard until later tonight. We might as well go back to the station. Or do you want me to drop you off at the inn?"

Emily was looking at something across the street and didn't answer.

"Farentino?"

Her head snapped back to Louis. "What?"

"I was asking you if you wanted me to drop you off at the inn."

"No." She hesitated. "Could we go get some dinner maybe?"

There was something in her voice that caught him off guard. She wasn't coming on to him; there wasn't even a hint of that kind of vibration. But she wanted something. Maybe she just didn't want to be alone. Shit. He kept forgetting that when he went home to the Dodies' cheerful company each night, she was stuck alone in a mildewed hotel room.

"I could use a burger or something," Louis said. "Come on, I know a good place."

Chapter Twenty-two

The clouds chased them over the Sereno causeway and onto the mainland. But the rain still had not made its appearance by the time Louis stopped to pay the toll at the Captiva causeway.

Emily had been quiet during the drive, and now she had closed her eyes. Louis let her doze and drove on. When he finally pulled into a parking lot and cut the engine, she stirred and looked around.

"Where are we?" she asked.

"Captiva," Louis said. "The Mucky Duck."

She nodded slowly. "Oh, right. Burgers."

They got out and started up to the restaurant. Louis pulled on the door but it was locked. He saw someone inside and knocked on the glass. The waiter looked up and then pointed to his wrist, mouthing the words "half hour."

"I forgot. They don't start serving until five-thirty," Louis said. "You want to wait or go somewhere else?"

Emily was looking at the beach. "Isn't this where he dumped the homeless man?" she asked.

Louis nodded. "Near here."

"Show me," Emily said.

He led the way through the sea oats and down the sandy slope. They walked the hundred yards or so to where the body had been found. The gulf water was churning gray-green, and the beach was deserted except for two elderly women walking in the surf with a bounding Irish setter.

Emily stood staring at the spot where the body had lain. Louis watched as her eyes traveled up toward the sea oats dancing in the wind.

"We think the beating and stabbing took place up there and then he was dragged down here," Louis said.

Emily's eyes narrowed. She walked slowly up to the sea oats. They came up nearly to her waist. She stood there, arms wrapped around herself, staring down at the sand. The sound of the setter's barking carried on the wind.

Louis went up to her. "Farentino," he said. "What's the matter?"

"Nothing," she said.

"Look, if it's something Dan—"

She shook her head quickly. "No, it's not Wainwright."

"Then what?"

She was looking now at the elderly women and their dog.

"I was thinking about the homeless man and wondering if anyone is missing him," she said.

Louis said nothing.

"He had to have someone, somewhere," Emily said.

The wind gusted, sending the sand swirling around them. Emily's slight body swayed with the sea oats.

"Someone is missing him," she said.

Her voice was soft, but without emotion somehow. Louis couldn't read it or her face. Was she talking as a cop or a woman? It was the closest she had come to saying anything personal. If, in fact, that was what she was even doing. For a second he considered trying to say something comforting. But for what? Did she even need it? Shit, she'd probably take his head off if he tried. Christ. He had come to appreciate the way her mind worked, but anything more than that would be like trying to cozy up to a porcupine.

"Let's go back," she said suddenly.

She started back up the beach toward the restaurant. Louis followed.

When they got back to the Mucky Duck, they still had ten minutes to spare. Emily retrieved her neon-green rain slicker from the car and they sat on a picnic table of the restaurant's patio. Emily was quiet, hunched down in the slicker like a bird, looking out at the gulf. Whatever the reason, she still didn't seem inclined to talk.

"This is ridiculous," Louis said finally.

"What is?"

"Eating at five-thirty," Louis said. "That's what blue hairs do. Next thing you know, I'll be wearing boxers."

Emily's lips tipped up. "So you're a briefs man?"

"None of your business, Farentino."

She shrugged. "You're the one who got personal, Kincaid."

They were quiet again.

"Back there with Roberta," Louis said. "You were good with her, you know."

"What do you mean?"

"That thing you said about your parents. It worked."

She turned to face him. "It's true," she said.

The challenge in her voice caught him off guard. He just stared at her.

"You think I made it up to get her to talk?" she asked.

"What? Hell no," Louis said quickly, his own anger sparking. "Jesus, Farentino . . ."

She turned away. A car pulled in behind them, a door opened and closed. The restaurant was open.

"So, you still want to eat or not?" Louis said.

"In a minute," she said quietly.

The wind was getting almost cold now. Louis burrowed down into his windbreaker. The sky was slate gray, with a smudge of pink faint on the horizon. It looked as bleak as a Michigan sky. So much for seeing another one of those great Florida beach sunsets Dodie was always yakking about it.

"Look, Kincaid," Emily said, "I'm sorry."

He stifled a sigh.

"What Roberta said about twenty years counting for something. That made me think about my parents, that's all." Emily paused. "And I haven't done that in a while."

"Why not?" Louis asked.

She smiled wryly. "I'm good at compartmentalizing."

"What do you mean?"

"Putting my feelings in neat little boxes."

There was the sound of more cars and voices in the lot behind them.

"Why weren't they married?" Louis asked.

The question had just popped out. He knew it was because his own parents hadn't been married either. His own father hadn't even stayed around long enough for his first birthday. And his alcoholic mother had lost all three of her kids to child services. He had grown up believing that white kids didn't have such secrets. Sure, those guys on *Bonanza* didn't have a mother. Neither did Opie or the kids on *My Three Sons,* unless you counted Uncle Charley. But white kids all had fathers, didn't they?

Black kids didn't. That's what the other kids used to say to him in school. *Where's your father, Louis? Why do you live with that white guy?* Shit, even Diahann Carroll's son didn't have a father on that stupid *Julia* show. They killed him off in Vietnam.

Dear old Dad . . . missing in action.

He waited for Emily to answer. He wanted to know.

"They didn't believe in marriage," she said. "It was the sixties, California, free love and all that crap. Me coming along wasn't enough of a reason for them to change their minds."

"But they stayed together," Louis said.

Emily nodded. "They loved each other. They loved me. Thirty-five years. Like I told Roberta, that counts. But kids can be cruel, you know? I guess a little part of me never got over feeling ashamed."

Louis looked out over the water. He was glad she didn't ask him about his own childhood. He was pretty damn good at compartmentalizing, too, and right now, he wanted to stick his past back in its box. He realized suddenly Emily had been speaking in the past tense.

"Your parents. They're dead?" Louis asked.

She nodded. "Car accident when I was a senior in college."

Louis watched as she pulled her slicker tighter around herself. "No other family?" he asked.

She shook her head. She took off her glasses and held them up in the waning light. "Salt spray. Got a Kleenex?" she asked.

"Sorry."

She slipped them back on. "I love the water," she said after a moment. "It fogs up my glasses, frizzes my hair, and clogs up my sinuses, but I love it."

"Does the ocean look like this?" Louis asked.

She looked at him. "You've never seen the Atlantic Ocean?"

"Nope."

She looked back out at the gulf. "It's similar. Biscayne Bay, near where I live, looks like this some. The ocean's a little wilder."

"I had a partner once who told me I should live near water," Louis said. "He was into astrology."

Emily nodded. "You're probably a water sign. I'm a Virgo. That's an air sign."

"I knew there was a reason we don't like each other."

She laughed. She had a great contralto laugh.

"So," she said after a moment, "where are you going when the case is over?"

Louis didn't answer. Why was everyone asking him that? He thought about his conversation with Candy. Candy, who had lived all his life in one place and couldn't wait to pull up his roots and get to the "real world." Candy, who believed that cops—or anyone—really had any control over how their lives played out.

Louis stared out at the water. The wind-whipped sea oats were whispering. Something else was whispering, there in his brain. *Where are you going, Louis?*

"Miami . . . you like it there?" Louis asked.

Emily smiled slightly. "I do now. It took a long time."

"Why?"

"I went to Miami after I graduated because it was the farthest I could get away from California after my parents died," she said. "Florida's a big escape destination and I hated the place. Old people, humidity, cockroaches the size of small Cessnas flying across my kitchen."

"But you stayed," Louis said.

"Yeah. You can put down roots. Not an easy thing to do in sand, but it can be done."

Louis waited a moment. "But you're alone."

She nodded slightly. "I have good friends, a few people who miss me when I'm gone. When you don't have family, sometimes you have to just build one."

She fell quiet again, burrowing into her rain slicker. Louis wanted to ask her more, though he wasn't sure about what. He glanced at her profile, just her nose and those big black glasses poking out of the slicker's collar. The moment was gone; she had retreated.

"Shitty sunset," she said. "Let's go eat."

Chapter Twenty-three

Queenie Avenue was a narrow street pulsating with neon and the sound of blues melting with the low rumble of the storm. It was raining lightly as Louis and Emily made their way down the slick sidewalk. Here, miles from the water, the street smelled only of city things. Dumpsters, car exhaust, vomit, piss, and the aroma of frying chicken.

They had been walking the street for an hour now, wandering in and out of the bars and take-out joints. So far, no one had recognized Walter Tatum's picture. Louis wondered if anyone would admit it even if they did. Queenie Avenue seemed like the kind of place that hid its secrets well.

They drew stares as they walked. Louis ignored them. Emily seemed nervous. He felt her inch closer as they approached the last bar. It didn't even have a sign, just a Budweiser sign glowing in the night.

"I guess you're in charge here," she said.

He looked down at her. Her hair was a wet helmet of curls around her small face. "Feeling a little out of place, Farentino?"

She gave a snort. "I went to high school in Santa Monica, California, where every girl is a blond Amazon and every guy is blinded by a C-cup. I was a short, freckled geek with braces, glasses, and no tits."

"Yeah, but you can change all that. Can't change your skin color. Come on, last stop, and then we'll hit a McDonald's for hot apple pie."

"There's something to look forward to," Emily murmured.

The bar was a small cavern, dense with smoke and dominated by a long bar. A jukebox glowed in the corner, illuminating an old table shuffleboard heaped with beer cartons. The place was packed, laughter mixing with the clink of bottles and Etta James singing "Losers Weepers."

Louis headed for the bar, Emily at his heels. Louis squeezed between two men seated on stools. He motioned to the bartender, a skinny guy in a lime-green tank top.

"Yo," the bartender said, "I didn't do it and I don't know who did."

"He ain't no cop, Jackie," piped up one customer.

"Sure he is." The bartender smiled at Louis. "Ain't you?"

Louis nodded. The bartender's eyes drifted behind Louis to Emily. "That your lady?"

Louis ignored him and held out the photo. "Do you know this man? His name is Walter Tatum."

The bartender looked at the photo. "That dude is dead."

"You know him then?"

"Everybody know Walter."

Louis felt Emily press in behind him. "He was a regular here?" Louis asked.

"Yup."

"Was he here March first?"

"Shit, that was three weeks ago, man . . ."

"It was a Tuesday."

"Tuesday? Why didn't you say so? Yeah, Walt was always here on Tuesdays."

"Are you sure?" Louis asked.

The bartender turned to the far end of the bar. "Hey, Lucille! Ain't Tuesday the night Walt Tatum always here?"

Louis looked to the end of the bar. Even in the gloom, he could see her, a large, tawny-skinned woman with an elaborate fountain of red braided hair and huge hoop earrings that glinted in the bar lights.

"Why you asking about Walter?" she yelled back.

"This man here is asking."

Emily sidled up. "You going to talk to her?"

Louis nodded and walked down the bar. The woman saw them coming and her eyes flared with contempt, but Louis suspected it was at Emily, and not him.

"Do you know Walter Tatum?" Louis asked.

A few other patrons had gathered, interested in what was going on. Lucille stared at Louis with heavily made up Cleopatra eyes. Then she looked down into her glass.

"Leave me be. I'm grieving here."

"For Walter Tatum?" Louis asked.

"Walter was my man," she said.

Louis caught Emily's eye.

"Was Walter here Tuesday, March first?" Louis asked.

Lucille didn't answer or look at him. Finally she nodded.

"Were you with him that night?"

Lucille nodded again. "He left about two," she said. "Said he couldn't stay."

Louis wondered if Lucille knew about Roberta. Or vice versa.

Lucille spun to face him suddenly. "You know who killed him?"

"No," Louis said.

"They saying in the papers a white man did it," Lucille said bitterly, "one of them skinheads or something."

"We don't know that for sure," Louis said. The crowd was pressing close around. Louis glanced up at Emily. She was standing very still, like she was trying hard to blend into the inky smoke. Her face looked very small and very white.

Louis looked back at Lucille. She was staring hard at Emily.

"What are you doing here?" Lucille demanded suddenly.

"I'm an FBI agent," Emily said. Her voice was firm but her hand fumbled as she reached for the badge that had disappeared into her raincoat.

"Did Walter leave alone?" Louis asked quickly.

Lucille looked back at Louis. "Yeah. He said he was tired and was going home to sleep." She smiled wanly. "He was always tired after I was done with him."

Her friends snickered.

"Is there anywhere he might have stopped?" Louis asked.

The bartender had wandered down and was listening. "Not much traffic out there after midnight. All the action's out on the beach and that's ten, twelve miles from here."

"Okay, thanks," Louis said.

They left the bar. It was raining harder, and they didn't talk as they hurried back to the car.

Emily let out a breath, leaning back into the seat.

"I would have come to your rescue," Louis said.

"Shut up," Emily said, wiping her face on her sleeve.

They sat there for several moments, the thumping bass from a nearby bar beating time to the rain on the roof. Finally, Louis started the car and they pulled out. He took the most direct route back toward Sereno, staying on busy Summerlin Road until they reached the causeway. At the boat trailer parking lot, Louis pulled in and stopped.

"What are you doing?" she asked.

"Just thinking."

For several minutes he just sat, watching each car as it made its way past, into the darkness toward Sereno Key.

"This was a waste of time," Louis said. "The killer did not stalk Tatum from Queenie Boulevard."

"How can you be so sure?"

"No white guy would hang out there," Louis said.

Emily nodded. "Zone of comfort," she said.

"What's that?"

"Serial killers operate within a zone of comfort," she said. "And you're right. If the killer is white, he would not have blended in or felt he could stalk his victim from Queenie Boulevard."

They were silent for a moment.

"Maybe he isn't white," Farentino said. "Have you considered that possibility?"

"Yeah . . . but just for Levon."

"Serial killers rarely choose victims outside their own race," Emily said. "It's part of the pattern."

Louis looked out at the water. Something Roberta Tatum said came back to him. Something about Wainwright believing the killer was black because it was easier to accept black genocide than white racists murdering out of hate.

He looked over at Farentino. Was it easier for her, too?

"My gut says the killer's white," Louis said.

"Is that a professional or personal point of view?" she asked.

He put the car in gear. "I don't know," he said.

Chapter Twenty-four

Louis took off his glasses and rubbed the bridge of his nose. There was too much information spinning in his mind. Did the killer stalk or was he an opportunist? Why did he paint them? Where did he live? What was his connection to Sereno Key? And why did he kill so viciously?

He rose, stretching his back muscles. He heard his bones crack as he made his way to the coffeepot. Wainwright was on a call on the south end of the Key, and Farentino hadn't shown up yet.

He poured a cup of coffee and stepped back to look at the bulletin board. Yesterday, they had moved it from Wainwright's office to a small adjoining conference room. That had been Emily Farentino's idea. She said she needed room for her files, room to work.

So rather than let her share his desk, Wainwright had moved everything to the conference room. She had immediately taken over the table, spreading out files, photographs, and papers.

The bulletin board was still covered with the color-coded note cards. Wainwright dutifully kept it maintained. Emily ignored it, sticking to her carefully organized files. Officer Candy had walked in this morning and nicknamed the whole mess "the war room."

Little did he know, Louis thought ruefully.

He stirred in three sugar packs. He took a sip, grimaced, and stirred in one more. His gaze drifted up to the photos on the bulletin board of the homeless man's pulverized face. The gruesome photo was becoming as familiar as his own face in the mirror. It was with him day and night. He stared at it now, his neck muscles tightening. Gone . . . just gone. No eyes, no mouth. It was as if the killer had wanted to erase him.

Nothing in his experience had prepared him for this. Not all the grisly pictures in the manuals, not the decomposed body found in a field that he had responded to back when he was a rookie. Not even what had happened in Michigan.

Was evil born or bred? He had heard other cops talk about it, but he had always figured it was something best left to shrinks and priests. But now, he found the question lurking in the back of his mind. The rational part of him, the part that had read all the books and heard all the experts, that part of him believed monsters were made, molded from short-circuited brain chemistry and society's illnesses.

But after he had seen the homeless man's brutalized face, the other part of him, that vestige that still held all the primal fears and the dark terrors of childhood, that part of him was feeling the brush of something cold.

"Louis!" Officer Candy hollered from the front office. "I think you better come out here."

Louis put the cup down and went to the door. The outer office was a square room with a couple of desks, a radio console, where the dispatcher sat, and a counter for complaints.

The double glass entrance doors were bleached with morning sunlight and all Louis could see was a giant silhouette against them. He knew who it was immediately and he tightened, adrenaline surging forward. But he didn't move.

The silhouette didn't move either.

He heard Candy's voice to his left. "Chief's five minutes away."

Louis kept his eyes on the doors. "What about the sheriff's department?" he asked softly.

"Ten minutes."

Louis squinted into the light, trying to decide how to play this. The dispatcher glanced at him and he motioned for her to stay still.

The silhouette shifted slightly and let out a breath that sounded like a heater fan kicking on.

"Levon," Louis said firmly. "Levon, come over here. Nice and slow."

Levon didn't move.

"Levon," Louis said, "did you hear me?"

"I hear you."

Louis took a step toward a chair. "Levon . . . please."

Levon hung his head, then started toward Louis.

He had to turn to get through the doorway. Louis kept his hand on the chair, but moved behind it.

Levon came into the light of the office and Louis could see his eyes were swollen and his lips were cracked and dry. He was barefoot and moved as if his legs were made of lead.

When he got to Louis, he held out his wrists. Louis stared at them, then glanced backward for Officer Candy. Candy stuck a set of his cuffs in his hand and Louis snapped them over Levon's large wrists.

Louis looked up into Levon's face. The whites of his eyes bulged like Ping-Pong balls, but Louis wasn't sure if it was from drugs or fear. But he wasn't taking any chances.

"Levon, I have to put you in a cell. Do you understand that?"

"I hear ya."

Louis took one arm and Candy hurried ahead to open all the doors. Levon moved along silently and by the time Louis got to the cell door, Candy was waiting.

Levon went inside and immediately lay down on the bunk, letting out a deep-throated groan. Candy closed the door and Louis followed him out. They closed the outer door.

"Shit," Candy breathed.

Louis glanced at him. "Right."

The front door opened and Farentino walked in. She wore white cotton pants that looked as if they had been wadded into a ball for weeks, and a purple shirt. She stopped short when she saw their faces.

"What's the matter?" she asked.

"We have Levon Baylis in custody," Louis said.

She swung her briefcase onto the counter. "Have you questioned him yet?"

"Waiting for Wainwright," Louis said.

They heard the screech of tires outside, and seconds later the glass doors opened and Wainwright came in. He stopped short, glancing around.

"Where is he?"

"In the lockup," Candy said.

"Anyone hurt?"

"He surrendered, Dan. Just like that."

Wainwright hurried past them, and they followed him back to the cell block. Wainwright stopped in front of the cell. Levon was curled into a ball on the bunk. They could hear his labored breathing.

"Anyone Mirandized him yet?" Wainwright asked.

"No, sir."

Wainwright began the speech. "You have the right—"

Levon let out a long, agonizing wail that ricocheted off the walls. Louis glanced at Wainwright. "Think he's sick?"

"You have the right to remain silent—"

"Ugghhgg!"

"Fuck," Wainwright said.

"Berta!" Levon screamed. "Ber-taaaaa!"

Louis turned. "I'm calling Mrs. Tatum."

They watched silently from the corridor, staring into the dimly lit cell. Levon had asked that the overhead light in his cell be turned out and at first Wainwright had objected. Louis had turned it off anyway.

Roberta had made them wait for Bledsoe before

questioning Levon, and he now stood next to Louis in the corridor, his eyes wide as he watched Levon.

Roberta was the only one Levon had allowed into the cell. She stood facing him, shoulders straight, hands clasped in front of her.

"Levon," she said, "it's Berta."

He emerged from the shadows of the lower bunk, planting his feet on the concrete floor. He sat hunched and frightened, his bald head shiny in the thin light.

"Levon," Roberta said again.

He lifted his face to hers. Louis thought he could see the dried streaks of tears on his cheeks, but wasn't sure.

"Why did you come here?" Roberta asked. "Why did you turn yourself in?"

"I'm guilty, Berta. You know I am."

"Guilty of what?" she asked.

"Walter's dead. Walter's dead. I'm guilty."

"Did you kill Walter?" Roberta asked.

Levon hung his shoulders, his long arms almost reaching the floor. "I must've."

Bledsoe nudged Louis. "He's crazy," he whispered. "No chair. Slam dunk."

Louis shot him a look to silence him. He looked back at Roberta.

She was leaning over Levon now. "Don't say that if you didn't do it, Levon. You either did or you didn't."

She took his chin and forced him to look up at her. "Tell me what happened to Walter," she said firmly.

"I killed him. I beat him with these," Levon said,

holding up both fists. "I beat him with these. I'm sorry, Berta. I'm so sorry."

Louis could see Roberta's body go rigid and he thought about intervening, but he waited.

"Why?" Roberta whispered.

Levon whimpered, choking on his words. "He was mean, Berta, mean."

She smacked him lightly above the ear. "Tell me the truth. Can't you for once tell the truth?"

Levon recoiled, grabbing his head. "Stop it. Stop it! I'm telling the truth. I killed Walter. I killed him. I *know* I did it. I just don't remember."

Louis let out a long sigh, glancing at Emily. She was watching intently, but was no longer writing in her notebook. Louis looked back at Roberta and caught her eye, motioning her toward the bars.

"Ask him about the others."

"Not so fast," Bledsoe said. "He confesses to the others, you'll fry his ass."

Emily pressed forward. "I don't think he knows about the others, Mr. Bledsoe. He won't be able to tell us anything."

Roberta eyed them hard, then glanced at Wainwright, standing by the edge of the cell, near the wall.

"You don't know Levon," Roberta said softly. "He's a confessing fool. All his life, always taking the blame. For me. For our daddy. For damn near everything. What makes you think this will be different?"

"Because we'll know if he's lying," Emily said.

Roberta moved away and walked back to Levon. "What about the others?" she asked.

"What others?"

"The others!" Roberta said loudly. "That man

from Ohio and the homeless man! What about them?''

Levon's eyes took on a confused, empty look. ''Did I kill them?'' he asked.

Louis came forward. ''Why did you paint them, Levon?''

Levon's vacant eyes shifted to Louis. ''Paint? Paint what?''

Louis glanced at Roberta. ''They were painted,'' he said softly.

''Painted?'' she said.

''I'll explain later,'' Louis said. ''If Levon did it, he would have known about it.''

Roberta's shoulders slumped slightly with relief and she moved to her brother. She pulled his head to her belly, and held his neck. Louis could hear his muffled whimpers.

Wainwright turned away. ''What a crock of shit,'' he muttered, moving past them. He shoved open the door to the office.

Louis and Farentino followed. Bledsoe stayed with Roberta. When Louis and Farentino went into Wainwright's office, he was sitting in his chair, staring at the wall.

''He seemed confused,'' Emily said.

''That doesn't prove anything,'' Wainwright said. ''It could all be a put-on. He's a damn good actor when he wants to be. Believe me. Last time I had him in this jail, one minute he was making sense, the next he was tearing the toilet off the wall.''

''He's disturbed,'' Emily said. ''I'd like to find out more about his illness.''

''It's not an illness, Agent, his brain is scrambled,'' Wainwright said. ''And you know what makes this

really tragic? He'll never see the chair or even a jail
for these murders."

"Mentally ill people don't belong in the chair,
Chief," Farentino said sharply.

"I suppose you think we should study them like
goddamn rats in a lab?"

"In a hospital."

"He confessed," Wainwright said firmly.

"I'd hardly call it a confession," Farentino said.

"He's guilty, I know the man. He's capable of
extreme violence."

"I'm not saying he's not. I just don't think he's
our killer."

"*Our* killer? Jesus . . ." Wainwright let out a low
laugh.

Louis stepped forward. "Enough!"

They both stared at him.

"Listen to you, both of you," Louis said. "We have
a suspect in there. Let's deal with him. And each
other, for Christ's sake."

Wainwright was still staring at Louis. "Do you agree
with her?" he asked.

Louis hesitated. "Everyone is a suspect until
cleared," he said. "Levon needs to be examined
and—"

"Take a stand, Kincaid," Emily said firmly.

Louis looked Wainwright in the eye. "I don't think
Levon's the killer."

Wainwright drew back, just a step. His eyes moved
from Louis to Emily with a sudden coolness Louis
could almost feel on his skin.

"We still hold him on the other charges—resisting
arrest and evading," Wainwright said in a tight whis-

per. "Is that okay with you, Agent, or do you want to send him home to Mommy?"

"Lock him up for the rest of his life, if you want. It's not going to make him guilty of these murders," Emily said.

Wainwright shook his head slowly. "I need some air," he said.

Louis waited until he had gone through the door before he turned to Emily.

"Why did you have to make it confrontational?" he said.

"What do you mean?" Emily said.

"We've got Levon. You could evaluate him, we could investigate Van Slate and anyone else. Why do you have to push so hard?"

"Someone has to," she said.

"Get off his back, Farentino," Louis said.

"He's in over his head," she snapped. She started toward the conference room. "Maybe you are, too."

Louis spun away in anger.

Damn her. Damn Wainwright. Damn Levon for not being the goddamn killer.

He drew in a breath, hands on hips. Shit, this was falling apart. Mobley was going to get the case by default if they kept this up. He went quickly into the conference room. Emily was sorting through some files.

"Hey, Farentino," he called.

She looked up. "What?"

"Truce. Come to the Dodies' for dinner. That's where I'm staying," he said. "Dan's coming. The Dodies would like to meet you."

She stared at him. "I . . . I'm not good at parties—"

"It's just us, Farentino," Louis said. "Just cops."

Her small shoulders rose and fell. She looked out toward the outer office, shook her head slowly, and looked back at Louis.

"I'll bring the wine," she said.

Chapter Twenty-five

Emily's glass of Chianti sat untouched on the patio table. She was sitting on the edge of her chair, elbows on knees, hands clasped. Wainwright was prone in a lounge chair, his beer on his belly, eyes closed.

Louis glanced back at Farentino, watching her from behind sunglasses that he would soon need to remove. The sun was setting behind her, casting her in a soft, orange light, turning her red hair copper.

The three of them had barely said a word in the last half hour.

Louis had not told Wainwright that Emily was coming, and when she had shown up—a half hour late—Wainwright simply cracked open his second beer and headed to the patio. Louis knew Wainwright was pissed that he had invited her. This patio had become their sanctuary, their platform for discussing the gruesome aspects of their case. Outsiders weren't allowed in, although Louis and Wainwright had given Dodie a sort of special dispensation. But women weren't welcome. Even Margaret understood that.

The small talk had died quickly. After that, Margaret had lured Dodie inside to help with dinner. Wainwright had downed his beer too quickly and retreated to the lounge. Louis wondered how in the hell they were going to get through dinner, let alone any productive discussion of the case.

Emily looked at him suddenly and he knew he had been caught staring at her. There was this strange look in her eyes, this plea for some kind of communication, some kind of acknowledgment that she was here.

Louis took off the glasses and stood up. "Refill, Farentino?"

She shook her head, her eyes flitting to the comatose Wainwright and then back out to the canal. Louis could hear Dodie and Margaret. They were arguing about something, trying hard to keep their voices low. But not low enough that Louis didn't hear Emily's name . . . and his own. To his horror, he realized that Margaret was talking about how he should ask Emily out.

He glanced at Emily and knew she had heard it.

"Margaret thinks I'm lonely," he said.

"I gather," she said with a small smile.

He was glad when she let it go at that.

After a moment, she reached down and dragged forward her huge briefcase.

"I have something to show you," she said, pulling out some manila folders. "It's why I was late."

She tossed the stack on the table between them with a *thunk*.

"I spent the day going through VI-CAP," she said. "He's killed before."

Louis stared at the folders, then slowly came forward and picked up the top one. "Where?" he said.

"I found three other cases, similar MOs. All unsolved."

Louis was scanning the first file, a report out of the Ocean County, New Jersey, Sheriff's Department. A black man, shotgun wound, beaten, stabbed, and painted. His body was found August twenty-eight of last year.

He picked up another file. The second and third cases were from Broward County, Florida, in November of last year. Both with the same MO, including that the two men were likely killed on Tuesdays.

Louis looked over at Wainwright. His eyes were open.

"There could be more, but this was all I found," Emily said.

Louis nodded as he read the Jersey file. He knew a little about VI-CAP. The Violent Criminal Apprehension Program was new, a national system designed to identify serial murderers. The idea behind it was to bring together the fragmented efforts of law enforcement agencies around the country so data could be fed into computers for analysis. The problem was, few police departments and agencies had the equipment and manpower to either input or access the pool of information. Things had gotten even more muddied two years ago when VI-CAP was merged into the FBI's labyrinthine control.

But Farentino had cut through the red tape. Louis

glanced again at Wainwright. He struggled up to a sitting position in the lounge chair and was looking at Emily.

"We have to start talking about patterns," Emily said.

"The only pattern is the day of week," Wainwright said.

"There's got to be more," Emily said.

"If there was, we'd have seen it," Wainwright said.

"Maybe you don't know what to look for," Emily said.

Louis shot her a glance. She looked away.

Wainwright stared at her for a moment, then slowly hoisted himself out of the chaise. "I need another beer," he said.

Louis waited until he went inside. "Farentino, he's got thirty years on you. For God's sake, show some respect."

She dropped her gaze, then started sorting through the papers in the briefcase sitting between her knees. "Okay, I'm sorry," she said after a moment.

"Tell it to Dan," Louis said. He went back to reading the file from New Jersey.

She waited a moment, then let out a long sigh. "This isn't easy, you know," she said. "Most cops think the stuff I do is voodoo, or that I'm like some weirdo psychic called out to the scene to pick up vibrations from the victim's shoe or something." She paused. "This is science and I believe in it. I believe it can help."

"Tell that to Dan, too," Louis said.

Wainwright shuffled back out onto the porch, a

fresh Budweiser clutched in his hand. He paused, then came over to the table. He picked up one of the files and squinted to read it in the spare light of the Japanese lanterns. Finally, he retreated back to the chaise, taking the file with him. Emily watched him.

"Maybe I should explain how profiling works," she said, walking over to him.

Wainwright didn't look up from his reading. With a glance at Louis, Emily cleared her throat.

"The basic principle we work on is that behavior is a reflection of the personality," she said. "Criminal investigators, like myself, are called in to analyze the data gathered by law enforcement agencies and provide a picture—a profile, if you will—of what the UNSUB or unknown subject is like."

Wainwright was still reading the file.

"It's like . . ." Emily paused. "You're the regular doctor and we're the specialists, called in to offer advice. We're usually called in as a last resort."

Emily and Louis both waited for Wainwright to say something.

When he didn't, Emily continued. "I know you aren't comfortable with this, either of you. Cops are used to dealing with facts. Shit, so's the rest of the bureau." She paused and ran a hand over her messy curls. "And then, suddenly, here I come, giving you nothing but my feelings."

Wainwright had put down the file and was looking at her.

"With what I do, I don't have the luxury of dealing in black and white," she said. "I'm dealing with human behavior, in all its perverse forms. And believe me, there is nothing black and white about that."

Wainwright took a long swig of beer and let out a soft belch.

"Maybe I should go through the steps of how this works exactly," Emily said.

She glanced at Louis. He gave her a small nod.

"First, I evaluate the criminal act itself, the crime scene, police reports, and autopsy protocol. I've done that already through the files you sent to the bureau." She looked at Wainwright. "Then I develop a profile of the offender, with critical characteristics, and offer suggestions."

"And we take this *profile* and just go out and magically match it up to some dirtbag," Wainwright said.

"There's nothing magical about it," Emily said quietly.

Wainwright took a drink of his beer. Louis came forward and took the chair next to Emily.

"Go on," he said.

"Serial murderers tend to have certain common denominators," Emily said. "They're usually products of abusive homes, they often torture animals or set fires as children. They have low self-esteem, hate authority, and blame the world for their problems. They crave control and believe by killing, they are calling the shots. They almost always kill strangers and they are almost always the same race as their victims."

"But you still don't think it's Levon," Wainwright said.

Emily seemed surprised to hear him ask a question.

She shook her head. "I talked to Roberta Tatum some more today, and Levon wasn't abused. He does, however, exhibit profound self-esteem problems and may be mentally ill."

Wainwright got up suddenly and headed for the canal, the file in his hand. He went out to stand by the barbecue, staring out at the canal. For a second, Louis was afraid he was going to heave the file into the water.

"What else?" Louis asked, drawing Emily's attention back.

"Serial killers generally can be divided into two categories—organized and disorganized offenders," she said. She paused. "You're sure you want to hear all this?"

Louis nodded, taking a drink of beer.

"Okay," Emily said. "The organized offender is basically what we know as the sociopath. He's methodical, smart, socially adept, able to manipulate his victims so they feel comfortable. He carefully selects and stalks his victims from his comfort zone. Often there is a ritual aspect to the murders, usually sexual. The place where he dumps them often has some symbolic importance. He knows police procedure and likes to taunt cops."

"Ted Bundy," Louis said.

"Exactly." Emily reached for her wineglass and took a drink.

"Now the unorganized offender is different," she said. "He usually has a psychotic disorder of some kind—schizophrenia, personality fragmentation—that creates delusions. These guys are below average intelligence, loners, unmarried, live near the crime scenes. They use a 'blitz' style of attack, catching their victims off guard. The crime scene is disorganized. This is the guy neighbors always describe as weird."

"Son of Sam?" Louis asked.

Emily nodded. She took another drink of her wine. "We also have to look at the MO and the signature."

"Okay," Louis said, "the MO is what the killer does to effect the crime. In these cases, the shotgun to the leg, the beatings and stabbings."

She nodded. "And the signature is a symbol," she said, "the thing that gives him emotional satisfaction."

"The black paint," Louis said.

Emily nodded.

Louis was quiet for a moment. "Well, our guy attacks quickly, but with precision. The killings are methodical and sequential, but not all the scenes are alike so I sure wouldn't call them 'organized.' And victims still don't have anything in common but sex and race. Could our guy be both types?"

Emily nodded again. "Sometimes the line blurs."

"Great. That's fucking great."

Emily and Louis looked out to where Wainwright stood. He was facing them, shaking his head. He came back onto the patio.

"So basically, you're saying you can't really tell us anything for sure about this motherfucker," he said.

"Dan—" Louis said.

"First Louis says he's white, then you say he's black but it can't be Levon because he didn't set his pet dog on fire." He threw up his hands. "Goddamn it, if we can't even figure out what color he is, what the hell can we figure out?"

Emily and Louis stared at him.

"He's black," Emily said firmly.

Wainwright looked down at the file folder in his hand, then tossed it on the table. He went inside the house.

Emily watched him go, then reached for her wine. She finished it quickly.

Louis went to the table, opened each file, and scanned the three police reports. One in New Jersey and five in Florida.

"Why do you think he came to Florida?" Louis asked.

"These guys often go underground when they feel the heat and resurface someplace new and start over again," she said. Louis looked closer at the faxed pages. The New Jersey body was found in a place called Barnegat Light, the first Florida body in a place called Coral Springs, and the third in Lauderdale Lakes.

"Where's Barnegat Light, New Jersey?"

"It's on a barrier island, north of Atlantic City."

"And the places in Florida?"

She paused. "Broward County. It's over on the East Coast, north of Miami. Both places are suburbs of Fort Lauderdale."

"Where were the bodies found?" Louis asked.

"I know where you're going with this," she said. "The Jersey one was right on the beach." She pulled out a fax. "The second and third ones were found in drainage canals."

Louis dropped the file back on the table and turned to look out at Dodie's boat.

"What is it?" Emily asked.

"I just remembered something Dan said when we

were over in Captiva," Louis said. "He was right about something and didn't realize it." He turned to face her. "He's dumped them all in water. It's water, Farentino. That's the thread. He likes water."

Chapter Twenty-six

Louis took a sip of coffee and set the cup on the small patio table. He was sitting forward on a lounge chair, his feet planted on either side of him, the files from the NAACP guys, Mills and Seaver, spread in front of him.

He could feel the sun climbing up his back, and checked his watch. It was almost seven A.M.

He picked up another folder, this one thick and banded with fat rubber bands. These were "tips," names of possible weirdos, offered by their mothers, brothers, sisters, and ex-wives. *My old boyfriend has a knife collection and hates black people. My neighbor once threatened to throw acid on the black guy down the block.*

He was trying to find a link—any link—between the NAACP list and the tips. But he wondered if he was wasting time.

He's black, Emily had said.

How could she be so sure?

He heard the sliding door open and looked up. Margaret was heading his way with a coffeepot. Her hair dangled with loose rollers and her cotton robe fluttered in the morning breeze.

She refilled his cup and set four sugars on the table.

"How long have you been up?" she asked.

He pulled off his reading glasses and rubbed his face. "Since four. Thanks for the refill."

"I can throw on a few eggs, if you want."

"That's okay, I can eat later."

Louis slipped his glasses back on, but could see her pink slippers out of the corner of his eyes. He looked up at her again.

"Really, I'm fine, Margaret."

"Louis, did it ever occur to you that I *like* taking care of you? I like cooking for you and Sam."

He took off his glasses again. "I don't want you to fuss, that's all."

She sat down in the chair across from him. "It's what I do. People have things they just do. You read those awful things and chase killers, I take care of people."

He smiled. "Well, then, I will take some eggs."

She didn't move. He started to put his glasses back on, but stopped, afraid she would take it as a dismissal.

"You need to let people take care of you sometimes, Louis," she said gently. "I heard you mention your foster mother the other day. I didn't know you were a foster child. When Sam told me why you went back to Mississippi, I just assumed that's where you were raised. What was she like, your foster mother?"

He straightened, setting his glasses on the files. "Her name is Frances. And she did take good care of me, Margaret," he said.

"As much as you would let her, right?"

Louis glanced toward the canal. Suddenly he remembered hanging over a toilet, sicker than a damn dog from the flu. He had locked both his foster parents out of the bathroom and had fallen asleep in his thin pajamas on the cold floor. Phillip had finally removed the lock to get in and carried him to bed.

There had been other locks, too. Locks that came after the one time Louis tried to run away. He was ten and had been with the Lawrences for less than a year. He took ten dollars from Frances's purse and jumped out the bedroom window at midnight. When he tried to buy a bus ticket to Mississippi, the clerk had called the police. Hours later, Phillip had shown up at the police station and brought him home. He didn't know at the time that his actions normally would have sent him straight back into the system. He didn't know that Phillip had pleaded with child services to give Louis a second chance. All he knew is that there were now locks on his bedroom windows. "We put them there because we want you to stay, Louis," Frances had told him. He never tried to leave again.

He looked back at Margaret. "Yeah, she took care of me. As much as I would let her, yes."

Margaret smiled. "You know, Sam and I talked about taking in foster kids, but I didn't think I could bear to let them go home," she said. "Plus, Black Pool didn't have much of that kind of thing."

She paused. "Did you have lots of brothers and sisters coming and going through the house?"

He knew she meant foster kids, kids he refused to make friends with, because even after he realized he wasn't going anywhere, he knew they were. But two others came to mind, too. A skinny kid with skin as dark as coffee beans and a big girl with a stiff ponytail and bright red lipstick—lipstick stolen from his mother's purse.

"I have a brother and sister," he said, immediately surprised that he had said anything. "When my family was split up, they stayed in Black Pool. They went to relatives."

Margaret didn't ask why.

"You should look them up," she said instead. "You can't ever replace family or friends."

He nodded. Another image came to mind. He was small, very small, and his sister Yolanda was putting curlers in his hair. He smiled. God, she'd be what . . . thirty-five now? Hell, he probably had nephews or nieces somewhere. And Robert would be thirty-one. Gulfport. That's where he'd heard they'd gone.

"Yeah," he said softly. "I should."

Issy strolled over to them and hopped onto Margaret's lap. The cat stared at Louis and he thought he detected a smirk.

"What about your friend who gave you the cat?" Margaret asking, stroking Issy.

She was fishing, he knew that. She was trying so hard to find out if there was a woman in his life— or had been.

"It didn't work out," he said simply.

"But you kept her cat," Margaret said.

He didn't answer.

Margaret smiled. "Well, it's nice to keep a part of something you lost," she said. "I have a baby blanket my grandmother gave me when I was pregnant. We lost the baby, but I couldn't get rid of the blanket, even after the doctor told me I wouldn't ever have more babies. What he said was just words. The blanket was something real."

Louis sensed she expected him to say something. "It must have been hard," he said. "I mean, as much as you wanted children."

"We were lucky," Margaret said. "We had enough of each other to keep going. But there are still nights we talk about how our lives might have been different."

He was silent. He wasn't thinking about Margaret and Sam now, or even about about Zoe and Michigan. He was thinking about Kyla, the girl he had gotten pregnant in college.

How can you say it's not yours, Louis?

It can't be, he had told her. But he was thinking, *It ruins everything. I'm twenty years old and I don't want this.*

I'll leave then, Louis. I'll get rid of it.

Go, he had thought.

"Louis?"

Margaret was talking to him, bringing him back. "That's why Sam likes you here," she said.

He looked at her. "I'm sorry?"

She touched his arm. "Sam," she said. "He likes having you here."

Louis didn't trust himself to say anything.

She rose, setting Issy aside. "I'll go get your eggs going now," she said.

The cat sat on the floor for a moment, staring up at him, then trotted after Margaret.

Chapter Twenty-seven

Louis rubbed his eyes and looked up at the wall clock. Twelve-ten in the morning.

"Well, it's officially Wednesday," he said quietly.

Farentino glanced up at him, then went back to the notes she was making. The table between them was littered with papers, files, photographs, Styrofoam cups, and half-empty cartons of Chinese take-out. They had been at it for fourteen hours straight, going through copies of police reports that had been flowing in since yesterday.

Louis took off his glasses, rubbing his eyes. His thoughts drifted back to the other night on Dodie's patio. Dinner had been just a continuation of what had gone on before—Wainwright drinking too much, Farentino bristling with indignation, Margaret and Dodie furiously refilling the wineglasses. And he himself sitting there not having the slightest idea of how to get Wainwright and Emily to pull together.

But by the end of the evening, even Wainwright had begun to come around to Emily's assertion that the killer was black. There was no choice really; they had to believe her. There was no evidence to the contrary.

When Louis had arrived at the station early the next morning, Emily was already at work. She had tapped back into VI-CAP searching for any other cases up in New Jersey with MO's similar to the Broward County and Ocean County cases—black victims who had been beaten, stabbed, and painted. When she found none, she had expanded her search to all East Coast states, specifically jurisdictions near water. Still drawing a blank, she expanded the MO to victims who matched any of the three criteria—stabbed, beaten, or painted. She was looking specifically for bodies that had been left in water.

They had pored over the faxes, looking for red flags. But so far, they had uncovered only a handful of cases that were similar to the six they already had. There were no more exact fits. There were a half dozen middle-aged black victims who had been stabbed to death, four who had beaten to death. Some had been left in lakes or rivers, one even in a swimming pool. But none had been painted.

Louis tossed the fax he was reading on the table. His ass ached from sitting, his eyes were fuzzy from reading. He pulled his legs off the table and slowly got up, stretching.

"We're never going to get through all this shit," he muttered, taking off his glasses.

She didn't look up.

"Farentino," he said, "shouldn't we be concentrating on evidence we have instead of evidence we don't have?"

"You don't have any evidence," she said, still not looking up. "You don't have prints, hairs, fibers, or witnesses, for God's sake."

"We could be trying to match the blade."

"You want to go visit pawnshops, be my guest."

"We could be looking for an expert, or a knife show or something. There's lots of things we could be doing besides sitting here looking at paper."

She looked up at him. "He's in here. I know he is." She paused. "I got the impression the other night you were interested in this."

He stared glumly at the mess of faxes that they hadn't even looked at yet. "I am," he said.

She smiled slightly. "But you want to be out there. You're a cop. You can't help it."

He heard the low murmur of the dispatcher's radio behind him. It was Candy, reporting in from the Sereno causeway. He heard Wainwright answer from his post out on Captiva. There were thirty men out tonight, counting the sheriff's department and extras from Fort Myers. Cruising, watching the beaches and the causeways. And she was right; he wanted to be out there with them, even though he knew they had no chance of catching him in the act.

There was really nothing to do now but wait for the next body to be found.

Louis went to the map on the bulletin board, staring at the pins that marked the places of the abductions and crime scenes. Yesterday, they had added maps of Ocean County, New Jersey, and Broward County, Florida.

"Maybe it's got something to do with his job," he said, staring at the pins.

"What does?"

"The water. Maybe it's part of his job."

She let out a sigh. "Possibly. Or maybe it's just part of his hunting ground. Bundy liked college campuses."

Louis fell quiet again. He could hear the scratch of Emily's pencil on paper.

"Why the gap?" he said quietly.

Farentino looked up at him.

"I mean, why did he kill up in Jersey, then wait almost nine months before he killed again in Fort Lauderdale? Then wait some more before he killed three men here?"

Emily gave a weary shrug. "It's common. Sometimes these guys can go for months or years without killing but then the stressor kicks in and sets them off."

Louis turned to look at her. "Stressor?"

"Yeah, it's like a trigger. Something that sets him off, some crisis in his life that he can't cope with."

"So something down here triggered him to kill Tatum?" Louis asked.

"Maybe. Or maybe there are cases in between we haven't found yet." She dropped the pencil and ran her hands roughly over her face. "What we really need to do is find the first case. You can usually tell a lot about the killer from that."

"You don't think the one up in New Jersey was the first?"

She shook her head slowly. "No, it was too much

like all the others. Serial killers aren't usually perfect on the first try. They get better at what they do. If we find earlier cases, I'll bet they are not as ... refined."

"Strange choice of words, Farentino."

She shrugged.

He picked up the files again, opening to the personal report on the Barnegat Light, New Jersey, victim. He was fifty-five years old, a high school geography teacher with a son. No known enemies, no odd lifestyle patterns, just didn't return home from work one night after coaching a Little League game. He looked at the black-and-white Xerox of the autopsy photograph. Specks of black paint could be seen on the man's face, but at least he had a face.

Louis opened the other two files from Broward County. One was a fifty-year-old janitor whose service truck was found in a bank parking lot, door open. The other was a forty-eight-year-old X-ray technician who walked five blocks to a store for a pack of cigarettes and never made it home.

Louis turned to the photographs. The same. The faces were beaten but intact.

"He didn't beat these men as badly," Louis said, sliding the photos over to Emily.

She didn't even look at them. "Like I said, he's getting better at his work."

They were silent again. The radio traffic hummed in the background. It was too quiet.

"Why does he leave the bodies out in the open? Why not hide them?" Louis asked.

Emily looked up again and gave him a small smile. "You ask a lot of questions."

"I have a lot to learn about this," he said.

She leaned back, stretching her arms above her head. "Some of these guys want their victims found because they are taunting police or—this is sick—they are really proud of their work." She paused. "Then there are some who want to be caught." She hunched back over the files and put her glasses back on. "But those are few and far between."

Louis remembered the debris on the causeway where Tatum was found. "I think he just thinks they're garbage," he said, tossing the photos back on the table.

Emily nodded thoughtfully. "I think you're right. How a killer disposes of the body is crucial to understanding him. This killer has no use for his victims, takes no souvenirs, and makes no effort to hide the bodies from us. When he's done, he's done."

The phone rang. It was Wainwright's line. Louis punched the button.

"Sereno Police Department."

"Dan?"

"No, this is Kincaid. Louis Kincaid."

"Shit. This is Chief Horton over in Fort Myers. Where's Dan?"

"On stakeout, Chief. I'm—"

"Get Dan on the radio. Now."

"What's—"

"We got another victim."

"Same MO?"

"Yeah. Except this one's alive."

Louis yanked open the door to the Fort Myers Police Station, and was met in the lobby by a short, muscular man with a brush cut and intense brown eyes. He wore gray uniform pants and a white shirt that stretched tightly across his chest. He thrust out his hand.

"Chief Horton," he said, pumping Louis's hand as he pulled him through a door. "You must be Kincaid."

"Right, and this is Agent Farentino," Louis said, nodding behind him. Horton gave her a cursory smile.

"Dan said you'd get here first. He's about five minutes out."

"Where's the victim?" Louis asked.

"Interrogation room one." Horton led him down a hallway, crowded with uniforms. "A passing patrol car picked him up. He was a mess when he got here. We bagged his shirt, pants, and apron."

"Apron?" Louis said.

"He's a waiter. We also scraped his nails and checked his hands. Maybe we'll pick up a skin sample, a fiber, who knows?"

They came to a stop in front of a window. Louis stared at him.

He looked to be in his mid-thirties, with tawny brown skin and a short-cropped tuft of dark brown hair. He was small-framed but wiry, his sinewy arms exposed in a white cotton T-shirt. His bare feet were visible beneath the baggy orange jail pants. His head was bowed and his hands were wrapped around a Styrofoam cup.

"Is he hurt?" Louis asked.

"Bruises on his neck, but that's all."

Louis glanced down the hall. He was anxious to get in there, but he knew he should wait for Wainwright.

Louis suddenly thought about Mobley. "Have you called the sheriff?" Louis asked.

Horton was staring at Emily, who had moved down the window for a better view of the victim's face.

"Chief?"

Horton looked at Louis. "What? Hell no. I'll roust his ass about five A.M." Horton's eyes moved back to Emily, and he leaned toward Louis. "Who's that?" he whispered.

"FBI. She's been assisting. She's a profiler."

"No shit?"

Someone called Horton's name and he disappeared. He was back a few seconds later with Wainwright. Wainwright looked as if he had run all the way from Sereno Key.

"This is him?" Wainwright asked, looking in the window.

Horton nodded. "Roscoe Webb. He's a waiter at the Pelican Restaurant."

"That place down on MacGregor by the outlet mall?" Wainwright asked.

Horton nodded.

"Outlet mall? Isn't that near Hibiscus Heights?" Louis asked.

"Yeah, I guess it's on the way," Horton said.

"What did you get from him?" Wainwright asked Horton.

"Just what I've told you. I wanted to wait till you got here to talk to him."

"Thanks, Al. I owe you one."

Horton opened the door and the four of them went inside, Emily sliding in just as the door closed.

Webb looked up them, his eyes skittering from one to the other.

Horton walked around behind him and patted his shoulder. "Sorry to leave you alone, Mr. Webb."

"It's okay," he whispered. His hands, clasped around the cup, were trembling.

"Mr. Webb, this is Chief Wainwright and Officer Kincaid from Sereno Key and Agent Farentino from the FBI. They want to ask you a few questions. That okay with you?"

Webb nodded.

Horton turned on a tape recorder and moved the mike closer to Roscoe. "Just talk normal."

Louis glanced at Wainwright, who nodded toward the table. Louis pulled up a chair and straddled it, across from Roscoe Webb.

"Let's back up, Mr. Webb. Where were you when he came up to you?" Horton began.

"Coming out of the restaurant. We close at midnight. It was about twenty after. I noticed the boss's car and this truck in the lot, which was weird 'cause there weren't any customers in there when I left. But I didn't see anyone so I just went to my car."

"What did the truck look like?"

"Dark pickup, maybe blue. Rust spots, old."

Webb took a deep breath and a drink from his cup.

"I was getting ready to unlock the door and I dropped my keys. I bent down to pick them up when I heard this explosion."

"Like a shotgun blast?" Louis asked.

Webb frowned slightly. "I've never heard a shotgun, but yeah, it sounded kinda like I heard on TV. Loud . . . real loud and close."

"It hit the car door," Horton said.

Webb ran a hand over his face. "I keep thinking . . . if I hadn't dropped those keys . . ."

"Did you see him, Mr. Webb?" Louis prodded gently.

Webb shook his head. "Before I could turn around, he grabbed me from behind."

Louis let out a breath, disappointed. "How exactly did he grab you?"

"Put an arm around my neck," Webb said, using his own arm to demonstrate. "I started clawing at his face, over my head, 'cause I read once how you could get away by scratching their eyes out, but I couldn't get ahold of anything. Except his hair. I grabbed that."

"Can you describe his hair, Mr. Webb?"

"I didn't see—"

"I know. What did it feel like?"

Webb blinked. "Greasy, it was greasy like."

Louis glanced at Horton. "Hair cream maybe?"

"I'll tell the techs to look," Horton said. He looked at Roscoe. "Mr. Webb, did you wash your hands yet?"

Webb's eyes went from Horton to the others. "Yeah, yeah, I did. I had to take a piss after that lab guy finished with me."

"Can you guess how long the hair was?" Louis asked.

"I got a good handful, so it couldn't be short. Maybe ear-length. I don't know."

"Thick or thin?"

"Thick, seemed like there was lots of it." Webb paused and brought the coffee slowly up to his lips again. He took a sip and set it back down. He stared at his trembling hands. "Man, I'm sorry . . ."

"That's all right, Mr. Webb, you're doing fine," Horton said. "Go on."

Webb pulled in a breath. "Well, then he pulls this pole up and levels it across my throat."

"A pole? What kind of pole?" Wainwright said.

"A long metal pole, like a pipe of some kind. It was maybe four or five feet long and he pulled it real tight against my throat. I barely got my fingers between it and my neck."

"Are you sure it wasn't a shotgun barrel?" Wainwright asked.

Webb shook his head. "No . . . no, I never seen no gun, just that pole."

"What about his hands? Can you describe them?"

"He was wearing gloves, tan, I think, looked like leather. And long sleeves. Denim."

Louis glanced at Wainwright. "Could you tell how tall he was?"

"Taller than me. I had the feeling my back was dead against his chest. And I could feel from his arm that he was pretty well muscled."

"How did you get away?" Louis asked.

Webb rubbed his face. It was quiet in the room for a moment except for Webb's labored breathing.

"Mr. Webb? You all right?" Horton asked quietly.

"Yeah, yeah . . ."

"Take your time."

Webb pulled in a deep shuddering breath. "I knew I was losing it," he said. "I couldn't breathe and I knew I was losing it and I was going to die." He paused. "I don't know what made me think of it, but I remembered my corkscrew in my apron. I reached down and pulled it out . . ."

He stopped, closing his eyes tight. His hands were

clenched. "I flipped it open and just brought it down as hard as I could. I . . . it hit his leg."

Webb opened his eyes. The room was air-conditioned to arctic, but he had sweated through his T-shirt.

"He let go," he said quietly. "He let go and I ran."

"Did he chase you?" Louis asked.

"I don't know. I was blocks down the road when I saw the cop car." He leaned back in the chair, spent, his eyes going from one man to the other.

Louis looked up at Horton. "Your guys see anyone?"

Horton shook his head. "The second unit was ten minutes out."

Louis sat back in his chair. Not much to go on. Maybe, if they were lucky, some hair or clothing fibers or a blood type off the corkscrew. He glanced at Emily, who was standing against the far wall. She was scribbling in her notebook.

"Anything else, Chief?" Louis asked Wainwright.

Wainwright hesitated, then came forward. "Mr. Webb, did he say anything?"

Webb looked up at him. "Oh, yes, sir."

"What did he say? And try to recall his exact words."

Webb swallowed hard. "Shit, it's hard to forget. He said, 'You're gonna die tonight, nigger.' "

"He used those exact words?" Louis asked.

Webb nodded.

Louis glanced at Wainwright, then leaned closer to Webb. "Mr. Webb, was this man black or white?"

Webb stared at Louis for a moment. "I didn't see his face—"

"I know. Was this man black or white, Mr. Webb?"

His eyes went from Louis, up to Wainwright and

Horton, and back to Louis. "I've been called a nigger by a black man and I've been called a nigger by a white man," he said firmly. "There's a difference." He paused. "This was a white man."

Louis held Roscoe's eyes for a moment, then leaned back, looking up at Wainwright and Horton. They were staring at Roscoe. Louis looked at Emily. She had stopped writing in her notebook. Her face was like ice.

"Thank you, Mr. Webb," Louis said, touching the man's arm. "You did fine."

Webb nodded, his eyes empty. "I guess," he said softly. "I'm alive."

They left the room, gathering just outside the door.

"We've got him a hotel room for the night with a uniform, in case this asshole tries to find him," Horton says. "We'll take good care of him."

"Good job, Al," Wainwright said.

Horton nodded and ran a hand through his hair. "Well, I guess I better go call Mobley and get this over with. I'll keep you posted, Dan."

Horton left and they made their way back to the lobby and outside. They stood on the sidewalk, breathing in the cool, damp night air.

"He might go underground after this," Wainwright said, breaking the silence.

"Why?" Louis asked.

"This one got away. It could make him nervous."

"Or just madder," Louis said. "I've got a feeling this isn't going to make a difference one way or the other. I think he's going right back out hunting."

Wainwright shook his head, looking at the squad cars parked at the curb.

"White," Louis said. "He said he's white."

"Yeah, a white guy with long, greasy hair," Wainwright said quietly. "Shit. I don't know what to think now."

Louis looked at Farentino. She was staring at the ground.

"What about you, Farentino?" Louis asked.

She wouldn't look up.

"Farentino?" Louis repeated.

Emily lifted her head. "I think we just wasted two days," she said.

Chapter Twenty-eight

"Tell me again about this guy, Van Slate," Farentino said, as she turned a corner.

Louis loosened his grip on the armrest and reached for his glasses. After the interview with Roscoe Webb last night, they had switched their focus back to white suspects. And now they were on their way to see Matthew Van Slate again. Louis had suggested to Wainwright that Emily come along this time to get a reading on Van Slate. Wainwright had agreed; he and Candy were following them in another squad car.

Emily was driving the Sereno Key cruiser and she seemed to have two speeds: fast and get-the-hell-outta-my-way. Louis tried not to look at the water as they sped across the causeway. He opened Van Slate's file.

"Matthew Van Slate. Arrested and convicted of a racially motivated beating last summer. Served ten months. His father, Hugh, is a high-profile local who helped get the sentence reduced."

Emily reached down and turned up the air conditioner. "Tell me the circumstances," she said.

"He and two friends followed a black man and white woman from a bar, ran them off the road, and beat the guy up."

"How bad?"

"Hospitalized him."

"What's his beef with blacks?"

"He thought his wife left him for a black guy."

Farentino was quiet for a minute, then asked, "Did they use weapons?"

Louis closed Van Slate's file. "Their fists and a board."

"Did they all participate?"

"Yes."

Farentino shook her head slightly. "Did he confess when he was caught?"

Louis reopened the file and read down the page. "Yes, after confronted with a witness."

"How many times has this guy told you to get lost?"

"Twice."

Farentino was quiet as they pulled up to Van Slate's apartment. She killed the engine and they sat there for a moment waiting for the second cruiser with Wainwright and Candy.

"What do you think?" Louis asked Emily.

"I'll tell you when we're done talking to him," Emily said.

Van Slate came out of his apartment just as Wainwright's cruiser pulled in. He was carrying a small cooler. He locked his door and turned, freezing when he saw the two cruisers in the lot.

"Is that him?" Emily asked.

"That's our hero," Louis said, getting out.

Van Slate turned back to his door, jiggling his keys, as if he was thinking about going back inside. But after a moment, he turned back and started out toward the parking lot, not even looking their way.

"Van Slate," Louis called out.

Van Slate kept going.

"Hold it, Van Slate."

He stopped and turned. Wainwright and Candy came forward. They formed a half circle around him and as Van Slate's eyes moved over them, Louis could see him tense.

"Who's dead now?" Van Slate asked.

"Stay cool, Van Slate. We just want to ask you a few questions," Wainwright said. "Why don't you come down to the station with us?"

Van Slate set the cooler on the top of a black pickup. He looked at Louis.

"What is your problem with me?" he said. "You're not even a cop and you got these guys—the real cops—believing I'm some sort of serial killer." Van Slate spat into the gravel. "And they call *me* the racist."

"We just want to ask a few questions," Louis said.

Van Slate spun around and slapped angrily at the bed of the truck, and took a few steps toward the apartment. Then he turned back. "All right. Ask. Right here. Right now. I'm not going anywhere."

Wainwright glanced at Louis, then rubbed his jaw. "Suit yourself," Wainwright said. "We got a witness that says the killer's truck is blue." Wainwright nodded at Van Slate's shiny blue truck parked a few spots away. "That's one piss-ass fairy color but to me, it looks blue."

"Fuck," Van Slate muttered, leaning against the black pickup. "Like I'm the only guy with a blue truck around here?"

"You're the only guy around here with a blue truck and a record," Wainwright said.

Louis looked at Emily and knew she was thinking the same thing, that Roscoe Webb said the truck he saw in the restaurant lot was dark, maybe blue, but definitely old and rusted.

"How long are you guys going to hassle me over that shit?" Van Slate asked, his voice rising. "This is fucking bullshit."

Louis looked at Farentino. She was taking notes.

"Own a knife, Van Slate?" Wainwright asked.

Van Slate eyed Wainwright. "Christ." He took a few steps and reached in the flatbed of the black truck he had been leaning against. He threw back the tarp and spread his arm toward it. "Be my guest."

"Is this your truck?" Louis asked.

"Hell no. This piece of shit is the boatyard truck. I just drive it for work."

Louis's eyes swept over the rust-pocked black pickup and then he glanced up at Wainwright. Louis stepped forward and looked inside the flatbed. It was filled with tools, white plastic tubs of paint. There was a large, plastic case that looked like a toolbox.

"How about you open that for us, Van Slate?" Wainwright said, pointing to it.

Van Slate reached in and popped it open. Louis peered inside. It was a tackle box, filled with the usual fishing paraphernalia. But there were also eight knives, different shapes and sizes.

"We'd like to have those knives, Van Slate," Wainwright said.

Van Slate threw up his hands. "Go ahead, take them! You'll get them eventually anyway." He leaned against the truck, his arms crossed. "You won't find anything on any of them, except maybe some fish guts and worm shit."

Wainwright nodded at Candy, who came forward, pulling a plastic evidence bag from his pocket. He carefully picked out the knives and bagged them.

"I want them back," Van Slate said.

Wainwright spoke again. "You got any spray paint, Van Slate?"

"Spray paint? Yeah, I got—" he stopped, his eyes narrowing. "Why?"

They didn't answer him. Louis could almost hear the gears in Van Slate's brains grinding. "Did this guy paint a message on the walls?" Van Slate asked. When no one answered, he smiled. "Manson did that, he painted 'Helter Skelter' on the walls. You know, the Beatles song?"

Van Slate started singing the song, but then stopped suddenly. "No, wait! I got it. He wrote a message on the bodies or something, right?"

"Can you go get the paint for us?" Wainwright asked.

"They had paint on them. What color was it?"

"You tell us," Wainwright said.

Van Slate shrugged. "White?"

Louis glanced at Emily. She was staring hard at Van Slate.

"Why white?" Wainwright asked.

Van Slate was suddenly interested in the conversation. "Well, it makes sense, don't it? I mean, these dead guys are all black, right? Why would anyone paint them black? They're already black." Van Slate locked eyes with Louis, and a slow grin came over his face. "Shit, if I was doing this, I'd paint 'em white. You know, make 'em lighter. Do a Michael Jackson on 'em. Improve on nature."

Louis resisted the urge to reach over and grab a handful of Van Slate's T-shirt.

Van Slate's grin widened. "This is a real kick in the ass, ain't it?" he said. "Me helping you guys."

"Go get the paint, Van Slate. That would be a help to us," Wainwright said.

"Get a warrant," he said.

"I will if I have to," Wainwright said.

Van Slate was shaking his head, still smiling. "You guys are fishing, aren't you? You don't know *who* the fuck you're looking for. You don't even know why these poor assholes were even offed in the first place."

He paused to pull a pack of Marlboros out of his jeans. "I read the paper. I know what they're saying, that some guy with a hard-on toward black guys is doing it. You know what I think? I think these guys were all asking for it some way."

Louis suddenly realized that here they were, four experienced cops, standing and listening to this scumbag's opinions. He knew that suspects who could manipulate an interrogation were dangerous to investigations. But he wasn't sure that's what Van Slate was doing.

"Shut up, Van Slate," Wainwright interrupted. "Nobody wants to hear your theories."

"I do," Louis said.

Van Slate's eyes snapped to Louis, along with Wainwright's. He lit his cigarette and blew the smoke over his head before he answered.

"*You* want to hear *my* opinion?"

"I do, too," Emily said.

Van Slate focused on her for a second, as if he had just now noticed she was there.

"I can't believe I'm helping you," he said, smiling. "Okay, here it is. None of these dead guys had it coming for the reasons you're thinking. From all appearances, they lived a very normal black life. They were no threat."

"To who?" Louis asked.

Van Slate met his eyes. "To guys like me." He took a quick drag on his cigarette. "Besides, no self-respecting racist—which I am not, by the way—would do these guys the way they were done."

"Enlighten us," Louis said tightly.

Van Slate's eyes focused for a moment on Emily, on the pad and pencil in her hands. "Let me put it this way, if I'm going to beat the shit out of somebody, I ain't going to get my hands dirty doing it."

"Is that why you used a board on Zengo?" Wainwright asked.

Van Slate looked at him, a smirk on his face. "You're learning."

Louis looked away, his gaze settling on a dandelion poking through the gravel.

"Plus," Van Slate said, "if this guy is a racist—which I am not, by the way—he'd be proud of what he did. He'd leave you a message. You know, like a dog pissing to show you he was there. And from what I hear, this guy leaves nada."

Louis had heard enough. He turned and started back to the squad car.

Van Slate was an idiot, but one thing he had said had stuck in Louis's mind: *And you call me a racist?*

A long time ago, he had learned not to turn a deaf ear when his instinct was trying to tell him something. But instinct—vibrations, gut feeling, whatever it was that had worked for him so well in the past—had failed him in Michigan. He'd been blindsided, not only by a killer, but by people he had grown to trust. He'd been wrong. Fatally wrong.

Was he wrong here, too? Was he going after Van Slate just because he was a small-minded bigot? Because he was white?

He heard Wainwright finishing up with Van Slate, but he didn't care. Van Slate hadn't murdered those men. Van Slate wanted no contact with blacks; he would never have gone to Queenie Boulevard. And his bigotry was too generalized, his hatred too unspecific. He had attacked Joshua Zengo, true, but it had come from some warped personal motive. These murders were seemingly without any reason. There was still no *why* —at least not that they had been able to see.

If a white man like Van Slate doesn't kill a black stranger out of hate, what else could it be?

Wainwright, Emily, and Candy were coming toward him. They all stood, watching as Van Slate busied himself rearranging the tarp in the flatbed.

"He made a good point," Emily said, closing her notebook.

"About what?" Wainwright said.

"About the murderer being proud of what he does," she said. "Whoever murdered Tatum, Quick, and the homeless man doesn't seem to care what we think. He hasn't contacted anyone, hasn't taken any souvenirs from his victims or left his mark. Most serial killers do.''

''You don't call the paint a mark?'' Wainwright said.

Emily shook her head. ''I agree with Louis. I think it's a symbol, something important to him alone. It's not a sign that he was there. He's not like the Zodiac killer. He's not saying, 'Remember me.' ''

''What's your take on Van Slate, Farentino?'' Louis asked.

''Well, he definitely doesn't fit the disorganized offender category. I guess a case could be made for organized—''

''In English, Farentino,'' Wainwright said patiently.

She sighed. ''I think Matt Van Slate is mean-spirited and a bigot. But I don't think he's a murderer. At least not this one.''

Wainwright looked at Louis. ''You agree?''

Louis nodded. ''I guess I couldn't see past my disgust of this guy.''

Van Slate gunned the black truck. He gave them a taunting wave as he peeled out, spraying gravel.

''What an asshole,'' Candy offered.

Wainwright watched the truck tear down the road. ''Yeah,'' he said. ''But unfortunately being an asshole isn't against the law.''

Chapter Twenty-nine

Wainwright came out of his bathroom, buttoning a fresh shirt. He stared at Louis and Emily, who were slumped in chairs around the conference table. It was heaped with files, faxes, and coffee cups.

"Why don't you two go home and change? You're starting to stink up the joint," Wainwright said.

Emily was on the phone, on hold, but she ignored him. Louis rubbed his bristly jaw and took a sip of coffee. It was cold.

They had been up all night. Emily had worked feverishly, still plowing through the VI-CAP files. She had also called everyone she had already contacted, telling them to switch their focus to white suspects and racially motivated crimes. New faxes had begun coming in around eleven this morning, forming a pile on the table next to the discarded ones that focused on black suspects. Every hour, Candy had come in and deposited new faxes on the table. Emily doggedly went through each one, methodically reading it and assigning it its own file.

Louis had felt sorry for her and stayed to help, even though he thought the chances of finding a related case this way was like trying to find a lost pearl on the beach. But he had to admire her stamina if nothing else.

In the background, Louis could hear the crackle of the radio. Another shift was signing on after a long night of surveillance. Now it was four in the afternoon. They were still waiting for a fresh body to turn up. And they were all running on adrenaline, stale coffee, and frayed nerves.

Wainwright picked a bear claw out of the Dunkin' Donuts box on the desk.

"Did the lab call back yet on whether Van Slate's knives match?"

"Not yet," Louis said. "They do have something on Roscoe Webb, though. No hairs, but they did find hair cream under his nails. It's standard Vitalis."

"Did Van Slate's alibi check out?"

Louis nodded. "The bartender at the Lob Lolly said he was there until it closed at two and then he left."

"So Van Slate couldn't have been in that parking lot with Webb," Wainwright said. He took a bite of the stale bear claw and tossed it back into the box.

"You find anything in the new VI-CAP stuff?" he asked.

"Nothing."

"Fuck. When are we going to catch a break on this?"

Emily slammed down the phone. Louis and Wainwright looked over at her.

"Assholes," she said. She felt them staring at her. "He says he doesn't have *time* to look up cases that are five years old."

"Farentino, look at it from their standpoint," Wainwright said. "You're asking them to stop whatever they're doing and search for a case you don't even know exists."

"We have to find the first murder," she said firmly. "It will tell us who he is."

"Goddamn it, we can't even solve *these* murders," Wainwright said. "If you want to waste time looking for something that might have happened five years ago, be my fucking guest."

Wainwright looked at Louis. "But don't tie up my men with your hocus-pocus bullshit."

"Dan—" Louis said.

Emily stared at Wainwright. "You narrow-minded old fart—"

"Farentino," Louis said quickly.

"You don't have a clue about what I'm doing here," Emily said. "And you don't want to know. You don't want to know anything new, anything that doesn't fit into your testosterone-poisoned world."

Wainwright took a step toward the table, his blue eyes boring into her. "Testosterone? You wanna talk hormones, lady? It takes testosterone to do this job," he said.

"And what does it take to work in OPR?" Emily shot back.

Louis stared at Wainwright. He thought he saw a flicker of embarrassment cross his face.

"Farentino, you're the one who has no clue," Wainwright said calmly.

Emily took off her glasses, pinching the bridge of her nose. She rose slowly, without looking at either of them. "I need some air," she said.

She left, closing the door hard.

"Shit," Wainwright muttered.

"She's working her ass off, Dan," Louis said.

"I know. I know." He went to the watercooler, poured a cup, and slurped it down.

The phone on the conference table rang. It was Wainwright's extension. Wainwright made no move to pick it up.

"You going to get that?" Louis said.

Wainwright grabbed the receiver. He listened, gave a few grunts in response, and hung up.

"That was the lab," he said. "Van Slate's knives aren't even close. But they did identify the foreign tissue on the broken blade. It's fish guts. Snapper, to be exact."

Louis rose quickly. "He's a fisherman."

"Maybe," Wainwright said. "The lab is still trying to match the blade, but they're pretty sure it's a fillet knife of some kind."

Louis glanced at his watch. "I'm going to the docks. Can I take unit three?"

"We'll take my car," Wainwright said.

Louis paused. "What about Farentino?"

Wainwright looked at the files on the table. "She's got her own work to do."

* * *

It was nearly five by the time they turned onto San Carlos Boulevard, heading south toward Fort Myers Beach. Louis wove impatiently through the heavy traffic.

"Slow down, Louis," Wainwright said.

"The boats get in around four-thirty at Fisherman's Wharf. If we miss them, we have to wait till morning."

"You know, that isn't the only marina here. There's dozens of them, and he could be working any one of them," Wainwright said. "There's a shitload of 'em near the beach here, a couple on Sanibel, more over in Cape Coral and up in Bokeelia, a couple on the river. And we got to consider the fact this guy could be back bay instead of ocean."

"Back bay? The clerk at the Holiday Inn mentioned that. What is it?" Louis asked.

"Fishing for snook or tarpon in the bays and flats in small boats, usually with a hired guide. If our guy is a guide, we'll never find him. There's hundreds of them operating around here." He let out a breath. "He could work at a bait shop or behind the fish counter at Winn-Dixie, for all we know."

"But Quick was seen at Fisherman's Wharf," Louis said. "We know that for a fact."

"So says your shrimp woman," Wainwright said.

They pulled into the lot at Fisherman's Wharf and got out. Beyond the snack bar, Louis could see four charter boats at dock, including the one with the broken generator he had seen on his first visit.

The wharf hummed with activity. Knots of sun-burned men in polo shirts and bermudas were watch-

ing the crews haul the day's catches out of the freezers
and onto cleaning tables. The tourists were joking
and gulping beer while crewmen silently and swiftly
went about the business of filleting the fish. Other
grim-faced crewmen hosed the decks and packed up
lines and poles. The sun was in a deep slant now,
and everyone just wanted to go home.

Louis watched the crewmen. They were all shapes
and sizes, some wiry, some beefy. Any one of them
could be the killer. Louis felt a spurt of adrenaline.
He could be watching him right now and not even
know it, but at least the net was finally narrowing.

He and Wainwright split up, each taking photos of
the blade and Anthony Quick.

At the first boat, the *Island Lady,* Louis showed the
photos of Quick and the blade to the captain and
two crewmen, but none of the men recognized either.
It was the same at the second boat, where one of the
crewmen said that in his twenty years in the business
he had never seen a fillet knife with a curved blade.

Louis waited near the bar for Wainwright to finish
with the final boat of the four. As Wainwright drew
near, Louis could tell he had had no luck either.

"Nothing," Wainwright said.

"Damn, I was so sure," Louis said. "You question
every crewman?"

"Yeah. Shit, he could be right here under our noses
but how are we going to tell?" Wainwright looked
out over the water, then up to where the cars inched
along on the skyway bridge. "I think we should head
over to Deebolts before they clear out for the day."

Louis nodded, not able to hide his disappointment.
Laughter drifted over to him. The tourists had taken
their party to the bar. Gulls circled overhead, their

raucous cries competing with the men's laughter and the thump-thump of Bob Seger singing "Night Moves."

Louis's gaze wandered out to the water again. He squinted. There was another charter boat coming in.

"Dan, look."

The boat was larger than the others, a huge red and white two-deck catamaran that growled and spat out diesel fumes like some sleek monster. As it inched into its moorings, Louis made out the name on the bow: *Miss Monica.*

"You take this one and I'll go to Deebolts and swing back and get you," Wainwright said. He headed off to the parking lot.

Louis stood on the dock, waiting as the lines were secured. The six tourists onboard stood quietly at the railing. A couple of them looked green and they all looked eager to get off. The engines were cut. As the tourists filed off, Louis watched the two crewmen go through a perfectly choreographed tango of cleaning and stowing the gear—rubber waders, nets, fishing poles with reels the size of small bike tires.

Louis approached the nearest crewman.

"I'd like to speak to the captain," he said.

The crewman, a tall wiry man with deeply tanned skin and bleached blond hair, eyed Louis. "What for?" he said.

"Just get him, please."

The man tossed the line to the deck and trudged off. A few moments later, a short man of about sixty came forward. He wore wrinkled white shorts, a sweat-stained madras shirt, and a red baseball cap stitched with the name *Miss Monica.*

"I'm George Lynch," he said. "What can I do for you?"

Louis introduced himself and explained that he was investigating the murders.

"I heard about it," Lynch said. He took off his baseball cap and ran a hand through his sparse hair. "We were just talking about it on the way in."

"We think the man who murdered these men might have some connection to the fishing business," Louis said.

Lynch looked shocked. "Jesus."

Louis stepped forward, holding out the photo of Anthony Quick. "Have you seen this man, Captain Lynch? He might have been a customer on your boat."

Lynch studied the photo, frowning. "Maybe. I can't say for sure. It's been real busy of late."

"Think hard. It would have been on March fourteenth, a Tuesday," Louis said.

Lynch shook his head. "Just a minute. Hey, Woody, Ty! Come here!"

Two crewmen came forward. One was the tall blond, his lanky hair visible beneath a sweat-stained *Miss Monica* cap. The other man was shorter, black, wearing the same cap.

"Either of you remember this guy being onboard about two weeks ago?"

The blond man was staring at the photo. "Yeah, I remember him. He was with that six-pack we took out in the gulf."

"Why do you remember him?" Louis asked.

" 'Cause he was really pissed that he didn't catch anything. I told him tough luck, that's why it was called fishin' and not catchin'."

"Woody—" Lynch interrupted.

"He was mouthing off, Cap," Woody said.

"I don't care. He paid his money." Lynch's mouth pulled into a tight line.

"Was he with anybody?" Louis asked, pulling out a notebook and pen.

"Nah, came on alone. Left alone."

"You saw him get into a car?"

Woody shook his head. "No, I sent him over to Dixie's to buy some fish to ship home." He stared at Louis. "Anything else?"

Louis shook his head.

"Go finish up," Lynch said.

The crewmen left. Louis watched them. Woody went back to coiling lines. Ty was manning the cleaning table, pulling glistening silver fish up onto the wooden board and slitting them open with one expert thrust of his knife. Louis focused on the fillet knife. It was only about eight inches in length and perfectly straight. He pulled out the photo of the broken blade.

"Have you ever seen a knife like this before?" he asked Lynch.

Lynch looked at the photo. "That a fillet knife?"

"We were hoping you could tell us that."

"Nothing like anything I've ever seen." Lynch called again for Woody and Ty, but Woody had disappeared below. Ty came over.

"Ty, you ever seen a knife like this before?"

The crewman wiped his hands on his dirty cutoffs and took the photo. He stared at the photo for a long time. "Yeah," he said softly. "I saw one like this once. A guy working in Montauk had one. It's German-made, I think."

"Montauk? That's New York, right?" Louis said. "You know his name?"

Ty shook his head. "He was here last winter. I haven't seen him around this season."

"Thanks, Ty," Lynch said. "Finish up and you can go."

"Okay," Ty said. He noticed Louis looking at him and gave him a reticent smile, his hazel eyes dropping to the dock. He went back to the fillet table, bagging the fish in plastic filled with ice. Louis looked for Woody, but he was nowhere to be seen.

"You think these fellows were killed with fillet knives?" Lynch asked.

"We're not sure. We haven't identified the weapon yet, but it's a good possibility."

Lynch nodded emphatically. "I can see that," he said. "We have to keep 'em sharp as razors." He held up his left hand. "Look at this. I was filleting a pompano once and slipped. Lost my pinkie. Sliced it clean off."

Louis stared at Lynch's callused hand, trying not to think of the defense-wound slash marks on Anthony Quick's hand.

"Captain Lynch," he said, "what can you tell me about your crew?"

"My crew? Do you—" He stopped. "You guys think someone down here did this?"

"We're just checking all possible leads," Louis said. "Tell me about your crewmen. How long have they been with you?"

Lynch looked uneasy. "Well, Ty's been with me, geez, it has to be nearly three years now. Woody . . . let's see. He came on this past November right here."

"What's both their full names and addresses?"

Lynch gave them to him.

Louis closed the notebook. "Thanks, Captain Lynch."

"I had a third man," Lynch said, "but he left a while back."

"He left? Why?" Louis asked.

Lynch shrugged. "Who knows? These guys, they're like Gypsies. It's a transient business, and we don't ask a lot of questions. The most important thing is just showing up."

"When did he leave?" Louis asked.

"Oh, two or three weeks ago. Left me short."

Louis flipped opened the notebook. "Name?"

"Gunther . . . Gunther Mayo."

"How long did he work for you?"

"He came on last April up in Barnegat Light."

Louis stopped taking notes. "Barnegat Light, New Jersey?"

Lynch nodded. "Yeah, that's where we go in the summer." When he saw the look on Louis's face, Lynch added, "Something wrong with that?"

"You split your time between here and Jersey?" Louis asked.

Lynch nodded again. "Winter here, summer up north. We call it following the tuna."

"Do all the charters here do that?"

"Nope. Just the bigger boats like the *Miss Monica* here." He waved a hand proudly at the fishing poles stowed behind him. "We go after the big stuff."

"Do you know where he might have gone?"

"Shit, he could be anywhere from Maine to Key West. That's the circuit."

"You know anything else about him?" Louis asked. "Where he lives?"

"I'm not sure. There's a lot of seasonal rentals over around Buttonwood Street. You can walk there from here."

Louis felt his patience drying up fast. "You don't keep records of your employees, Mr. Lynch?"

"Not unless I have to."

"What about Mayo's vehicle?"

"Don't know. Never saw him drive anything."

Louis sighed. "Okay, let me ask you this. Did you ever hear Mayo make any racial slurs? Threats against blacks? Anything like that?"

Lynch shook his head. "He didn't say much about anyone or anything. Quiet, moody kind of guy."

"I don't suppose you'd have a picture of him."

Lynch started to shake his head, then paused. "You know, I might, I just might. Hold on."

Lynch disappeared and came back with a stack of photos. He sifted through them and held one out to Louis. "That's him behind the fat guy, holding the hose."

It was a photo of four tourists standing at the rail of the *Miss Monica,* holding up their catches. Mayo was visible in the background, a blur of profile and dark hair worn in a ponytail.

"Can I see the others?" Louis asked, nodding at the stack in Lynch's hand.

"You can have them," Lynch said, handing them over. "These are just extras the tourists didn't buy."

Louis stuck the photos in his pocket. His fingers closed around a business card and he pulled it out. It was one of Farentino's FBI cards on which she had scribbled the Sereno Key Police Department number. He printed his own name on the back and handed it to Lynch.

"Call me if you think of anything else or if Mayo shows up," Louis said.

Lynch looked at the card. "Wow . . . FBI."

Louis turned to leave. His eyes locked on the fishing gear now stowed neatly on the aftdeck. A question floated into his mind, but he knew no matter how he asked it, it would sound stupid. What the hell.

"Captain Lynch?"

The captain turned back to him.

"Do you ever have reason to use guns when you fish?"

"What?"

"Do you ever use a shotgun onboard?"

For a moment, Lynch looked at him like he was nuts; then he held up a hand. "Hang on."

He went below and when he came back on deck, he was holding a slender metal pole about six feet long. Louis instantly knew it was the pole Roscoe Webb had seen.

"What is it?" he asked Lynch.

"A bang stick. We use it on sharks mainly."

Louis came forward and gingerly took the pole.

"It ain't loaded," Lynch said.

"How—"

Lynch pointed to a cylinder on the top. "You load the shell in here and it kind of sits cocked on a spring device that is triggered by touching the tip to the target. In our case, the shark." He pointed to a pin. "That's the safety pin. Keeps you from shooting yourself in the foot."

"It takes a shotgun shell?" Louis asked.

"Standard variety."

"What about blanks?"

Lynch frowned. "Well, I heard of alligator hunters

using blanks 'cause they don't want the hides messed up. But a blank would only stun a shark."

"Or a man," Louis said, staring at the pole's lethal tip. "Do all of your crewmen have one of these things?"

Lynch shook his head. "No need to. Most boats just keep one onboard."

"Can I borrow this?" Louis asked.

Lynch shrugged. "Sure, we don't use them much down here. But bring it back, okay? We need it for up North."

Louis heard a car horn and looked to the lot. Wainwright was waiting in the squad car. Louis took one last look around the docks. For the first time, he felt a sense of progress. They had a fresh suspect. They had a weapon. Now all they had to do was put together the *why* behind it.

The shrieks of seagulls drew his eye back to the *Miss Monica*. Ty was washing down the cleaning bench, tossing the fish guts into the water. The gulls swarmed on them, screaming.

Chapter Thirty

When they got back to the office, Candy was waiting for them. Wainwright took one look at his officer's face and asked, "Now what?"

"There's a woman waiting to see you."

"About what?"

Candy was staring at the bang stick in Louis's hand. "She says she might know who the homeless man is. I put her in your office, Chief."

Wainwright went into the office. Louis detoured to pick up the case file and joined him. The woman was sitting in a chair in front of Wainwright's desk and turned to look as they came in. She was about twenty-five, a pretty woman in a green business suit, with close-cropped black hair, gold earrings, and the same tawny-toned skin as the homeless man. Her large brown eyes went expectantly from Wainwright to Louis.

Wainwright extended his hand. "I'm Sheriff Wainwright. You're here about a possible identification?"

She took his hand, nodding. "My father," she said softly.

Wainwright glanced back at Louis. Louis set the bang stick against a cabinet and came forward.

"I'm June Childers," she said. "My father's name is Harold. Is he—" She paused, seeing the look on Wainwright's face. Her eyes filled with tears.

Wainwright pulled his handkerchief from his pocket, saw it was stained, and wadded it up. Louis rose, went to the bathroom, and came back with some tissues. Shit, he prayed June Childers wouldn't lose it like Anita Quick did. He couldn't stand another one.

But June Childers's eyes were dry and she managed to give Louis a small smile as she took the Kleenex. "I saw an article in the *Palm Beach Post*," she said. "I live over in West Palm." She hesitated. "It said you had a man here with a tattoo of a dog on his arm."

"There's also a word." Wainwright said. "Can you tell us what it was?"

"Bosco," she said softly.

Wainwright glanced over at Louis. He rose and went to the watercooler. For a long time, it was quiet in the room.

Then Wainwright spoke, without turning. "Miss Childers, did your father have any other identifying marks?"

She turned to look at Wainwright. So did Louis. Other identifying marks? Wainwright knew there were none except the tattoo. What was going on here?

"No," she said.

Wainwright filled a Dixie cup and slowly took a drink. He stood there, sipping and staring at the wall. June Childers looked back at Louis, her eyes questioning. Louis pulled a photo out of the file.

"Is this the tattoo?" he asked.

The photo showed only a forearm with a ruler lying next to it, but something changed in June Childers's eyes as she stared at it.

"It was our dog's name," she whispered. "Bosco . . . you know, like that chocolate stuff kids drink." Her eyes welled again.

Louis looked up at Wainwright. There were still routine questions that needed to be asked, but Wainwright was just standing there, staring at the wall.

"Dan—" Louis said.

Wainwright looked at him, as if coming out of a trance. "Let me know when you're done," he said. He tossed the cup in the trash and left, closing the door behind him. Louis stared at the door in disbelief for a moment.

Shit. Not again.

For a second, he considered going after Wainwright. But he turned back to June Childers. She wasn't crying, but she still had the spent look of someone who had just come to the end of a long and wearisome journey.

"Miss Childers, do you know where your father was living?" he asked.

She shook her head. "I haven't seen him in almost ten years," she said softly. "We—my brother Billy and I—we lost track of him. He wasn't himself after Mama died and we looked, but we lost . . ." Her eyes welled but she pulled in a deep breath, keeping her emotions inside.

"He was from West Palm Beach?"

She shook her head. "We grew up in Clewiston, west of there."

"Why do you think he came over here?" Louis asked gently.

"When we were kids, he used to bring us here," she said. "Daddy loved it here. He loved the water."

"If you could, can you please supply us with any other records you have . . . dental or medical records, maybe?"

She nodded.

Louis hesitated, not knowing what else to ask. There was nothing she could really help them with. She pulled in a deep breath and looked at him.

"Is there something I have to do . . . somewhere?" she asked.

He shook his head. "It's not necessary to identify him in person." He saw the next question in her eyes. "I think it's better if you don't see him. But I'll take you there if you want."

For a second, she just looked at him. "I understand," she said softly, looking down at the wad of tissue in her hands. She rose slowly and slipped the strap of her purse over her shoulder.

"Is there someplace I can make a call?" she asked. "My brother wanted to know."

Louis nodded to the phone on the table. "Just dial nine. I'll be outside if you need anything."

She gave him a small smile and held out her hand. "Thank you, Officer—"

"Kincaid," he said, taking her hand.

He left, taking the case file with him. Wainwright

wasn't in the outer office. Louis went to the conference room. The door was ajar.

Wainwright was standing at the bulletin board, looking at the photos of Tatum and Quick.

"Dan?"

Wainwright didn't move.

Louis came closer. "Dan, what happened back there?"

Wainwright turned. "Let's walk over to the Flamingo. I'll buy you a beer."

The bar was nearly deserted, just a few locals draped on the bar and a family eating burgers at one of the wooden tables. A hockey game was on the TV above the grill, sound turned off. "Sea of Love" was playing on the jukebox. Louis watched the Red Wings forward glide across the ice in perfect sync with the song.

Louis waited until the waitress took their order, then leveled his eyes at Wainwright.

"Okay, what?"

Wainwright was looking at the family. "This is a nice place," he said softly.

Louis started to say something, but decided he needed to stay quiet.

"Sereno Key," Wainwright said, "it's a nice place."

Wainwright fell silent again, his eyes drifting up to the TV and finally back to Louis. "I knew the moment I saw this place, it was where I needed to be."

"My foster mother thinks everyone has a place like that," Louis said.

Wainwright nodded slightly. "When I retired from the bureau, I stayed in Detroit for a while. But I knew

I needed to find someplace else. I heard about the chief's opening here and I looked up the town in the atlas. I saw this little green island sitting in all that blue water, and I fired off my letter."

The waitress brought their beers, some fries, and a bucket of steamed shrimp. Wainwright picked out a shrimp and began to slowly peel off the shell.

"Dan, what does—"

"I know. You want to know what this has to do with what went on back there with June Childers."

"And Anita Quick," Louis added.

Wainwright held his gaze for a moment, then nodded. He ate the shrimp and took a drink of his beer.

"I was with the bureau for eighteen years."

"I know. The Office of Professional Responsibility," Louis said.

Wainwright paused. "You'd like to know exactly what that is, wouldn't you?"

Louis took a swig of beer, then nodded.

"OPR is an inspection team that evaluates misconduct and efficiency problems, kind of an internal affairs department," he said. "It was put together as a response to all the corruption in the early years. Lot of the guys were there on temporary assignments." He gave a wan smile. "We called ourselves rent-a-goons."

Louis couldn't decide who felt more ill at ease, he himself or Wainwright.

"You said it was temporary?" Louis said.

Wainwright nodded. He pushed the bucket toward Louis but Louis shook his head.

"You're missing a treat here," Wainwright said.

"They look too much like crawfish."

Wainwright pulled the bucket back and peeled another shrimp, chewing it slowly.

"My first real assignment was as a field agent working out of Jackson, Michigan."

"Jackson? That's farm country," Louis said.

"It was a satellite office. The bureau has hundreds of them in small towns. They're called RAs—resident agencies."

"What the hell do FBI agents do in places like Jackson?"

"Not much," Wainwright said. "I had a few bank robberies and one custodial kidnapping, but those years were pretty quiet at first."

Louis picked at his fries.

"Then in 1973 a girl was murdered in Albion, a town nearby," Wainwright said. "Everyone in that town knew who did it—a snot-nosed college kid named Carson. But no one seemed to want to prosecute one of the town's favorite sons."

Wainwright paused to take a drink. "Then another girl turned up dead. Both the mothers were begging me to step in. Because the girls appeared to be forcibly taken, I was able to call it a kidnapping and took it over."

"Did you catch Carson?"

"Yeah, after he killed a third time." Wainwright pushed the shrimp bucket away and finished his beer.

Louis signaled the waitress for another round.

"I got lucky in that case, Louis," Wainwright said, "made a few right turns here and there. Before I knew it, I was being asked to advise on other similiar cases. This was before anyone really knew much about serial murders. Shit, we just called them multiples in those days."

He paused. "I worked nine or ten cases. Then we caught a case in seventy-eight near Adrian. Ever heard of the Raisin River Killings?"

Louis sat upright. "Harlan Skeen?"

Wainwright nodded, his eyes drifting. "Skeen raped and murdered twelve little girls. We found the first body in April of seventy-eight. The second one turned up around July Fourth. By Thanksgiving, we had found four."

The waitress put the fresh beers in front of them. Wainwright took a drink before he went on.

"I was assigned to the task force. We put everything humanly possible into that case for nine months."

Louis waited. It was a full minute before Wainwright went on.

"Toward the end of winter, we had another girl go missing," he said. "A week later, we finally got a break. Someone saw a man taking a girl into his car and got a license number. That night, he was spotted at a traffic light and ran. We chased the fucker into a park." Wainwright shook his head. "I had this wild idea that maybe we'd get lucky, that maybe we'd find this kid alive."

Wainwright stopped again.

"What happened?" Louis prodded.

"We cornered Skeen in the bathroom." Wainwright took a drink of beer. "I had to shoot him."

The flatness in Wainwright's eyes was chilling. "What about the girl?" Louis asked.

"We found her when we popped his trunk. She was dead."

Louis looked away.

"The other bodies turned up one by one when the snow started melting. I was called out for every single one." He paused. "Then, one Saturday afternoon, I got the call again. I didn't want to go because my kid had a basketball game, but I went. It was raining, windy, still cold like it can be in April. I drove down to Adrian, out to the woods. I parked at the bottom of the hill with all the other units."

Wainwright stopped, staring at this hands, clasped around the sweating beer bottle.

"I got out and looked up the hill. It was foggy and all I could see was that damn yellow tape flapping in the wind." He looked up at Louis. "Something happened. I couldn't go up. I just couldn't go up there and look at one more of those damn little bones."

A burst of laughter drifted over from the family at the next table.

Wainwright cleared his throat. "The next day I asked to be reassigned. They sent me to OPR."

His blue eyes remained locked on Louis for a moment; then he raised the bottle to his lips. He closed his eyes as he drank. When he finally put the bottle down, it was empty.

"Almost every agent I worked with paid a price in some way," he said. "Ulcers, heart scares, divorce. It's not so much dealing with the evil as what the evil leaves behind."

"Anita Quick and June Childers," Louis said quietly.

Wainwright nodded slowly. "The families," he said. "That was the worst part for me, dealing with the families."

They fell quiet.

"Dan, this thing with you and Farentino—"

"What about it?"

"You want me to talk to her, try to smooth things over?"

"Why?"

"Because we have to work together," Louis said.

Wainwright picked at the Bud label. "Do what you think is necessary," he said.

Louis wanted to say more, but he could tell from Wainwright's eyes that the subject was closed.

The bartender ambled over to the jukebox. A few seconds later, the bar filled up with the sound of Frankie Goes to Hollywood singing "Relax."

Wainwright was staring at the window. It was raining lightly, the neon Bud sign forming red streaks on the glass. Wainwright looked back at Louis.

"What the fuck is this song about?" he asked.

"Jerking off," Louis said.

Wainwright shook his head. "Man, I'm getting old." He stood up, tossing a twenty on the table. "Let's get out of here."

Chapter Thirty-one

Patsy Cline's contralto drifted out of the house, floated over the canal, and dissipated in the balmy night air. The mangroves were black lace against a lavender sky.

Louis watched the family across the canal cleaning up after their barbecue, the kids rolling on the grass like puppies while the mother tried to herd them inside. They appeared to be acting out parts in a silent movie, their movements overlaid with music.

The sliding glass door opened and Louis looked up to see Dodie coming out, a sandwich and beer in his hand.

"I didn't know you were home," Dodie said. "We didn't wait supper on ya. You ate yet?"

Louis shook his head. "Not hungry, thanks."

"Mind if I sit?"

Louis motioned toward the lounge. Patsy Cline had launched into "How Can I Face Tomorrow?" Louis heard Margaret's voice warble in sync with Patsy's.

"Margaret really likes her country music," Louis said.

Dodie stared at him. "You don't?"

"It's all about drunks and losers and ugly dogs. Pretty pathetic stuff, don't you think?"

"Some folks would think cop work is pretty pathetic, too. It's just life."

"And death," Louis said.

Dodie nodded. "I suppose."

Louis stood up and went to the edge of the patio. The thick curtain of night had descended. The family across the way had gone in, turning off their porch lights. The glow of their television danced in the darkness.

"Sam, I need some advice," Louis said.

"Sure."

"Dan's not who I thought he was."

"Folk seldom are."

Louis turned. "No, I mean, he's not strong as I thought. I think he's losing his grip on this case."

"What's wrong with him?" Dodie asked. "Is he sick?"

"No, but he's not handling things well," Louis said. "He blew up at Mobley and today, he took off Farentino's head. Told her she didn't have a clue about what she was doing. But Farentino provokes him. Called him an old fart."

Dodie made a face.

"They're at each other's throats, Sam," Louis said, "and I'm sick of playing referee."

"You can't talk to them?" Dodie asked.

Louis shook his head. "But that's not all. Dan told me some stuff today, some things that happened on the job in the past. He left the bureau as a burn-out after a tough case. He came down here to escape and for five years that's what he's done. Now this shit has hit him in the face and I think it's getting to him."

Dodie had set his sandwich aside. "You saying he doesn't know what he's doing?"

Louis frowned. "Not exactly. He's worked a dozen homicides, but it's like he's lost his nerve. I'm not so sure he won't break completely if we can't catch this guy pretty soon."

"Maybe you ought to convince him to hand it off to that Sheriff Mobley fella."

Louis shook his head. "That would make things worse. Mobley's an idiot."

"Well, somebody's gotta lead, Louis."

"There's Chief Horton over in Fort Myers," Louis said. "He's a good cop but he really doesn't have a stake in this whole thing." He drew in a breath. "This is a fucking mess."

Margaret had turned off the music inside. The frogs had filled the silence with their own chorus of creaks and peeps.

"Louis," Dodie said.

Louis turned.

"Come sit down."

Louis came back and took the chair next to Dodie. The Japanese lanterns weren't lit and Louis could barely make out Dodie's face in the light coming in from the kitchen. He was lying back in the lounge chair, the beer in his hand.

"I was seventeen when my daddy was shot and killed," Dodie said. "It happened real sudden and everyone in the family rushed over to the house, and there was a might good number of them, too. Aunts, uncles, nephews, and even my sister managed to get herself home that weekend."

Louis was glad Dodie couldn't see his face clearly. He really didn't want to hear one of Dodie's old stories right now.

"They all sat around crying and making promises to Momma," Dodie went on. "Promises about taking care of the farm, making the car payments, bringing her food, and just plain making sure she didn't suffer too much. I had an Uncle Isaac who said he'd take care of the finances for her."

Dodie looked down at his beer bottle. "A few weeks after the burial, the casseroles stopped coming, the car was repossessed, and Momma found out Uncle Isaac had taken all her money out of the bank and headed to New Orleans."

"What did you do?" Louis asked.

Dodie pressed his lips together. "I wasn't known for taking charge of things in those days, but I knew I couldn't let the land go to the bank. So I quit school and went to work. Most folks thought I dropped out to marry Margie, but that wasn't it."

A long-forgotten image came back to Louis. Ethel Mulcahey, hunched over her high school annual, showing him pictures of her classmate, Sam Dodie. *He dropped out of school to marry Margaret Sue Purdy. We all knew she was pregnant.*

Louis shook his head. Small towns and their small secrets.

"I did it to save that farm for Momma, so she could

pass on there," Dodie said. "Which she did eight years later."

"You gave up a lot," Louis said.

Dodie gave a small shrug. "It wasn't just saving the farm. It was saving Momma."

They sat for a few minutes, listening to the frogs. Louis lifted his bottle to his lips. It was empty. He heard the scrape of the lounge and looked over to see Dodie hoisting himself up.

"Well, I'm going in," he said.

"Sam."

Dodie looked down.

"What should I do?" Louis asked.

"Save the farm," Dodie said. He picked up the sandwich plate and the empty beer bottles. "See you in the morning, Louis."

Dodie went inside. Louis leaned his head back on the chair, closing his eyes. Save the farm. Okay, so maybe he had to take charge. But how? He had no real authority here. He didn't even have a badge, just a damn ID card.

He couldn't do an end run around Wainwright. But he couldn't just sit back and do nothing, hoping Dan could hold the investigation—and himself—together long enough to catch this monster.

He felt something brush his leg and he looked down. Issy was curling against his shin. The cat sat down and looked up at him, its eyes catching the kitchen light like road reflectors.

Damn. He knew what he had to do. The only problem was getting up the guts to do it. He glanced at his watch. With a sigh, he hoisted himself up from the chair, went inside, and grabbed the car keys off the kitchen counter.

* * *

The porch light went on and the door opened.

"Kincaid, what are you doing here?" Wainwright asked.

"I'd like to talk, Dan. Can I come in?"

Wainwright swung the screen wide. "Sure, sure."

Louis paused in the small foyer. The living room off to his right was small but comfortable looking. The worn furniture looked more suited to a northern colonial than a Florida bungalow. There were a few generic landscapes on the walls and a bookcase filled with books that looked untouched. On the mantel above the coral rock fireplace there were three framed photographs, a teenage boy and girl that looked like graduation pictures, and a formal portrait of a pretty brunette woman. A TV tray was set up in front of a battered Barcalounger. *Cheers* was on.

"Am I interrupting your dinner?" Louis asked.

"No, I'm finished," Wainwright said, going to the tray and picking up his plate. He started to the kitchen. "You want anything? Beer? Soda?"

"No, nothing. Thanks."

Wainwright reappeared. "Sit down, sit down," he said, moving a stack of papers off a chair and turning the sound off on the TV.

Louis perched on the edge of the chair, his eyes wandering to the television screen. Carla was beating Cliff Clavin on the head with a dishrag.

"So?" Wainwright said.

"What do you think of the idea of forming a task force?" Louis asked.

Wainwright looked down at his beer, pursing his lips. "Okay," he said quietly.

"I think we need to coordinate all the efforts, Dan," Louis said. "We're spinning our wheels here."

Wainwright looked up at him. "Is that all?"

"What do you mean?" Louis asked.

"I mean, is that your only reason?"

"We need—" Louis looked over at the television for a moment, then came back to Wainwright. "We need all the help we can get on this."

"And who do you see heading this task force?" Wainwright asked.

Louis forced himself to meet Wainwright's eyes. "Someone neutral," he said.

"Horton," Wainwright said.

"I think that would be best," Louis said.

Wainwright's blue eyes didn't blink. But he gave an almost imperceivable nod of his head. "You sure you don't want a beer?" he asked.

Louis shook his head.

"Well, I do." He rose slowly and went to the kitchen. Louis heard the refrigerator opening. He glanced down and saw a stack of case files on the floor next to the lounger. They looked untouched.

Wainwright came back, holding the can of beer. He didn't sit down.

"We'll call Horton in the morning." He paused. "Thanks for coming by."

Louis hesitated. Wainwright's voice had a slightly clipped sound to it. Louis was being dismissed. He started to say something, but changed his mind. He rose and went to the door. Wainwright followed him.

As he stepped outside, Louis turned. "Dan—"

"Good night, Louis."

Wainwright closed the door.

Chapter Thirty-two

The cruiser crested the top of the causeway and Louis looked over at Wainwright. His eyes were focused straight ahead and his hands were loose on the wheel. If he was still pissed about last night, at least he was being enough of a pro not to show it. Louis hadn't been in the office when Wainwright made the call to Al Horton. But later, Wainwright had come out and announced simply, "Let's go, Al's waiting."

Still, the ride across the causeway had been silent.

There was a flutter of papers in the backseat. "Damn it, can you please close your window, Kincaid?" Emily said.

Louis rolled up the window, glancing back at her. She had her briefcase open at her feet, and a lap full of faxes and files.

"Here it is," she said, shaking a paper at him. "I knew it was in here."

"What is it?" Louis asked.

"Gunther Mayo's sheet. It came in just as we were leaving."

"Read it," Wainwright said.

"Burglary in seventy-eight, assault in eighty, possession in eighty-one, and indecent exposure in eighty-two. I've dug up some personal stuff—"

Louis looked at her. "Can I see that?"

She handed him the papers. Louis flipped through them. "Dan, listen. Gunther joined up with a boat called the *Liberty Belle* in eighty-two, then boat-hopped for four years, working up and down the coast. He hooked up with Lynch in Barnegat Light last April."

"Was he ever questioned in any of the murders up North?" Wainwright asked.

"I've been through those files and I never saw his name," Emily said.

Wainwright stopped at a traffic light. "Where's this creep from?"

Emily stuck her head in between them. "He was born in Camden, New Jersey."

Louis looked up from reading Mayo's dossier. "Dan, this guy was a member of a gang called The Brotherhood. Ever heard of it?"

Wainwright shook his head.

"It was a teenage white supremacist gang from South Philly," Emily said from the back.

"No shit?" Louis said.

"It was a short-lived venture," Emily said. "They were busted by the local cops for spray-painting racial slurs on churches. Mayo was fifteen."

Louis glanced back at her. "Farentino, this guy fits your profile, doesn't he?"

She looked at him over her glasses, arms crossed. "He's a white male, age twenty-eight, low achiever, unskilled laborer, seventh of eight kids, father a drunk and felon. What do you think?"

Louis pointed to a date in June of last year. "Why is this underlined?"

Emily came forward. "It's when his grandmother died."

"So?"

"Mayo was thirteen when his father went to prison and he was shipped off to live with his grandmother. They were close."

"His stressor?" Louis said.

"That's what I think," Farentino said, falling back into the seat.

"Farentino, what's your guess on where he lives?" Wainwright asked.

Emily hesitated. Louis knew it was because she was surprised Wainwright was asking her for an opinion.

"I'm convinced it's Fort Myers Beach, Chief," she said. "It's in his comfort zone. Even if it's not out in the beach area itself, it'll be close by."

Wainwright was nodding thoughtfully.

"Lynch told me there are a lot of seasonal rentals near the wharf," Louis said. "I sent Candy over to Buttonwood Street to show Mayo's picture around." He paused. "I hope we don't scare the bastard away."

Farentino leaned forward again. "We may do just that if you swarm the neighborhood or wharf with uniforms. I think a more subtle approach is necessary."

"It ain't gonna look like a military parade, Farentino," Wainwright said.

Wainwright pulled into the parking lot of the Fort Myers PD and jerked the car to a stop. "Okay, first and ten," Wainwright said without looking at either of them. "Let's go see if we can turn this game around."

Inside the lobby of the station, the receptionist behind the glass recognized Wainwright and buzzed them through. Al Horton was waiting for them at his open door. "Come on in, Dan. Mobley's not here yet."

"But he agreed to come?" Louis asked.

"I told him you and I were thinking about working together on the case," Horton said. "He'll show."

They all took chairs around Horton's desk.

"Anything new on this Mayo character?" Horton asked.

Louis quickly filled him in. Emily was about to add something when there was a noise in the hallway. A moment later, Lance Mobley appeared at the door. Driggs was behind him.

Mobley surveyed the office and turned to Driggs. "Wait outside," he said. He came in, shutting the door. He leaned back against it, folding his arms. "Okay, I'm here, Al. What's this all about?"

Horton was sitting on the edge of his desk. With a glance at Wainwright, he looked at Mobley.

"We're forming a task force, Lance," he said.

Mobley's eyes went from Wainwright to Louis, bounced across Emily, and came to rest back on Horton. He smiled.

"Okay . . . " he said.

"And I'm in charge," Horton said.

Mobley's smile faded. "Is this some kind of joke?"

"Six dead men," Horton said. "It's time to start working together."

"Six?" Mobley said.

"Yeah, six," Wainwright said. "Not exactly up to speed, are you, Lance?"

"We found three related cases in New Jersey and over in Broward," Emily said.

Mobley turned to Emily. "Who are you?" he demanded.

"FBI Agent Farentino. I'm a forensic psychologist."

Mobley stared at Emily, then looked back at Horton. "Look, if you think I'm going to sit back and let a case like this be run by amateurs and psychics, you're nuts."

Louis and Wainwright got up. Horton slid off the desk.

"Sheriff Mobley, I think we should—" Emily began.

"Go play with your tarot cards, lady," Mobley snapped. "And take Virgil Tibbs here with you."

Louis started toward Mobley but Wainwright was quicker. In two strides he was chest-to-chest with Mobley. "Listen, you prick," Wainwright said, his voice low. "While you've been baking in the tanning salon, this *lady* has been busting her hump plowing paper to track down three other cases. And Louis here has found a weapon and a suspect. If you got a problem with me, that's fine." He jabbed a finger into Mobley's chest. "But until you have something to offer in this case, keep your fucking mouth shut."

Mobley stared at Wainwright, his jaw muscles pulsating.

"You have a suspect?" he asked tightly.

Horton came forward and handed Mobley a copy of Gunther Mayo's sheet.

"Where is he?" Mobley said, after scanning it quickly.

"He disappeared about a week ago," Louis said.

Before Mobley could say anything else, there was a knock and the door opened a crack, hitting Mobley in the back. He moved and a woman's face appeared.

"Chief, the press is here," she said.

"Thanks, Karen. Put them in the briefing room. We'll be right in."

The door closed. Mobley stared at Horton. "You called a press conference?"

Horton nodded. "You in or out, Lance?"

Mobley's eyes went to Wainwright and back to Horton. "All right," he said quietly. "You'll get every man I can give. But I get the collar."

Horton glanced at Wainwright, who looked away. Horton nodded to Mobley. "I'll take the lead here," Horton said. "There are things we're not telling them, you hear me, Lance?"

"I hear you." He reached into his pocket and pulled out a tin of Altoids. He popped one into his mouth, surveyed the room, and gave them a smile.

"Shall we?" he said.

The briefing room was not very large, and there were ten reporters, photographers, and cameramen waiting when Horton led them all in. Horton went to the lectern at the front of the room, motioning Wainwright and Mobley to his sides. Louis, Emily, Driggs, the Fort Myers Public Information Officer, and a few uniforms hovered in the background.

Horton glanced at the four mikes that had been

set up on the lectern. All three local stations were here, WEVU, WBBH, WINK, plus the usual familiar faces from the *News-Press, Sanibel Island Reporter, The Naples Daily News,* and others.

"You guys ready?" Horton said.

"Sooner the better, Chief," someone called out. "We're trying to make the noon broadcast."

The camera lights went on and Horton blinked in the glare. "Karen here has kept you all up to speed on the details so far in these three murder cases," Horton began, nodding to his PIO.

"But I am here today to announce the formation of a task force," he went on. "Its purpose is to better coordinate the efforts of the three law enforcement agencies involved in the case, and to make better use of our manpower. We've also established a hot line for tips, so we can coordinate our information. That number will be given to all of you at the conclusion of this press conference."

Louis, standing behind Wainwright, watched as Horton went on to introduce Wainwright and Mobley. Wainwright stepped forward to add a few innocuous standard comments, looking ill at ease. Mobley took his turn before the mikes, cool as a Beltway pol, adding his assurances that the killer would be apprehended.

"Chief, who are your other players here?" a reporter asked, pointing a pencil at Louis and Emily.

Horton motioned to Wainwright. "This is Louis Kincaid, a special investigator temporarily attached to my office," Wainwright said, drawing Louis forward by the arm.

Wainwright paused. "To my right is Agent Emily Farentino, a forensics psychologist with the FBI."

Louis saw the cameras swing to Emily. "Spell the last name, please," someone called out.

"F-a-r-r-e-n-t-i-n-o," Wainwright said.

Emily leaned into the mike. "One R. Farentino with one R." She backed away.

"Chief, do you have any new leads since Roscoe Webb's escape?"

"We have a good lead on a new suspect we are looking at, but I can't give you any details," Horton said.

"Does he live here?"

Louis tensed, his eyes going to the Mayo sheet still in Mobley's hand. He prayed Mobley had enough brains not to say anything. The last thing they needed now was for Gunther Mayo to get squirrelly and move on to new hunting grounds.

"No details," Horton said.

Mobley didn't move.

"Chief, have you figured out yet why all the murders have taken place on Tuesdays?"

"No, not yet. We're still working on it."

"Chief Horton," a woman called out, "do you have any response to the NAACP charges that these are racially motivated crimes and your department is not doing enough?"

Louis could see Horton's neck muscles tighten. "I gave you my response to that when it came out, Cheryl," he said calmly. "This new task force is evidence that we are determined to do whatever it takes to catch this murderer. Now, if there's nothing else—"

"I have a question for Agent Farentino."

Louis blinked in the glare of the lights, finally

seeing the source of the voice, a tall man standing in the back.

"What exactly is your role in this investigation?" the reporter asked.

Emily hesitated and slowly came to the mike. She had to stand on her tiptoes to reach it. "My role is to assist the officers in any way I can," she said.

Louis glanced at Wainwright. He was staring at the floor.

"You do what's called profiling, right?"

All the heads in the room had swung to the reporter now. Louis heard a Nikon motor drive whir off a couple of frames.

"Profiling is a layman's term," Emily said. "I—"

"What kind of man do you think this killer is?"

Emily glanced at Wainwright, then cleared her throat. "Serial killers are usually white men, twenty to thirty years old, unskilled workers, and loners."

"But what kind of man do you think *this* killer is?"

Emily hesitated again. Louis could see a bead of sweat on her forehead. Shit, they were all sweating. *Stay cool, Farentino, stay cool.*

"I think he is a man who will eventually make a mistake," Emily said. "A mistake that will lead to his apprehension. That's all I am prepared to say right now."

Louis let out a breath.

Horton took a few final questions and then turned it over to the PIO. They filed out of the room through a back door and paused in the hall.

"Next time you call a press conference, Al, I want more notice," Mobley said. "And I want to be brought up to speed on everything you have—now."

"You know where my office is, Lance," Horton said. "I'll be right there."

Mobley stalked off, Driggs at his heels. Horton turned to Wainwright. "You don't need to stay. I'll handle this," he said.

Wainwright nodded. Horton left, leaving the three of them standing alone in the hall.

"The press conference went well," Louis said.

Wainwright looked at Emily. "It could have been worse. Come on, we've got work to do."

Chapter Thirty-three

Damn it. Where'd the game go?

He squinted up at the television above the bar. Who the hell was this asshole?

He looked down the bar, but nobody else seemed to care. He took a quick drink of beer and looked back up at the television.

What the fuck was this? An old man that looked like an army guy. A stupid-looking guy in a cop uniform. Some bitch with red hair. And a black guy standing in the background.

He strained his ears to hear what they were saying.

Task force. Cops. FBI. Task force?

For me?

He resisted the urge to smile, resisted the urge to laugh.

They were so stupid.

He heard the word "Tuesday." They were telling people he killed on Tuesdays. But they didn't know why.

Stupid fuckers. It was his day off. It was the only time he had. What other reason could there be?

The bitch was talking now . . . she was calling him a serial killer. She was describing the killer. Describing *him.*

White, twenty to thirty, unskilled work. What the fuck did they mean, unskilled work? It was his work. His *life.* Unskilled. Like it meant nothing. *Fuck them.*

He took a drink.

But she did say white. That was important.

Last week he had read they thought he was black.

They were learning.

His eyes focused on the black man again. The camera came in for a quick close-up.

Wait . . . wait . . . .

Yes . . . yes!

The camera picking up the white cop now. *Damn it! No! Go back to the black guy!*

There! There he is again, in the background.

He looked . . . what? Uncomfortable . . . nervous . . . like he didn't belong. That tan face there among the other white faces. He *knew* he didn't belong. Oh, yes, he *knew.* He just didn't see it yet.

He wouldn't be easy.

He'd have a gun.

And he'd fight back.

But that was okay. That was part of the plan.

He took another drink, staring at the black cop over the rim of his glass.

Yes. Perfect. He's perfect.

The army guy finished talking. He was asking the public for help. He was done. He was fucking done!

The paint!

They didn't talk about the paint! Why didn't they talk about the paint?

He gripped the glass.

What the fuck was wrong with them? Didn't they know? Didn't they see it?

It was everything . . . the paint. It was everything!

He tightened, glaring into his beer.

Maybe the paint had washed off. Maybe he shouldn't have gotten them wet. But he had to get them wet.

Fuck.

Maybe he should tell them.

No. It didn't matter. They weren't important. They weren't part of the plan and they didn't matter.

He looked up, his eyes boring into the black cop.

He mattered.

But still . . . the paint was important.

His brain started pounding. This wasn't supposed to happen now.

No . . . not now. Stop. . . .

He put his hands to his temples. *Stop. Stop.*

Water. He needed the water. The sound of the water.

He needed a kill.

And he would make sure they didn't miss the paint next time. He would make damn sure.

Chapter Thirty-four

Emily came out of the bathroom and paused in front of the table, where Gunther Mayo's life was spread out before her. She picked up a mug shot of him, courtesy of the Atlantic City PD.

He had a frizzy bush of black hair and a ragged mustache. His gray eyes, too light for his hair, seemed to bore through the camera lens.

Emily tossed the photo down and looked at the clock. It was after eleven P.M. And it was Tuesday night.

Again they waited. Only tonight she was alone, stuck in the office with her notes, files, and Gunther Mayo.

Damn them, anyway.

After two weeks of hard work, it was still "them"

on one side and her on the other, looking in. Even after Wainwright's defense of her work in Horton's office. Louis had seemed to accept her and Wainwright was coming around. But when it came down to the real work, the street work, they still didn't trust her to pull her weight.

Like tonight. Every available cop and detective, Lee County, Fort Myers, Sereno, was out tonight on surveillance, trying to track down Gunther Mayo.

She looked up at the wall map with a sigh. The canvassing of the rental neighborhoods around the wharf had yielded nothing, so they had expanded the search to the rentals and motel rooms over on the beach. At least they had listened to her on that.

"Evening, Agent Farentino," Greg Candy said, coming through the door.

Emily looked at him. "You stuck here, too?"

"Hell no. I'm just coming off ten hours over on the beach." He looked beat. "Why aren't you out there with the rest of them?"

"I'm still in detention," she said, sliding into a chair and staring down at Gunther Mayo.

Candy gave her a frown. "Detention?"

"Never mind," Emily said.

"Well, I'm dead on my feet. Going home to catch a nap."

Candy disappeared. Emily lowered her head to her arms. She closed her eyes, and lost herself in the beat of her heart and the light ticking of the clock on the wall.

Tuesday night. Would she ever be able to think of it in a normal light after this was all over?

The phone rang and she jumped, then picked it up.

"Agent Farentino," she said.

"Officer Kincaid, please," a man said.

Emily rubbed her eyes. "He's on patrol. Can I help you?"

The man hesitated. "Are you a police officer?"

She rolled her eyes. "Yes, I am."

"My name is George Lynch and my man is missing."

"Your man?"

"My employee, Ty. We were supposed to meet for dinner and he was just going home to clean up. But it's been two hours and I think something's happened to him."

Emily picked up a pen and pulled her notepad closer. "How old is he?"

"Twenty-five."

She tossed the pen down. *Christ.*

"Mr. Lynch, two hours is hardly enough time to report someone missing. Why don't you call us back—"

"Is that other cop there?" Lynch said.

"No, you're stuck with me."

"Then why can't you take some kind of report or whatever it is you do? What's wrong with you people?"

Emily picked up the pen. "Okay, tell me about your friend."

"His name is Ty Heller and he's a black man who works for me. We were supposed to have dinner at the Dockside Pub and he never showed."

Emily wrote down the name. A man going missing for two hours was no big deal. But a black man going missing on a Tuesday could be. Even if he was too young to fit the victim profile.

"Your name again, sir?"

"George Lynch. You gonna do something or not?"

"Just a minute, please." She put a hand over the receiver, thinking she would call Candy. But then she remembered he said he was tired and heading home. She thought of radioing to Louis or Wainwright, but she knew Wainwright would probably dismiss whatever she had to offer. Sending an officer to talk to this guy could waste valuable time and manpower.

Shit, she would go talk to Lynch herself, calm him down. She would go take the report herself.

"Where are you, Mr. Lynch?"

"I'm still at the bar. It's in Fort Myers Beach, on First Street, just under the bridge. I'll be out on the porch."

"I'll be there in twenty minutes."

When Emily got to the Dockside Pub the lot was filled, so she parked across the road in front of a closed bait shop. She got out of the car. It was dark, but she could see the lights of the marina flickering on the water. Across Matanza Pass, she could see the empty, dark charter boats at their docks at Fisherman's Wharf.

She shoved a police radio in her briefcase and started across the street, shifting the heavy bag to her left shoulder. Eleven forty-five. It had taken her longer than she had expected to get over to the beach. She hoped this Lynch guy had waited. Hell, if he hadn't, at least she'd get a burger or something. She hadn't eaten since breakfast.

The Dockside Pub was a rustic tavern with a screened porch facing the docks. She went in, hoping Lynch would signal her.

He did, giving her a small wave from a table across the room. She moved toward him, half hoping to see that his employee had arrived safely. But when she got there, the other side of the table was empty. She sat down and stuck out her hand.

"Mr. Lynch?"

"Yeah." His weathered face looked stricken as he shook her hand.

"I'm Agent Farentino, FBI." She slid into a chair, hoisting her briefcase up into an empty chair beside her. "I take it your friend's still not here?"

Lynch shook his head and watched Emily dig through her briefcase for a notebook and pen. When she looked up, he leaned forward. "You ready?" he asked.

"What do you do for a living, Mr. Lynch?"

"I'm a charter boat captain. Tyrone is one of my crewmen."

Emily looked up at him. "You work on the docks?"

Lynch nodded. "Yeah, thirty years now. I'm retiring in May and—"

"Your employee's name is Heller?"

"Yeah, Tyrone Heller. I call him Ty. I've always called him Ty, for all the years he's been with me." There was an untouched glass of beer in front of Lynch. He was picking at a cocktail napkin.

"So you and your employee were meeting here for dinner?" Emily asked.

He nodded, his eyes intent on Emily. "Shouldn't you put out one of those bulletins for him?"

"First things first, Mr. Lynch."

Lynch tossed down the shredded napkin and ran a hand over his face. "Look, miss, I'm sure something's happened to Ty. He's a good kid, a real good kid. He's kinda like a son to me, you know?''

"When did you last speak to him?'' Emily asked.

"About six, when we closed down for the day. We always come here for dinner every Tuesday night, ever since we've been coming to Fort Myers. Tonight, at the last minute, Woody changed his mind so it was just Ty and me. Ty wanted to go get cleaned up. He said he'd meet me back here at nine.''

"Have you tried to contact him?''

"He doesn't have a phone. I went over to his place about nine-thirty, but he wasn't there.''

"His address, please?''

Lynch gave it to her. "So I came back here, hoping I just missed him.'' He paused. "I didn't want to call the police right away, but with these killings and all . . .'' He hesitated. "Ty can sometimes be too damn trusting, you know what I mean?''

"Describe him, please.''

"Jeez . . . about six-foot, with brown hair and light skin, for a black man. He was wearing cutoffs and a white T-shirt when he left work. Probably would be wearing the same thing, just clean if he changed.''

"Tell me about Woody. Real name? Address?''

"Woody? Why do you need to know about Woody?''

"He might be with him.''

Lynch shook his head. "Woody said he had a date.''

"Why don't you give me his name and address anyway?'' After Lynch did, she asked, "Does Tyrone have any relatives here?''

"None that I know of.''

Emily looked up from her notes. "If you were to guess, where do you think he might go?''

"If he's not home, he's usually on the boat. He's kind of a simple guy."

"Is there anything else you can tell me about Tyrone?" Emily said.

"Just that he's a fine young man." Lynch was picking at the shredded napkin again.

"Does he own a vehicle?"

"A truck, I think. I don't know the make."

"How can I reach you, Mr. Lynch?"

Lynch gave her a number. "Or over at Fisherman's Wharf, the *Miss Monica.*"

Emily blinked. "The *Miss Monica*?"

"Yeah," Lynch said.

"You have another employee . . . Gunther Mayo?" Emily asked.

"Did. Haven't seen him in weeks. What's that got—"

Emily slid the notebook back into her briefcase. She needed to call Wainwright, but she couldn't do it here in front of Lynch. The guy was alarmed enough already.

"Mr. Lynch, I think you should go home," she said, rising quickly.

"Home? What—"

"We'll check it out and call you if we find anything."

"But—"

Farentino hurried away, hefting her briefcase to her shoulder. As she started to the parking lot, she rummaged through the briefcase for the police radio. She couldn't find it and stopped short.

"Shit!" she said.

She plunked the briefcase down on the hood of the nearest car and yanked the briefcase wide open, digging for the radio. Finally, her fingers found it and she pulled it out.

Suddenly everything went dark. There was something slick and damp over her head and an arm under her throat. A hand clamped down on her mouth.

Her heart surged up against her sternum. Her hands shot to her face as she tried to claw at the cloth. She twisted, trying to get free, but the hands tightened.

She felt a sudden sharp blow to her head. Her knees buckled and she went out.

Chapter Thirty-five

Louis screeched the cruiser to a stop, grabbed a flashlight, and climbed out. A man standing at the rear of a car came forward as he saw Louis emerge.

"It's over there," the man said, pointing.

Louis hurried to the red Honda. He immediately saw Farentino's briefcase on the hood.

"I didn't touch it," the man said quickly, coming up behind him. "I mean, I didn't move it after I started looking inside for a wallet. As soon as I saw that police radio I called you guys."

"Did you see anyone?" Louis asked. "A woman, about five-two, red hair—"

But the man was shaking his head. "The lot across the street was full when I got here, so I parked over here. It was deserted when I came out. I figured some broad just left it on my hood and drove off—"

"This Honda is your car?"

The man nodded.

Louis surveyed the area. They were standing in a small parking lot in front of a bait store. There were only two cars in the lot, the red Honda and, about twenty feet away, Farentino's rental, a black Nissan. The entrance to the Dockside Pub was about thirty yards away, across the street. The pub's entrance faced the street, but there were no other businesses open and the street was quiet. The pub's own parking lot was around the side. If someone had been standing in the pub's lot, they would not have seen what was going on in the lot of the bait shop.

His heart was racing. There was no way Farentino would have left that briefcase. He could hear approaching sirens.

He went quickly to Farentino's Nissan and shined the light inside. Still locked. He swung the light to the ground, looking for signs of struggle, keys, anything.

He returned to the red Honda, swinging his flashlight over the ground. The beam picked up a flash. Farentino's glasses on the asphalt, just under the Honda. He gingerly picked them up with his shirttail and placed them on the hood of the Honda next to the briefcase.

The whoop of the sirens became deafening and the lot lit up with whirling lights. Louis looked over to see Lance Mobley bound out of a patrol car and sprint over to Louis. A deputy trailed behind.

"What do we got?" he asked tersely.

"Farentino's missing."

"Farentino?"

"The FBI agent."

Mobley nodded quickly. "How do you know?"

Louis pointed the light at the glasses on the hood. "Those are hers. So's the briefcase."

Mobley peered into the open briefcase. Louis saw Wainwright hurrying toward them.

"You got gloves on you?" Louis asked as Wainwright came up to him.

Wainwright pulled a pair of latex gloves from his hind pocket and handed them to Louis.

"You should wait for CSU," Mobley said.

"We don't have time," Wainwright said. "Put the briefcase on the ground, Louis. We need to dust the car."

The man who had found the briefcase pressed forward. "What? What you going to do to my car?"

"Just look for fingerprints," Wainwright said. "Please step back, sir."

"Oh, man . . ."

Louis pulled on the gloves and set the briefcase on the asphalt. He gingerly began going through the briefcase as Wainwright held the flashlight.

"I think she stopped here and set the briefcase down to look for something and that's when she was abducted," Louis said.

"Why didn't he take the briefcase?" Mobley said.

"He didn't want it. He wanted her," Louis said.

"That's her rental," Wainwright said, pointing to the Nissan. "Why don't you go check it out, Lance?"

"It's still locked," Louis said.

Mobley stared at Wainwright for a moment, then moved away, yelling to his deputy, "Howard, bring me the punch."

Louis pulled Emily's wallet out of the briefcase. "Money's still here," he said, laying the wallet on the ground. He took out the folders of case files and laid them aside. He set a small makeup bag and a hairbrush next to the files.

"No keys," he said.

He pulled out a small notepad. It was open, and he scanned the top page. Farentino had tiny, hen-scratch handwriting.

"Dan, shine that here."

The words jumped out at him. *Dockside Inn. George Lynch. Tyrone Heller. Miss Monica. Missing since eight* P.M. *Twenty-five years old.*

"Jesus, Dan," Louis said. "She was here to meet Lynch."

"Why?" Wainwright asked.

Louis rose. "I think Lynch called the station to report his crewman missing. Farentino came here to take the report."

"What the fuck was she doing down here taking a report?"

"Maybe she was just trying to help."

Wainwright turned away. "Shit . . ."

"Dan," Louis said, "we have two missing." When Wainwright looked at him, Louis went on. "This crew-man—his name is Tyrone Heller—he's black."

Mobley came back. "There's nothing in the car or trunk."

"Sheriff," Louis said, "we need to find a man named George Lynch."

"Who's Lynch? A suspect?"

Louis paused just a beat. "Damn it, do you read anything we send over?"

"You badgeless punk," Mobley said. "I have a hun-dred men under my command."

Louis wanted to slug him. "Then fucking use them."

"What for?" Mobley shouted.

"Lynch is a boat captain. His black crewman is missing. Someone needs to get to Lynch fast."

"What's the hurry? If this sicko did this, his crewman is already dead. So's the woman," Mobley said.

He snatched his radio from his belt and walked away, barking out commands.

Louis yanked off the latex gloves. He looked at Wainwright and knew he was thinking the same thing. Mobley was right.

Chapter Thirty-six

Blackness. She was floating up from the blackness to consciousness. She opened her eyes. The blackness was still there and she gave a terrified jerk. The thing . . . it was the thing covering her face. The cloth was still there. She could smell its musky odor, and when she drew in a breath, the soft fabric touched her lips.

She became aware of a sharp throbbing in her head, and a faint nausea boiling in her stomach. Her heart was pounding. But she had to stay calm.

Think, think! Calm down . . . use your head, use your senses.

She tried to move her arms. They were bound at the wrists, palms up. She could feel the hard wood of the chair. She strained to hear something or someone.

Nothing. Just water lapping and a soft groaning sound. Pilings? The air was still and smelled of mildew and fish. An old building of some kind near the docks? Was she still near the wharf? Something kicked on . . . like a motor, faint.

She tried to make herself calmer, tried to quiet the pounding of the blood in her ears so she could hear better. Nothing. No cars, no voices. Just the droning motor sound. It stopped and it was quiet again, except for the lapping water.

The floor creaked. She jumped.

Footsteps on wood. Coming closer.

Then it stopped. But she could hear someone moving.

Who was it? Gunther Mayo?

"Motherfucker . . ."

The voice made her jump. A man, it was a man.

"Damn it. Damn it."

More footsteps. Pacing.

Louder this time. She tried to draw on what she knew, tried to remember what the books said. But nothing was coming. Just the feeling of panic gathering slowly in her gut. She gulped in several breaths of the fetid air to push the panic back down. The cloth billowed against her face. She uttered a small cry and suddenly the agitated pacing stopped. It was quiet. Water lapping. She held her breath.

"Where was he?" he asked.

The voice had changed. Calmer now, almost benign.

"Where was he?" Louder.

She didn't answer. Couldn't.

"You can talk to me, lady," he said. "It's just you and me. You can talk now."

"Take this off and I'll talk to you," she whispered.

Footsteps moving away. "I can't do that," he said.

It was quiet for a minute; then she heard a scraping sound, like he was dragging something. It stopped. The floor creaked.

"Listen to me," he said.

She froze.

"Are you listening to me?"

She nodded quickly.

"I want you to tell them. You tell them that I had to do this. Everything is ruined now and this is the only way."

What?

"I had to change my plan. You understand that, right?"

She squeezed her eyes shut.

"He left me no choice," he said.

It was very quiet. She strained her ears and she could hear him breathing. But she thought she heard someone else, too. A different rhythm to the breaths, slower, labored, congested.

Then—another sound. A thudding noise. What was it? It went on, turning wet, like the slapping of a soggy sponge against something. And groans, soft, agonizing.

She felt a sprinkle of water. No. Not water.

Blood. *Dear God.* He was hitting someone.

"Motherfucking piece of shit! Don't talk to me! Don't look at me!"

She bit her lip to keep from screaming.

Flesh against flesh. Bone cracking.

The groaning had stopped. Just grunts now, sharp grunts and panting.

Tears ran down her cheeks as she drew blood from her own lip.

She heard a hissing sound and smelled paint. The fumes filled the room.

"Get it right this time," he said. "You fucking idiots. Get it right."

Then it stopped.

She could hear his breath slowing. He let out a soft groan. Something fell against wood. She was shaking, her heart hammering, the wet cloth stuck to her face.

It was silent. She wasn't sure how long.

"Fuck . . ." he whispered. "No . . . no."

Tears? Regret?

She heard footsteps and he came closer. "He made me do it!" he yelled. "Do you understand? He made me!"

Her brain was racing, trying to think of some way to calm him. What? What could work? Talk? Did he want to talk?

"Who?" she asked. "Who made you?"

He screamed at her. "Him!"

She drew back in the chair. Retreating footsteps. She heard the dragging sound again, a door opening, and felt a waft of fresh air. She pulled at her wrists, but they were bound tight.

Minutes passed. Or was it seconds? She couldn't tell anymore. But then, she heard the door close and the fresh air was gone. He was back.

He was pacing, muttering. She heard his footsteps come nearer.

"Who are you?" he asked.

"I'm . . . I'm . . ." She could hear her voice. It sounded faint, childlike. "I'm an FBI agent."

"Why were you there?"

There? Where . . . the pub?

"I was there to take a missing person's report from someone," she said.

"I didn't—" He stopped. "Who's missing?"

Why was he asking this? He knew it was Tyrone Heller. He had just killed him.

"Who?" he demanded.

"A man named Tyrone Heller."

"Ty Heller." The voice grew louder, impatient. "*Ty* Heller! Who said he was missing? *Cap?*"

Cap? Captain Lynch? He knew about Lynch? Had he followed her there? She swallowed dryly. "Yes . . . yes, Lynch. He was worried about Heller. He thought he may be in danger."

"What did he say about him?"

"Him?"

"Ty Heller. What did he *say* about him?"

She was quiet, her shallow breathing pulling the cloth against her skin. She didn't know how to answer this.

"Did he say he was smart? A good worker? What did he *say*?"

Emily searched her memory for the right words. "He said he was a fine young man."

"Did he say a black man?"

"Yes . . . yes . . . he did."

It was quiet for several minutes. She could hear a boat horn, faintly. The quiet seemed to go on forever, but she knew it had to be only a minute or two.

"I have to finish it."

His voice had gone flat.

The panic began to rise up inside her. She struggled against the ropes at her wrists, her breath coming faster now. She started to cry and screwed her eyes shut, concentrating on staying still and quiet so he wouldn't hear her. Her nose was running, the cloth over her face becoming wetter with each breath she took.

The footsteps came closer.

She let go. The sobs poured out. "Why? Why?" she pleaded. "I'm not like the others! I'm not black!"

"Do you think about it?"

"What?"

"What it's like to be black?" he shouted.

"No," she sobbed.

Quick, heavy footsteps. The air stirred and she instinctively pulled back. "Have you ever fucked a black man?" he demanded.

Dear God . . .

"No . . ."

"You know what happens when you do?"

"No . . . no. Please . . ."

"You get freaks. Disgusting little monkeys that should've been scraped out of their mothers' wombs with a spoon."

For a second, she heard nothing but the pounding of her pulse in her head.

Then, suddenly he was there and she jerked back. The air around her stirred with his breathing and she could smell him. Sweat and dead fish.

She screamed as she felt the blade on her skin.

Chapter Thirty-seven

He stared at their faces.

They stared back, silent images tacked on a bulletin board. Walter Tatum. Anthony Quick. Harold Childers. Roscoe Webb.

Louis walked slowly to the desk, opened the drawer, and pulled out the stack of photos Captain Lynch had given him. He rifled through them until he found a photo of Tyrone Heller. It was blurry, and he was standing behind Woody, but it was all he had.

He walked back to the board and tacked it next to Roscoe Webb's photo. Now there were eight. Emily Farentino didn't fit but she was still number nine.

Louis felt himself tighten but he refused to turn away from the board. His eyes moved over the maps, the color-coded cards, the pushpins and faces, his mind straining to find that one piece, that single strand, that might give them a break.

The door opened and Louis turned. Wainwright came in, his face drawn, his eyes vacant. No one had gotten much sleep in the last two days, but Wainwright looked like he had aged ten years overnight.

"I thought you were out there with the rest of them," Wainwright said. He went to the coffee urn and poured a cup.

"I thought maybe I could do more here." Louis hesitated. "Anything? Any word?"

Wainwright shook his head. He slumped into a chair at the table.

"We'll find her, Dan," Louis said. He said it, but he wasn't sure he believed it himself.

Wainwright didn't look up. Louis couldn't stand seeing the guilt in Wainwright's eyes. He turned back to the board.

"Tyrone Heller doesn't fit," Louis said quietly.

"What do you mean?" Wainwright asked.

"Farentino's profile. He doesn't fit." Louis pointed to one of the cards. "Mayo knows this kid Heller. He worked with him on the same boat for almost a year. Farentino says this guy only kills strangers."

"It's Tuesday," Wainwright said flatly. "Gunther knew their routine, knew they went to dinner at the Dockside. He knew exactly where to find Heller."

Louis concentrated again on the victims' photographs. They began to mutate into brown blurs. He rubbed his gritty eyes.

"Dan, you have the photos of the other cases?" Louis asked.

Wainwright sifted through a folder and handed the three photos to Louis. They were color copies of autopsy photos. Louis tacked them up next to the others, in the order of their abductions. He took a step back and looked at them.

Nothing. Nothing was coming.

His eyes moved from the first—Barnegat Light, New Jersey—to the last—Roscoe Webb. His eyes lingered on the blurry snapshot of Tyrone Heller. Heller was . . . young, younger than the others. That didn't fit either.

He went back to the New Jersey and Fort Lauderdale files, snatched them up, and returned to the board. He wrote the victims' ages on each photo. The man in New Jersey was fifty-five; the two in Fort Lauderdale were fifty and forty-eight. Tatum was forty-five, Quick was forty, Harry Childers was forty-eight, and Tyrone Heller was twenty-five.

They were getting younger.

But there was something else, something right there in front of him that he wasn't seeing.

Then, suddenly, he saw it.

The skin colors. The Barnegat Light victim's skin was ink black. The Coral Springs, Florida, man was maybe a shade lighter. The man from Lauderdale Lakes looked mahogany-toned. Tatum's skin was the color of maple syrup. Quick was cinnamon-skinned. Harold Childers was tawny. Roscoe Webb was a medium tan. And Heller . . .

Louis stared at Heller's picture. He was as light as he himself was.

"They're getting lighter," Louis said quietly.

"What?" Wainwright said.

"The victims," Louis said. "Their skin colors are getting lighter."

Wainwright eyed the board over the rim of the cup. "So?"

"It means something."

"What?"

Louis tried to get his brain in gear. He was tired; it was hard.

Wainwright came up behind him. "I don't see what it could mean," he said, but he was studying the faces carefully.

"I think I do," Louis said. "The killer is aware of skin color, of the importance that people put on shades of skin color. The lighter the skin, the more prized it is."

Wainwright was looking at Louis now. But Louis was staring at the faces on the bulletin board.

"Black people with lighter skin get preferential treatment," Louis said quietly. "The lighter the skin, the less threatening the person is to the white power structure."

Louis paused, his eyes locking on Tyrone Heller's tawny skin. "We do it, too. To ourselves. No darker than a brown paper bag," he said softly. "That's the ideal."

Louis turned away from the bulletin board. He went to the table, dropping into a chair, rubbing his tired eyes.

"You think the killer picks these men based on the exact *shade* their skin is?" Wainwright asked.

"Yes. It's too big a coincidence."

"But how many white men really notice shit like that?"

"I don't know. Maybe . . ." The thought was there, on the tip of his tongue, but he couldn't make sense of it. "Maybe he's working toward someone who looks like the real object of his hatred."

"A white man?"

Louis nodded.

"Then why involve the black guys at all? Why not just kill a white guy?" Wainwright said sharply. "Shit, this makes no sense. This guy is hung up on race one way or the other. It's what drives him."

Louis turned, his own frustration bubbling over. "Then explain the faces getting lighter. I'm telling you he knows exactly who he wants and in what order."

Wainwright leaned on his desk and drew in a deep breath. The room was quiet except for the occasional spatter of radio traffic.

Finally, Wainwright spoke. "So you think his last victim will be white?"

Louis nodded.

"I don't know, Louis. That sounds kind of far-fetched."

Louis looked at Wainwright tiredly. "Not if that white man is himself."

Wainwright blinked. "Suicide?"

Louis didn't answer.

"But what if he's not on self-destruct?" Wainwright asked. "What if it's some other white person? What if it's Farentino?"

Louis stared at him. Jesus. He hadn't thought of that.

Sleep was impossible.

Around six, Louis took out a squad car and headed to the wharf. He saw other cruisers—Sereno, Lee

County, Fort Myers, they were all out, searching. The radio traffic was muted. Too quiet.

He went across the bridge and turned down Estero Boulevard. The street was almost empty, the tourists still asleep, the honky-tonk neon silent. The radio traffic had deteriorated to the occasional unit just checking in. The stretches of silence had grown longer.

He pulled into a parking lot and got out of the car. He walked to the beach and stood gazing out at the dark expanse of sand and water. The sky was a murky gray, that soft blanket of half-light that covered the earth just before dawn.

Quiet. Just the sweet lap of the waves curling gently against the shore and stretching endlessly into the darkness.

He walked slowly across the sand, stopping at the water's edge.

He had grit behind his eyes, his neck and shoulder muscles throbbed. And his head ... his head pounded, and he couldn't think, couldn't even move now, couldn't do anything that would make any difference.

His mind was gripped by images of what he might be doing to her. He couldn't erase them, couldn't change them.

It would almost be easier to be in her place, have some measure of control, no matter how small.

Oh Jesus, he hurt.

And he knew now what lay behind the emptiness in the eyes of June Childers, Anita Quick, and Roberta Tatum. He knew now what haunted Wainwright.

Dealing with what the evil leaves behind.

He tightened, against the sense of impotency and

the vivid images that had been building all night in his head. He felt pain, as if his gut had been taken and twisted into a knot. He sank to his knees in the sand.

He felt a coolness on his knees and opened his eyes to see that the waves had crawled to his knees.

The waves retreated and came again, and he watched their rhythm numbly, finding a strange comfort in it. For a long time he didn't move, lost in the cool, bleak grayness of the dawn.

From somewhere in the distance, he heard a voice. It was Wainwright. The radio in the cruiser. They were calling him.

He stood and trudged back to the car. He grabbed the portable and responded.

"Kincaid to Sereno One."

Wainwright's voice sliced through the silence. "They found her, Louis. She's status four."

Chapter Thirty-eight

The street in front of the Fort Myers Police Station was blocked with TV news trucks: WEVU, WBBH, WINK. A crowd of reporters and photographers milled around the entrance: the *News-Press, Naples Daily News, Tampa Tribune, St. Petersburg Times*. Even *USA Today* and the East Coast papers had made the trip this time. Louis pushed his way through and burst through the door.

A burly patrolman stopped him just inside. "You Kincaid?"

Louis nodded and the man pointed down the hall. Al Horton and Wainwright were coming out of Horton's office. They saw Louis approach and pulled the door shut.

"How is she?" Louis asked.

"Good shape overall," Wainwright said. "She's got a laceration on her left forearm she won't let us fix."

"Mentally?"

"Cool as ice. I couldn't believe it," Horton said, shaking his head slowly. "I mean, this bastard had her in a shack of some kind, bound in a chair, a hood over her face. He cut her arm just before he let her go."

"Jesus," Louis whispered.

"That isn't all," Horton said. "She says he killed Heller while she was there."

"She saw it?" Louis asked.

"No. She heard it."

Louis ran a hand over his face. "How'd she get away?"

"He left her in the shack and she eventually wiggled her hands from under the rope," Horton said. "When she got out, she found a phone and called 911."

"Where was she?" Louis asked.

"About a mile from Fisherman's Wharf, in an abandoned storage shack. It's near where the shrimp boats put in. Our guys are already there."

Horton shook his head again. "You should've seen her when they brought her in, Louis. She refused to go to the hospital, just kept telling us that she was 'evidence.' "

"Evidence?"

Horton nodded. "She asked for a crime scene tech, a change of clothes, and a pad to write down her statement. The CSU guy is in there with her now."

Louis glanced anxiously at the door.

"We have paramedics on standby," Wainwright added.

The door opened and the tech man come out, carrying a black case, a plastic bag holding Emily's clothes, and a smaller bag holding a wadded black cloth.

"I've got all I could," he said.

Horton nodded and the tech left. Louis moved by Wainwright and went into the office.

Emily was seated in an armchair, facing Horton's desk. She was wearing an oversized gray sweatshirt that said FORT MYERS POLICE and sweatpants that billowed over her bare feet. Her helmet of red curls was crushed from where the tech had combed for evidence and her face was streaked with a mixture of dried sweat and tears.

Louis stared at her. Something was different. Her glasses. He had never seen her without them. He noticed now that her eyes were brown, underscored with shadows. A two-inch bandage circled her left forearm. Louis could see blood seeping through the gauze.

He slid into the chair across from her.

"How you doing, Farentino?" he asked softly.

She looked at him, her eyes slightly dazed, but steady. "Hey, Kincaid," she said softly. "Have you found my glasses?"

Louis nodded. "Yes, but . . . I'm sorry . . . I didn't think . . ."

She looked away. "That's okay."

Louis glanced back at Wainwright, standing behind him, then back at Emily. Tentatively, he reached over and took her hand. She didn't seem to notice.

"He came up behind me in the lot at the bar," she said. She stopped and looked over at Horton.

"You'd better turn on the tape," she said.

"It's already on," Horton said.

She nodded woodenly and looked back at Louis. "He threw something over my head and coldcocked me," she said. "I woke up, tied to a chair, with the cloth still over my head." She looked at Horton again. "Forensics has it, right?"

Horton nodded.

"Go slow," Louis said. "Tell us what happened, whatever you can remember."

She took a deep breath. "I heard him pacing and swearing, like he was talking to himself. Then a dragging sound." She paused. "I didn't know what it was. It was probably Heller."

"Did he talk to you?" Louis asked.

She nodded. "He told me to listen, that he wanted to say something. Then he said that he had to change his plan, something like, 'It's all ruined.' "

"Then what?"

Tears welled in her eyes and she brushed them roughly away. "I heard him stabbing Heller. It went on for a long time. I started to get sick."

Emily drew in several slow breaths. Her hand, resting on the arm of the chair, was trembling. "He started beating him after that," she said, the words pouring out. "I could hear that, too."

She ran a shaky hand over her brow. "Then it stopped and it was quiet. There was a sound, like a hiss. He was painting him. I could smell it."

"Did you hear him say anything while he was doing it?"

She nodded. "He said, 'Motherfucking piece of shit.' " She hesitated. "And something else . . . 'Get it right this time, you fucking idiot.' "

Louis laid his hand over hers. "Then what?"

"He said, 'No, no,' like he was sorry about something. But then he started yelling, 'He made me do it.'"

"He said this to you?"

"I'm not sure. Sometimes I couldn't tell if he was talking to himself or me." She drew in another shaky breath. "Then I heard a door open and I think he dragged Heller out. Then he was back."

"Then what?"

"He asked me who I was and what I was doing there."

"At the Dockside?"

She nodded. "I told him I was an FBI agent and went there to take a missing person's report."

She paused. "Wait ... wait. He said something strange then. He asked me who was missing."

"Who?"

"Yes. I told him Tyrone Heller and he asked if Captain Lynch had been the one reporting him missing." She ran a shaking hand across her forehead. "He sounded angry, not making any sense, and he asked me what Lynch said about Heller."

"What do you mean?"

"I think he wanted to know what Lynch thought of Heller. So I told him Lynch described him as a fine young man." She paused. "It almost sounded like jealousy."

Louis glanced up at Wainwright and Horton. Neither man had moved a muscle.

Emily drew in another deep breath. "He started pacing again, saying things like, 'I didn't want to do this.' And then—"

She closed her eyes. The room was quiet.

"Then he said, 'I have to finish it.'"

Her fingers wove through Louis's and she squeezed tight. "I . . . I thought he was going to kill me and I lost it." A tear made its way down her cheek. She withdrew her hand from Louis's and wiped it quickly away.

"I was pleading with him, telling him I wasn't black. Oh, God . . ." She covered her face.

"It's okay, Emily," Louis said quietly.

She shook her head rapidly, looking at him. "He wanted to know if I had ever slept with a black man."

Her voice grew tight. "No, no . . . he said, exactly, 'Have you ever fucked a black man?' And when I said no, he said, 'Good, all you get from that are monkeys who should've been scraped from their mothers' wombs with a spoon.' "

Louis glanced back at Wainwright. He was shaking his head.

"That was all," Emily said softly. She was staring at the floor. "Until he cut me."

Louis took a deep breath. "Why do you think he cut you?"

She closed her eyes.

"Farentino?" He touched her arm. "Emily . . ."

She looked up at him, tears welling again. "I don't know, Louis. He cut me and then I felt him put his hand over it to stop the bleeding. Then he was gone."

The room was quiet. Emily was slumped in the chair, her face like chalk. She brought up a hand to shield her eyes and sat motionless for a long time. Horton turned off the tape.

"I think—" Horton began.

"I was so stupid," Emily whispered.

"What?" Louis said.

She removed her hand, looking at him. "I blew it, Louis. I blew everything."

"Emily—"

"I was in the same room with him," she said. "I should've been able to talk to him. I should've been able to get more out of him."

"Emily, stop."

She curled her hands into fists and leaned on her knees. "That is what I *do!* It's what I was trained to do and I couldn't get past my fear. I just sat there paralyzed!"

Blood oozed from under the bandage.

Louis leaned forward, hands on her shoulders. "Emily, listen to me. It's not your fault."

"I should've been smarter," she said.

"Stop this."

"I am so sorry . . . so sorry."

"You have nothing to be sorry about."

Her eyes bore into his. "No!" she said. "I should've seen it coming."

"Listen to me. It doesn't work that way. I know."

She was shaking her head.

"Something happened to me," Louis said. "Up in Michigan. Men are dead because of something I missed."

She was quiet now, looking at the floor.

"We all miss things," he said. "But you can't keep beating yourself up over it. You go on with your life. You do better next time. You *deal* with it."

She looked up at him. He couldn't tell if she was hearing him or not. He glanced at her arm. The gauze was soaked through.

"Emily," he said, "go get yourself stitched up."

She looked down at her arm and nodded slightly.

Louis heard the door open and looked back to see the paramedic standing there. Louis eased Farentino up from the chair. The paramedic came forward, took her arm, and led her out.

"When you're ready, why don't you guys leave by the back," Horton said.

Wainwright nodded. A young woman poked her head in the door. It was Karen, the public information officer.

"Chief, it's getting ugly out there," she said.

Horton glanced at his watch. "I'm not waiting for Mobley," he said. "Come on, Karen. Let's go throw 'em some meat."

Louis and Wainwright left Horton's office and went out the back entrance. The morning sun was still low in the sky but the day was already warm. Louis and Wainwright stood just outside the door for a moment, neither saying a word.

Wainwright moved away, going to a nearby bench and sinking down onto it. Louis joined him. Two uniformed patrolmen came up the walk, stared at Wainwright's wrinkled uniform, and went in.

"Think she'll be all right?" Wainwright asked.

"Yes," Louis said. He leaned his head back against the brick building, closing his eyes.

For several minutes, neither man moved or said a word. Louis knew they were both long past exhaustion.

"Louis," Wainwright said finally, "what were you talking about back there?"

"When?"

"When you were telling her what happened in Michigan," Wainwright said. "When you said you should have seen it coming."

Louis opened his eyes. Wainwright wasn't looking at him. He was staring straight ahead.

"I made a lot of mistakes," Louis said.

He could feel Wainwright's eyes on him now. He drew in a long breath. "Mistakes I could have prevented if I had seen it coming."

Wainwright said nothing. Finally, Louis looked at him. Wainwright was staring straight ahead again, but his eyes were unfocused, distant.

"Remember Skeen?" Wainwright asked after a moment.

"The Raisin River killer."

"Right before the end, right before the last little girl was murdered, my wife Sarah committed suicide," Wainwright said.

Louis waited.

"She had been depressed for a long time," Wainwright went on. "I was away all the time then. She was holding everything together with the kids, the house, and she never said anything."

Louis remembered the photograph on the mantel back at Wainwright's house, the one of the pretty brunette woman.

"The signs were there," Wainwright said quietly. "I saw that eventually. But I didn't at the time. I didn't see it coming."

Louis stared at Wainwright's profile. For a long time, Wainwright just sat there, looking off at the parking lot across the street.

"I've buried it, just buried it, for a lot of years," Wainwright said. "It's why I came down here, because I didn't want to deal with it. My kids—" He stopped, wiping a hand roughly over his face. "I haven't seen them for a while," he went on. "After Sarah died, my oldest—Kevin—I think he blamed me. Gina didn't, but Kevin . . . he was the one who found Sarah and . . ." His voice trailed off.

Louis waited. Finally, when he was sure Wainwright was not going to say anything more, he put a hand on Wainwright's shoulder.

"Let's go," Louis said quietly.

Wainwright shook his head. "I can't sleep."

"I can't either. Let's go take a look at that shack."

Wainwright nodded. "Yeah . . . yeah. Good idea. Thanks."

Chapter Thirty-nine

They stood at the door to the storage shack.

The crime scene techs were almost finished. Louis had watched as they meticulously dusted every inch of the walls, the wooden table, the wooden crab traps, and the chair that still sat in the middle.

Under the chair, they had scraped up blood Louis guessed would turn out to be Emily's. From another area, they took samples of blood that Louis was sure belonged to Tyrone Heller. The techs had also found tiny specks of dried blood, probably from the tread of a shoe.

Bags of evidence had been removed: fish scales and shrimp shells, hairs, fibers, some rusted cans, crumpled pieces of tissue, blue and white buoys, and some cigarette butts. On both arms of the chair, there were several loops of yellow plastic rope.

Louis's eyes swept over the tiny room, trying to get a feel for what had happened. No . . . a feel for the killer's mind, that's what he wanted. He focused for a moment on the chair, then moved to the bloodstain, rimmed with black paint. It was smaller than the bloodstain from Quick up on the overlook. But Mayo had dragged Heller out right after killing him. Louis's eyes went now to the walls. The old gray planks were splattered with blood. There was more on the ceiling.

He realized he was feeling nothing. No vibrations. And worse, no emotion.

"We need something out of this mess to tie Mayo in," Wainwright said. "We need proof he was here."

"Mayo's prints are on file," Louis said. "Maybe we'll get a match from here."

"He's using gloves. He hasn't left his prints anywhere else."

Louis was looking at the bloodstain again, noticing something new. There was less blood than at the overlook but more paint.

"He used a lot of paint on Heller," Louis said.

"I was thinking the same thing," Wainwright said. "Why do you think he went overboard this time?"

"Remember what Farentino said she heard him say? 'Get it right this time, you fucking idiot.' Maybe she heard it wrong. Maybe he said 'idiots.' "

"Plural?" Wainwright asked.

Louis nodded. "Maybe he was talking to us."

"What do you mean?"

"Maybe he saw the press conference. Maybe he's pissed that we didn't mention the paint. It's important to him and he wants us to notice it this time."

Wainwright nodded. "Farentino said he might react to anything. I guess we found out."

The techs moved out, taking the table. They told Wainwright they would return for the chair and to tear up the stained floorboards and walls.

Louis's eyes went back to the chair. "Why didn't he kill her?" he asked.

"Maybe your theory about the skin shades is wrong and he's not working toward a white victim," Wainwright said.

Louis shook his head. "No, I still think there's something to it. Heller is lighter than the others and he killed him."

"Then why did he even bother to take Farentino in the first place?" Wainwright asked.

"Maybe she was just in the way," Louis said. "Maybe he was going to kill her but changed his mind."

"Doesn't make sense. Doesn't fit his profile." Wainwright paused. "Maybe it's like all the paint this time. Maybe he wants to tell us something and Farentino was just the messenger."

"What's the message?"

Wainwright let out a weary sigh. "I don't know. We're both so fucking tired we can't think straight."

They were silent for a moment. "He's not finished," Louis said. "I still think he's moving toward something."

Wainwright's eyes were focused on the bloodstain. "The question is, what?"

Louis woke and immediately looked at the clock. Two-thirty in the afternoon. He had fallen into bed after coming home from the storage shack and gotten a couple hours of fitful sleep. There was still grit behind his eyes but he knew he couldn't sleep any more.

He showered, dressed, and went out to the kitchen. Empty. Issy looked up at him from her bowl of kibbles.

Louis heard country music from the patio and went outside. Margaret was cutting the dead blooms off one of her orchids.

"You're up," she said, turning.

"Anybody call?" he asked.

Margaret shook her head and slipped her pruning shears into her apron.

"How 'bout I fix you a sandwich?" she said, starting for the kitchen.

"No, Margaret, I'm fine," he said quickly.

"Didn't we talk about this before?"

Louis sighed. "Whatever you want to fix is fine. Where's Sam?"

"Fishing," Margaret said with a grimace.

Louis followed her into the kitchen. He picked up the wall phone and dialed Horton's office. Horton picked up immediately.

"Any news?" Louis asked.

"Still no sign of Heller. The other crewman— Woody something—said Heller didn't show for work this morning. We did a welfare check at Heller's trailer. No sign of anything out of the ordinary. No sign of Heller's truck either. We've got a BOLO out on it."

"Mayo probably followed Heller to the Dockside," Louis said. "Maybe he used the truck to take Heller to the storage shack and then abandoned it."

"We thought of that. Got the whole wharf area covered. Nothing."

Margaret came into the kitchen and began to busy

herself at the refrigerator. Louis turned away and lowered his voice. "How's Farentino?"

"Sleeping at her hotel," Horton said. "I put a uniform outside her door."

"Anything back from the scene yet?"

"There was a lot of old trash but nothing fresh. The owner says the place used to be a storage shed for the shrimping company nearby, but it's been abandoned for years."

Louis could hear Horton flipping some papers. "Let's see . . . shrimp shells, rusted cans, fish scales, specifically snapper, spot-tail, king mackerel. Dozens of prints, but the only fresh ones were on the chair and we're running them."

"What about the blood?"

"AB-negative under the chair. Rare stuff," Horton said. "It matches Farentino's. The big stain was O-positive, but we don't know what Heller is. The specks of blood on the floor turned out to be from king mackerel."

Louis sighed. "Is there anything I can do?"

"I'll tell you the same thing I told Dan this morning," Horton said. "Get some rest. We'll call."

Louis hung up. When he turned, Margaret was standing there holding a plate.

"Eat this, damn it," she said.

He thanked her and took the peanut butter and jelly sandwich out to the patio. Margaret came out a moment later and set a Dr Pepper at his side. She went to the small cassette player and turned her tape over. The song "Luckenbach, Texas" started playing.

Louis wolfed down the sandwich and set the plate aside, wishing Margaret had made two sandwiches. He tried to remember the last time he ate.

He laid his head back, closing his eyes, thinking about the events of the last twenty-four hours. What a night.

He had a sudden picture of Farentino's tear-streaked face in his mind. She must be a wreck. Alone, in a strange town, scared to death. He wondered if she'd slept, if she'd be up for a visit.

He got up. Margaret looked over. "Where you going?"

"To visit Farentino," he said.

Margaret wiped her hands on her apron. "I've got some fudge you can take her."

Chapter Forty

The Sereno Key Inn was a clot of wooden cabins clustered around a marina not far from the town center. It had a funky, fifties air, like time had not quite caught up. He spotted a Fort Myers patrol car in front of one of the cabins and parked next to it. An officer was sitting on a lawn chair on the porch and rose as Louis came forward.

"Louis Kincaid, Sereno Key PD," he said.

"Some ID, sir?"

Louis took out the card Wainwright had given him. The officer eyed it suspiciously.

"Just a moment, sir." He keyed his radio. Louis waited patiently while he talked to his office.

"Sorry, sir," he said, handing the card back. "Go ahead."

Louis knocked on the door. It took a while for it to open. Farentino stood there, hair wet like she had just gotten out of a shower.

"Hey, Farentino."

She smiled. "Hey, Kincaid. Come in."

The cabin was furnished with old rattan and color prints of flamingos that looked like they had been lifted from a Miami Beach hotel, circa Jackie Gleason. The Mr. Coffee machine in the kitchenette was spurting out a fresh pot.

"Want some?" Farentino asked, seeing him eyeing it.

Louis shook his head. "Too much lately. I think my kidneys are shot."

She smiled. She was wearing a black-and-red kimono that looked like it came from a thrift store. Her face was still pink from her shower. She was squinting at him.

"Oh, almost forgot," he said. "Got some presents for you." He pulled a Baggie from his pocket. "Fudge, from Margaret."

"Nice lady," Emily said, taking it.

"And from me," he said, pulling her glasses out of his breast pocket.

Her grin widened. "Thank God," she said, taking them and slipping them on. She glanced around the room. "Shit, this place is uglier than I remember."

Louis laughed, then sobered, his eyes going to the gauze wrap on her arm. "So, how you doing?" he asked.

She shrugged. "I'm okay. Six stitches." She went to the coffeemaker and poured a cup. "You didn't bring my briefcase," she said, turning back to him.

"It's still in evidence."

"Shit. I need it."

"You'll get it back."

"I mean now. I want to get back to work."

"Farentino—"

She held up a hand. "Look, Kincaid, I'm okay. The best thing I can do now is get my mind in gear again. I'm going crazy here, just staring at the walls, thinking . . . " Her voice trailed off.

"Thinking about what?" Louis asked.

She sat down at the small table, setting the coffee aside. "Thinking about everything Mayo said. I've been turning it over and over in my head, trying to figure out if I've missed anything. I know there has to be more than what I told you. If I had the files here, maybe it would trigger something." She shook her head. "I don't know."

"You did the best you could, Farentino," Louis said.

She looked up at him. "But I keep going back to the same question—why me? Why did he take me? And why did he let me go?"

The last words came out shaky. She wasn't all right. He could hear from her voice that she was really thinking, *Why am I still alive?*

"He said, 'Why were you there?' " she said quietly.

"You already told us that," Louis said.

"No, you don't understand. It was 'why were *you* there?' Like I wasn't supposed to be." She shook her head. "It means something."

Louis hesitated. He thought about telling her what he and Wainwright had discussed, that her abduction and release was some kind of message on Gunther Mayo's part. But he didn't want her getting too worked up about it.

"It means you were just in the way," Louis said. "That's why he let you go."

She looked up at him, then nodded slightly. "You haven't found Heller's body yet?"

"No. We're concentrating on the water. Everyone's out looking—marine patrol, coast guard. I'll call you the moment we have news."

"I want to help," she said.

"It's too early," he said.

She was quiet, staring at her coffee cup. He sensed she wanted to say something.

"Farentino, what's the matter?" he asked.

"Wainwright was right," she said softly. "I didn't have a clue what I was doing out there. I could have ridden with the NYPD for two years and still not had a clue."

"No cop really does until it happens," Louis said. "Stop beating yourself up." He paused, realizing she looked tired. He wondered how much she had slept.

"I've got to get going," Louis said. "I'll check in with you tomorrow, okay?"

"Bring my briefcase," she said.

By the time he got back to the Dodies', it was nearly four. Margaret was nowhere to be seen so he grabbed a Dr Pepper and a leg of leftover chicken from the refrigerator and headed out to the patio. Issy followed him, patiently waiting at his feet until he tossed her a sliver of chicken.

A boat was motoring slowly toward the dock. It was Dodie, his burnt face bright beneath the aqua Miami Dolphins cap. Louis went down to the dock.

"Need some help?" he asked.

"Yeah, tie that off," Dodie said, tossing a line and cutting the engine.

Louis hesitated, then started to wrap the line around a piling. Dodie gave an impatient grunt and stepped onto the dock. He took the line and, in one quick move, knotted it off.

"I'm telling you, Louis, you gotta come fishing with me," Dodie said, holding out a cooler.

Louis took the cooler while Dodie hauled up his gear and his catch for the day—two puny-looking gray fish.

"Why should I?" Louis said. "Doesn't strike me as worth the effort."

"Well, with fishing, it ain't the destination, it's the journey," Dodie said, heading toward the house.

Louis deposited the cooler on the patio. Dodie dropped into his lounge chair and pulled a beer can from the cooler. "Last one. You want it?" he asked, holding it out.

"Got my soda," Louis said.

"Where's Margaret?" Dodie whispered.

"I heard the washer go on," Louis said.

"Good." He popped the top and took a swig.

Louis sat down in the nearby chair.

"I saw the news this morning," Dodie said. "You found Miss Farentino. TV said she's okay."

"He didn't hurt her," Louis said.

"Thank God."

"I went over to see her earlier. She's doing as good as can be expected."

Dodie shook his head. "Seems kinda weird, don't it?"

"What?"

"That he didn't kill her?"

"We thought the same thing." Louis shook his head in frustration. "We seem to be just one step behind him."

"You want to bounce some stuff off me?" Dodie asked.

Louis looked at Dodie. He was leaning forward, his eyes avid. Louis sighed. He told Dodie about the shrimp shack.

"You find anything helpful there?" Dodie asked.

"Blood, paint. Fresh prints. They're not back yet."

"What else?"

"Nothing . . . just some trash, shrimp shit, and fish scales."

"What kind of fish scales?"

"Jesus, Sam—snapper, mackerel, spit-tail, or something. What difference does it make? We *know* he's a fisherman."

Dodie sat back and took a sip of beer.

"What kind of mackerel?"

Louis closed his eyes. "I'm not sure. King?"

"King mackerel? Well. Them kings are big-ass fish," Dodie said.

Louis put his hand over his eyes.

"I seen a king once," Dodie went on. "We were out on one of them deep-sea boats. This was up near Tampa after I took Margie to Bush Gardens."

Dodie leaned forward. "You should have seen it, Louis. Even the crew guys were excited 'cuz I guess it was a pretty rare bird, that fish. Fifty pounds. You ever seen a fifty-pound fish, Louis?"

Louis shook his head.

"Shit, it took that guy an hour to land that sucker. And it bled all over the damn boat." He paused.

"Damn trip cost me fifty bucks and I didn't catch jack-shit."

Louis didn't say anything.

"Well, I'm going in to shower," Dodie said. He rose and went inside.

Louis lowered his hand from his brow and stared after Dodie. Through the kitchen window, he could see him kiss Margaret and wander away.

Christ. That had been a pretty shitty thing to do. Dodie only wanted to help.

He shook his head. Big-ass fish.

Big fish. Rare bird. King mackerel. Deep sea.

Suddenly his brain kicked into a new gear.

He got up and went inside, going to the bathroom door. He opened it an inch.

"Sam!" he called.

"What the . . . Louis?"

"Where did that deep-sea boat take you?"

Dodie stuck his head out of the curtain. "Where? Clear out to the Gulf of Mexico."

Chapter Forty-one

Louis walked into the war room and drew up short. The bulletin board was gone. The table was clear. There was one box on the table.

Wainwright came out of his bathroom, saw the look on Louis's face, and shrugged. "I had it all carted over to Horton's office. We'll work out of there."

Louis nodded, understanding but not liking it. It had been their work. The faces on that bulletin board had kept him going.

"Dan," Louis said, "I think I can put Mayo in the shrimp shack."

"How?"

"Blood from a king mackerel was found in the shack. It was fresh, Dan. And the only place you can catch that fish is in the gulf. I checked with a guide today. There are five boats at the wharf. Only one—the *Miss Monica*—goes to the Gulf of Mexico. We know Mayo worked on the *Miss Monica.*"

Wainwright sat down. "Not bad. But I'd rather have something concrete, like Mayo's prints on the chair."

"Nothing back on that yet?"

Wainwright shook his head.

Louis sighed and looked back at the empty space where the board had been. "Horton have anything for us to do?" he asked.

Wainwright shook his head again.

Louis looked down at the box on the table. "What's in this?"

"Just some of Farentino's personal papers and useless files. I didn't want to toss them. She wouldn't be too happy about that."

"Won't be happy about what?" a voice said from behind them.

They turned to see Emily standing in the doorway. Louis went over to her.

"Hey, Farentino. How you doing?" he said.

"Hey, Kincaid. Not bad." Her smile faded as she noticed the blank bulletin board. "Where's all our stuff?" she asked.

"Everything's downtown," Wainwright said.

Emily looked at them. "Then why are *we* here?"

Louis slid his hip on a desk. "We're on standby."

"You mean we're out of it," Emily said.

Neither answered her.

"Louis has a theory," Wainwright said.

Louis told her about the shrimp shack connection to Mayo. Emily looked unimpressed.

"What?" Louis asked.

"Fresh blood?" she asked. "Louis, Mayo hasn't

been on a boat in almost a month. We know that. We have every boat under surveillance."

Louis paused, then turned away. "Fuck!" he said. He kicked a chair. It rolled and crashed into the wall. Wainwright and Emily just stared at him.

"Goddamn it," Louis said, shaking his head, hands on hips.

"Louis—" Wainwright said.

"I was so fucking sure," Louis said, staring at the empty bulletin board. They were all silent for a moment.

"Louis," Wainwright said finally, "we'll find another way to place him there."

"Don't try to handle me, Dan," Louis said. "Please. Not now."

"Look, if we have to go back to square one, turn over every lousy piece of evidence, we will," Wainwright said.

Louis threw his arm out to the empty bulletin board. "We don't *have* any fucking evidence!"

"Hold on," Emily said.

She reached into the box, pulled out a legal pad, and tossed it at Wainwright. He caught it in his lap.

She turned to Louis. "Interview me again."

"What?"

She pulled a chair up to the desk and sat down. "I've been thinking, trying to remember more details. I want to try something. Interview me again."

"Are you sure?" Louis asked.

"Yes."

Louis glanced at Wainwright and came back to the desk. He sat on the edge, facing Emily. Emily drew in a breath and closed her eyes. Louis waited, giving her a moment.

"Tell me what you hear," he said.

She pressed her lips together. "I hear a motor running . . . like a refrigerator kicking on."

"That would be the freezer truck generator," Wainwright said. "There was one a few feet away."

"What else?" Louis asked.

She was silent for several seconds. "Nothing. Just water lapping."

"What does it smell like?" Louis asked.

She shook her head. "It stunk, like fish but . . ."

Louis waited.

She squeezed her eyes shut.

The sounds of the outer office drifted in. Phones. Voices. Traffic outside the window. It was distracting her. Louis glanced around and saw a sweatshirt hanging on a hook behind the door. He walked over and grabbed it.

She opened her eyes as he approached her and saw him holding the shirt.

He hesitated. She nodded and he placed the sweatshirt over her head, backing away. Her breath quickened.

"You okay, Farentino?"

"Yes."

He moved to her and placed her wrists on the arms of the chair, palms up. He waited almost a full minute.

"What does it smell like?"

"Old wet wood and fish—no, shrimp. I know it's shrimp."

"What is the first thing you hear?"

"He's talking, to himself. And he's dragging Heller. Then . . . he starts talking to me."

"What is he saying?"

" 'I want you to tell them something. Tell them I had to do this.' "

"You're sure he said 'them'?"

She nodded. "Yes . . . I think he meant us. He wanted us to understand something about him. He was . . . his voice sounded urgent. Then he said that thing about having to change his plan. And . . . 'He left me no choice.' "

Louis glanced at Wainwright. That was new. "Who do you think he was referring to?"

"I don't know . . . Heller?"

"What happened next? The stabbing?"

She nodded. "It went on for a while . . . the stabbing. And the beating."

"Did Mayo say anything during this time?"

It took her a minute to answer. "He said, 'Motherfucking piece of shit. Don't look at me.' It must have been Heller he was talking to."

She paused. "And he said, 'Get it right this time, you idiots.' "

" 'Idiots'? Plural?"

She nodded slowly. "Yes, *idiots.*"

"You were right, Louis," Wainwright whispered.

"What happened next?" Louis asked.

"He dragged Heller out. I heard the door and Mayo came back. He asked me who I was and I told him I was an FBI agent and that I was there to take the missing person's report." She hesitated.

"What is it?"

"I'm not sure," she said slowly. "It was his voice. There was something in his voice that made me think I *shouldn't* have been there."

"Then what?" Louis asked.

She hung her head slightly. Louis watched the shirt breathe with her.

"I . . . oh. Oh. He wanted to know what Lynch said about Tyrone Heller. He seemed very interested in *how* Lynch described Heller."

Louis looked over at Wainwright, who was still taking notes. "What did you tell him Lynch said?"

"I told him Lynch thought Tyrone was a fine young man."

"Did that seem to anger him?"

"No . . . no. Wait . . . wait. But then he asked me if Lynch had described Tyrone as a black man. He stressed *black*. I heard it in his voice."

Louis glanced at Wainwright. This was new, too. But what did it mean? Louis waited for Emily to go on.

"At some point . . ." she said, "it was near the end . . . he said that he didn't want to do this. He was . . ." She paused. "He was almost kind about it, like he was apologizing."

Her voice had grown small.

"What did that mean to you?" Louis asked.

"That he didn't want to kill Heller . . . or me. I'm not sure."

"Go on."

She was quiet for a minute. Wainwright stood up and came over to them.

"Farentino?" Louis said gently.

Her breath quickened. "He got mad. He was furious and he wanted to know if I knew what it was like to be black."

Emily stopped but Louis didn't say a word.

"He was shouting," Emily said, "and then he asked me about fucking a black man." Her words rushed out. "And then he said that thing about scraping people from wombs." She shook her head slowly. "It was like a different person had come into the room."

Her chest was heaving and Wainwright looked at Louis, concerned. Louis held up a hand to him.

"Then what?"

Her hands were curled into fists. "Nothing."

"Think. What else did he say?"

She bowed her head. "I don't know. Nothing. There was no more talk."

Louis glanced at Wainwright, mouthing the word "gloves." Wainwright understood immediately and rose. He returned from his office a few moments later with a pair of brown leather gloves. Louis slipped them on.

Louis picked up a letter opener and ran the tip lightly across Emily's forearm. Her head shot up, and she sucked the cloth to her face, but she didn't move.

He wrapped his gloved hand around the invisible cut, held it there for a second, and backed away. They waited.

"No," she said softly.

A few more seconds passed.

"No, that's not right," she said finally. "Do it again. Without the gloves. He wasn't wearing gloves when he touched me."

Louis took them off and repeated the move, wrapping his fingers around her wrist.

Emily shook her head.

Louis looked down at his fingers wrapped around her arm. Tan against white. Suddenly he knew.

"What about this?" he asked.

He made the "cut" again with the opener, this time placing his own wrist flat against hers, rubbing.

"Yes!" she said. "That's it. That's what he did."

Louis turned away. There was a rock in his stomach. The germ of an idea was there, but his brain couldn't work fast enough to make sense of it.

It was like a different person had come into the room.

He stood with his back to them, eyes closed.

Do you ever think about what it must be like to be black?

Emily, on Dodie's patio: *He's black.*

Roscoe Webb: *This was a white man talking to me.*

"Louis?" Wainwright asked.

He turned. Emily had taken the shirt off her head. She was staring at him. So was Wainwright.

"He's not white," Louis said. "And he's not black. He's both."

"Explain," Wainwright said.

"He's biracial," Louis said.

"How do you know?" Emily asked.

"All of it," Louis said. "He has two sides, almost like two people, living inside him."

He paused. A sudden image rushed into his head. A man at the wharf. A knife flashing in the sun. Fish guts being dumped into the water.

He looked at Emily and Wainwright. "Tyrone Heller isn't a victim," he said. "He's the killer."

Chapter Forty-two

The rain beat down on the windows. Louis and Emily sat silent at the table, both lost in their own thoughts.

Wainwright hung up the phone and looked at Louis. "I told Horton what you said. He wants us downtown immediately. And there's something new. They found Heller's truck abandoned in a canal east of the airport. No body, no Heller."

Wainwright got up and left the room.

"He might have skipped," Emily said.

Louis was silent.

"If he goes underground again, we could lose him until he resurfaces," Emily said.

"Shit," Louis muttered.

Wainwright came back, carrying a computer printout. "Horton sent over Heller's sheet. He's got a history. Manslaughter conviction, 1979, Broward County, Florida. Served three years."

"We need more," Louis said.

"I'll call over to Broward," Wainwright said, picking up the phone.

"We may not have to," Emily said.

They looked over at her. She was standing over the box on the table, holding a file. "He's in here," she said.

Wainwright stared at the file in her hand. "How did we miss it?" he asked.

"It was in the stack of black suspects," she said. "We put them aside after Roscoe Webb, after we decided we were looking for a white man."

She flipped it open and scanned it quickly. Wainwright and Louis waited.

"It's the first case," she said. "Heller's first murder—his own father."

"Jesus," Wainwright said.

"It's from the Pompano Beach PD," Emily said. "It's where Heller was born, just north of Fort Lauderdale."

She adjusted her glasses. "In 1979, when he was eighteen, Tyrone Heller stabbed his father four times. He fled, and the father died hours later. Heller was charged with manslaughter." She paused. "Listen to this. His public defender wanted to plead him out on diminished capacity and got him a psych exam."

"Is the medical report in there?" Wainwright asked.

Emily nodded. "Here's the family history. Heller's

mother was white, father black. They weren't married and Heller's father denied paternity and abandoned the family. Heller was raised by the mother, whose three other children were white. He was the youngest. Here's what the psychiatrist wrote: 'As child, subject was target of emotional abuse and isolation by mother and siblings. Subject expresses rage against absent father and displays extreme episodes of depression and self-loathing.' "

She paused, looking up at Louis and Wainwright.

"Like he should've been scraped from his mother's womb," Louis said.

"All through his teenaged years, Heller tried to locate his father," Emily went on. "He finally found him living in Fort Lauderdale, but the father again rejected him. That's when Heller attacked." She looked up. "They found the body in a bathtub, with the faucet running."

"In water," Louis said.

Emily let out a sigh. "There's quite a bit from the psychiatrist here," she said. " 'The subject, Tyrone Heller, exhibits reaction formation and confabulation.' "

"Translate, Farentino," Louis said.

She looked up at them. "Reaction formation is a kind of defensive mechanism, a way of dealing with negative and unacceptable feelings by substituting thoughts or behaviors that are completely opposite of the bad feelings."

"I don't get it," Wainwright said.

"Normal people, healthy people, can channel negative feelings into something positive," Emily went on. "But people like Heller can't, so they almost turn against themselves." She paused. "Like the closet homosexual who covers up true feelings about himself by acting like a homophobe or gay basher."

"So to Heller the *unacceptable* fact is that he looks black?" Louis asked.

Emily was nodding, remembering something. "It's why he asked me what Lynch said about him. It's why he asked me if Lynch said he was black. I think Heller truly believes he is white." She paused. "It explains his racism toward his black victims."

"And why Roscoe Webb was so certain he heard a white man talking to him when Heller called him a nigger," Louis said.

"What's confabulation?" Wainwright asked.

"Lying," Louis said.

Emily hesitated. "Not really," she said. "It's more like filling in the gaps in your memory with unconscious fiction. It's making up stories to cover up the fact that you don't know the truth. Alzheimer patients do it to hide the fact that they can't remember things they know they should be able to."

Wainwright shook his head. "But you said Heller really believed he was white. So was he was kidding himself? Is that what confabulating is?"

"In Heller's case, I'm guessing that the unacceptable fact of his black side caused him to suppress many of his memories about growing up and he has invented a more acceptable past—and identity."

"As a white man," Louis said tightly. He got up and went to the window, his back to them.

They were silent. The rain pounded on the windows. Wainwright was watching Louis but finally he turned back to Emily.

"Anything else in there we need to know?" Wainwright asked.

Emily scanned the rest of the medical report. "Diagnosis: antisocial personality disorder, substance abuse disorder, substance-induced psychosis versus paranoid schizophrenia." She took off her glasses, rubbing the bridge of her nose. "No wonder I thought I heard two men talking to me."

"Jesus, he isn't one of those multiple personalities, like that Sybil woman?" Wainwright said.

Emily shook her head. She slipped her glasses back on. "I think I know what set him off—Lynch," she said quietly.

"Lynch?" Wainwright said.

"Lynch told me he was retiring after the fishing season was over. Tyrone Heller probably knew that. And Lynch was Heller's *acceptable* father figure."

Wainwright was staring at her. "Bullshit," he said softly. "Some people are just born bad and this asshole is one of them. I don't buy it."

"I do," Louis said, turning.

They both looked at him.

"Heller was raised by people who told him that being black was inferior," Louis said. "He grew up believing it, believing that being black was less than . . . that it was garbage."

He paused. "His father was gone, his black side was gone. He wanted to be accepted, but to do that he had to change the one thing he couldn't change—his skin. In his mind, he became white."

Louis paused. He realized he was clenching his fists. He turned away, flexing his fingers.

Wainwright glanced at Emily.

"Louis," Emily said quietly, "go on. Please."

He didn't turn. He didn't speak.

Wainwright cleared his throat. "Why did he kill his father then?" he asked.

"Abandoned children sometimes kill out of rejection," Emily began.

Louis turned. "Heller didn't search for his father because he wanted acceptance. He searched for him—hunted him down—to kill him. When he realized the world wasn't going to accept him as white, he blamed his father. He saw his father as something that had infected him."

He came back toward the table and sat down.

"Is that why he cut Farentino?" Wainwright asked. "Was he trying to *infect* her with his black blood?"

Emily looked at Louis. When he didn't say anything, she shook her head. "Heller might have moments of reality. I might have been there for one, and he might have been trying to make me feel his pain."

"It still doesn't explain why he killed those men," Wainwright said. "Or why he painted them. What? Is he trying to show the world that they deserve to die just because they're black?"

Emily thought about that for a moment, then shook her head. "I think his victims are symbolic fathers. Heller stabbed his father but he never actually saw him die. Maybe the paint is his way of trying to erase him over and over again."

Louis had fallen quiet again. Emily looked over at him.

"I think it's more," Louis said. "I think it's tied in to why the victims' skin colors got lighter."

Emily nodded. She was on the same track.

"Maybe he started out trying to kill his father,"

Louis said, "but even after he kills these men, his father's face is still there. That's why he beats them so badly, and when that doesn't erase the face, he paints them."

"But it isn't working for him," Emily said.

"No," Louis said. "They are still there. *He* is still there. His self-hatred is catching up with him. Some part of him knows the face he is trying to erase is his own."

"Okay," Wainwright said quietly. "I have one more question. Who was killed in that shack?"

They fell silent suddenly, as if they had forgotten there was an unidentified victim still out there somewhere. Louis turned back to face the bulletin board. The rain beat a steady tattoo on the windows.

"We ruined his plan," Emily said. "He told me that. There's no telling who he killed in that shack."

She closed the file and slid it across the table to Wainwright. "You'd better get this to Horton," she said.

"You'd better come with me and explain it," Wainwright said, rising.

Emily rose and slipped on her green rain slicker. They both stopped and looked at Louis. He was still staring at the empty bulletin board. The phone on the table rang. Wainwright picked it, spoke briefly, and hung up.

"That was Horton. They got the search warrant for Heller's trailer. Mobley's men are on their way there now."

"I want to be there," Louis said, turning.

"Take Candy with you," Wainwright said. "We'll meet you downtown later."

Chapter Forty-three

Candy jerked the cruiser to a stop behind the Lee County Sheriff's Department car. Louis could see Sheriff Mobley and a deputy standing under an awning at Heller's door. They had already checked the tiny trailer twice before, first doing a routine welfare check the night Heller went missing and then again the next day. And there had been a sheriff's deputy posted out front since last Tuesday.

But now they were here to look with different eyes, armed with a search warrant.

Louis got out of the cruiser and hurried through the driving rain to the door. Candy came up behind him and pulled off his cap, shaking the water from it. The four men stood huddled under the listing awning.

Mobley stared at Louis. "Wainwright couldn't come?"

"He's with Horton," Louis said. He had to speak up to be heard over the rain beating on the metal awning. He debated whether to fill Mobley in on what they had just learned about Heller from Emily's file. He decided not to bother. He wasn't sure he understood it well enough himself.

"There's no reason for Dan to be here when we know Heller isn't here," Louis said.

"You're not even sure Heller is a killer. He could be dead," Mobley said.

"We're sure."

"Tell me why."

"It's complicated," Louis said, watching the deputy pry the door open.

"Then tell me this. If Heller wasn't killed in the shrimp shack, who the hell was?"

"We don't know."

"There seems to be a lot you don't know," Mobley said.

The door popped open.

Louis trailed the other three men inside and stopped, wiping the rain from his face. The trailer was stuffy and smelled of fish, and he sensed it came from the unwashed clothes he saw piled in a corner. All the blinds were drawn and the television was on. He wondered if Heller had been watching the press conference from here.

The deputy switched on a lamp and the tiny trailer was revealed in all its cramped mess. Louis took it in quickly, but decided Heller had not brought any of his victims here. The mess seemed to be just the usual squalor of daily living; there was no sign of a struggle.

Besides, he doubted that someone like Heller would have allowed those men inside his home in the first place.

They started in the living room, tossing cushions and rifling through drawers. Louis wandered to the kitchen, opening cupboards. Cereal. Macaroni and cheese. Canned chili.

In the sink, a few food-encrusted dishes and a dead cockroach. On the counter empty beer cans. Louis spotted a beer mug with red lettering on it. He carefully turned it around. It said SMOKEY'S HAPPY HOUR 2 FOR 1 DRINKS 4 TO 6.

Emily had been right. Heller had stalked Walter Tatum from Queenie Boulevard. How had Heller felt walking that street, sitting in that bar, among all the black people? As a "white" man, he must have been uncomfortable. Or had he felt simply invisible?

Louis moved on to the refrigerator. Pepsi. Gatorade. Eggs. He checked the freezer, half expecting to find some human body part. There was nothing. He stood for a moment, listening to the rain batter the metal roof, wondering how anyone could stand the racket.

He moved past Mobley to the narrow hall and entered a small room. It was a bedroom, but also had been used as an office and storage room. It was packed with papers and clothes strewn around a cheap particleboard desk lodged under the window.

Heller's bed was small, a twin with plain wooden posts that resembled pilings at the dock. The bed was made, covered with a plain green blanket. On the dresser Louis could see a hairbrush and a bottle of Vitalis.

He moved to the closet. It was open, the sliding

door off its runner and propped against the wall. The inside was crammed with boxes and clothes. Louis sifted through the boxes carefully, finding more crumpled clothes and an array of old fishing gear—tangled line, rusted hooks, and lures.

At the bottom of the box of clothes, hidden beneath a sweater, he saw a wadded denim shirt. Gingerly he pulled it out and laid it over the bed. It was covered with blood, brown and dried stiff.

He looked for more. There were three, all long-sleeved shirts, all with blood splattered across the front and down the sleeves. Then came the pants, worn old jeans, two pairs, both stained dark brown on the groin area and thighs. One pair had a blood splotch on the upper leg and a small puncture in the denim. The puncture Roscoe would have made when he stabbed Heller in the thigh.

"Sheriff," Louis called, "better get in here."

Mobley appeared at the door, ducking slightly to come into the tiny room. He stared at the clothing, curling his lip.

"Christ," Mobley said. "I guess you were right."

He snatched the radio from the belt, barking at his dispatcher to speed up the crime scene techs. He shoved the radio back, looking slowly around the room. "This fucker needs to fry," he said.

Louis went to the desk and started opening drawers. "He's in the right state for it," he said.

"Not anymore. Texas is doing one a month," Mobley said, peeking into the closet. "We'll never catch them now."

Louis opened the top drawer. It was stuffed with old newspapers, and Louis looked through them quickly, searching for articles about the murders. All the sec-

tions were from the *News-Press*, but there was nothing
in the pages about the murders. Under the newspapers, Louis spotted a worn manila envelope. He
pulled it out, sliding the contents to the desk.

On top was a letter. It appeared to have been typed
on an old typewriter and it was stained with water
spots. It was dated June 23, 1981, and addressed to
the Florida Department of Health, Vital Statistics. It
read *To Whom it May Concern, My name is Ty Calvin
Heller and my birth certificate has a mistake on it. Under
race it should say Caucasian. I would like this corrected
immediately.*

Louis swallowed dryly and set it aside.

Next was a copy of Heller's birth certificate. The
box titled RACE had been whited out with Wite-Out
and the word *Caucasian* written in.

Beneath the certificate was a small stack of drawings
done with colored marker pens on loose-leaf paper.
They were childlike scrawls of stick men, but the
heads were round black circles with no facial features.

Finally, Louis pulled out four snapshots, yellowed
with age, their edges curled. The first one was a white
woman and three white kids, standing on a beach.
The second one showed the same thin blond woman
in front of a truck—laughing with two men who could
have been friends, lovers, or uncles. The third picture
was another shot of the woman and the kids, sitting
on a brown sofa with a dog. Louis was suddenly very
sure the blond woman was Heller's mother.

There was no sign of Tyrone in any of the shots—
except in the last picture. It had been taken in front
of a gray house. It showed the white woman and
the three white kids, but someone had painstakingly

glued on a cutout of another child—a child with dark brown hair and tan skin.

Mobley came up behind him, staring at the drawings. "What's that?" he asked.

"Family album," Louis said, tossing the pictures on the desk.

"Kincaid, I just got off the radio with Horton. Why didn't you tell me about the damn file on Heller you found?"

"I figured Horton would."

"Yeah, he did. And he told me it says Heller killed his own father."

"So?"

"So, what the fuck is this then?"

Mobley was holding a greeting card. "We found a Father's Day card. Doesn't look that old."

"Maybe Heller has a kid somewhere," Louis said.

"It's *from* Heller," Mobley said, handing it to Louis.

Louis looked at the signature beneath the greeting inside. It had been written with a black marker and simply said *Ty.* He lowered it and glanced around the bedroom.

Had it been meant for his dead father, a man who still lived in his mind? Or a phantom father, an invented father whom Heller could call his own?

"Until I read that file, I don't know what I'm looking for in all this shit," Mobley said. "We need to wait for the CSU guys." He started to the door and turned back.

"Don't move anything else, Kincaid."

Louis didn't reply. He had seen enough anyway. He walked from the bedroom, back out to the dingy kitchen. He felt someone behind him and turned. It was Candy.

"Dispatch called. You have a message waiting for you at the station."

"From who?"

"A Captain Lynch. Said he needs to talk to you about Tyrone. Said it was urgent."

Louis sighed. "He's heard the news. Damn it. I should've gone to tell him myself."

Candy nodded toward Mobley. "They got this covered. We know who we're chasing and we know he did it. Let's go see Lynch now."

Louis nodded, slipping past the deputy who was sorting through stuff from a kitchen drawer. Louis stopped in the living room.

The rotting fish odor hit him again, only this time it was different, tinged with the stink of bloody clothes and an almost palpable feeling of despair. The rain beat on the metal, pounding like Heller's fists against faceless men.

The photographs came back to him. That small brown face, pasted into the family photos.

The anger he had felt back at the station was coming into sharper focus now. But what had he been angry about? Heller and his inability to deal with his reality, his blackness? The woman who had killed a child's soul? The father who wasn't there to save him? He was angry at all of them.

In some small, strange, distant way, he understood Heller. He hated him, hated what he had done, but he could understand. The need to be part of something more than himself, the need to belong to someone. He had lived it himself. He knew what it felt like to be different . . . and ignored because of it.

He had felt it back in Mississippi, even at age seven, seeing people staring at his light skin. He had felt it in the foster homes, hearing the other kids whisper. He had spent so much time searching for acceptance and finding only turned heads. Finally, he had stopped looking. By the time Phillip Lawrence had come along, he had almost closed up completely.

Louis realized he was still holding the Father's Day card. He set it on the kitchen counter.

"Louis, let's go," Candy said. "This place gives me the creeps."

Chapter Forty-four

Candy let the car idle for a minute, watching the rain pummel the windshield. Louis could barely make out the white blur of the *Miss Monica*.

"This rain is what they call a Palmetto Pounder," Candy said.

Louis didn't reply. He was too preoccupied, trying to figure out something that had been bugging him during the short drive from Heller's trailer to the wharf. Heller had set up his own disappearance. But why?

To see if Captain Lynch reacted with concern? Or to see who showed up to take the report?

"Sereno base to Sereno three, come in."

Candy keyed the radio. "Go ahead, base."

It was Myrna the dispatcher. "Is Louis with you?"

"Right here."

"Emily Farentino wants to talk to him. Switch to channel three, please."

Candy handed Louis the mike. Louis waited. Now what?

"Louis, this is Emily."

"Go ahead," he said.

"I had a thought after you left," Emily said. "It's about Heller."

Louis had to lean in toward the radio to hear her over the sound of the rain on the roof of the car. "Go ahead," he said.

"Something's been bothering me and I haven't been able to figure it out," she said. "Something Heller said in the shack. I mentioned it to you when you came to see me at the hotel."

Louis felt Candy's eyes on him. "What is it, Farentino?"

"When Heller asked me why I was there . . . I had the feeling he was expecting someone else."

"You told me that already."

"I know, but I think he was expecting someone else to show up and take the report. I just remembered something else he said to me. He said, 'Where is he, where is he?' It was the first thing he said to me. It didn't register. I guess I was too scared." She paused. "He was expecting one of you."

Louis hesitated, his finger poised on the mike button.

"Do you understand what I'm saying?" she asked.

He did. Heller had been expecting him to show up that night.

"Be careful," Emily said.

"We will," Louis said. He clicked off and glanced at Candy.

"Are we getting out or are we going to sit here?" Candy asked, reaching for his rain cap.

Louis turned off the engine. "Let's go," he said.

He slid out, squinting into the rain, hoping Lynch was still onboard and that he still had not heard the news about Heller. Television wouldn't have had it yet, unless someone had leaked it. There was still time for Lynch to get the bad news the right way.

They hurried toward the docks and Louis stopped at the rear of the *Miss Monica*. He could hear the engines idling. He hesitated, a knot gathering in his gut. What was wrong? He had always been able to deliver bad news before. But now, now he was seeing Roberta Tatum, Anita Quick, and June Childers. And he didn't want to see Lynch's face when he told him. For the first time, he was really beginning to understand why Wainwright had refused to walk up that last hill in Michigan.

"Man, I hate getting wet," Candy said. "Let's get this over with."

Louis glanced at Candy, who was huddled down into the upturned collar of his yellow raincoat. Louis looked at the open bar. There were only a handful of customers, including a sheriff's deputy. Louis saw a second sheriff's department car swing into the parking lot.

"Why don't you get a cup of coffee," Louis said. "It might be better if I talk to Lynch alone."

"I hate coffee," Candy said. He stopped fumbling for the latch on the boat's railing and hopped over.

Louis climbed over the rail after Candy. He slipped

and his feet hit the metal flooring with a thud and a skid before he caught himself.

"Lynch!" he called out.

Louis shaded his eyes from the rain and looked around the boat. There was a large enclosed cabin, its roof forming a second deck. A steel ladder connected the two.

Candy ventured to the left toward the bow, easing down the narrow walkway that ran along the side of the boat. Louis could barely see the blur of his yellow raincoat.

"Lynch!" Louis called again.

No answer. He squinted, trying to see inside the cabin. He saw another yellow blur moving around inside. Lynch couldn't hear him over the rain.

Louis stepped over some large spools of fishing line and slid open the heavy steel door of the cabin. He stepped inside, wiping the water off his face.

There were ten or more rows of padded red benches and tables. Large rectangular windows paneled both sides, under them knee-high metal storage boxes. Life jackets and looped twine hung on three posts that ran along the center.

But no Lynch. He had gone back outside, or maybe down below.

The door behind him clanged shut.

Louis spun around, seeing only a blur of yellow move by a window. What the hell was going on?

Another flash of yellow at the side windows. Two of them. Candy . . . he could make out his rain hat. But who . . . ?

The other man's face flashed against the glass. It wasn't Lynch. It was Heller.

Louis's heart began to pound.

A blur of yellow slammed against the window. Heller and Candy fighting.

Louis grabbed the radio from his pocket and keyed it as he rushed to the door.

"Chief! Chief! This is Kincaid! We've been ambushed on the *Miss Monica!*"

He jerked at the door. It didn't budge.

He keyed the radio again, cutting off the frantic dispatcher. "I'm locked in the cabin," Louis said, his words rushing out. "Officer Candy is on deck with the suspect. Repeat—we are separated!"

Louis ran to the other door at the front of the cabin. It was locked.

He hurried back to the left-side window. Up near the bow, he could see a man, lying facedown, in a yellow raincoat. But he couldn't tell who it was.

He could feel the vibrations under his feet growing stronger.

Louis slammed his palms against the glass. "Candy!"

The body didn't move.

Louis spun around, his eyes sweeping over the room. He could see no one, hear no one. The rain was deafening against the roof, the engines growling beneath his feet.

He scanned the cabin for a weapon. Fishing poles, rope, life jackets, and nets. Wainwright's voice drifted up to him and he lifted the radio.

"Louis, status. What's your status?"

"We're moving. Repeat—we're moving." He glanced back at the window. He couldn't tell Wainwright that Candy was probably dead, not over the radio. "Chief, Sereno forty-five is injured. We need assistance. Now!"

"We're on it."

Louis lowered the radio, drawing in deep breaths. *Stay calm. Stay calm.*

He walked slowly through the cabin, taking in every inch of the room. Every few steps he would stop at one of the windows to see if Candy had moved. He had not.

He spotted another ladder in the middle of the room, a small one that seemed to disappear into the top deck. He moved to it slowly and looked up. It opened up onto a small hatch. He could see what looked like a blanket and maybe a bunk above.

A face suddenly appeared in the square.

Heller. But not the shy-eyed young man he had met a few weeks ago. This man stared down at him with unnerving dark eyes and long, dark wet hair that hung to his jaw.

Louis didn't move, locking eyes with Heller. His heart was hammering, but he forced his words out slowly and evenly.

"Why'd you hurt him?" Louis demanded.

"He didn't have to come," Heller said. "He was stupid."

Louis turned, grabbed a fishing pole, and came around swinging. He slammed it against the open hatch. Heller's face disappeared and the hatch slammed shut.

Louis swallowed hard and moved back to the windows, throwing the rod aside. The shoreline was growing more distant. Lights flickered as the darkness crept in.

Louis moved back to the ladder.

"Heller!" he shouted.

No answer.

"Tyrone Heller!"

The hatch opened and a face reappeared. "It's Ty!" he screamed. "You going to talk to me, you call me Ty, you stupid motherfucking piece of shit!"

Then he was gone. The hatch slammed shut. A click of a lock this time. The lights in the cabin went out.

How far would he take him? How long would it take Wainwright to get the coast guard out here? How long did he have to stay alive?

He moved back to the ladder.

"Ty!" he shouted. "Stop the boat and we'll talk." No answer.

Louis moved around the room. The cupboards were padlocked, the windows too thick to shatter. He tossed pads from the benches, finding only storage and life jackets underneath.

Finally, as darkness engulfed the boat, he sat down, positioning himself in a corner, listening to the traffic on his radio. The coast guard had been notified. Wainwright was on his way to the wharf.

Suddenly, the vibrations under his feet stopped.

He stood up.

He could hear footsteps above him, then saw Heller descend the outside ladder in the back. He had a portable battery-powered light in one hand and a bang stick in the other.

Heller unlocked the door and slid it open. Water was streaming off the upper deck onto his rain cap.

"You didn't come the first time. Why?" Heller demanded.

Louis kept his eyes on the bang stick in Heller's right hand. He forced himself to speak calmly.

"I didn't get the message."

"You should have come! You ruined the plan! You should have come!"

"What plan?"

"It doesn't matter. I changed it." Heller set the light on a table just inside the door. "You came this time. Now I can finish the plan."

Louis raised his hand, backing up slowly. "No, you don't have to," he said. "You have a choice."

Heller's face changed suddenly. "I never had a choice!" he screamed, waving the bang stick. "I never had a fucking choice!"

Louis backed around a post, his heart hammering, his breath shallow. His eyes searched the floor for a weapon, a pole, anything.

"Ty, they know we're out here. They'll be waiting for you when you get back."

"I'm not going back!" Heller shouted. He turned, and then spun back, his face distorted. "You should know that! What's wrong with you? What the fuck is wrong with you? Why do you pretend you're different?"

Louis stared at him, trying to get a grip on his fear. He knew there were two people inside Heller, but he didn't know which one he was talking to. But he needed to say something. Anything.

"Different than who?" he asked.

"Me!" Heller screamed. "Me!"

Different? Jesus . . . he wasn't different. He was as close to Heller as anyone could get. In age, in build, and in color.

What did he say? What could he say to this man?

"I'm not different than you," Louis said loudly. "I understand you. I understand everything."

Heller shook his head violently, spraying water.

"No one understands!" he screamed. "I have things I need to do! I have things inside me other people don't have! And I can't get rid of them. Do you hear me? I can't get rid of them!"

Heller's voice had turned thick with rage.

"That's why I'm doing this. That's why I'm taking the boat. He doesn't want it anymore. He doesn't want anything anymore."

"Including you?" Louis asked.

Heller's face tightened, the muscles stretched hard against the bone.

"Stupid piece of shit . . . stupid piece of shit," Heller said, repeating it over and over, as he walked toward him.

"Heller, listen to me—"

Heller stopped talking, his eyes drifting to the floor. His breathing slowed.

"Heller . . ."

Heller didn't move for several seconds; then he lifted his eyes slowly. "You came to me. Do you hear me? You tell them, *you came to me.*"

This was crazy. How was he going to tell anyone anything?

"Ty . . ."

Heller started shaking his head, coming closer. "Stop talking to me. You're not supposed to talk."

Louis backed up again, only a couple of the benches separating them. Heller leveled the bang stick.

Louis felt the wall against his back. His hands searched for something he could grab but there was nothing.

The tip of the stick inched toward him. He thought

about kicking up, trying to knock the bang stick out of Heller's hand, but knew he would be too slow.

His eyes flicked between the tip of the bang stick and Heller's face, hoping he could see a sign—a flinch—something that would tell him when Heller was about to thrust the stick into him.

Heller stepped closer. His eyes jumped down to Louis's legs.

Now!

Louis threw out his hand just as Heller lunged. The tip smashed into the wall and exploded.

The blast echoed against the metal, and Heller stumbled backward.

Louis dove to the floor. He sucked in a breath. He was alive. And not hit.

Heller was in the shadows, trying to reload the stick. Louis could hear him. "Shit . . . shit."

Louis felt along the cold floor until he found a fishing pole. He pulled it to him, easing himself into the darkness behind the post. He curled around it, coming up behind Heller as he was trying to shove another shell into the bang stick.

Louis held the pole in the center, the huge metal reel hanging heavy on the far end. With both hands, he swung.

The reel smashed into Heller's cheek. Heller yelped and threw his hand to his face. He dropped the bang stick and the shell bounced out.

Louis backtracked toward the open rear door. He would lock the son of a bitch in.

Outside, water rushed off the top deck, pouring over him, and he couldn't get a good grip on the metal door. He pulled harder, inching it along with each jerk.

A knife shot out the narrow opening, ripping blindly at his arm, slicing into it. Louis jerked back, his hand over the wound, blood between his fingers.

Heller shoved the door open.

Louis staggered back. Candy—his gun. He had to get to it. He had no choice but to make a complete circle around the boat and pray Heller didn't know what he was after.

Louis ran to his right, slipping down the walkway, away from Heller.

His arm throbbed, he couldn't see, couldn't hear anything over the roar of the rain. The gun . . . he needed to get around the boat to the other side.

Something hit him hard from above, crashing into his shoulders, crushing him into the deck. Heller had jumped him from the top deck.

Louis jerked up, gasping, pedaling backward, until he was pressed against the cabin wall.

Heller came at him, knife raised.

Nowhere to go. No time even to draw up his feet to push him away.

Heller thrust the knife toward his chest.

No choice! Grab it!

Louis grabbed the blade. It sliced into his palm and he let out a yell, gritting his teeth against the pain. He gripped the blade tighter, fighting to angle it away from him. Heller tried to draw it back, wrench it away, but Louis held tight, blood streaming down his arm.

Heller jerked to his right.

Louis snapped the knife to the left. It broke off in his hand and Louis tossed it over the railing.

For an instant, Heller stood there, his eyes riveted to the broken knife butt.

Now!

Louis hit him in the face. Heller fell sideways, the butt skittering across the deck.

He hit him again, and again, but Heller was unfazed, coming back at him. Heller lunged forward, smashing his fists into Louis's face. Slammed backward, Louis could get no leverage, draw no strength. He started grappling for Heller's throat, anything to restrain him.

Oh, Jesus. Jesus.

Heller was pummeling him with blows to the face and head. Louis rolled to his side, shielding his face, inching away, pounded now by punches to his back.

Fighting him off with his elbows and legs, Louis pulled himself up on the rail. The boat lurched and for just a moment the pounding stopped.

A spool of fishing line was at his feet. Louis grabbed it and spun, swinging it upward. The heavy wooden spool crashed into Heller's head. Heller fell against the cabin wall, then slipped to the deck, blood pouring down his face.

Louis wiped the bloody water from his eyes.

Lights! Flashing blue lights far off in the distance. *Hold on . . . just five more minutes. Hold on!*

He staggered toward the back of the boat, holding his bleeding palm. He heard Heller behind him and he knew he would never make it around to Candy. He found the open door and fell inside, struggling to close it. It shut and he stumbled toward the rear of the cabin. He heard the door slam open and looked up to see Heller standing in the opening, the broken knife in his hand.

The flashing blue lights were coming closer, swirling faintly in the cabin now. Heller swept a hand over the table and the battery-powered portable light crashed to the floor.

Louis inched backward, his eyes on Heller. Heller moved slowly forward, his bloody face intent on Louis, his chest heaving, the broken knife in his hand.

Back . . . back. There was no way out. Back . . . back. Blue lights swirling. And white now, the searchlight from the coast guard boat.

His heel hit something and he fell, catching himself against a bench as he hit the floor.

The bang stick.

He snatched it up, thrusting it out lengthwise across his chest to ward off the knife butt's blows. He could hear Wainwright's voice calling to him on the radio from across the room.

Heller inched forward. White light swept the room. Louis pressed back, squinting in the light, blinded each time it moved over the room. Each time he saw Heller's bulky form above him, coming closer.

God . . . they weren't going to make it in time!

Then he saw it. There in the beam thrown out by the portable light, he saw the shell.

He grabbed it and pulled the open tip of the bang stick to him. He tried to jam the shell inside, but his fingers were stiff with blood. His hand was shaking, his eyes darting from the shell to Heller.

Damn it! Damn it!

The shell dropped in and he swung it around, pointing it at Heller.

Heller stopped, the knife butt in the air. Louis could hear him panting.

The white lights swept over them again.

Louis got up slowly, using the wall for support, keeping the bang stick aimed at Heller's chest.

Heller took two more steps closer, drawing deep, raspy breaths.

Jesus Christ! He wasn't going to stop.

Louis drew in the stick as far he could. Heller finally stopped. He looked down at the end of the stick, only inches from his heart, then back at Louis.

Louis stared at him, holding the bang stick with trembling arms.

Suddenly, it was clear. He had been right. Heller wanted to die. He had been trying to kill himself all along, trying to erase himself, and now he wanted Louis to do it for him.

Heller moved, leaning into the stick.

Louis jerked the bang stick downward and it exploded into Heller's thigh.

Heller went down with a groan, disappearing between the benches. Louis fell back against the steel wall, slumping to the floor, sucking in air. Heller lifted his head.

Stay down! Stay down, you bastard!

Heller grabbed his ankle, and Louis jerked away, bringing the bang stick down on Heller's shoulders. He kept coming, clawing at Louis's legs, unfazed by the pounding of the rod. Heller was on him, swinging blindly, spewing blood.

Louis twisted sharply, and Heller rolled to his side, his shoulders caught for just a second under the bench. Louis yanked him back by his collar, then brought the bang stick across the front of his throat. He pulled back with every ounce of strength he had left.

Heller started gagging, his fingers curling around the stick. Louis jerked again. Heller writhed against him.

The white lights swept over the walls. The metal bar was thick with blood from his hands. He could hear sirens and voices.

Suddenly, Heller dropped his hands. His body went limp. "Finish it," he gasped.

Louis froze.

Heller's face snapped toward his. "Finish it!"

You son of a bitch! I'm not going to do it for you!

Louis shoved him away, slamming his head into a bench post. He grabbed Heller's hair and slammed it again.

Heller went limp.

Louis struggled to his feet, panting. He saw a reel and stumbled to it, bringing it back to Heller. He jerked the line loose and wrapped it around Heller's wrists and arms, pushing it through the legs of the bench and back again. Then yanked it tight, wedging the pole between the bench and the wall.

The lights sprayed the cabin in white.

He pulled himself to his feet, reeling toward the door.

The coast guard boat was abreast the starboard side of the *Miss Monica* now. Somebody was yelling over a megaphone, somebody was calling his name. Louis ignored the voice and staggered around to the port-side gangway.

He made his way to where Candy lay, dropping next to him on the deck. He rolled him over. Candy's eyes were closed. His face looked like wet clay.

Louis pressed a finger to his neck. He felt a weak pulse.

He ripped open Candy's raincoat. Blood was running from his belly down the deck. Louis pressed a hand to the wound, pulling Candy to him, using his body to shield him from the rain.

Oh God, no . . . please. Not again.

The white lights swept over them again.

Chapter Forty-five

Someone draped a blanket around his shoulders. He didn't look up. He kept his eyes on the distant wharf. He could see it now, make it out through the rain. He could see the muted colors of the boats, the gray of the restaurant. He could see the blue bubble lights.

They were waiting for him.

The engines of the coast guard boat vibrated with power under his feet. He heard the door of the cabin slide open and footsteps come near.

"We're almost back."

Louis nodded.

"Your friend, the other officer ... what's his name?"

"Candy," Louis said. "Greg Candy."

He could see yellow raincoats swarming the docks now. He got up slowly, wincing in pain, holding the blanket around him as best he could with his bandaged hands. Slowly, he went over to the stretcher.

Candy's eyes were closed, his face ashen. Louis watched for the rise and fall of his chest but saw nothing beneath the dark blue wool blanket.

"He's lost a lot of blood," a voice behind him said.

Louis turned to look at the young coast guard officer. "Is he going to make it?"

"We're doing what we can. We're almost back."

Hang in there, Candy. . . .

His eyes drifted to the other stretcher where Tyrone Heller lay strapped in. He was moaning, muttering something incoherent.

Like fragments from a dream, the details started swirling back to Louis in that moment. The heaviness of Heller's body, the fury of his fists, the feel of the blade as it cut through his palm.

His stomach begin to churn.

The cold wet metal of the bang stick in his hand. The trembling in his arms as he held it against Heller's throat.

Die, you fucker! Die!

No . . . no. I'm not going to help you commit suicide.

The agonizing relief when Heller's head crashed into the floor and he went limp.

Louis moved slowly away, going to stand at the window. They were at the dock. Men were throwing lines. Voices were barking out commands. The sounds of boots on the metal deck outside. The door opened again and four paramedics came in, followed by two cops. The cops wore heavy slickers and Louis couldn't make out where they were from. They swarmed the stretchers, the paramedics picking up Candy and carefully carrying him out. The cops pushed by the other two paramedics, cuffing Heller to the gurney. Louis watched as they moved as a group to the ambulances waiting out in the lot.

The young coast guard officer was standing there holding out a raincoat.

"Paramedics are standing by for you, Officer Kincaid," he said.

Louis nodded woodenly and allowed the man to drape the raincoat over his shoulders.

The first person he saw was Wainwright, hovering over Candy until they closed the doors on the ambulance. Then Wainwright's eyes swiveled back to the boat. He moved forward, waiting at the end of the dock for Louis. Emily was a small figure in bright green behind him. He went to them.

"Jesus," Wainwright said, his expression going slack.

Emily's eyes filled with tears as she stared at his face.

"I'm okay," Louis mumbled.

Wainwright took his arm and led him toward the ambulance. The paramedics hurried to get the stretcher out, but Louis waved them off and they opened the door for him.

An officer in a Fort Myers raincoat came rushing up. "Chief, the coast guard says they found a body onboard the *Miss Monica*."

"Who is it?" Wainwright asked.

"They don't know. It was down in the hold, wrapped in a blanket. Looks like it had been there for a while. The face has black paint all over it, but it looks to be a white male, about sixty."

Louis shut his eyes briefly, then looked at the officer. "Tell them to look at his left hand," he said slowly. "Ask them if there's a finger missing."

The cop stared at Louis for a moment, then keyed his radio. A moment later, he heard the reply come back.

"That's affirmative. Left pinkie missing."

"It's Lynch," he said softly.

Emily turned away. Louis closed his eyes.

He heard a siren and opened his eyes in time to see a Lee County sheriff's car swing into the lot. Mobley climbed out and hurried toward Heller as they were lifting him into the ambulance.

Wainwright watched him. "He's too late again," he said. "My guys have him in custody. It's our collar."

Louis nodded, grabbing the edge of the door to climb into the ambulance. Another siren made them turn.

Candy's ambulance was moving. Louis watched it until it pulled from the lot.

"He'll make it, Louis," Wainwright said. "You get in there and I'll see you at the hospital. I've got to go ride with Heller."

Louis nodded.

"I'll go with Louis," Emily said quickly.

"Good," Wainwright said.

The paramedics helped Louis into the ambulance. He didn't protest as they strapped him into the stretcher and started an IV. The doors closed, the sirens wailed.

Emily sat hunched across from him, her wet hair plastered to her head, her eyes locked on him. She took off her glasses to try to wipe them dry. He saw the tears in her eyes.

"Farentino, I'm going to be all right," he said softly. "It's over."

"I feel like this is my fault," she said.

He saw the guilt etched in her face. He knew it would be a while before it would fade.

Chapter Forty-six

Louis woke to the smell of strong coffee. He grimaced as he sat up, and looked down at his hand.

The tips of his fingers protruded from a thick bandage. His palm still throbbed. His forearm was bandaged in thick gauze. He hurt everywhere.

He slid his legs gingerly over the side of the bed and looked at the clock on the nightstand. Four-fifteen. Jesus, he had slept almost all day.

He used the bedpost to stand. Issy was curled in the covers at the foot of the bed. Someone had left an old plaid robe on the bedpost. He slipped it on and shuffled to the kitchen.

Dodie jumped up from his chair. "Here, lemme help you, Louis."

He put a hand on Louis's arm, pulling out a chair.

Louis sat, letting out a sigh that rippled through his bruised muscles.

"Coffee?"

Louis nodded. He pulled the newspaper over to him.

Heller was being arraigned today. He saw his own picture on the bottom of the page. He pushed the newspaper away as Dodie came back with the coffee. Margaret was on his heels.

"You shouldn't be up," she said.

"I've slept for two days," Louis said. The pain in his jaw began to pound again. He sipped at the coffee, but it burned the cuts on his lips.

"You hungry? I can fix you something," Margaret said.

Louis shook his head. He wasn't sure he could chew.

"Scrambled eggs," Margaret said. "Soft scrambled eggs."

She disappeared.

Louis's eyes flicked to Dodie sitting across the table. He was staring at him.

"I'm okay, Sam."

"Just checking."

The smell of eggs filled the kitchen. It made Louis's stomach churn.

"Oh, Louis," Margaret said, "Emily Farentino called. She came over yesterday but you were asleep. She has to leave today and she wants to say good-bye. She said you could reach her at Dan's office till five tonight."

"Thanks, Margaret."

Dodie was staring at him again. "You decide yet

what you're going to do?" he asked. "I mean, after you heal up and all."

"I don't know. Go home for a while, I guess."

"Why? You can't work there."

Louis tried another sip of coffee. "I have applications out, Chicago PD, Cleveland. I'll find something."

Dodie stirred his coffee.

"Besides, my car's up there," Louis said.

"Go get it."

Louis sighed.

Margaret returned with the eggs. She started to tuck a napkin into Louis's pajama top, and he let her, too tired to argue. He started to eat slowly.

"You could find work here, Louis," Dodie said.

"Sam's right," Margaret added quickly.

He looked up at them. "I'm not a PI." He looked away, shaking his head. "It wouldn't work."

"Well, what about Dan?" Dodie pressed.

Louis shook his head again.

"Dan could find something for you, Louis. Lord knows he could use a good man and—"

Margaret put a hand on Dodie's arm. "Sam, you've been chewing on his ear for two days now about this. Let the man be."

Dodie sat back in his chair. Margaret moved back to the stove.

Louis felt something rub his leg. He looked down to see Issy. The cat looked up at him, then trotted off toward the laundry room. Louis glanced up at the wall clock. It was after four-thirty.

He took another bite of eggs, then slowly rose.

"Where you going?" Dodie asked.

"To say good-bye to Farentino."

* * *

Emily was sitting in the chair facing Wainwright when Louis came in. They were laughing. Wainwright sobered when he saw Louis at the door. Emily turned.

"You still look like shit," she said.

"You should see me from this side," Louis said. "What were you two laughing about?"

"Mobley," Wainwright said. "He's still pissed he didn't get the collar."

"He'll live," Louis said. He eased into a chair and looked over at Emily. The briefcase was sitting next to her chair. She saw him looking at it.

She shrugged. "I dunno. Maybe I'll write my memoirs someday," she said.

He studied her face. She looked like she hadn't slept well. Or maybe like she wouldn't ever truly sleep well again. He didn't know what to say. He didn't want her to leave, but he didn't know what to say that could keep her here any longer. She hadn't been a partner, at least not in the real sense. But he knew he was going to miss her. He'd miss her energy and dedication, the way her mind worked. He smiled slightly. Shit, he was even going to miss her balls.

She was looking at him. "Well, I've got a long drive ahead," she said. She hesitated, then held out her hand to Wainwright.

"Thanks, Chief," she said. "It's been . . . an education."

Wainwright stood up and took her hand. "For both of us."

She turned to Louis and extended her hand. "Hey, Kincaid."

He held up his bandaged hand. She smiled and shook his thumb.

"Hey, Farentino," he said.

"Drive careful," Wainwright said.

She picked up her green rain slicker and started to the door.

"Farentino," Louis said.

She turned.

"Got time to go get some coffee or something?"

She smiled. "Sorry. Got a date with Vinny. Later, guys."

She left.

Louis turned to look at Wainwright. "Vinny?" he asked.

"Vince. The ME," Wainwright said.

Louis shook his head, smiling.

"I went to see Candy this morning," Wainwright said. "He was asking about you."

"I feel bad I haven't been over to see him yet," Louis said.

"Don't be. He wasn't really up for visitors until today." Wainwright paused. "He's going to be all right, by the way. The knife missed everything important."

"Thank God."

"He said he can't wait to come back to work," Wainwright said. "Said something weird, too. Said he was rethinking the Miami thing. You know what he meant?"

Louis nodded, smiling slightly.

His eyes wandered over the office, falling finally on the bulletin board. It was empty. His gaze came to the framed photograph of Wainwright's two kids. He looked up to see Wainwright looking at him.

"You feeling any better?" Wainwright asked.

Louis shrugged. "How about you?" he asked.

Wainwright nodded slowly. "Better."

It was quiet except for the rain on the window and voices filtering in from the outer office.

"I found out something interesting today," Wainwright said. "It's about the Broward cases. I found out why there was a gap between the first New Jersey killing and the two near Fort Lauderdale. After the Jersey fishing season was over, the *Miss Monica* headed south and put in at Fort Lauderdale for repairs. They were there for a month."

"Enough time for Heller to kill twice," Louis said.

"And then the boat came here for the winter," Wainwright said.

They were quiet again for a moment.

"They're saying Heller's mentally incompetent, that he won't get the death penalty," Louis said.

"I know," Wainwright said. "I still think he should fry." He leaned back in his chair.

Wainwright let a moment or two pass. "Why didn't you do it?" he asked.

"Do what?"

"Kill him."

Louis held Wainwright's gaze, then looked away. He had asked himself the same question in the last two days. He couldn't come up with an answer. He couldn't come up with an answer either about why he felt nothing but ambivalence when he thought of Tyrone Heller being locked up for life rather than dying in the chair.

He looked back at Wainwright. "That day you had Skeen cornered in the bathroom," he said. "You said you killed him. Why?"

"I told you," Wainwright said softly, his eyes unwavering. "I had to."

Louis nodded slowly. It fell silent again. Voices drifted in from the outer office. There was a knock.

"Yeah?" Wainwright called out.

Myrna poked her head in the door. "Chief? This just came for Louis." She handed Louis a paper and left.

Louis unfolded the paper and read it. "Goddamn it," he said softly.

"What?"

"Mobley," Louis said. "It's a summons. He's busting me for not having a goddamn PI license."

He crumpled it and threw it across the room.

"Don't sweat it," Wainwright said. "It's just a small fine."

The room was quiet again. Louis knew it was time to say his good-byes and get out, but he didn't want to leave.

"So, what will you do now, Louis?" Wainwright asked finally.

"I don't know."

"I'd offer you something, but—"

"It's okay, Dan."

Louis's gaze drifted to the window.

"Oh, I almost forgot," Wainwright said. "Roberta Tatum called this morning. Wanted me to give you a message."

"What?" Louis asked.

"She said, 'Tell the cookie to come get his money.' "

Louis stared at Wainwright.

"It's twenty grand, Louis. You earned it."

Louis didn't answer. He rose slowly and held out his hand.

"Thanks, Dan," he said. "For everything."

Wainwright rose, hesitated, then came around the desk. He gave Louis a quick but gentle clasp around the shoulders.

"Thanks for all your help," Wainwright said. "Keep in touch. Let me know when you get settled somewhere or if you ever come back to Sereno."

Louis nodded quickly and went to the door, closing it softly behind him.

The rain was finally letting up as Louis stopped to pay the toll. He went across the causeway and headed slowly down the tree-tunneled road through Sanibel. He crossed the low-slung bridge over Blind Man's Pass onto Captiva Island.

By the time the road took a bend toward the water, the rain had stopped. He glanced to his left as he drove, watching the orange smudge of sun creep toward the gray-green water.

At the tiny town center, he pulled up in front of the Island Deli and Liquor and went in. A bell tinkled over his head as he closed the door.

The store's narrow aisles were crammed with boxes. More boxes were stacked along the back in front of the coolers of wine and beer. To his right there was a shelf crowded with cheap ceramic birds, dolphins, and assorted shells. Colorful beach towels, embroidered with the words *Captiva Island*, hung along a wall.

Roberta was behind the counter ringing up a loaf of bread and a six-pack of Bud for a man in a flowered shirt. She glanced at Louis as she took the man's money. The man gathered up his bag and moved past Louis, out the door. The bell tinkled again.

There was no anger in Roberta's eyes as she looked at him across the counter. Fatigue maybe. Or relief. But the anger was gone.

"Evening," he said.

She came around the counter. "I see you got my message."

Louis nodded.

Roberta hollered toward the back. "Levon!"

Levon came around a corner. "Yeah?"

"Levon, you remember Mr. Kincaid, don't you?"

Levon came forward slowly, an apron around his waist, a price-punch in his hand. His eyes settled on Louis's bruised face. "Did I do that to you?"

Louis shook his head. "No."

Levon sighed. "Good."

Roberta tapped him on the arm. "Tell the man."

"I'm sorry. It won't happen again. I got my meds back now."

Louis nodded slightly. "I hope not."

Roberta turned toward the cash register. "Watch the front, Levon. I'll be right back."

Roberta motioned for Louis to follow her to the back. She led him to an office that was so small he could barely get the door closed behind him.

"Sorry for the mess. Today's delivery day." She sat down at a desk and opened her checkbook.

"You look like shit," she said, writing. "You doing okay?"

"I'll be fine," he said.

She scribbled her name with elaborate curves and

ripped the check from the book, holding it out to him.

"There you go."

He looked down at it. All the way over here he had thought about what he would do with the money. He had told himself it was his, fair and square. But now it wasn't that easy. He lifted his gaze to her face and let out a small sigh.

She heard it and narrowed her eyes. "Take it."

Louis hesitated. "Mrs. Tatum . . ."

She stood and slapped it in his hand. "Don't be stupid. Somebody offers you money, you take it."

He fingered it, then met her eyes. "It just doesn't seem right to take money from you when you've lost . . . your husband."

Roberta put her hands on her hips. "You had nothing to do with me losing Walter. But you have a whole lot to do with how I get past it. Put the damn money in your pocket."

She reached for the door, then looked at him. "I can afford it. Does that make you feel better?"

Louis smiled. "I guess. Thank you."

She pulled open the door. "Now get out of here. I got a shitload of stuff to get out on those shelves out there."

He followed her out, toward the front, putting the check in his pocket. She moved to a box of canned peas and he paused to watch her. She bent to rip open the box and started stacking the cans on the shelf. If she knew he was still there, she wasn't going to say anything. Life was moving forward, he was now a part of her past.

"Excuse me, please."

He turned to see a woman standing behind him.

Her round body was draped in a bright muumuu, her eyes hidden behind black sunglasses. Silver bracelets tinkled on her wrists like the bell above the door.

"I just want to get to those," she said, pointing.

Louis moved so she could get to the shelf of plastic trinkets.

"What do you think about this?" the woman said, holding out an ugly bird made out of shells.

"Very nice," Louis said.

"I want to get a souvenir of this place," the woman said. "I've enjoyed it so. It's so nice and peaceful here."

She put the bird back and plucked out a conch shell instead. She stared at it, heaving a heavy sigh.

"It's so hard to go back to Wisconsin. All that snow and everything." She looked up at him. "You know what I mean?"

"Yeah, I do," he said.

Chapter Forty-seven

He left the car in the deli's lot and walked down the street to the beach. The cloud cover had broken and shards of pink sun cut through the gray, but the beach was empty, the shell seekers abandoning the sand, the tourists retreating to the bars. Only a few hardy souls were walking along the surf, waiting to see if there might yet be a sunset worth witnessing.

Louis paused on the crest of the small dune. He hadn't been back here since the day he and Emily had talked. He was remembering what she had said about being alone, about having to build a family if you didn't have one. It occurred to him that he had never done that. As much as he cared for Phillip and Frances, he had always kept them at arm's length, as if he didn't quite trust himself to love them. They had put locks on his doors, always afraid he would run away. But he had anyway, even without leaving.

The storm had left the water green and churning, and the surf crashed and foamed on the hard, wet sand.

Down the beach, a little to the south, he could see the place where Harold Childers's body had been found. He went to it and looked down. The sand was washed of footprints. It looked clean, pristine, untouched, and new.

He sat down among the swaying sea oats. He watched a group of sandpipers play tag with the surf and then turned his gaze out to the gulf.

So what will you do, Louis?

Go home.

To what? The rented cabin in Loon Lake? Another empty apartment in Detroit or some other city where he knew no one? The hope that, in ten or fifteen years, he might have a gold shield to hang on his shirt?

Twenty grand . . .

A cop didn't take rewards. But he wasn't a cop.

Well, what the hell am I then?

"Excuse me."

Louis turned. A man was standing on the dune behind him, hands on hips. He was wearing shorts, a bulky white sweater, and a plaid tam on his head. It took Louis a moment to recognize him. It was the Frenchman who had come down to the beach the morning they had found Harold Childers's body.

"You can't be here," the Frenchman said. "This is *propriété privée.*"

"Can I sit down there?" Louis asked, pointing down toward the water.

"If you want," the Frenchman said with a shrug. He paused, peering at Louis.

"I know you," he said. "You were here with the dead man. You are *le flic.*"

"Yeah, I'm the flic," Louis said.

"Things are better now, no?"

"Things are better now, yes."

"*Bon.*"

Louis started to get up.

"No," the Frenchman said. "You stay here."

Louis nodded, easing himself back down to the sand. He looked back out at the churning green gulf. The wind was picking up and he zipped his jacket up to his chin. The pink streaks that had promised a sunset had faded, leaving only the gray bank of clouds low over the water.

"I don't think there's going to be a sunset," Louis said.

The Frenchman shrugged. "There will be another tomorrow." He turned and trudged back up toward the cabins.

Louis watched him go. He looked back out at the water.

Okay. All right. Maybe . . .

Maybe it was time to stop running away.

He glanced at his watch. Margaret would be waiting dinner on him. He could make it if he hurried.

He rose, dusting the sand from his jeans. He took one more look out at the water. The sun had slipped below the gray cloud bank. Maybe there would be a real sunset tomorrow.

He would come back and see.

ABOUT THE AUTHOR

P.J. Parrish has worked as a newspaper reporter and editor, arts reviewer, blackjack dealer, and personnel director in a Mississippi casino. The author currently resides in Southaven, Mississippi, and Fort Lauderdale, Florida, and is married with three children, three grandchildren, and five cats. P.J. Parrish is currently at work on the next Louis Kincaid thriller, which will be published in 2006. Please visit the author's Web site at www.pj parrish.com.